# Life and Gabriella

*Publd. 1916.*

by

# Ellen Glasgow

*1873 - 1945.*

The Echo Library 2006

Published by

The Echo Library

Echo Library
131 High St.
Teddington
Middlesex  TW11 8HH

www.echo-library.com

Please report serious faults in the text to complaints@echo-library.com

ISBN  1-40681-042-8

# CONTENTS

**BOOK FIRST—THE AGE OF FAITH**

**CHAPTER**

**BOOK SECOND—THE AGE OF KNOWLEDGE**

# BOOK FIRST

## THE AGE OF FAITH

## CHAPTER I

## PRESENTS A SHAMELESS HEROINE

After a day of rain the sun came out suddenly at five o'clock and threw a golden bar into the deep Victorian gloom of the front parlour. On the window-sill, midway between the white curtains, a pot of blue hyacinths stood in a cracked china plate, and as the sunlight shone into the room, the scent of the blossoms floated to the corner where Gabriella was patiently pulling basting threads out of the hem of a skirt. For a minute her capable hands stopped at their work, and raising her smooth dark head she looked compassionately at her sister Jane, who was sitting, like a frozen image of martyrdom, in the middle of the long horsehair sofa. Three times within the last twelve months Jane had fled from her husband's roof to the protection of her widowed mother, a weak person of excellent ancestry, who could hardly have protected a sparrow had one taken refuge beneath her skirt. Twice before Mrs. Carr had wept over her daughter's woes and returned her, a sullen saint, to the arms of the discreetly repentant Charley; but to-day, while the four older children were bribed to good behaviour with bread and damson preserves in the pantry, and the baby was contentedly playing with his rubber ring in his mother's arms, Gabriella had passionately declared that "Jane must never, never go back!" Nothing so dreadful as this had ever happened before, for the repentant Charley had been discovered making love to his wife's dressmaker, a pretty French girl whom Jane had engaged for her spring sewing because she had more "style" than had fallen to the austerely virtuous lot of the Carr's regular seamstress, Miss Folly Hatch. "I might have known she was too pretty to be good," moaned Jane, while Mrs. Carr, in her willow rocking-chair by the window, wiped her reddened eyelids on the strip of cambric ruffling she was hemming.

Unmoved among them the baby beat methodically on his mother's breast with his rubber ring, as indifferent to her sobs as to the intermittent tearful "coos" of his grandmother. He had a smooth bald head, fringed, like the head of a very old man, with pale silken hair that was almost white in the sunshine, and his eyes, as expressionless as marbles, stared over the pot of hyacinths at a sparrow perched against the deep blue sky on the red brick wall of the opposite house. From beneath his starched little skirt his feet, in pink crocheted shoes, protruded with a forlorn and helpless air as if they hardly belonged to him.

"Oh, my poor child, what are we going to do?" asked Mrs. Carr in a resigned voice as she returned to her hemming.

"There's nothing to do, mother," answered Jane, without lifting her eyes from the baby's head, without moving an inch out of the position she had dropped into when she entered the room. Then, after a sobbing pause, she defined in a classic formula her whole philosophy of life: "It wasn't my fault," she said.

"But one can always do something if it's only to scream," rejoined Gabriella with spirit.

"I wouldn't scream," replied Jane, while the pale cast of resolution hardened her small flat features, "not—not if he killed me. My one comfort," she added pathetically, "is that only you and mother know how he treats me."

Her pretty vacant face with its faded bloom resembled a pastel portrait in which the artist had forgotten to paint an expression. "Poor Jane Gracey," as she was generally called, had wasted the last ten years in a futile effort to hide the fact of an unfortunate marriage beneath an excessively cheerful manner. She talked continually because talking seemed to her the most successful way of "keeping up an appearance." Though everybody who knew her knew also that Charley Gracey neglected her shamefully, she spent twelve hours of the twenty-four pretending that she was perfectly happy. At nineteen she had been a belle and beauty of the willowy sort; but at thirty she had relapsed into one of the women whom men admire in theory and despise in reality. She had started with a natural tendency to clinging sweetness; as the years went on the sweetness, instead of growing fainter, had become almost cloying, while the clinging had hysterically tightened into a clutch. Charley Gracey, who had married her under the mistaken impression that her type was restful for a reforming rake, (not realizing that there is nothing so mentally disturbing as a fool) had been changed by marriage from a gay bird of the barnyard into a veritable hawk of the air. His behaviour was the scandal of the town, yet the greater his sins, the intenser grew Jane's sweetness, the more twining her hold. "Nobody will ever think of blaming you, darling," said Mrs. Carr consolingly. "You have behaved beautifully from the beginning. We all know what a perfect wife you have been."

"I've tried to do my duty even if Charley failed in his," replied the perfect wife, unfastening the hooks of her small heliotrope wrap trimmed with tarnished silver passementerie. Above her short flaxen "bang" she wore a crumpled purple hat ornamented with bunches of velvet pansies; and though it was two years old, and out of fashion at a period when fashions changed less rapidly, it lent an air of indecent festivity to her tearful face. Her youth was already gone, for her beauty had been of the fragile kind that breaks early, and her wan, aristocratic features had settled into the downward droop which comes to the faces of people who habitually "expect the worst."

"I know, Jane, I know," murmured Mrs. Carr, dropping her thimble as she nervously tried to hasten her sewing. "But don't you think it would be a comfort, dear, to have the advice of a man about Charley? Won't you let me send Marthy for your Cousin Jimmy Wrenn?"

"Oh, mother, I couldn't. It would kill me to have everybody know I'm unhappy!" wailed Jane, breaking down.

"But everybody knows anyway, Jane," said Gabriella, sticking the point of her scissors into a strip of buckram, for she was stiffening the bottom of the skirt after the fashion of the middle 'nineties.

"Of course I'm foolishly sensitive," returned Jane, while she lifted the baby from her lap and placed him in a pile of cushions by the deep arm of the sofa, where he sat imperturbably gazing at the blue sky and the red wall from which the sparrow had flown. "You can never understand my feelings because you are so different."

"Gabriella is not married," observed Mrs. Carr, with sentimental finality. "But I'm sure, Jane—I'm just as sure as I can be of anything that it wouldn't do a bit of harm to speak to Cousin Jimmy Wrenn. Men know so much more than women about such matters."

In her effort to recover her thimble she dropped her spool of thread, which rolled under the sofa on which Jane was sitting, and while she waited for Gabriella to find it, she gazed pensively into the almost deserted street where the slender shadows of poplar trees slanted over the wet cobblestones. Though Mrs. Carr worked every instant of her time, except the few hours when she lay in bed trying to sleep, and the few minutes when she sat at the table trying to eat, nothing that she began was ever finished until Gabriella took it out of her hands. She did her best, for she was as conscientious in her way as poor Jane, yet through some tragic perversity of fate her best seemed always to fall short of the simplest requirements of life. Her face, like Jane's, was long and thin, with a pathetic droop at the corners of the mouth, a small bony nose, always slightly reddened at the tip, and faded blue eyes beneath an even row of little flat round curls which looked as if they were plastered on her forehead.

Thirty-three years before, in the romantic and fiery 'sixties, she had married dashing young Gabriel Carr for no better reason apparently than that she was falling vaguely in love with love; and the marriage, which had been one of reckless passion on his side, had been for her scarcely more than the dreamer's hesitating compromise with reality. Passion, which she had been taught to regard as an unholy attribute implanted by the Creator, with inscrutable wisdom, in the nature of man, and left out of the nature of woman, had never troubled her gentle and affectionate soul; and not until the sudden death of her husband did she begin even remotely to fall in love with the man. But when he was once safely dead she worshipped his memory with an ardour which would have seemed to her indelicate had he been still alive. For sixteen years she had worn a crape veil on her bonnet, and she still went occasionally, after the morning service was over on Sunday, to place fresh flowers on his grave. Now that his "earthly nature," against which she had struggled so earnestly while he was living, was no longer in need of the pious exorcisms with which she had treated its frequent manifestations, she remembered only the dark beauty of his face, his robust and vigorous youth, the tenderness and gallantry of his passion. For her daughters she had drawn an imaginary portrait of him which combined the pagan beauty of Antinous with the militant purity of Saint Paul; and this romantic blending of the heathen and the Presbyterian virtues had passed through her young imagination into the awakening soul of Gabriella.

By the town at large Mrs. Carr's sorrow was alluded to as "a beautiful grief," yet so deeply rooted in her being was the instinct to twine, that for the first few years of her bereavement she had simply sat in her widow's weeds, with her rent paid by Cousin Jimmy Wrenn and her market bills settled monthly by Uncle Beverly Blair, and waited patiently for some man to come and support her.

When no man came, and Uncle Beverly died of a stroke of apoplexy with his will unsigned, she had turned, with the wasted energy of the unfit and the incompetent, to solve the inexplicable problem of indigent ladyhood. And it was at this crucial instant that Becky Bollingbroke had put her awful question: "Have you made up your mind, Fanny, what you are going to do?" That was twelve years ago, but deep down in some secret cave of Fanny's being the ghastly echo of the words still reverberated through the emptiness and the silence.

"Don't you think, darling," she pleaded now, as she had pleaded to Becky on that other dreadful occasion, "that we had better send immediately for Cousin Jimmy Wrenn?"

"I—I can't think," gasped Jane, "but you may if you want to, mother."

"Send, Gabriella," said Mrs. Carr quickly, and she added tenderly, while Gabriella dropped her work and ran to the outside kitchen for Marthy, the coloured drudge, "you will feel so much better, Jane, after you have had his advice."

Then at the sight of Jane's stricken face, which had turned blue as if from a sudden chill, she hurriedly opened the drawer of her sewing machine, and taking out a bottle of camphor she kept there, began tremulously rubbing her daughter's forehead. As she did so, she remembered, with the startling irrelevance of the intellectually untrained, the way Jane had looked in her veil and orange blossoms on the day of her wedding.

"I wonder what on earth we have done to deserve our troubles?" she found herself thinking while she put the stopper back into the bottle and returned to her sewing.

"Marthy has gone, mother," said Gabriella, with her cheerful air as she came back into the room, "and I shut the children in the laundry with Dolly who is doing the washing."

"I hope they won't make themselves sick with preserves," remarked Jane, with the first dart of energy she had shown. "Perhaps I'd better go and see. If Fanny eats too much we'll be up all night with her."

"I told Dolly not to let them stuff," answered Gabriella, as she sat down by the window and threaded her needle. She was a tall, dark girl, slender and straight as a young poplar, with a face that was frank and pleasant rather than pretty, and sparkling brown eyes which turned golden and grew bright as swords when she was angry. Seen by the strong light of the window, her face showed sallow in tone, with a certain nobility about the bony structure beneath the soft girlish flesh, and a look of almost stern decision in the square chin and in the full rich curve of the mouth. Her hair, which was too fine and soft to show its thickness, drooped from its parting at the side in a dark wing over her forehead, where it shadowed her arched black eyebrows and the clear sweet gravity of her eyes. As she bent over her sewing the thin pure lines of her body had a look of arrested energy, of relaxed but exuberant vitality.

"You won't go to the dance to-night, will you, Gabriella?" inquired Mrs. Carr nervously.

"No, I'm not going," answered the girl regretfully, for she loved dancing, and her white organdie dress, trimmed with quillings of blue ribbon, lay upstairs on the bed. "I'll never dance again if only Jane won't go back to Charley. I'll work my fingers to the bone to help her take care of the children."

"I'll never, never go back," chanted Jane with feverish passion.

"But I thought Arthur Peyton was coming for you," said Mrs. Carr. "He will be so disappointed."

"Oh, he'll understand—he'll have to," replied Gabriella carelessly.

The sunshine faded slowly from the hyacinths on the window-sill, and drawing her crocheted cape of purple wool closer about her, Mrs. Carr moved a little nearer the fireplace. Outside the March wind was blowing with a melancholy sound up the long straight street, and rocking the glossy boughs of an old magnolia tree in the yard From the shining leaves of the tree a few drops of water ·fell on the brick pavement, where several joyous sparrows were drinking, and farther off, as bright as silver in the clear wind, a solitary church spire rose above the huddled roofs of the town. When the wind lulled, as it did now and then, a warm breath seemed to stir in the sunshine, which grew suddenly brighter, while a promise of spring floated like a faint provocative scent on the air. And this scent, so vague, so roving, that it was like the ghostly perfume of flowers, stole at last into the memory, and made the old dream of youth and the young grow restless at the call of Life, which sang to the music of flutes in the brain. But the wind, rising afresh, drove the spirit of spring from the street, and swept the broken leaves of the magnolia tree over the drenched grass to the green-painted iron urns on either side of the steps.

The house, a small brick dwelling, set midway of an expressionless row and wearing on its front a look of desiccated gentility, stood in one of those forgotten streets where needy gentlewomen do "light housekeeping" in an obscure hinterland of respectability. Hill Street, which had once known fashion, and that only yesterday, as old ladies count, had sunk at last into a humble state of decay. Here and there the edges of porches had crumbled; grass was beginning to sprout by the curbstone; and the once comfortable homes had opened their doors to boarders or let their large, high-ceiled rooms to the impoverished relics of Confederate soldiers. Only a few blocks away the stream of modern progress, sweeping along Broad Street, was rapidly changing the old Southern city into one of those bustling centres of activity which the press of the community agreed to describe as "a metropolis"; but this river of industrialism was spanned by no social bridge connecting Hill Street and its wistful relics with the statelier dignities and the more ephemeral gaieties of the opposite side. To be really "in society" one must cross over, either for good and all, or in the dilapidated "hack" which carried Gabriella to the parties of her schoolmates in West Franklin Street.

For in the middle 'nineties, before social life in Richmond had become both complicated and expensive, it was still possible for a girl in Gabriella's position—provided, of course, she came of a "good family"—to sew all day over the plain sewing of her relatives, and in the evening to reign as the acknowledged belle of a ball. "Society," it is true, did not reach any longer, except in the historic sense, to Hill Street; but the inhabitants of Hill Street, if they were young and energetic, not infrequently made triumphant excursions into "society." Though Gabriella was poor and sewed for her living, she had been, from the moment she left school, one of the most popular girls in town. To be sure, she was neither so pretty as Florrie Spencer nor so clever as Julia Caperton, but in the words of Julia's brother Algernon, she was "the sort you could count on." Even in her childhood it had become the habit of those about her to count on Gabriella. Without Gabriella, her mother was fond of saying, it would have been impossible to keep a roof over their heads.

Twelve years before, when they had moved into the house in Hill Street, Mrs. Carr had accepted from Jimmy Wrenn the rent of the first floor and the outside kitchen, which was connected with the back porch by a winding brick walk, overgrown with wild violets, while the upper story was let to two elderly spinsters, bearing the lordly, though fallen, name of Peterborough. These spinsters, like Mrs. Carr, spent their lives in a beautiful and futile pretence—the pretence of keeping up an appearance. They also took in the plain sewing of their richer relatives, who lived in Franklin Street, and sent them little trays of sweet things as soon as the midday dinner was over on Sunday. Sometimes they would drop in to see Mrs. Carr just before supper was ready, and then they would pretend that they lived on tea and toast because they were naturally "light eaters," and that they sewed all day, not for the money, but because they liked to have "something to do with their hands" They were tall thin women in organdie caps and black alpaca dresses made with long basques which showed a greenish cast in the daylight. The walls of their rooms were covered with family portraits of the colonial period, and Mrs. Carr, who had parted with most of her treasures, often wondered how they had preserved so many proofs of a distinguished descent. Even her silver had gone—first the quaint old service with the Bolton crest, which had belonged to her mother; then, one by one, the forks and spoons; and, last of all, Gabriella's silver mug, which was carried, wrapped in a shawl, to the shop of old Mr. Camberwell. She was a woman who loved inanimate things with the passion which other women give only to children, and a thousand delicate fibres of sentiment knit her soul to the portraits on the wall, to the furniture with which she lived, to the silver and glass that had once belonged to her mother. When one after one these things went from her, she felt as if the very roots of her being were torn up from the warm familiar earth in which they had grown. "There's nothing left in the parlour that I shouldn't be ashamed to have your grandmother look at," she had once confessed to her daughters.

Seen by the light of history, this parlour, in which so much of Gabriella's childhood was spent, was not without interest as an archaic survival of the fundamental errors of the mid-Victorian mind. The walls were covered with bottle-green paper on which endless processions of dwarfed blue peacocks marched relentlessly toward an embossed border—the result of an artistic frenzy of the early 'eighties. Neither Mrs. Carr nor Jimmy Wrenn, who paid the rent, had chosen this paper, but having been left on the dealer's hands, it had come under the eye of the landlord, who, since he did not have to live with it had secured it at a bargain. Too unused to remonstrance to make it effective, Mrs. Carr had suffered the offending decoration in meekness, while Jimmy, having a taste for embossment, honestly regarded the peacocks as "handsome." From the centre of the ceiling a massive gilt chandelier, elaborately festooned with damaged garlands, shed, when it was lighted, a dim and troubled gloom down on the threadbare Axminster carpet. Above the white marble mantelpiece, the old French mirror, one of the few good things left over from a public sale of Mrs. Carr's possessions, reflected a pair of bronze candelabra with crystal pendants, and a mahogany clock, which had kept excellent time for half a century and then had stopped suddenly one day while Marthy was cleaning. In the corner, between the door and the window, there was a rosewood bookcase, with the bare shelves hidden behind plaited magenta silk, and directly above it hung an engraving of a group of amiable children feeding fish in a pond. Across the room, over the walnut whatnot, a companion picture represented the same group of children scattering crumbs before a polite brood of chickens in a barnyard. Between the windows a third engraving immortalized the "Burial of Latané" in the presence of several sad and resigned ladies in crinolines, while the sofa on which Jane sat was presided over by a Sully portrait of the beautiful Angelica Carr, wearing a white scarf on her head and holding a single rose in her hand. This portrait and a Saint Memin drawing of Mrs. Carr's grandfather, the Reverend Bartholomew Berkeley as a young man in a high stock, were the solitary existing relics of that consecrated past when Fanny Berkeley was "not brought up to do anything."

To Mrs. Carr, whose mind was so constituted that any change in her surroundings produced a sensation of shock, the room was hallowed by the simple fact that she had lived in it for a number of years. That an object or a custom had existed in the past appeared to her to be an incontestible reason why it should continue to exist in the present. It was distressing to her to be obliged to move a picture or to alter the position of a piece of furniture, and she had worn one shape of bonnet and one style of hairdressing, slightly modified to suit the changing fashions, for almost twenty years. Her long pale face, her pensive blue eyes, and her look of anxious sweetness, made a touching picture of feminine incompetence; and yet it was from this pallid warmth, this gentle inefficiency of soul, that the buoyant spirit of Gabriella had sprung.

For Gabriella was the incarnation of energy. From the moment of her birth when, in the words of her negro "mammy" she had looked "as peart as life," she had begun her battle against the enveloping twin powers of decay and inertia. To the intense secret mortification of her mother, who had prayed for a second waxlike infant after the fashion of poor Jane, she had been a notoriously ugly baby (almost as ugly as her Aunt Becky Bollingbroke who had never married), and as she grew up, this ugliness was barely redeemed by what Jane, in her vague way, described as "the something else in her face." According to Cousin Jimmy, who never recognized charm unless its manifestations were soft and purring, this "something else" was merely "a sunny temper"; and one of the constant afflictions of Gabriella's childhood was overhearing her mother remark to visitors: "No, she isn't so pretty as poor Jane, but, as Cousin Jimmy tells us, she is blessed with a sunny temper."

"Give me that ruffle, mother, and I'll whip the lace on while we're waiting," she said now, laying aside the skirt of her Easter dress, and stretching out her hand for the strip of cambric in her mother's lap. But Mrs. Carr did not hear, for she was gazing, with the concentrated stare of Jane's baby, at a beautiful old lady who was walking slowly through the faint sunshine on the opposite pavement.

"I wonder where Mrs. Peyton can be coming from in her best dress?" she remarked, forgetting Jane for an instant while her sense of tragedy yielded to the keener impulse of curiosity.

"She never goes anywhere but to church or to the Old Ladies' home," replied Gabriella. "Arthur says she hasn't paid a call since her husband's death."

"Well, I haven't made one, except of course to my relatives, for fifteen years," rejoined Mrs. Carr a trifle tartly. Then her manner lost its unusual asperity, and she added excitedly, "They're coming now, Jane. There's Cousin Jimmy and he's bringing Cousin Pussy and Uncle Meriweather!"

"Oh, mother, I can't possibly see them! I feel as if it would kill me!" cried Jane in desperation.

"Give her the camphor, mother," said Gabriella with grim humour as she went to open the door.

"Brace yourself, my darling. They are coming," pleaded Mrs. Carr, as she slipped her arm under Jane's head. At the first hint of any excitement she invariably lost her presence of mind and became distracted; and Jane's hysterical outbursts never failed to convince her, though they usually left the more skeptical Gabriella unmoved. "Don't you think you would feel better if you lay back on the pillows?" she urged.

Then the bell rang, and before Jane could swallow her sobs, her sister ushered in Jimmy and Pussy Wrenn, who were closely followed by the ponderous figure of Uncle Meriweather, a gouty but benign old gentleman, whose jet-black eyebrows and white imperial gave him a misleading military air.

"Well, well, my dear, what's this I hear about Charley?" demanded Cousin Jimmy, whose sprightly manner was never sprightlier than in the hour of tragedy or the house of mourning. "What does he mean by letting you run away from him?"

"I've done my duty by Charley. I've never, never failed in my duty!" wept Jane, breaking down on Pussy's tender bosom, and waking the sleeping baby.

"We know, darling, we know," said Pussy, patting Jane's shoulder, while Jimmy drew a white silk handkerchief from his pocket, and hid his face under the pretence of blowing his nose.

To see a woman cry never failed to wring a sympathetic tear from Jimmy. Though he was a man of hard common sense, possessed of an inflexible determination to make money, there was a soft spot inside of him which was reached only by the distress of one of the opposite sex. The suffering—particularly the financial suffering—of men left him unmoved. He could foreclose a mortgage or press a debt (as long as the debtor's wife or daughter did not appeal to him) as well as another; but the instant a skirt fluttered on the horizon that soft something inside of him appeared, as he expressed it, "to give way." Apart from their afflictions, he had an eye, he used to boast, for but one woman in the world, and she, thank God, was his wife. Handsome, portly, full-blooded, and slightly overfed, he had let Pussy twine him about her little finger ever since the afternoon when he had first seen her, small, trim, and with "a way with her," at the age of six.

"Poor, poor child," said Pussy, cuddling Jane and the baby together against her sympathetic bosom. "Something must be done, Cousin Fanny. Something must be done, as Mr. Wrenn said on the way down, if it's only for the satisfaction of letting Charley know what we think of him."

"We've got to put down our pride and take some step," declared Jimmy, wondering vaguely how he could have forgotten the spirited utterance his wife attributed to him. "I'm all for the authority of the husband, of course, and the sanctity of the home, and everything according to the Bible and all that—but, bless my soul, there's got to be a limit to what a woman is expected to stand. There're some things, and I know Uncle Meriweather will agree with me, that it isn't in human nature to put up with."

"If I were forty years younger I'd call him out and give him a whipping he wouldn't forget in a jiffy," blustered Uncle Meriweather, feebly violent. "There's no way of defending a lady in these Godforsaken days. Why, I remember when I was a boy, my poor father—God bless him!—you recollect him, don't you Fanny?—never used a walking stick in his life and could read print without glasses at ninety—"

"Making love to the dressmaker," pursued Jimmy, whose righteous anger refused to be turned aside from its end.

"Don't you think, Cousin Fanny," whispered Pussy, "that Gabriella had better leave the room?"

"Gabriella? Why, how on earth can we spare her?" Mrs. Carr whispered back rather nervously. Then, beneath Pussy's compelling glance, she added timidly: "Hadn't you better go, darling, and see what the children are doing?"

"They are playing in the laundry," replied Gabriella reassuringly. "I told Dolly not to let them go out of her sight."

"She knows so much already for her age," murmured Mrs. Carr apologetically to Pussy.

"I don't know what Mr. Wrenn will think of your staying, dear," said Pussy, smiling archly at the girl. "Mr. Wrenn, I was just saying that I didn't know what you would think of Gabriella's staying in the room."

Jimmy's large handsome face, with its look of perpetual innocence—the incorruptible innocence of a man who has never imagined anything—turned helplessly in the direction of his wife. All things relating to propriety came, he felt instinctively, within the natural sphere of woman, and to be forced, on the spur of the moment, to decide a delicate question of manners, awoke in him the dismay of one who sees his accustomed prop of authority beginning to crumble. Surely Pussy knew best about things like that! He would as soon have thought of interfering with her housekeeping as of instructing her in the details of ladylike conduct. And, indeed, he had not observed that Gabriella was in the room until his wife, for her own purpose, had adroitly presented the fact to his notice.

"Gabriella in the room?" he repeated in perplexity. "Why, you'd better go, hadn't you, Gabriella? Oughtn't she to go, Pussy?"

"Just as you think best, dear, but it seems to me—"

"Certainly she ought to go," said Uncle Meriweather decisively. "The less women and girls know about such matters, the better. I don't understand, Fanny, how you could possibly have consented to Gabriella's being present."

"I didn't consent, Uncle Meriweather," protested poor Mrs. Carr, who could not bear the mildest rebuke without tears; "I only said to Pussy that Gabriella knew a great deal more already than she ought to, and I'm sure I'm not to blame for it. If I'd had my way she would have been just as sheltered as other girls."

"Don't cry, mother, it isn't your fault," said Gabriella. "Uncle Meriweather, if you make mother cry I'll never forgive you. How can she help all these dreadful things going on?"

She was sensible, she was composed, she was perfectly sweet about it; but, and this fact made Pussy gasp with dismay, she did not budge an inch from her position. With her clear grave eyes, which lost their sparkle when she grew serious, and her manner of eager sympathy, she appeared, indeed, to be the only one in the room who was capable of facing the situation with frankness. That she meant to face it to the end, Pussy could not doubt while she looked at her.

"Oh, it doesn't matter about Gabriella. She knows everything," said Jane, with the prickly sweetness of suffering virtue.

"But she's a young girl—young girls oughtn't to hear such things," argued Uncle Meriweather, feeling helplessly that something was wrong with the universe, and that, since it was different from anything he had ever known in the past, he was unable to cope with it. Into his eyes, gentle and bloodshot above his fierce white moustache—the eyes of one who has never suffered the painful process of thinking things out, but has accepted his opinions as unquestioningly as he has accepted his religion or the cut of his clothes—there came the troubled look of one who is struggling against forces that he does not understand. For Gabriella was serious. There was not the slightest hope in the disturbed mind of Uncle Meriweather that she was anything but perfectly serious. Caprice, being a womanly quality, was not without a certain charm for him. He was quite used to it; he knew how to take it; he had been taught to recognize it from his childhood up. It was pretty, it was playful; and his mind, if so ponderous a vehicle could indulge in such activity, was fond of play. But after the first perplexed minute or two he had relinquished forever the hope that Gabriella was merely capricious. Clearly the girl knew what she was talking about; and this knowledge, so surprising in one of her age and sex, gave him a strange dreamy sense of having just awakened from sleep.

"I must say I like girls to be girls, Fanny," he pursued testily; "I reckon I'm only an old fogy, but I like girls to be girls. When a woman loses her innocence, she loses her greatest charm in the eyes of a man—of the right sort of a man. Pluck the peach with the bloom on it, my poor father used to say. He didn't believe in all this new-fangled nonsense about the higher education of women— none of his daughters could do more I than read and write and spell after a fashion, and yet look what wives and mothers they made! Pokey married three times, and was the mother of fourteen children, nine of them sons. And are we any better off now than then, I ask? Whoever heard of a woman running away from her husband before the war, and now here is poor Jane—"

"But it isn't my fault, Uncle Meriweather!" cried Jane, in desperation at his obtuseness. "I've tried to be the best wife I could—ask Charley if I haven't. He neglected me long before I let any one know—even mother. I forgave him again and again, and I'd go on forgiving him forever if he would let me. I've told him over and over that I was going to be a faithful wife to him if he killed me."

"Of course, my dear, I'm not meaning to reproach you," said Uncle Meriweather, overcome by the effect of his words. "We all know that you've stood as much as any woman could and keep her self-respect. It isn't possible, I suppose, for you to go on living with Charley?"

"Oh, I couldn't bear a separation, not a legal one at any rate," groaned Mrs. Carr. "Of course she must come away for a time, but nobody must hear of it or it would kill me. They are one in the sight of God, and my dear old father had such a horror of separations."

"Well, I'd kick him out—I'd kick him out so quickly he wouldn't know it," declared Jimmy. "If a daughter of mine were married to that scamp, she'd never lay eyes on him except over my dead body. I reckon God would enjoy the sight of his getting his deserts."

Deep down in Cousin Jimmy, deeper than sentiment, deeper than tradition, deeper even than the solid bedrock of common sense, there was the romantic essence of his soul, which hated baseness with a fiery hatred. His ruddy face, still boyish in spite of his fifty years, blanched slowly, and there came into his soft dark eyes the look he had worn at Malvern Hill under the fire of the enemy.

At the sight Gabriella thrilled as she did when drums were beating and armies were marching. "Oh, Cousin Jimmy, don't let her go back!" she cried.

"I can't go back to him now! I can never, never go back to him again!" intoned Jane with passionate energy.

"No, God bless her, she shan't go back," declared Jimmy, as profoundly stirred as Gabriella.

"But the children? What will become of the children?" demanded Mrs. Carr, not of Jimmy, but of the universe. Her helpless gaze, roving wildly from face to face, and resting nowhere, was like the gaze of a small animal caught in a trap. "If Jane separates the children from their father what will people think of her?" she asked, still vainly addressing Heaven.

"As long as she is right it doesn't matter what people think," retorted Gabriella; but her protest, unlike her mother's, was directed to the visible rather than to the invisible powers. The thought of Jane's children—of the innocent souls so unaware of the awful predicament in which they were placed that their bodies could be devouring bread and damson preserves in the laundry. The poignant thought of these children moved her more deeply than she had ever been moved before in her twenty years. A passion for self-sacrifice rushed through her with the piercing sweetness of religious ecstasy. Nothing like this had ever happened to her before—not when she was confirmed, not when she had stood at the head of her class, not when she had engaged herself to Arthur Peyton two years before. It was the pure flame of experience at its highest point that burned in her.

"I will take care of the children," she said breathlessly. "I will give up my whole life to them. I will get a place in a store and work my fingers to the bone, if only Jane will never go back."

For a moment there was silence; but while Gabriella waited for somebody to answer, she felt that it was a silence which had become vocal with inexpressible things. The traditions of Uncle Meriweather, the conventions of Mrs. Carr, the prejudices of Jimmy, and the weak impulses of Jane, all these filled the dusk through which the blank faces of her family stared back at her. Then, while she stood white and trembling with her resolve—with the passionate desire to give herself, body and soul, to Jane and to Jane's children—the voice of Experience spoke pleasantly, but firmly, through Cousin Pussy's lips, and it dealt with Gabriella's outburst as Experience usually deals with Youth.

"You are a dear child, Gabriella," it said; "but how in the world could you help Jane by going into a store?"

In the midst of the emotional scene, Cousin Pussy alone remained sweetly matter-of-fact. Though she was not without orderly sentiments, her character had long ago been swept of heroics, and from her arched gray hair, worn à la Pompadour, to her pretty foot in its small neat boot, she was a practical soul who had as little use for religious ecstasy as she had for downright infidelity. There seemed to her something positively unnatural in Gabriella's manner—a hint of that "sudden conversion" she associated with the lower classes or with the negroes.

"You are a dear child," she repeated, biting her fresh lips; "but how will you help Jane by going into a store?"

"I can trim hats," returned Gabriella stubbornly. "Mr. Brandywine will take me into his new millinery department, I know, for I said something to him about it the other day."

"Oh, Gabriella, not in a store! It would kill mother!" cried Jane, with the prophetic wail of Cassandra.

"Not in a store!" echoed Mrs. Carr; "you couldn't work in a store. If you want to work," she concluded feebly, "why can't you work just as well in your home?"

"But it isn't the same thing, mother," explained Gabriella, with angelic patience. "Nobody will get me to make hats at home, and, besides, I've got to learn how to do it. I've got to learn business methods."

"But not in a shop, my dear," protested Uncle Meriweather in the precise English of his youth.

"Bless my heart!" chuckled Cousin Jimmy. "Business methods! You're as good as a show, Gabriella, and, by George! you've plenty of pluck. I like pluck in man or woman."

"I shouldn't encourage her if I were you, Mr. Wrenn," said Cousin Pussy, almost forgetting to be indirect.

"Well, of course, I don't approve of that store business," replied Jimmy, deprecatingly, "but I can't help liking pluck when I see it. Look here, Gabriella, if you're bent on working, why don't you turn in and teach?"

"Yes, let her teach by all means," agreed Uncle Meriweather, with genuine enthusiasm for the idea. "I've always regarded teaching as an occupation that ought to be restricted by law to needy ladies."

"But I can't teach, I don't know enough, and, besides, I'd hate it," protested Gabriella.

"I'm sure you might start a school for very little children," said Mrs. Carr. "You don't have to know much, to teach them, and you write a very good hand."

"What about plain sewing?" asked Pussy in her ready way. "Couldn't you learn to make those new waists all the girls are wearing?"

"I haven't the patience to sew well. Look how hard mother works, making buttonholes with stitches so fine you can hardly see them, and yet she doesn't get enough to put bread into her mouth, and but for her relatives she'd have been in the poorhouse long ago. I'm tired of being on charity just because we are women. Now that Jane has come home for good I am simply obliged to find something to do."

"I don't mind your wanting to work, dear, I think it's splendid of you," returned Pussy, "but I do feel that you ought to work in a ladylike way—a way that wouldn't interfere with your social position and your going to germans and having attention from young men and all that."

"Why don't you make lampshades, Gabriella?" demanded Jane in an emphatic burst of inspiration. "Sophy Madison earns enough from lampshades to send her sister and herself to the White Sulphur Springs every summer."

"Sophy makes all the lampshades that anybody wants, and, besides, she gets orders from the North—she told me so yesterday."

"Gabriella crochets beautifully," remarked Mrs. Carr a little nervously because of the failure of her first suggestion. "The last time I went to see Miss Matoaca Chambers in the Old Ladies' Home, she told me she made quite a nice little sum for her church by crocheting mats."

"And Gabriella can cook, too," rejoined Pussy, with exaggerated sprightliness, for she felt that Mrs. Carr's solution of the problem had not been entirely felicitous. "Why doesn't she try sending some of her angel food to the Woman's Exchange?"

Jimmy, who had listened to this advice with the expression of tolerant amusement he always wore when women began to talk about the more serious affairs of life in his presence, made an honest, if vulgar, attempt to lighten the solemnity of the situation with a joke.

"Gabriella isn't trying to earn church money. You're out gunning for a living, aren't you, Ella?" he inquired.

"I'm sick of being dependent," repeated Gabriella, while her face grew stern. "Do you think if Jane had had enough money to live on that she would ever have stood Charley so long?"

"Oh, yes, I should, Gabriella. Marriage is sacred to me!" exclaimed Jane, whose perfect wifeliness atoned, even in the opinion of Jimmy, for any discrepancies in logic. "Nothing on earth could have induced me to leave him until—until this happened."

The conviction that she had never at any moment since her marriage "failed in her duty to Charley" lent a touching sanctity to her expression, while the bitter lines around her mouth faded in the wan glow that flooded her face. Whatever her affliction, however intense her humiliation, Jane was supported always by the most comforting of beliefs—the belief that she had been absolutely right and Charley absolutely wrong through the ten disillusioning years of their married life. Never for an instant—never even in a nightmare—had she been visited by the disquieting suspicion that she was not entirely blameless.

"Well, you've left him now anyway," said Gabriella, with the disarming candour which delighted Jimmy and perplexed Uncle Meriweather, "so somebody has got to help you take care of the children."

"She shall never come to want as long as Pussy and I have a cent left," declared Cousin Jimmy, and his voice expressed what Mrs. Carr described afterward as "proper feeling."

"And we'd really rather that you'd earn less and keep in your own station of life," said Pussy decisively.

"If you mean that you'd rather I'd work buttonholes or crochet mats than go into a store and earn a salary, then I can't do it," answered Gabriella, as resolute, though not so right-minded, as poor Jane. "I'd rather die than be dependent all my life, and I'm going to earn my living if I have to break rocks to do it."

# CHAPTER II

## POOR JANE

Supper was over, and Gabriella, still in the dress she had worn all day, was picking up the children's clothes from the floor of her room. According to Mrs. Carr's hereditary habit in sorrow or sickness, Jane had been served in bed with tea and toast, while several small hard cots had been brought down from the attic and arranged in the available space in the two bedrooms. As Gabriella looked at the sleeping children, who had kicked the covering away, and lay with round rosy limbs gleaming in the lamplight, she remembered that Arthur Peyton was coming at nine o'clock to take her to Florrie's party, and she told herself with grim determination that she would never go to a party again. The Berkeley conscience, that vein of iron which lay beneath the outward softness and incompetence of her mother and sister, held her, in spite of her tempting youth, to the resolution she had made. She had told Jimmy that she meant to earn her living if she had to break rocks to do it, and Gabriella, like Pussy, came of a race that "did not easily change its mind."

Turning to the bureau, she smoothed out the children's hair ribbons and pinned them, in two tight little blue and pink rolls, to the pincushion. Then taking up a broken comb, she ran it through the soft lock of hair that fell like a brown wing over her forehead. Her bright dark eyes, fringed in short thick lashes and set wide apart under arched eyebrows, gazed questioningly back at her from a row of german favours with which she had decorated the glass; and it was as if the face of youth, flickering with a flamelike glow and intensity, swam there for an instant in the dim greenish pool of the mirror. Beneath the charm of the face there was the character which one associates, not with youth, but with age and experience. Beneath the fine, clear lines of her head and limbs, the tall slenderness of her figure, the look of swiftness and of energy, which was almost birdlike in its grace and poise, there was a strength and vigour which suggested a gallant boy rather than the slighter and softer frame of a girl.

While she stood there, Gabriella thought regretfully of all that it would mean to give up her half-dependent and wholly ladylike existence and go to work in a shop. Necessity not choice was driving her; and in spirit she looked back almost wistfully to the securely circumscribed lot of her grandmother. For there was little of the rebel in her temperament; and had she been free to choose, she would have instinctively selected, guided by generations of gregarious ancestors, the festive girlhood which Cousin Pussy had so ardently described. She wanted passionately all the things that other girls had, and her only quarrel, indeed, with the sheltered life was that she couldn't afford it. In the expressive phrase of Cousin Jimmy, the sheltered life "cost money," and to cost money was to be beyond the eager grasp of Gabriella.

The door opened as if yielding under protest, and Marthy entered, still hurriedly tying the strings of the clean apron she had slipped on over her soiled one before answering the door-bell.

"Yo' beau done come, Miss Ella. Ain't you gwine?"

"No, I'm not going to the party, Marthy, but ask him to wait just a minute."

"He's settin' over yonder in de parlour wid his overcoat on."

"Well, ask him to take it off; I'll be there in a moment." She spoke as gravely as Marthy had done, yet in her face there was a light play of humour.

Two years ago she would have thrilled with joy at the thought that Arthur was waiting for her; but in those two years since her engagement she had grown to look upon her first love as the gossamer, fairylike romance of a child. For months she had known that the engagement must be broken sooner or later; and she knew now, while she listened to Marthy's shuffling feet hastening to deliver her message, that she must break it to-night. In the dim pool of her mirror a face looked back at her that was not the face of Arthur Peyton; she saw it take form there as one sees a face grow gradually into life from the dimness of dreams. It was, she told herself to-night, the very face of her dream that she saw.

"Well, I must get it over," she said with a sternness which gave her a passing resemblance to the Saint Memin portrait of the Reverend Bartholomew Berkeley; "I've got to get it over to-night, and whatever happens I've got to be honest." Then, with a last glance at the sleeping children, she lowered the gas, and went across the darkened hail, which smelt of pickles and bacon because one end of it was used as a storeroom.

The parlour had been swept since the family council had deliberated there over Jane's destiny. The scraps of cambric had been gathered up from the threadbare arabesques in the carpet; the chairs had been placed at respectable distances apart; the gas-jets in the chandelier were flaming extravagantly under the damaged garlands; and the sewing machine had been wheeled into the obscurity of the hail, for it would have humiliated Gabriella's mother to think that her daughter received young men in a room which looked as if somebody had worked there.

When Gabriella entered, Arthur Peyton was standing in front of the fireplace, gazing abstractedly at his reflection in the French mirror. Though his chestnut hair was carefully brushed, he had instinctively lifted his hand to smooth down an imaginary lock, and while he did this, he frowned slightly as if at a recollection that had ruffled his temper. His features were straight and very narrow, with the look of sensitiveness one associates with the thoroughbred, and the delicate texture of his skin emphasized this quality of high-breeding, which was the only thing that one remembered about him. In his light-gray eyes there was a sympathetic expression which invariably won the hearts of old ladies, and these old ladies were certain to say of him afterward, "such a gentleman, my dear—almost of the old school, you know, and we haven't many of them left in this hurrying age."

He had done well, though not brilliantly, at college, for his mind, if unoriginal, had never given anybody, not even his mother, the least bit of trouble. For three years he had worked with admirable regularity in the office of his uncle, Carter Peyton, one of the most distinguished lawyers in the Virginia of his period, and it was generally felt that young Arthur Peyton would have "a brilliant future." For the present, however, he lived an uneventful life with his widowed mother in a charming old house, surrounded by a walled garden, in Franklin Street. Like the house, he was always in perfect order; and everything about him, from his loosely fitting clothes and his immaculate linen to his inherited conceptions of life, was arranged with such exquisite precision that it was impossible to improve it in any way. He knew exactly what he thought, and he knew also his reason, which was usually a precedent in law or custom, for thinking as he did. His opinions, which were both active and abundant, were all perfectly legitimate descendants of tradition, and the phrase "nobody ever heard of such a thing," was quite as convincing to him as to Mrs. Carr or to Cousin Jimmy Wrenn.

"Gabriella, aren't you going?" he asked reproachfully as the girl entered.

"Oh, Arthur, we've had such a dreadful day! Poor Jane has left Charley for good and has come home, with all the children. We've been busy dividing them among us, and we're going to turn the dining-room into a nursery.

"Left Charley? That's bad, isn't it?" asked Arthur doubtfully.

"I feel so sorry for her, Arthur. It must be terrible to have love end like that."

"But she isn't to blame. Everybody knows that she has forgiven him again and again."

"Yes, everybody knows it," repeated Gabriella, as if she drew bitter comfort from the knowledge, "and she says now that she will never, never go back to him."

For the first time a shadow appeared in Arthur's clear eyes.

"Do you think she ought to make up her mind, darling, until she sees whether or not he will reform? After all, she is his wife."

"That's what mother says, and yet I believe Charley is the only person on earth mother really hates. Now Cousin Jimmy and I will do everything we can to keep her away from him."

"I think I shouldn't meddle if I were you, dearest. She'll probably go back to him in the end because of the children."

"But I am going to help her take care of the children," replied Gabriella stanchly. "Of course, my life will be entirely different now, Arthur," she added gently. "Everything is altered for me, too, since yesterday. I have thought it all over for hours, and I am going to try to get a place in Brandywine's store."

"In a store?" repeated Arthur slowly, and she saw the muscles of his mouth tighten and grow rigid.

"Mother doesn't like the idea any more than you do, but what are we to come to if we go on in the old aimless way? One can't make a living out of plain sewing, and though, of course, Charley will be supposed to provide for his children, he isn't exactly the sort one can count on. Brandywine's, you see, is only a beginning. What I mean is that I am obliged to learn how to support myself."

"But couldn't you work just as well in your home, darling?

"People don't pay anything for home work. You must see what I mean, Arthur."

"Yes, I see," he replied tenderly; but after a moment's thought, he went on again with the gentle obstinacy of a man whose thinking had all been done for him before he was born. "I wish, though, that you would try to hold out a little longer, working at home with your mother. In a year or two we shall be able to marry."

"I couldn't," said Gabriella, shaking her head. "Don't urge me, Arthur."

"If you would only consent to live with mother, we might marry now," he pursued, after a minute, as if he had not heard her.

"But it wouldn't be fair to her, and how could I ask her to take mother and Jane and the children? No, I've thought it all out, dear, and I must go to work."

"But I'll work for them, Gabriella. I'll do anything on earth rather than see you ordered about by old Brandywine."

"He won't order me about," answered Gabriella cheerfully; "but mother feels just as you do. She says I am going out of my class because I won't stay at home and work buttonholes."

"You couldn't go out of your class," replied Arthur, with an instinctive gallantry which even his distress could not overcome; "but I can't get used to the thought of it, darling—I simply can't. You're so sacred to me. There's something about the woman a man loves that's different from every other woman, and the bare idea of your working in a shop sickens me. I always think of you as apart from the workaday world. I always think of you as a star shining serenely above the sordid struggle—" Overwhelmed by the glowing train of his rhetoric, he broke down suddenly and caught passionately at the cool hand of Gabriella.

As he looked at her slender finger, on which he had placed her engagement ring two years before, it seemed to him that the situation was becoming intolerable—that it was an affront not only to his ideal of Gabriella, as something essentially starlike and remote, but to that peculiar veneration for women which he always spoke and thought of as "Southern." His ideal woman was gentle, clinging, so perfectly a "lady" that she would have perished had she been put into a shop; and, though he was aware that Gabriella was a girl of much character and determination, his mind was so constructed that he was able, without difficulty, to think of her as corresponding to this exalted type of her sex. By the simple act of falling in love with her he had endowed her with every virtue except the ones that she actually possessed.

"I know, I know," said Gabriella tenderly, for she saw that he suffered. Her training had been a hard one, though she had got it at home, and in a violent reaction from the sentimentality of her mother and Jane she had become suspicious of any language that sounded "flowery" to her sensitive ears. With her clear-sighted judgment, she knew perfectly well that by no stretch of mind or metaphor could she be supposed to resemble a star—that she was not shining, not remote, not even "ideal" in Arthur's delicate sense of the word. She had known the horrors of poverty, of that bitter genteel poverty which must keep up an appearance at any cost; and she could never forget the grim days, after the death of Uncle Beverly Blair, when they had shivered in fireless rooms and gone for weeks without butter on their bread. For the one strong quality in Mrs. Carr's character was the feeling she spoke of complacently, though modestly, as "proper pride"; and this proper pride, which was now resisting Gabriella's struggle for independence, had in the past resisted quite as stubbornly the thought of an appeal to the ready charity of her masculine relatives. To seek a man's advice had been from her girlhood the primal impulse of Mrs. Carr's nature; but, until Fate had starved her into sincerity, she had kept alive the ladylike fiction that she was in need of moral, not material, assistance.

"Of course, if there were any other way, Arthur," said Gabriella, remembering the earlier battles with her mother, and eager to compromise when she could do so with dignity; "but how can I go on being dependent on Cousin Jimmy and Uncle Meriweather. Neither of them is rich, and Cousin Jimmy has a large family."

Of course she was reasonable. The most disagreeable thing about Gabriella, Jane had once said, was her inveterate habit of being reasonable. But then Jane, who was of an exquisite sensibility, felt that Gabriella's reasonableness belonged to a distinctly lower order of intelligence. When all was said, Gabriella saw clearly because she had a practical mind, and a practical mind is usually engrossed with material matters.

"I understand exactly how you feel, dear, but if only you could go on just as you are for a few years longer," said Arthur, sticking to his original idea with a tenacity which made it possible for him to argue for hours and yet remain exactly where he had started. Though they talked all night, though she convinced him according to all the laws and principles of logic, she knew that he would still think precisely what he had thought in the beginning, for his conviction was rooted, deeper than reason, in the unconquerable prejudices which had passed from the brain into the very blood of his race. He would probably say at the end: "I admit all that you tell me, Gabriella, but my sentiment is against it;" and this sentiment, overruling sense, would insist, with sublime obstinacy, that Gabriella must not work in a shop. It would ignore, after the exalted habit of sentiment, such merely sordid facts as poverty and starvation (who ever heard of a woman of good family starving in Virginia?), and, at last, if Gabriella were really in love with Arthur, it would triumph over her finer judgment and reduce her to submission. But while she watched him, in the very minute when, failing for words, he caught her in his arms, she said to herself, suddenly chilled and determined: "I must get it over to-night, and I've got to be honest." The scent of the hyacinths floated to her again, but it seemed to bring a cold wind, as if a draught had blown in through the closed slats of the shutters.

"Everything has changed, Arthur," she said, "and I don't think I ought to go on being engaged." Then because her words sounded insincere, she added sternly: "Even if we could be married—and of course we can't be—I—I don't feel that I should want to marry. I am not sure that I love you enough to marry you."

It was all so unromantic, so unemotional, so utterly different from the scene she had pictured when she imagined what "breaking her engagement" would be like. Then she had always thought of herself as dissolving in tears on the horsehair sofa, which had become sacred to the tragedy of poor Jane; but, to her surprise, she did not feel now the faintest inclination to cry. It ought to have been theatrical, but it wasn't—not even when she took off her engagement ring, as she had read in novels that girls did at the decisive instant, and laid it down on the table. When she remembered this afterwards, it appeared rather foolish, but Arthur seemed not to notice it, and when Marthy came in to light the fire in the morning, she found the ring lying on a copy of Gray's Elegy and brought it back to Gabriella.

"I'll never give you up," said Arthur stubbornly, and knowing his character, she felt that he had spoken the truth. He could not give her up even had he wished it, for, like a belief, she had passed from his brain into the fibre of his being. She had become a habit to him, and not love, but the inability to change, to cease thinking what he had always thought, to break a fixed manner of life, would keep him faithful to her in his heart.

"I'm sorry—oh, I'm sorry," she murmured, longing to have it over and to return to Jane and the children. It occurred to her almost resentfully that love was not always an unmixed delight.

"Is there any one else, Gabriella?" he asked with a sudden choking sound in his voice. "I have sometimes thought—in the last four or five months—that there might be—that you had changed—that—" He stopped abruptly, and she answered him with a beautiful frankness which would have horrified the imperishable, if desiccated, coquetry of her mother.

"There is some one else and there isn't," she replied simply. "I mean I think of some one else very often—of some one who isn't in my life at all—from whom I never hear—"

"Is it George Fowler?"

She bowed her head, and, though she did not blush, her eyes grew radiant.

"And you have known him less than a year?"

Again she bowed her head without speaking. What was there, after all, that she could say in justification of her behaviour?

A groan escaped him, smothered into a gentle murmur of protest. "And I thought women were more constant than men!" he exclaimed with something of the baffled and helpless feeling which had overtaken Uncle Meriweather while he regarded Gabriella.

The generalization was not without interest for Gabriella.

"I thought so, too," she observed dispassionately. "I thought so, too, and that is why it was such a dreadful surprise to me when it happened. You yourself aren't more shocked and surprised than I was in the beginning," she added.

"But you've got used to the thought, I suppose?"

"Well, one has to, you see. What else is there to do? I always understood from mother"—she went on with the same eager interest, as if she were stumbling upon new and important intellectual discoveries—"I always understood that women never fell in love with men first—I mean until they had had positive proof that their love would be returned. But in this case that didn't seem to matter at all. Nothing mattered, and the more I fought against it and tried to be true to my engagement, the more I found myself being false. It's all very strange," she concluded, "but that is just how it happened."

"And he knows nothing about it?"

"Oh, no. I told him I was engaged to you, and then he went away."

For an instant he was silent, and watching his face, so carefully guarded and controlled by habit that it had the curious blank look of a statue's, Gabriella could form no idea of the suppressed inarticulate suffering in his heart.

"And if he came back would you marry him?" he asked.

Before replying she sat for a minute gazing down on her folded hands and weighing each separate word of her answer.

"I should try not to, Arthur," she said at last, "but—but I am not sure that I should be able to help it."

When at last he had said "good-bye" rather grimly, and gone out of the door without looking back, she was conscious of an immense relief, of a feeling that she could breathe freely again after an age of oppression. There was a curious sense of unreality about the hour she had just passed through, as if it belonged not to actual life, but to a play she had been rehearsing. She had felt nothing. The breaking of her engagement had failed utterly to move her.

After bolting the front door, she turned out the gas in the parlour, pushed back the lump of coal in the grate in the hope of saving it for the morrow, and went cautiously down the hall to her room. As she passed her mother's door, a glimmer of light along the threshold made her pause for a minute, and while she hesitated, an anxious voice floated out to her:

"Gabriella, is that you?"

"Yes, Mother, do you want anything?"

"Jane has one of her heart attacks. I put her to bed in my room because it is more comfortable than the dining-room. Don't you think you had better go back and wake Marthy?"

"Is she ill? Let me come in," answered Gabriella, pushing open the door and brushing by Mrs. Carr, who stood, shrunken and shivering, in a gray flannel wrapper and felt slippers.

Though Jane's attacks were familiar occurrences, they never failed to produce an immediate panic in the household. As a child of nine, Gabriella remembered being aroused in the middle of a bitter night, hastily wrapped in her mother's shawl and a blanket, and hurried up the staircase to Jane, who had broken her engagement to Charley the evening before. Jane, pale, angelic, palpitating, appeared to draw her last breath as they entered, while the old doctor supported her in his arms, and Marthy, in a frenzy of service, rattled the dead embers in the grate. It had all been horribly vivid, and when Jane had murmured Charley's name in a dying voice, they had stood, trembling and blue with cold, around her bed, waiting for the end. But the end had not come, and three months later Jane was married to Charley Gracey.

After that scene, Gabriella had associated Jane's attacks with a freezing January night and a fireless grate (though the last but one had occurred in mid-August), and she was relieved now to find a fire burning in her mother's room and a kettle singing merrily on the fender. The elder children, with their flannel petticoats pinned over their thin little shoulders, were sitting straight and stiff on a box couch which had been turned into a bed, and their strange little faces looked wan and peaked in the firelight.

Jane was really ill, Gabriella decided, after a glance at her sister. Nothing except acute suffering could have given her that ghastly pallor or made her eyes sink so far back in her head. She lay quite motionless on the far side of the big tester bed, staring straight up at the ceiling with an expression which terrified Gabriella, though she had seen it on her sister's face at least a dozen times before to-night.

"Has Arthur gone?" asked Mrs. Carr in a voice that sounded as if she were running.

"Yes. Did you want him, mother?"

"I thought we might send him for the doctor and for Charley. Don't you think Charley ought to be told of her condition? She has asked for the children."

"Have you given her the digitalis?"

"I can't make her swallow it. There are the drops on the table by the bed. My hands tremble so I had to measure them three times."

Taking the glass from the table, Gabriella bent over her sister and implored her to swallow the drops, but, without appearing to hear her voice, Jane still stared blankly upward, with the rigid, convulsed look of a woman who has been stricken with dumbness. Her flaxen hair, damp with camphor, which Mrs. Carr had wildly splashed on her forehead, clung flat and close to her head, while the only pulse in her body seemed to beat in irregular, spasmodic throbs in her throat.

"Don't go, mother. I'll wake Marthy," cried Gabriella, for Mrs. Carr, inspired by the spirit of panic, was darting out of the door in her felt slippers. Then, while the children, crying distractedly, rushed to Jane's bedside, the girl ran out of the house and along the brick walk to the kitchen and the room above it where Marthy lived the little life she had apart from her work. In answer to Gabriella's call she emerged entirely dressed from the darkness; and at the news of Jane's illness she was seized with the spurious energy which visits her race in the moment of tragedy. She offered at once to run for the doctor, and suggested, without a hint from Gabriella, that she had better leave word, on her way home, for Marse Charley.

"I knowed 'twuz comin' jez ez soon ez I lay eyes on 'er," she muttered, for she was an old family servant. "Dar ain' no use 'n tryin' ter come betweenst dem de good Lawd is done jine tergedder fur worse. A baid husban'! Hi! Dar ain't un 'oman erlive, I reckon, dat 'ouldn't ruther own a baid husban' den no husban' at all. You all is got to teck 'em de way dey's made, en dar's moughty few un um dat is made right."

Still muttering, she stumbled down the walk and out of the gate, while Gabriella returned to her mother's room and hurried the weeping children into their shoes and stockings. Mrs. Carr, still in her flannel wrapper, with her little flat gray curls screwed up on pins for the night, and her thin ankles showing pathetically above her felt slippers, ran nervously to and fro with mustard plasters and bottles of hot water which she continually refilled from the kettle on the fender. Occasionally she paused long enough to hold the camphor to Jane's nose or to lift the quilt from the bottom of the bed and then put it carefully back in the very spot where it had lain before she had touched it. And because she was born to take two steps to every one that was necessary, because she could not accomplish the simplest act without a prodigious waste of energy and emotion, because she died twenty deaths over the slightest anxiety, and, most of all, because she was the last person on earth who ought to have been burdened with poverty and hard work and an unhappily married daughter—because of all these things Mrs. Carr wore herself to a shadow in the quarter of an hour they spent waiting for the doctor and Charley Gracey.

Though she had brought Jane through at least a dozen "attacks," she still lost her presence of mind as completely as on that January night when, utterly distraught, she had hurried Gabriella to the first death-bed scene of her sister; she still grew as forgetful of herself and her own feelings, and, in obedience to some profound law of her nature, she still as confidently "expected the worst." For Mrs. Carr's philosophy, like Jane's, was of that active but dreary sort that thrives best upon misery. Just as Jane, who had lost every illusion about Charley, went on loving him in spite of it, so Mrs. Carr, having lost her illusions about life, retained a kind of wistful fondness for the thing that had wounded her.

The door-bell rang sharply, and Gabriella went to let in the doctor, a brisk, authoritative young man of the new school, who had learned everything there was to be known about medicine except the way to behave in a sickroom, and who abhorred a bedside manner as heartily as if it were calomel or castor oil. His name was Darrow, and he was the assistant of old Dr. Walker, Mrs. Carr's family physician, who never went out at night since he had passed his seventieth birthday. Gabriella, who liked him because he was not anecdotal and gave small doses of medicine, hastily led the way to her mother's room before she ran back to meet Charley Gracey at the door of the dark parlour.

"You can't see her now. The doctor is with her," she whispered. "I'll make a light in here and you can wait."

"Let me," said Charley, quite as pleasantly as if he were not a bad husband, while he found a match and struck it on the sole of his foot. Then, as the gas flared up, he exclaimed, with a low whistle, "By Jove, you're a sight, Gabriella!"

"Well, it's your fault," replied Gabriella sharply, letting him see, as she told herself, exactly what she thought of him. "You've made Jane so ill we thought she was dying."

"I'm sorry for that," he said, suddenly smitten with gravity. "Is she really so bad?"

His charming freckled face, with its irrepressible humour, grew almost grotesquely solemn, while the habitual merriment faded slowly from his light-gray eyes, leaving them empty of expression. He was a short, rather thick-set man, not particularly good-looking, not particularly clever, but possessing a singular, if unaccountable, charm. Everybody liked Charley, though nobody respected him. He was a scamp, but a lovable scamp, while Jane, with the best intentions in the world, had managed to make every virtue unattractive. When people condemned him, they said that he was "utterly unprincipled"; when they softened in their judgment, they admitted that he had "the best heart in the world."

"I suppose it isn't any worse than other attacks," answered Gabriella, "but you know what they are like."

"Yes, I know," replied Charley. "Oh, Lord, don't I?"

"She asked mother to send for you," continued Gabriella. "She wants you to know that she has forgiven you."

"Has she?" said Charley, without elation. Turning away, he stared for a minute or two at the engraving of the children feeding fish in a pond; then, with his eyes still glued to the picture, he burst out passionately: "Gabriella, I'd hoped she wouldn't this time!"

"If I were she," retorted Gabriella crushingly, "I would never speak to you again until the day of my death."

"If she were you," rejoined Charley, with barefaced audacity, "I'd have been a good husband. Why, I was simply starving to be a good husband when I married Jane. It's my ideal in life. I'm all for the domestic thing by nature. I was tired—positively dog-tired of the other kind. I wanted a wife. I adored—I've always adored babies—"

"If that is true," returned Gabriella sternly, for she was not disposed to soften to Charley, and in her heart she deeply resented what she called Jane's "weakness," "if that is true why do you behave so outrageously to Jane and the children? Why can't you be decent?"

"I could," answered Charley, with engaging lucidity, "if she were less so. It's her infernal virtue I can't stand, Gabriella. No man could stand it without taking to drink."

"But you knew she was that way. She was always trying to make people better. It is her mission. Why, I remember one winter night before you were married mother got me out of bed in the cold to come and hear Jane forgive you beautifully about something."

"That was the first time, and it was very touching. I suppose the first time always is touching. Of course, I didn't know she meant to keep it up. No man could possibly have kept it up," said Charley, with bitterness, "but she married me to reform me, and it is the only thing she has really enjoyed about her marriage. She's a born reformer. I haven't eaten a thing I cared about, nor drank a drop I wanted, nor used a bad word I was fond of, since I married, without being nagged at about it. She loved me for my vices, and yet she hasn't let me keep a single one—not even the smallest—not even cigarettes. Nag! Good God!

She's nagged me to perfection ever since the day of our wedding when she made me sign the pledge before she let me kiss her!"

"Well, that doesn't make it any easier for us or for the children," replied Gabriella, without sympathy; "and if you don't think of Jane, you might at least think of your children."

"Of course it's hard on the kids," admitted Charley ruefully. "But as for Jane—now, will you tell me what would become of Jane after she had reformed me? Why, she'd be bored to death. She'd be a martyr without any martyrdom. When she made me give up tobacco, she lost interest in everything for a week. She was like your Uncle Meriweather after the surrender. There wasn't anything left to fight about, and fighting was all he could do—"

"I believe—I really believe you have been drinking," interrupted Gabriella with cold disgust. "Suppose Jane were to die?"

"She won't die. She'll be all right as soon as she has forgiven me."

He was not only bad, she told herself, he was perfectly shameless. He appeared to have been born without the faintest sense of responsibility. And yet, while Gabriella listened to him, she realized that, in some ways, he might be a less trying companion than poor Jane. His candour was as simple, as unaffected, as the serene artlessness of a child. It was impossible not to believe in his sincerity. Though she "despised him," as she told herself, still she was obliged to admit that there was something to be said on his side. The harsh judgment of youth—of youth that never tries to understand, that never makes allowances—softened under the influence of Charley's reprehensible charm. Even badness, Gabriella conceded grudgingly, might be easier to live with in some circumstances than a too exalted self-righteousness.

"If you'll bring Jane to that way of thinking," retorted Charley, with vulgar frankness, "I'll give you five hundred dollars down. If you'll thoroughly corrupt her mind and persuade her to neglect her duty to me, I'll make it a thousand."

He was jesting! It was monstrous, with Jane lying ill in her mother's room; it was indecent; it was grossly immoral; but he was actually jesting! Not even scandal, not even the doctor's presence in the house, could suppress his incorrigible spirit of levity. "If I were Jane, I'd never speak to him," thought Gabriella, and the question flashed through her mind, "how in the world could she ever have loved him?" It was impossible for her to conceive of any situation when Charley could have made a girl fall in love with him. Though she had heard stories of his early conquests, she had never believed them. There were times when she almost liked him, but it was the kind of liking one gave to an inferior, not to an equal. She admitted his charm, but it was the charm of an irresponsible creature—the capricious attraction of a child or an animal. Her common sense, she told herself, would keep her from making a mistake such as Jane had made with her life; and, besides, she was utterly devoid of the missionary instinct which had lured Jane to destruction. "If I ever marry, it will be different from that," she thought passionately. "It will be utterly different!"

The door of Mrs. Carr's room opened suddenly, Marthy's name was called in a high voice, and the doctor was heard saying reassuringly: "She is over the worst. There is no need to worry."

"Don't send me in there alone, Gabriella," begged Charley piteously. "I'd rather face bullets than Jane in an attack." His bravado had deserted him, and he appeared positively craven. The stiffness seemed to have gone not only out of his character, but out of his clothes also. Even his collar had become limp with emotion.

"Well, I don't care," answered Gabriella, "you've got to stand it. There's no use squirming when you've only yourself to blame." With a malicious pleasure, she watched the consternation in Charley's face, while the doctor's footsteps came rapidly down the hall and stopped at the threshold of the parlour.

"You may go in, Mr. Gracey—your wife is asking for you; but be very careful not to say anything that might disturb her. Just keep her as quiet as you can for a few hours."

Then the door in the distance opened again, and Mrs. Carr, in the hollow tones of destiny, called: "Gabriella, Jane is waiting to speak to her husband."

"Come, Charley," ordered Gabriella, grimly, and a moment later she pushed him across her mother's threshold and turned back into the hall. "I hope she'll make him squirm," she said to herself, with relish. Nothing, she felt, except the certainty of Charley's squirming, could make up to her for the half-hour she had just spent with him.

She was still standing there when Jane's medicine came from the druggist at the corner, and for a while she waited outside the door, fearing to lighten Charley's punishment by her entrance. The medicine had to be measured in drops, and she went into the dining-room, where the children were huddled together in an improvised bed, and diluted the mixture with water before she could persuade herself to go into her mother's room. Even then she hesitated until she remembered that the doctor had said Jane must take the first dose immediately. Not by her, if she could help it, should the divine wrath of the furies be appeased.

But with the first touch of her hand on the knob, Charley's flippant voice greeted her with, "Won't you come in, Gabriella?" and swallowing her angry retort, she entered stiffly, with the glass held out straight before her. Charley, on his knees beside the bed, with his arm under his wife's pillow, stared up at his sister-in-law with the guilty look of a whipped terrier, while Jane, pallid, suffering, saintly, rested one thin blue-veined hand on his shoulder. Her face was the colour of the sheet, her eyes were unnaturally large and surrounded by violet circles; and her hair, drenched with camphor, spread over the pillow like the hair of a drowned woman. Never had she appeared so broken, so resigned, so ineffably spiritual; and Gabriella's solitary comfort was the thought that Jane's attack had conquered Charley as completely as it had conquered the rest of them.

"Gabriella, I've forgiven him," said Jane, with fainting sweetness, "and he wants you and mother to do so. He has promised to be good in the future."

"Well, I shan't forgive him for keeping me up all night," answered Gabriella resentfully, and she felt that even if it killed Jane, she could not keep back her reply. "I can't answer for mother, but I haven't forgiven him and I never shall." She felt her anger hardened to a rock inside of her, and it hurt her so that she put the glass hurriedly down on the table and ran out of the room. As she closed the door behind her she heard Jane saying gently: "Yes, I forgive you, Charley, but I can't help feeling that you don't love me as you ought to."

An old cape of her mother's was lying on a chair in the hall, and, throwing it over her shoulders, Gabriella went out on the porch and stood breathing quickly in the cold air, with her hand pressed on her bosom, which rose and fell as if she had been running. She was not only furious, she was grossly affronted, though she had known from the beginning, she said to herself, exactly how it would end. She had never trusted Jane—no, not a minute; she had never really trusted her mother. Something had told her that Jane had never meant in her heart to leave Charley, that she was only making a scene, after the immemorial habit of women, before going back to him. And yet, though she had suspected this all along, she was as indignant as if she had been deceived by a conspiracy of the three of them. Her sense of decency was outraged. She despised Jane because she had no strength of character; but even while this thought was still in her mind, she admitted that Jane had had sufficient strength of character to upset the household, bring Charley to repentance, and emerge, faint but victorious, from the wreck of their peace. Yes, she despised Jane, though it was impossible to deny that Jane's methods were successful, since she had got what she wanted.

The street was very quiet, for it was in the small gray hours between midnight and dawn, and a solitary policeman, strolling by on his beat, appeared as wan and spectral as the bare boughs of the poplar trees beneath which he moved. The wind was still blowing over the brow of the hill, and now and then it tossed a wisp of straw or a handful of dust on the porch where Gabriella was standing. As it swept onward it drove a flock of shadows, like black birds, up the open street into the clear space under the old-fashioned gas lamp at the corner. All the lights were out in the neighbouring houses, but from a boarding-house down the block there floated suddenly the gay snatch of a waltz played on a banjo with a broken string. Then the music stopped, the policeman passed, and Gabriella and the wind were alone in the street. Overhead the stars shone dimly through a web of mist; and it seemed to her that the sadness of the sky and the sadness of the earth had mingled there in the long straight street where the wind blew with a melancholy sound between rows of silent and darkened houses.

A noise in the hall made her turn, and, looking up, she saw the gaunt figure of Miss Amelia Peterborough standing in the bend of the staircase. In her hand the old maid held a twisted candlestick of greenish brass, and the yellow flame of the candle cast a trembling, fantastic shadow on the wall at her back. Her head, shorn of the false "front" she wore in the day, appeared to have become all forehead and beaked nose; her eyes had dwindled to mere points of blackness; her mouth, sunken and drawn over toothless gums, was like the mouth of a witch. The wind, blowing in gusts through the open door, inflated her gray shawl and the skirt of her dressing-gown, while, with each flutter of her garments, the grotesque shadow on the white wall danced and gibbered behind her. And, as she gazed down on the girl, it was as if the end of life, with its pathos, its cruelties, its bitterness and its disillusionment, had stopped for a fleeting instant to look back at life in the pride and ignorance of its beginning.

"There was so much moving about, I thought something might have happened," said Miss Amelia apologetically, while Gabriella, closing the door, shut the draught from the staircase.

"Jane had one of her heart attacks," answered the girl. "I'm so sorry we waked you."

But she was thinking while she spoke, "So that is old age—so that is what it means to be old?" There is a vague compassion in the thought, but it held no terror, for the decay of Miss Amelia seemed as utterly remote and detached from her own life as one of the past ages in history. The youth in her brain created a radiant illusion of immortality. By no stretch of imagination could she picture herself like the infirm and loveless creature before her. Yet she knew, without realizing it, that Miss Amelia had once been young, that she had once even been beautiful. There was a legend, fading now into tradition, that her lover had been killed in a duel, fought for her while she was still a girl, and that she had worn only white or black since that day—she who was now well over eighty. She had known love; a man had died for her; it was said that she had been a famous coquette in the 'thirties; and now she stood there, grotesque and sexless, with her eyes empty of dreams and of memories, and her face as gray and sinister as the face of her shadow.

"I hope she is better, poor child," she said, for, like the rest of Richmond, she believed Jane to be all saint and Charley all sinner. "If I can be of any help, be sure to let me know."

"Yes, I'll let you know, thank you. I hope we didn't disturb Miss Jemima."

The younger Miss Peterborough—called "the happy one" by Gabriella and Mrs. Carr because she was always cheerful, though, as far as any one could tell, she had nothing and had never had anything to be cheerful about—was named Jemima. A chronic invalid, from some obscure trouble which had not left her for twenty years, she was seldom free from pain, and yet Gabriella had never seen her (except at funerals, for which she entertained a perfectly healthy fondness as diversions free to the poor) without a smile on her face.

"Sister Jemima doesn't wake easily. She is a sound sleeper and she's getting a little hard of hearing"; and lifting the candlestick to light her way, Miss Amelia turned back up the stairs, while the flame flitted like a golden moth into the dimness.

"Poor old thing," thought Gabriella, imagining in her ignorance that she could understand the tragedy of Miss Amelia's life; "poor old thing, she must have had a terrible time."

As she approached her mother's door, Charley came out, glanced at her sheepishly, and hurried to where his hat hung on the walnut hatrack in the front hall. Then, as if overcoming his first impulse to avoid her, he beckoned to her furtively, and said in a sepulchral whisper: "Gabriella, be very careful what you say to her."

The audacity of it! This from Charley, the abandoned, the depraved, the unutterably abhorrent in her sight. Without replying, she turned indignantly away and opened her mother's door.

Lying in the middle of the bed now, and slightly propped with pillows, Jane was sipping a second dose of medicine from a glass Mrs. Carr held to her lips.

"I know you don't understand my forgiving him, Gabriella," she said very gently, "but some day, after you are married, you will realize that I do it from a sacred duty—from a sacred duty," she repeated firmly, while the shining light of martyrdom illumined her features.

"Well, it's none of my business," answered Gabriella crossly, "but the sooner you do it, I suppose the sooner you will have to do it again." If only for once Jane would be direct, if only she would be natural, if only she would speak the truth and not fiction.

"Oh, no, dear, you don't understand him any better than you do me," said Jane as sweetly as ever in spite of Gabriella's deplorable loss of temper. "He is really dreadfully penitent, and he sees that he hasn't always treated me as he ought to have done. But you'll know what I mean when you marry, Gabriella. She'll understand me then, won't she, mother?"

"I'm sometimes tempted to hope that Gabriella will never marry," replied Mrs. Carr with the uncompromising bitterness of abject despair; "the Carrs all seem to marry so badly."

In her normal mood she would never have uttered this heresy, for she belonged to a generation that regarded even a bad marriage as better for a woman than no marriage at all; but the night had worn her out, and one of her spells of neuralgia, which followed fatigue, was already beginning in her face. The purple crocheted "fascinator" she had caught up at the doctor's entrance was still on her head, and her long pale face, beneath the airy scallops, appeared frozen in an expression of incurable melancholy. For the rest she had been too frightened, too forgetful of herself and her own comfort even to put on her stockings, though Gabriella had begged her to do so. "Don't think about me. Attend to poor Jane," she had repeated over and over.

"Mother, go into my room and get into bed," commanded Gabriella, whose patience, never abundant, was ebbing low. "If you don't get some sleep your neuralgia won't be any better."

"It isn't any better. I don't expect it to be any better."

"Well, you must go to bed or it will get worse. I'll heat you a cup of milk and wrap you up in warm blankets."

"Don't worry about me, dear. Think of poor Jane."

"We've been thinking of Jane all night, and you need it now more than she does. I can tell by your eyes how you are suffering."

In the first streak of dawn, which was beginning to glimmer faintly on the window-panes, Mrs. Carr looked as if she had withered overnight.

"It's only my left temple," she said dully, "otherwise I am quite well. No, dear, I must rub Jane's forehead until she falls asleep. The doctor said it was important that we should keep her soothed."

But it was a law of Gabriella's nature that she never knew when she was beaten. Failure aroused the sleeping forces within her, and when these forces were once liberated, the spasmodic efforts of Mrs. Carr and the indirect methods of Jane were alike powerless to oppose them. At such times a faint flush rose to her pale cheeks, her eyes shone with a burning darkness, while her mouth lost its fresh young red and grew hard in outline.

"You must go to bed, mother," she repeated in a voice which Mrs. Carr would have obeyed had it issued from the wall or a piece of furniture.

Fifteen minutes later Gabriella stood authoritatively beside the bed, while her mother, with a mustard plaster at the back of her neck, obediently sipped hot milk from a teacup. Mrs. Carr had surrendered to the conquering spirit of her daughter, but her surrender, which was unwilling and weakly defiant, gave out presently a last feeble flicker of resistance.

"Don't you think, Gabriella, we might arrange to live with Jane?" she asked. "It would be a saving of expense for us both, and we might be so helpful about the children."

"And about Charley, too, I suppose," suggested Gabriella maliciously.

Mrs. Carr, having been born without a sense of humour, never understood the broadest joke unless it was illustrated; but even to her it became evident, after a moment's anxious thought, that Gabriella was teasing her.

"You seem to forget that he is her husband," she replied, with a pathetic clutch at her dignity, which, owing perhaps to the purple "fascinator" and the mustard plaster, she failed completely to recapture. Then, as she finished the milk and handed back the empty cup to her daughter, she added wearily, for life, as she often said to herself of late, was becoming almost too much for her, and she was feeling worn out and old:

"My one comfort, Gabriella, is the thought that Arthur Peyton loves you. There couldn't be anybody more unlike Charley."

"There couldn't be," agreed Gabriella mildly, for she felt that another blow would prostrate her mother.

# CHAPTER III

## A START IN LIFE

In the late 'seventies and early 'eighties the most important shop in the town of Gabriella's birth was known to its patrons (chiefly ladies in long basques, tightly tied back skirts, and small eccentric bonnets) as Brandywine & Plummer's drygoods store. At that period, when old Mrs. Carr, just completing her ninetieth year with a mind fixed upon heaven, would have dropped dead at the idea that her granddaughter should ever step out of her class, Gabriella's mother bought her dresses (grosgrain of the very best quality) from Major Brandywine. To be sure, even in those days, there were other shops in the city—for was not Broad Street already alluded to in the newspapers as "the shopping thoroughfare of the South?"—but, though they were as numerous as dandelions in June, these places were by no means patronized so widely by "the best people." Small shops, of course, carrying a single line of goods and supplying their particular products to an exacting and discriminating class, held their own even against the established reputation of Brandywine & Plummer's. O'Connell's linen store, Twitlow's china store, Mrs. Tonk's doll store, and Green & Brady's store for notions—all these were situated in Broad Street hardly a stone's throw from the Second Market. But none of these, excellent as they were, could bear comparison with the refined atmosphere, so different from the vulgar bustle of a modern department store, which enveloped one in the quiet gloom of Brandywine & Plummer's. In the first place, one could be perfectly sure that one would be waited on by a lady—for Brandywine & Plummer's, with a distinguished Confederate soldier at its head and front, provided an almost conventual shelter for distressed feminine gentility. There was, for instance, Miss Marye of the black silk counter, whose father had belonged to Stuart's cavalry and had fallen at Yellow Tavern; there was Miss Meason of the glove counter, and there was Mrs. Burwell Smith of the ribbon counter—for, though she had married beneath her, it was impossible to forget that she was a direct descendant of Colonel Micajah Burwell, of Crow's Nest Plantation.

Then, if one happened to be in search of cotton goods, one would be almost certain to remark on the way home: "Miss Peters, who waited on me in Brandywine's this morning, has unmistakably the manner of a lady," or "that Mrs. Jones in Brandywine's must be related to the real Joneses, she has such a refined appearance." And, at last, in the middle 'nineties, after the opening of the new millinery department, which was reached by a short flight of steps, decorated at discreet intervals with baskets of pink paper roses, customers were beginning to ask: "May I speak to Miss Gabriella for a minute? I wish to speak to Miss Gabriella about the hat she is having trimmed for me."

For here, also, because of what poor Jane called her "practical mind," the patrons of Brandywine & Plummer's were learning that Gabriella was "the sort you could count on." As far as the actual work went, she could not, of course, hold a candle (this was Mr. Plummer's way of putting it) to Miss Kemp or Miss

Treadway, who had a decided talent for trimming; but no customer in balloon sleeves and bell-shaped skirt was ever heard to remark of these young women as they remarked of Gabriella, "No, I don't want anybody else, please. She takes such an interest." To take an interest in other people might become quite as marketable an asset, Mr. Plummer was discovering, after fifty years of adherence to strictly business methods, as a gift for the needle; and, added to her engaging interest, Gabriella appeared to know by instinct exactly what a customer wanted.

"I declare Miss Kemp had almost persuaded me to take that brown straw with the green velvet bandeau before I thought of asking Gabriella's advice," Mrs. Spencer was overheard saying to her daughter, as she paused, panting and breathless, at the head of the short flight of steps.

"Oh, Gabriella always had taste; I'll ask her about mine," Florrie tossed back gaily in the high fluting notes which expressed so perfectly the brilliant, if slightly metallic, quality of her personality.

Beside her mother, a plump, bouncing person, with a noisy though imperfectly articulate habit of speech, and the prominent hips and bust which composed the "fine figure" of the period, Florrie seemed to float with all the elusive, magic loveliness of a sunbeam. From the shining nimbus of her hair to her small tripping feet she was the incarnation of girlhood—of that white and gold girlhood which has intoxicated the imagination of man. She shed the allurement of sex as unconsciously as a flower sheds its perfume. Though her eyes were softly veiled by her lashes, every male clerk in Brandywine & Plummer's was dazzled by the deep blue light of her glances. In her red mouth, with its parted lips, in the pure rose and white of her flesh, in the rich curve of her bosom, which promised already the "fine figure" of her mother, youth and summer were calling as they called in the velvet softness of the June breeze. Innocent though she was, the powers of Life had selected her as a vehicle for their inscrutable ends.

"Where is Miss Carr? I must speak to Miss Carr, please," she said to one of the shop girls who came up, eager to serve her. "Will you tell her that Miss Spencer is waiting to speak to her?"

Responding to the girl's artless stare of admiration, she threw a friendly glance at her before she turned away to try on a monstrous white Leghorn hat decorated around the crown with a trellis of pink roses. Unless she happened to be in a particularly bad humour—and this was not often the case—Florrie was imperturbably amiable. She enjoyed flattery as a cat enjoys the firelight on its back, and while she purred happily in the pleasant warmth, she had something of the sleek and glossy look of a pretty kitten.

"How does this look on me, mother?" she asked over her shoulder of Mrs. Spencer, who was babbling cheerfully in her loud tones to Miss Lancaster, the forewoman.

Though some of the best blood in Virginia, profusely diluted with some of the worst, flowed comfortably in Mrs. Spencer's veins, it was impossible even for her relatives to deny that she could be at times decidedly vulgar. Having been a conspicuous belle and beauty of a bold and dashing type in her youth, she now devoted her middle-age to the enjoyment of those pleasures which she had formerly sacrificed to the preservation of her figure and her complexion. Though she still dyed her somewhat damaged hair, and strenuously pinched in her widening waist, she had ceased, since her fiftieth birthday, to forego the lesser comforts of the body. As she was a person of small imagination, and of no sentiment, it is probable that she was happier now than she had been in the days when she suffered the deprivations and enjoyed the triumphs of beauty.

"What's that, Florrie?" she inquired shrilly. "No, I shouldn't get that if I were you. It doesn't flare enough. I'm crazy about a flare."

"But I want a pink bandeau, mother," replied Florrie a little pettishly, as she patted her golden-red fringe. "I wonder where Gabriella is? Isn't she ever coming, Miss Lancaster?"

"I thought I saw her when I came in," observed Mrs. Spencer, craning her handsome neck, which was running to fat, in the direction of the trimming room. "Florrie, just turn your head after a minute and look at the hat Patty Carrington is buying—pea green, and it makes her face look like a walnut. She hasn't the faintest idea how to dress. Do you think I ought to speak to her about it?"

"No, let her alone," replied Florrie impatiently. "Is this any better than the Leghorn?"

"Well, I must say I don't think there is much style about it, though, of course, with your hair, you can carry off anything. Isn't it odd how exactly she inherited my hair, Miss Lancaster? I remember her father used to say that he would have fallen in love with a gatepost if it had had golden-red hair."

Miss Lancaster, a thin, erect woman of fifty, with impassive features, and iron-gray hair that looked as if it were rolled over wood, glanced resignedly from Mrs. Spencer's orange-coloured crimps to the imprisoned sunlight in Florrie's hair.

"I'd know you were mother and daughter anywhere," she remarked in the noncommittal manner she had acquired in thirty years of independence; "and she is going to have your beautiful figure, too, Mrs. Spencer."

"Well, I reckon I'll lose my figure now that I've stopped dieting," remarked the lively lady, casting an appreciative glance in the mirror. "Florrie tells me I wear my sleeves too large, but I think they make me look smaller."

"They are wearing them very large in Paris," replied Miss Lancaster, as if she were reciting a verse out of a catalogue. She had, as she sometimes found occasion to remark, been "born tired," and this temperamental weariness showed now in her handsome face, so wrinkled and dark around her bravely smiling eyes. Where she came from, or how she spent her time between the hour she left the shop and the hour she returned to it, the two women knew as little as they knew the intimate personal history of the Leghorn hat on the peg by the mirror. Beyond the fact that she played the part of a sympathetic chorus, they were without curiosity about her life. Their own personalities absorbed them, and for the time at least appeared to absorb Miss Lancaster.

"I like the Leghorn hat," said Florrie decisively, as she tried it on for the third time, "but I'll wait till I ask Gabriella's opinion."

"I hope she's getting on well here," said Mrs. Spencer, who found it impossible to concentrate on Florrie's hat. "Don't you think it was very brave of her to go to work, Miss Lancaster?"

"I understood that she was obliged to," rejoined Miss Lancaster, with the weary amiability of her professional manner.

"She might have married, I happen to know that," returned Mrs. Spencer. "Arthur Peyton has been in love with her ever since she was a child, and there was a young man from New York last winter who seemed crazy about her. Florrie, don't you think George Fowler was just crazy about Gabriella?"

"I'm sure I don't know, mother. He paid her a great deal of attention, but you never can tell about men."

"Julia Caperton told me, and, of course, she's very intimate with George's sister, that he went back to New York because he heard that Gabriella was engaged to Arthur. Florrie, do you suppose she is really engaged to Arthur?"

Thus appealed to, Florrie removed the Leghorn hat from her head, and answered abstractedly: "Jane thought so, but if she is engaged, I don't see why she should have started to work. I know Arthur would hate it."

"But isn't he too poor to marry?" inquired Mrs. Spencer, whose curiosity was as robust as her constitution. "Haven't you always understood that the Peytons were poor, Miss Lancaster, in spite of the lovely house they live in?"

Her large, good-humoured face, which had once been as delicate as a flower, but was now growing puffed and mottled under a plentiful layer of rice powder, became almost violently animated, while she adjusted her belt with a single effective jerk of her waist. Though Bessie Spencer was admitted to have one of the kindest hearts in the world, she was chiefly remarkable for her unhappy faculty of saying the wrong thing at the wrong time. An inveterate, though benevolent, gossip, she would babble on for hours, reciting the private affairs of her relatives, her friends, and her neighbours. Everybody feared her, and yet everybody was assured that "she never meant any harm." The secrets of the town flowed through her mind as grist flows through a mill, and though she was entirely without malice, she contrived, in the most innocent manner, to do an incalculable amount of injury. Possessing a singularly active intelligence, and having reached middle-age without acquiring sufficient concentration to enjoy books, she directed a vigorous, if casual, understanding toward the human beings among whom she lived. She knew everything that it was possible to know about the people who lived in Franklin Street, and yet her mind was so constituted that she never by any chance knew it correctly. Though she was not old, she had already passed into a proverb. To receive any statement with the remark, "You have heard that from Bessie Spencer," was to cast doubt upon it.

"You don't think I'm getting any stouter, do you, Miss Lancaster?" she inquired dubiously, with her hands on her hips and her eyes measuring the dimensions of her waist. "I'm making up my mind to try one of those B. and T.

corsets that Mrs. Murray is wearing. She told me it reduced her waist at least three inches."

"Oh, you aren't like Mrs. Murray—she didn't measure a fraction under thirty inches," replied Miss Lancaster, with her patient politeness. Then, after a pause, which Mrs. Spencer's nimble wit filled with a story about the amazing number of mint juleps Mrs. Murray was seen to drink at the White Sulphur Springs last summer, Florrie exclaimed eagerly:

"Why, there is Gabriella! Won't you get her for us, Miss Lancaster?"

Near one of the long windows, beyond which large greenish flies were buzzing around the branch of a mulberry tree in the alley, Gabriella was trying a purple hat on a prim-looking lady who regarded herself in the mirror with a furtive and deprecating air as if she were afraid of being unjustly blamed for her appearance. "I'm not sure—but I don't think it suits me exactly," she appeared to murmur in a strangled whisper, while she twisted her mouth, which held a jet-headed hatpin, into a quivering grimace.

"She's waiting on Matty French," said Mrs. Spencer, and she added impulsively, "I wonder what it is that men see in Gabriella. You wouldn't call her really pretty, would you, Miss Lancaster?"

"Well, not exactly pretty, but she has an interesting face. It is so full of life."

"Can't you get her, mother?" asked Florrie; and Mrs. Spencer, always eager to oblige, rustled across the room and pounced vivaciously upon the prim lady and Gabriella.

"We've been looking for you everywhere, Gabriella," she began, nodding agreeably to Miss French. "Florrie has tried on all the hats in the room, and she wants you to tell her if that white Leghorn is becoming. Good morning, Matty! That blue wing is so stylish. I think you are very sensible to wear colours and not to stick to black as Susie Chamberlain does. It makes her look as old as the hills, and I believe she does it just to depress people. Life is too short, as I said when I left off mourning, to be an ink blot wherever you go. And it doesn't mean that she grieves a bit more for her husband than anybody else does. Everybody knows they led a cat and dog's life together, and I've even heard, though I can't remember who told me, that she was on the point of getting a divorce when he died. Are you going? Well, I'm glad you decided on that blue hat. I don't believe you'll ever regret it. Good-bye. Be sure and come to see me soon. Gabriella, will you help Florrie about her hat now? I declare, I thought Matty would never get through with you. And, of course, we didn't want anybody but you to wait on us. We were just saying that you had the most beautiful taste, and it is so wise of you to go out to work and not sit down and sew at home in order to support your position. A position that can't support itself isn't much of a prop, my husband used to say. But I don't believe you'll stay here long, you sly piece. You'll be married before the year is up, mark my word. The men are all crazy about you, everybody knows that. Why, Florrie met George Fowler in the street this morning, and when he asked after you, his face turned as hot as fire, she said—"

Gabriella's face, above her starched collar with its neat red tie, was slowly flooded with colour. Her brown eyes shone golden under her dark lashes, and Mrs. Spencer told herself that the girl looked almost pretty for a minute. "If she wasn't so sallow, she'd be really good looking."

Happily unaware that her face had betrayed her, Gabriella slid back a glass door, took a hat out of the case, and answered indifferently, while she adjusted the ribbon bow on one side of the crown:

"I didn't know Mr. Fowler had come back. I haven't seen him for ages."

From her small, smooth head to her slender feet she had acquired in three months the composed efficiency of Miss Lancaster; and one might have imagined, as Mrs. Spencer remarked to Florrie afterwards, that "she had been born in a hat shop."

But instead of the weary patience of Miss Lancaster, she brought to her work the brimming energy and the joyous self-confidence of youth. It was impossible to watch her and not realize that she had given both ability and the finer gift of personality to the selling of hats. Had she started life as a funeral director instead of a milliner, it is probable that she would have infused into the dreary business something of the living quality of genius.

"Oh, Florrie hadn't seen him for ages either," chirped Mrs. Spencer, with her restless eyes on the hat in Gabriella's hand. "I don't know whether I ought to tell you or not, but you and Florrie are so intimate I suppose I might as well—Julia Caperton told Florrie that George came back because he heard in some way that you had broken your engagement to Arthur. Of course, as I told Julia afterwards, you hadn't mentioned a word of it to me, but I've got eyes and I can't help using them. I was obliged to see that George was simply out of his mind about you. It would be a splendid match, too, for they say his father has made quite a large fortune since he went to New York—"

"Mother!" interrupted Florrie sternly, over her shoulder, "you know Julia told you not to breathe a single word as coming from her. She is the bosom friend of George's sister."

"But, Florrie, I haven't told a soul except Gabriella, and I know she wouldn't repeat a thing that I said to her."

"Now, isn't that exactly like mother?" observed Florrie, with the casual disapprobation of youth. "She was on the point of telling Miss Lancaster all about it when I stopped her."

"Why, Florrie, I didn't say a word except that men were crazy about Gabriella—you know I didn't. Of course, I talk a great deal," she pursued in an aggrieved, explanatory tone to Gabriella, "but I never repeat a word—not a single word that is told me in confidence. If Julia had asked me not to tell Gabriella what she said, I shouldn't have dreamed of doing so."

"Oh, it doesn't matter in the least, Mrs. Spencer," said Gabriella hastily, "only there isn't a word of truth in it."

The becoming flush was still in her cheeks, and she poised a hat over Florrie's head with a swift, flying grace which Mrs. Spencer had never noticed in her before. "I wonder if Gabriella can really care about George?" she thought quickly. "But if it is George she is in love with, why on earth did she start to work in a shop?" Then suddenly, following a flash of light, she reasoned it out to her complete satisfaction. "It must have been that she didn't know that George cared—that is why she is blushing so at this minute."

An hour or so later, when Florrie and her mother had fluttered volubly downstairs, and the exhausted assistants were putting the hats away before closing the cases, Gabriella went into the dressing-room, where Miss Nash, a stout, pleasant-looking girl, was sitting in a broken chair, with her shoes off, her blue serge skirt rolled back from her knees, and her head bowed, over her crossed arms, on the window-sill.

At Gabriella's entrance she glanced up, and remarked cheerfully: "My feet were killing me. I just had to take off my shoes."

"They do get dreadfully tired," assented Gabriella in the tone of sympathetic intimacy she had caught from the other girls.

Her naturally friendly spirit had refused to "hold aloof" from her companions, as her mother had begged her to do, and at the end of three months she had learned things about most of them which interested her profoundly. One supported an invalid father, another had a family of six little brothers and sisters to care for, and still another had lost her lover through a railroad accident only two days before her marriage. Several of them were extravagantly loud, one or two were inclined to be vulgar; but the others were quite as refined and gentle as the girls with whom she had grown up, and what impressed her about them all was their courageous and yet essentially light-hearted Southern spirit. To her surprise, she found an utter absence of jealousy among them. The elder women were invariably kind and helpful, and though she liked the girls, she soon discovered in herself a growing feeling of respect for these older women. They represented a different type, for the hardness she noticed in some of the younger girls was entirely lacking in the women of Miss Lancaster's generation. Many of them even her mother would have called well born, and one and all, they were almost painfully ladylike. With their thin, erect figures, their wan, colourless faces, their graying hair, and their sweet Southern voices, they imparted a delicate social air to the shop.

Usually Gabriella stopped to talk to the girls who crowded in from the workroom, brushing shreds of silk or ribbon from their skirts, but to-day her mind wandered while she answered Miss Nash, and when, a minute later, Miss Lancaster spoke to her on her way out, and asked her to match the flowers for Florrie's hat, she was obliged to make an effort before she could recall her roving attention. She was thinking not of Florrie's hat, but of Mrs. Spencer's words, "He has come back because he heard that your engagement was broken." And at the first insurgent rise of emotion, she ceased to be the business woman and became merely an imaginative girl, dreaming of love.

"They aren't quite the right shade, are they?" she asked with an uncertainty which was tactful rather than sincere, "or, perhaps, the ribbon might be darker?"

Her eyes questioned Miss Lancaster, who moved a step nearer the window as she held the bolt of ribbon toward the daylight.

"Well, we'd better look at it again in the morning. You are in a hurry, Miss Carr?"

"Oh, no, I've all the time in the world," answered Gabriella, though she longed to be out with the June scents and her dreams, "but I am sure the ribbon ought to be a deeper blue to tone with the ragged robins."

"You've a wonderful eye for colour, that's why I ask your advice," said the other, and a sudden friendliness shone in her tired eyes, for she had liked Gabriella from the beginning. That the girl possessed a genuine gift of taste, the elder woman had already discovered. For herself, Miss Lancaster had always hated the sight of hats, and had taken up the work merely because a place in Brandywine & Plummer's had been offered her shortly after her father, a gallant fighter but a poor worker, had gone to end his kindly anecdotal days in the Home for Confederate Soldiers. She was a repressed, conscientious woman, who had never been younger than she was now at fifty, and who regarded youth, not with envy, but with admiring awe. For she, also, patient and uncomplaining creature, belonged to that world of decay and inertia from which Gabriella had revolted. It was a world where things happened to-day just as they happened yesterday, where no miracles had occurred since the miracles of Scripture, where people hated change, not because they were satisfied, but because they were incapable of imagination. Miss Lancaster, who had never wanted anything with passion, except to be a perfect lady, was proud of the fact that she had been twenty years in business without losing her "shrinking manner."

"Yes, you have an eye for colour," she repeated gently; "if you could only learn to sew, you might command a most desirable position."

"I despise sewing," replied Gabriella, with serene good-humour, "and I could never learn, even at school, anything that I despised. But I suppose I can always tell somebody else how it ought to be done."

Then, because her work always interested her, she forgot the disturbing words Mrs. Spencer had spoken—she forgot even her impatience to feel the June air in her face. Her best gift, the power of mental control, enabled her to bring the needed discipline to her emotion; and when the moment of her release came, she found that the brief restlessness had passed from her mind. "There's no use letting myself get impatient," she thought; "I've got to stick to it, so it won't do a bit of good to begin wriggling."

All the other girls had gone home before her, and on the sidewalk Miss Meason, of the glove counter, stood talking about the spring sales to Mr. Brandywine. As Gabriella passed them, in her white shirtwaist and dark belted skirt, they looked thoughtfully after her until her sailor hat, with the scarlet band, crossed Broad Street and disappeared on the opposite side.

"She's a remarkable girl," observed Mr. Brandywine, with his paternal manner. "I hope she is beginning to feel at home with us."

"I believe she'd feel at home anywhere," replied Miss Meason, "and she's obliged to get on. There's no doubt of it."

"A pleasant face, too. Not exactly pretty, I suppose, but you would call it a pleasant face."

"Oh, well, I'd call her pretty in her way," answered Miss Meason. "Her eyes are lovely, and she has a singularly bright expression. I always say that a bright expression makes up for anything."

"Her mother was a beauty in her day," said Mr. Brandywine reminiscently; "she was the snow and roses sort, and her eldest daughter took after her, though she is a wreck now, poor lady."

"That's Charley Gracey," remarked Miss Meason tartly, for she had the self-supporting woman's contempt for the rake. "Yes, she was lovely as a girl. I remember as well as if it were yesterday how happy she looked when I sold her her wedding gloves. She is a beautiful character, too, they say, but somehow Gabriella, even as a child, appealed to me more. She has three times the sense of her sister."

Then they shook hands and parted, while Gabriella, tripping through the Second Market, was saying to herself: "There's not the least bit of sense in your thinking about him, Gabriella."

In Hill Street, maple and poplar trees were in full leaf, and little flakes of sunshine, as soft as flowers, were scattered over the brick pavement. Beyond the housetops the sky was golden, and at the corner the rusty ironwork of an old balcony had turned to the colour of bronze. The burning light of the sunset blinded her eyes, while an intense sweetness came to her from the honeysuckle clambering over a low white porch; and this light and this sweetness possessed an ineffable quality. Life, which had been merely placid a few hours before, had become suddenly poignant—every instant was pregnant with happiness, every detail was piercingly vivid. Her whole being was flooded with a sensation of richness and wonder, as if she had awakened with surprise to a different world from the one she had closed her eyes on a minute before.

As she crossed the street she saw her mother's head above a box of clove pinks in the window; and a little later the front door opened and Miss Polly Hatch, a small, indomitable spinster who sewed out by the day, walked rapidly between the iron urns and stopped under the creamy blossoms of the old magnolia tree in the yard.

"It's too late for your ma to be workin', Gabriella. You'd better stop her."

Pausing in the middle of the walk, she comfortably tucked under her arm an unwieldy bundle she carried, and added, with the shrewdness which was the result of a long and painful experience with human nature: "It's funny—ain't it?—how downright mulish your ma can be when she wants to?"

"I can't do a thing on earth with her," answered Gabriella in distress. "You have more influence over her than I have, Miss Polly."

Miss Polly, who had the composed and efficient bearing of a machine, shook her head discouragingly as she opened the gate and passed out.

"I reckon she's set for good and all," she remarked emphatically, and went on her way.

"Mother, it's time to stop sewing and think about supper," called Gabriella gaily, as she ran into the room and bent to kiss her mother, who turned a flat, soft cheek in her direction, and remarked gloomily: "Gabriella, you've had a visitor."

Not for worlds would Mrs. Carr have surrendered to the disarming cheerfulness of her daughter's manner; for since Gabriella had gone to work in a shop, her mother's countenance implied that she was piously resigned to disgrace as well as to poverty. It was inconceivable to her that any girl with Berkeley blood in her veins could be so utterly devoid of proper pride as Gabriella had proved herself to be; and the shock of this discovery had left a hurt look in her face. There were days when she hardly spoke to the girl, when refusing food, she opened her lips only to moisten her thread, when the slow tears seemed forever welling between her reddened eyelids. As they had just passed through one of these painful periods, Gabriella was surprised to find that, for the moment at least, her mother appeared to have forgotten her righteous resentment. Though it could hardly be said that Mrs. Carr spoke cheerfully—since cheerfulness was foreign to her nature—at least she had spoken. Of her own accord, unquestioned and unurged, she had volunteered a remark to her daughter; and Gabriella felt that, for a brief respite, the universe had ceased to be menacing.

"Gabriella, you have had a visitor," repeated Mrs. Carr, and it was clear that her sorrow (she never yielded to passion) had been overcome by a natural human eagerness to tell her news.

"Not Cousin Jimmy?" asked the girl lightly.

"No, you could never guess, if you guessed all night."

"Not Charley Gracey surely? I wouldn't speak to him for the world."

Though Jane had returned to Charley, and even Mrs. Carr, feeling in her heart that her younger daughter had dealt her the hardest blow, had been heard to say that she "pitied her son-in-law more than she censured him," Gabriella had not softened in her implacable judgment.

"Of course it wasn't Charley. I shouldn't have mentioned it if it had been, because you are so bitter against him. But it was somebody you haven't seen for months. Do you remember Evelyn Randolph's son who paid you so much attention last winter?"

"George Fowler! Has he been here?" asked Gabriella, and her voice quivered like a harp.

"I told Marthy to say you were out. Of course I wasn't fit to see company, but he caught sight of me on his way to the gate and came back on the porch to speak to me. He remembered all about my having gone to school with his mother, and it seems she had told him about the time she was Queen of May and I maid of honour. I asked him how Evelyn stood living in New York, but he said she likes it better than his father does. Archie Fowler insists that he is coming back to Virginia to end his days. They seem to have plenty of money. I expect Archie has made a fortune up there or he wouldn't be satisfied to live out of Virginia."

"Did George ask when I'd be at home?" inquired Gabriella.

Though she knew that it was unwise to divert her mother's attention from the main narrative, her whole body ached with the longing to hear what George had said of her, and she felt that it was impossible to resist the temptation to question.

"He said something about you as he was going away, but I can't remember whether he asked when you would be in or not." In spite of the fact that Mrs. Carr had the most tenacious memory for useless detail, she was never able to recall the significant points of an interview.

"He didn't ask where I was?"

The question was indiscreet, for it jerked Mrs. Carr's mind back with violence from its innocent ramble into the past, while it reminded her of Gabriella's present unladylike occupation. She shut her lips with soft but obstinate determination, and Gabriella, watching her closely, told herself that "wild horses couldn't drag another word out of her mother to-night." The girl longed to talk it over; but she might have tried as successfully to gossip with the angel on a marble tombstone. She wanted to hear what George had said, to ask how he was looking, and to wonder aloud why he had come back. She wanted to throw herself into her mother's arms and listen to all the little important things that filled the world for her. If only the aloof virtue in Mrs. Carr's face would relax into a human expression!

Taking off her hat, Gabriella went into the bedroom, and then, coming back again after a short absence, remarked with forced gaiety: "I suppose he didn't have anything interesting to tell you, did he?"

"No." Though the light had almost waned, Mrs. Carr broke off a fresh piece of thread and leaned nearer the window, while she tried to find the eye of the needle.

"Let me thread your needle, mother. It is too late to work, anyway. You will ruin your eyesight."

"I have never considered my eyesight, Gabriella."

"I know you haven't, and that's why you ought to begin."

As it was really growing too dark to see, Mrs. Carr rolled the thread back on the spool, stuck the needle into the last buttonhole, and folding the infant's dress on which she was working, laid it away in her straw work-basket.

"Will you light the gas, Gabriella?"

"Don't work any more to-night, mother. It is almost supper time."

Without replying, Mrs. Carr moved with her basket to a chair under the chandelier. Once seated there, she unfolded the dress, took the needle from the unfinished buttonhole, and tried again unsuccessfully to run the thread through the eye. Then, while Gabriella rushed to her aid, she removed her glasses and patiently polished them on a bit of chamois skin she kept in her basket.

"Don't you feel as if you could eat a chop to-night, mother?"

"I haven't been able to swallow a morsel all day, Gabriella."

"I've saved you a little cream. Shall I make you a toddy?"

"I don't want it. Drink it yourself, dear."

After this there followed one of those pauses which fill not only the room, but the universe with a fury of sound. There were times when Gabriella felt that she could stand anything if only her mother would fly into a rage—when she positively envied Florrie Spencer because her plebeian parent scolded her at the top of her voice instead of maintaining a calm and ladylike reticence. But Mrs. Carr was one of those women who never, even in the most trying circumstances, cease to be patient, who never lose for an instant so much as the palest or the thinnest of the Christian virtues.

Going into the bedroom, Gabriella changed from her shirtwaist into a gown of flowered muslin, with sleeves that looked small beside the balloon ones of the season, and a skirt which was shrunken and pale from many washings the summer before. She had worn the frock when she met George, and though it was old, she knew it was becoming, and she told herself joyfully that if she put it on to-night, "something must come of it." As she smoothed her hair by the dim gas-jet over the mirror, she saw again the face of George as it had first smiled down on her beneath the boughs of a mimosa tree in Mrs. Spencer's front garden. At the time, a year ago, she was engaged to Arthur—she had even called the placid preference she felt for him "being in love"—but while she talked to George she had found herself thinking, "I wonder how it would feel to be engaged to a man like this instead of to Arthur?" Then, since all Southern engagements of the period were secret, she had seen a good deal of George during the summer; and in the autumn, while she was still trying to make believe that it was merely a friendship, he had gone back to New York without saying good-bye. She had tried her best to stop thinking of him, and until this evening, she had never really let herself confess that she cared. But if she didn't care why was she so happy to-night? If she didn't care why was there such intoxicating sweetness in the thought of his return? If she didn't care why had she dressed herself so carefully in the flowered muslin he had once said that he liked? Her face, smiling back at her from the mirror, was suffused with a delicate glow—not pink, not white, but softly luminous as if a lamp, shining behind it, enkindled its expression. She had never seen herself so nearly pretty, and with this thought in her mind, she went back to her mother, who was still working buttonholes under the chandelier.

"Marthy has brought the lamp, mother. Why don't you move over to the table?"

"I can see perfectly, thank you, Gabriella."

"I hate to see you working. Let me finish those buttonholes."

"I'd rather get through them myself, dear."

"Have you seen Jane to-day?"

"No."

"Has Cousin Pussy been here?"

"No."

"Did you get out for a walk?"

"No."

The appalling silence again filled the room like a fog, and Gabriella, moving cautiously about in it, began straightening chairs and picking up shreds of cambric from the carpet. She felt suddenly that she could not endure the strain for another minute, and glancing at Mrs. Carr's bent head, where the thin hair was wound into a tight knot and held in place by a tortoise-shell comb with a carved top, she wondered how her mother could possibly keep it up day after day as she did? But, if she had only known it, this silence, which tried her nerves to the breaking point, was positively soothing to her mother. Mrs. Carr could keep it up not only for days and weeks, but, had it been necessary, she could have kept it up with equal success for half a lifetime. While she sat there, working buttonholes in a bad light, she thought quite as passionately as Gabriella, though her mental processes were different. She thought sadly, but firmly, with a pensive melancholy not untinged with pleasure, that "life was becoming almost too much for her." It seemed incredible to her that after all her struggles to keep up an appearance things should have turned out as they had; it seemed incredible that after all her sacrifices her children should not consider her more. "They have no consideration for me," she reflected, while she took the finest stitch possible to the needle she held. "If Jane had considered me she would never have married Charley. If Gabriella had considered me, or anybody but herself, she would not have gone to work in a store." No, they had never considered her, they had never asked her advice before acting, though she had brought them into the world and had worked like a slave in order to keep them in that respected station of life in which they had been born. Then, her sorrow getting the better of her resolution, she turned her head and spoke:

"I know you never tell me anything on purpose, Gabriella, but I think I have a right to know whether or not you have discarded Arthur for good."

"I told you all about it, mother. I told you I found I was mistaken."

"I suppose you never thought for a moment how much it would distress me? Though Lydia Peyton is so much older than I am, she was always my best friend—we often stayed in the room together when we were girls. I had set my heart on your marrying her son."

"I know that, mother, and I am very sorry, but when it came to the point I couldn't marry him. You can't make yourself care—"

"I should have thought that my wishes might influence you. I should never wish you to do anything that wasn't for your good, Gabriella."

"Of course, mother, you've given up your life to us. I know that, and Jane knows it as well as I do. That's why I want to earn money enough to let you rest. I want you to stop work for good and be happy."

"There are worse things than work," replied Mrs. Carr in a tone which implied that Gabriella had brought them upon her.

After a pause, in which her needle flew mournfully, she added: "I hope for your own sake that you will marry some good man before you lose your attractions. Poor Becky Bollingbroke proved to me how unfortunate it is for a woman to remain unmarried."

For an instant Gabriella looked at her mother without replying. She felt tempted—strongly tempted, she told herself—to say something cross. Then the sight of the bent gray head, of the bowed shoulders, of the knotted needle-pricked fingers, pierced her heart. Though she could not always agree with her mother, she loved her devotedly, and the thought that she must lose her some day had been the most terrible nightmare of her childhood.

"Don't worry about me, mother, dear," she answered tenderly. "I can always take care of myself. I can manage my life, you know that, don't you?" Then she stopped quickly while her heart gave a single bound and lay quiet. She had heard the click of the gate, and a minute later, as Mrs. Carr gathered up her sewing, there was a ring at the bell.

"It can't be a visitor before supper, can it, Gabriella?"

"I think not, mother, but I shouldn't run away if I were you."

"I'd better go. I don't feel dressed. Wait a minute, Marthy, and let me get out of the room before you open the door." She fled, clutching her work-basket, while Gabriella, turning to lower the flaming wick of the lamp, heard George's voice at the door and his footsteps crossing the hall.

"I knew something would happen," she thought wildly, as she went forward to meet him.

"I saw you pull down the shade as I was going by," he began rather lamely; and she hardly heard his words because of the divine tumult in her brain. Her heart sang; her pulses throbbed; every drop of her blood seemed to become suddenly alive with ecstasy. Under the tarnished garlands of the chandelier his face looked younger, gayer, more intensely vivid than it had looked in her dreams. It was the face of her dreams made real; but with what a difference! She saw his crisp brown hair brushed smoothly back from its parting, his blue eyes, with their gay and conquering look, the firm red brown of his cheek, and even the bluish shadow encircling his shaven mouth. In his eyes, which said enchanting things, she could not read the trivial and commonplace quality of his soul—for he was not only a man, he was romance, he was adventure, he was the radiant miracle of youth!

"Florrie told me this morning that you had come back," she answered coldly, as she held out her hand.

Her words seemed to come to her from a distance—from the next room, from the street outside, from the farthest star—but while she uttered them, she knew that her words meant nothing. She shed her joy as if it were fragrance; and her softness was like the magnolia-scented softness of the June night. Even her mother would not have known her, so greatly had she changed in a minute. Of the businesslike figure in the sailor hat and trim shirtwaist—of the Gabriella who had said, "I can manage my life"—there remained only an outline. The very feet of the capable woman had changed into the shrinking and timid feet of a lovesick girl. She was afraid to go forward, afraid to move, afraid to breathe lest she break the wonderful spell of the magic. Not only her basic common sense, but the very soul that shaped her body had become as light, as sweet, as formless as liquid honey.

But of course, she knew nothing of this. She was innocent of deception; she was innocent even of any definite purpose to allure. The thought in her mind, if there were any thought, which is doubtful, was that she must be composed, she must be indifferent if it killed her.

"I know I've come at an awkward hour, but I simply couldn't go by after I saw you."

"Won't you stay?" she asked, trying in vain to shut out the ominous sound of Marthy bringing their scant supper. She remembered, with horror, that she had ordered only two chops, and a wave of rebellion swept over her because life always spoiled its divine instants.

"No, I can't stay. I've an engagement for supper. I merely wanted to see you. You've no idea how I've wanted to see you."

"Have you?" said Gabriella in so low a voice that he hardly heard her. Then, lifting her glowing eyes, she added softly, "I am glad that you wanted to."

"There were times when I simply couldn't get you out of my mind," he responded, and went on almost joyously, with the romantic look which had first enchanted her imagination. "You see I believed that you were going to marry Arthur Peyton. Julia told me that your engagement was broken. That was why I came back. Didn't you guess it?"

"Yes, I guessed it," she answered simply, and all the softness, the sweetness, the beauty of her feeling passed into her voice.

Then, in the very midst of her happiness, there occurred one of those sordid facts which appear to spring, like vultures, upon the ineffable moments. She heard the bell—the awful supper bell which her mother insisted upon having rung because her parents had had it rung for generations before her. As the horrible sound reverberated through the house, Gabriella felt that the noise passed through her ears, not into her brain, but into the very depths of her suffering soul.

"There, I must go," said George, without embarrassment, for which she blessed him. From his manner, the supper bell might have made a delightful harmony instead of a hideous discord. "I'll see you to-morrow, if I may. May I, Gabriella?"

He smiled charmingly as he went, and looking after him, a minute later, over the clove pinks in the window-box, she saw him turn and gaze back at her from the opposite pavement.

# CHAPTER IV

## MIRAGE

On a bright Sunday in October Mrs. Carr stopped on her way from church to tell Mrs. Peyton of Gabriella's engagement. A crape veil, slightly scented with camphor, hung from her bonnet, and in her gloved hands she carried a bunch of yellow chrysanthemums, for she intended to go on to Hollywood, where her husband was buried. The sermon had been unusually inspiring, and there was a pensive exaltation in her look as she laid her hand on the gate of the walled garden.

"If it couldn't be Arthur—and of course my heart was set on her marrying Arthur—I suppose George is the one I should have chosen," she said to Mrs. Peyton with tender melancholy as she turned her soft, clammy cheek, which was never warm even in summer, to be kissed.

There was nothing against George that she could advance even to Gabriella. He was well born, for his mother had been a Randolph; he was comfortably rich (at least his father was); he was good-looking; he was almost arrogantly healthy—yet because she was obliged to regret something, she found herself clinging fondly to the memory of Arthur. "If it could only have been Arthur," she repeated sadly, gazing through the French window of the drawing-room to the garden where beds of scarlet sage flaunted brilliantly in the sunshine.

"I hope and pray that dear Gabriella will be happy," replied Mrs. Peyton, a beautiful old lady, with wonderful white hair under the widow's ruching in her bonnet. The exquisite simplicity of her soul was reflected in the rose-leaf delicacy of her skin, in her benignant and innocent smile, in the serene and joyous glance of her eyes. Never in her life had she thought evil of any one, and she did not mean to begin on the verge of the grave, with the hope of a peaceful eternity before her. If dear Gabriella had "discarded" dear Arthur, then she could only hope and pray that dear Gabriella would not live to regret it.

"She will be married at once, I suppose?" she said, and beamed as happily as if Gabriella had not disappointed the dearest hope of her heart. "There is no need to wait, is there?"

"They have decided on the 17th of November. I wanted you to know it first of all, Lydia, so I haven't mentioned it to a soul except to Cousin Jimmy Wrenn."

"You will live with dear Jane, will you not? Poor child, what a blessing you will be to her."

"No, I shall be with Jane only for a month or two until Gabriella and George have taken a house in New York. She wouldn't consent to be married so soon until I promised to live with them. But how on earth shall I ever manage to go so far away, Lydia? To think of being so far from Hollywood almost breaks my heart, and yet what can I do?"

Mrs. Peyton's loving gaze enfolded not only her visitor, but the house and the dreamy garden where frost was already blighting the flowers.

"I understand your feeling, of course, Fanny," she said, "but you must think of Gabriella. How different it will be for her if her mother is with her. I shall miss you every minute, but for the sake of that splendid child of yours, I must not allow myself to be sorry."

If Mrs. Carr's features could have lost the fixed impression of a lifetime, they would have appeared almost cheerful while her old friend held her hand and gazed benignly upon her; but so relaxed had the muscles of her face become that, even when her spirits rose, her countenance did not alter, and the flicker of light in her smile only served to illumine its profound melancholy.

"I try to think of Gabriella," she answered, "but I oughtn't to forget poor Jane. Whenever I remember her, I begin to reproach myself."

"Don't reproach yourself, Fanny. There is nothing on earth for which you can justly be blamed. I am sure you have never considered your own wishes for a minute in your life. If ever a mother gave up everything for her children, you have done so, Fanny, and you needn't deny it. But tell me about Gabriella. How thankful you ought to be that she has given up that work in a store!"

"If it had been God's will, I suppose I must have borne it, Lydia, but I felt as if it was killing me."

"The dear child has a strong character," observed Mrs. Peyton, and it seemed to her, while she thought of Gabriella, that a strong character was a beautiful and wonderful thing.

"You would hardly know Gabriella, she is so changed," replied Mrs. Carr. "I declare I sometimes think that I never saw a girl so wildly in love as she is. She positively worships George, and when I look at her, I remember Becky Bollingbroke's saying that a smart woman in love is worse than a silly one. She has that much more to get foolish with, poor Becky used to say.

"How happy it must make you," murmured the other. "There is nothing in life I'd rather see than my Arthur happily married."

"I always thought that he and Gabriella were made for each other, but one never can tell—"

"That must be Gabriella now," said Mrs. Peyton as the bell rang. "Is she coming for you?"

"Yes, Cousin Jimmy was to bring her, and then drive me out to Hollywood. Isn't that Arthur's voice talking to her?"

"Poor boy," whispered Mrs. Peyton, and then she rustled forward and enveloped Gabriella in a warm embrace. "My darling girl, your mother has just told me," she said.

"And Gabriella has just told me," added Arthur at her elbow. Though there was a hurt look in his eyes, his manner was perfect. Years afterwards, whenever Gabriella thought of him, she remembered how perfect his manner was on that morning.

"I wanted you to know first of all," said Gabriella.

As the old lady looked at her with loving eyes, it seemed to her that the girl was softly glowing with happiness. She accepted joy as she accepted sorrow, with quietness, but there was a look in her face which made her appear, for the moment, transfigured. A radiance like that of a veiled flame shone in her eyes; the cool tones of her voice had grown richer and gentler; and at last, as Mrs. Peyton said to herself, Gabriella, the sensible and practical Gabriella, was sweet with the honeysuckle sweetness of Jane.

"She must be over head and ears in love," she thought; and the next minute, "I wonder how it will end?"

The question brought a pang to her kind old heart, which longed to make everybody, and particularly her boy Arthur, happy. Then, because her eyes were filling, she stroked the girl's arm gently, and said:

"That's a pretty dress, my dear. I never saw you look better."

"She's really getting pretty," remarked Mrs. Carr. "Cousin Jimmy was saying only yesterday that if Gabriella keeps it up, she'll be a better looking old lady than Jane."

"Well, I think her a very pretty young one," replied Mrs. Peyton. "She hasn't such small features as Jane has, but there is more in her face. Now, I'm willing to wager that George thinks her a beauty."

Gabriella laughed happily. "He hasn't the faintest idea what I look like, but he declares he won't be a bit disappointed if he finds out some day that I am ugly."

The glow of youth, of hope, of love, gave to her expressive face an almost unearthly brightness. She seemed to draw to her all that was vital and alive in the dim old house, so filled with memories, and in the October pageantry of the garden. It was the day of her miracle, and against the splendour of the scarlet sage, she shone with an unforgettable radiance.

When, a little later, Mrs. Carr, in Cousin Jimmy's buggy, with her bunch of chrysanthemums held rigidly in her lap, drove off at an amble to Hollywood, and Gabriella, turning to wave her hand, had vanished behind the corner of the gray wall, Mrs. Peyton said gently:

"She looked very happy, dear boy. You and I must pray for her happiness."

The beauty which all her life she had created through faith awoke in Arthur's suffering heart while she spoke to him. She demanded nobility of being, and it existed; she exacted generosity of nature, and it was there. By her mere presence, by the overflowing love in her heart, she not only banished jealousy and envy, but made the very idea of them unthinkable.

"She is obliged to be happy. It is her nature," answered Arthur, for his disposition was hardly less perfect than his manner.

Crossing Broad Street, which wore its look of Sabbath sleepiness, Gabriella hurried on to Hill Street, and saw George waiting for her between the two green-painted urns filled with the summer's fading bloom of portulaca.

He was staring straight upward at one of the poplar trees, where a gray squirrel was playing among the branches, and for several minutes before he was aware of her presence, she watched him with her impassioned, yet not wholly uncritical, gaze. The sunlight sparkled in his eyes, which shone brightly blue against the red brown of his flesh; and between his smiling lips, which were thick and somewhat loosely moulded, she saw the gleaming whiteness of his teeth. She could not explain—she had never even tried to understand—why this face, which was not in the least a remarkable one, should so profoundly appeal to her. When George was absent, his look haunted her with the intensity of an hallucination; when at last she saw it again, she felt that nothing else in the world mattered to her, so supreme was the contentment that swept over her. Though she was more intelligent than Jane, not even Jane herself had surrendered so unconditionally to the primal force. At least Jane had made exactions, but so complete was the subjugation of Gabriella that she exacted nothing, not even a return of her love. To give was all she asked, and in the giving she bloomed into a beauty and fullness of nature which Jane's small, closed soul could never attain.

"George!" she called, and went swiftly toward him.

He turned, threw away the cigar in his hand, and held open the gate while she entered.

"There's a jolly little beggar up in the poplar," he said; "I've been watching him for ten minutes."

Then, as she passed before him into the parlour, he shut the door, and catching her in his arms, kissed the back of her neck.

"Oh, George!" she murmured, and her voice was like music. Even to his short-sighted vision there was pathos at the heart of her happiness—the pathos of ignorance, Of innocence, of the reckless generosity of soul that spends its best for the pure joy of spending. With the instinctive miserliness of the man who realizes that passion to last must be hoarded, not scattered, he had drawn back almost unconsciously from the simple abandonment of her love. He wanted her because the deep discomfort of his nature could not be satisfied without her; but in possessing her he did not mean to give up anything else. Never for an instant had he deluded himself with the mystic ecstasies of Gabriella. The passion which had changed her whole being as if by a miracle, had altered neither his fundamental egoism nor his superficial philosophy. He loved her, he knew, as much as it was possible for him to love any woman; but he was still able to take a profound and healthy interest in his physical comfort. In one thing, however, they were passionately agreed, and that was that the aim and end of their marriage was to make George perfectly happy.

"You are sweet enough to eat this morning," he said as he kissed her.

"I told Mrs. Peyton that you didn't know whether I was pretty or ugly," she answered merrily.

"It isn't beauty that takes a man, though women think so," he rejoined lightly, and yet as if he were imparting one of the basic facts of experience. "I don't know what it is—but it's something else, and you've got it, Gabriella."

She looked at him with luminous eyes.

"I've got you," she answered in a whisper; "that's all—nothing else on earth matters. I want nothing but love."

"But you let me go away for six months. I could never understand that."

"I had to, George. I couldn't be mean even for you, could I?"

"Well, I don't know." His gaze dwelt on her moodily. "Sometimes I wonder if you haven't too much conscience in your body?"

Careless as were his words, they brought stinging tears to her eyes. Her throat ached with the longing to pour out her love; but it seemed to her suddenly that a wall of personality had risen between them, and that she could only beat blindly against the impenetrable mass that divided them. She knew now that he could never understand, and yet the knowledge of this intensified rather than diminished her love. The mere physical attraction, which she had glorified into passion, was invested with the beauty and the mystery of an unattainable ideal.

"I believe you are going to cry, darling. Don't be so serious," he said, laughing.

"But you know—tell me you know that I love you."

"Of course I know it. Am I blind or a fool?"

Then before the glowing worship in her face, he caught her in his arms, while he said over and over, "I love you! I love you!"

He held her close, thrilling at her touch, seeking her warm lips with an eagerness which comforted her because she was too inexperienced to understand how ephemeral was its nature and its sweetness.

"Promise to love me always, George, as you do now," she said, passionately trying to make the fugitive joy immortal.

"If you'll tell me how to help it, I shall be grateful," he retorted as gaily as if her eyes had not filled with tears.

"Swear it!"

"I swear it. Now, are you satisfied?"

"I don't believe it. I'll never believe that you love me as much as I love you. Nobody could."

In his heart he agreed with her. That Gabriella loved him more than he loved her was a fact to which he was easily reconciled. He loved her quite as much as he could love anybody except himself and be comfortable, and if she demanded more, she merely proved herself to be an unreasonable person. Women did love more than men, he supposed, but what else were they here for? During the six months when he had thought that she belonged to another, she had, he told himself, almost driven him out of his mind; but possession once assured, he had speedily recovered his health and his sanity. Her worship flattered him, and in this flattery she had, perhaps, her strongest hold on his heart. Nothing in his engagement had pleased him more than the readiness with which she had given up her work at his request. He abhorred independence in a wife; and Gabriella's immediate and unresisting acquiescence in his desire appeared to him to establish the fact of her essential and inherent femininity. Had not all laws, as well as all religions, proclaimed that woman should be content to lay down not only her life but her very identity for love; and that Gabriella was womanly to the core of her nature, in spite of her work in Brandywine's millinery department, it was impossible to doubt while he kissed her. There were times, indeed, when the exaltation of Gabriella's womanliness seemed to have left her without a will of her own; when, in a divine submission to love, she appeared to exist only for the laudable purpose of making her lover happy.

"I'd do anything on earth for you, Gabriella," said George suddenly. "I wonder if you would make a sacrifice for me if I asked it?" From his face as he looked down on her it was evident that he was not speaking from impulse, but that he had seized an opportune moment.

"You know I would, George. I'd give up the whole world for you. I'd beg my bread with you by the roadside."

"Well, it isn't so bad as that, darling—it's only about your mother coming to us so soon. I've had a letter from home, and it seems that father has had losses and can't help me out as he intended to do. He's always either losing or making piles of money, so don't bother your precious head about that. In six months he'll probably be making piles again, but, in the meantime, mother suggests that we should postpone taking a house, and come and live with her for a few months."

"I'd rather live on your income, George, no matter how small it is. I'm an awfully good manager, and you'd be surprised to see how far I can make a little money go. Why can't we take an apartment somewhere in an inexpensive neighbourhood—one just big enough for mother and you and me?"

"We couldn't live half so well in the first place, and, besides, I'd hate like the devil to see you working yourself to death and losing your looks. That's just exactly what Patty is doing. She was the family's greatest investment, you know. Everything we had for years was spent on her because she was such a ripping beauty, and mother set her heart on her marrying nothing less than a duke. So we sent her abroad to be educated and squandered a fortune on her clothes, and then, just as mother was gloating over her triumphs, the very day after the Duke of Toxbridge proposed to her, Patty walked out one morning and married Billy King at the Little Church Around the Corner. Billy, of course, hasn't a cent to his name except what he makes painting blue pictures, and that's precious little. They're up on the West Side now, living in four rooms with neighbours who fry onions at nine o'clock in the morning next door to them, and half the time Patty hasn't even a maid, I believe, and has to do her work with the help of a charwoman."

"And is she happy?" There was eagerness in Gabriella's voice, for she was sure that she should love Patty.

"Oh, yes, Patty is happy, but mother isn't. It's rough on mother."

"I think she ought to have told your mother before she married."

"Well, Patty thought she could stand the fuss better after she'd done it than she could before. She said she needed the support of knowing they couldn't stop it. Cheeky, wasn't it?"

"And is she really so beautiful?"

"Ripping," said George; "simply ripping."

"I know I shall love her. Is she dark or fair?"

"I never thought about it, but she's a towering beauty—something between dark and fair, I suppose. She has golden hair, you know."

His arm was around her, and lifting her earnest face to his, Gabriella began in her softest voice: "I shouldn't mind a bit living like that, George—honestly I shouldn't."

"Yes, you would. It would be rotten."

"I wish you would tell me just how much we shall have to live on, dear. Even if it is very, very little, it would be so much better not to expect anything from your father. If the worst comes to the worst, I can always go back to work, you know, and I feel as if I ought to help because you are so generous about wanting mother to live with us."

He frowned slightly, while a dark flush rose to his forehead. Already Gabriella was learning how dangerously easy it was to irritate George. Serious discussions always appeared to disturb him, and at the first allusion to the responsibilities he had assumed, she could see the look of bored restlessness creep into his face. It was evidently abhorrent to him to hear her talk about business; but with her practical nature and her fundamental common sense it was impossible that she should be content to remain in a fool's paradise of financial mysteries. She had only the vaguest idea how he earned a living, and a still vaguer one of what that living represented. There was an impression in her mind that he worked in his father's office somewhere in Wall Street—he had once given her the number—and that he went "downtown" every morning after breakfast and did not get home to luncheon. Cousin Jimmy had once told her that George's father was a stockbroker, but this information conveyed little to her mind. The men she knew in Richmond were lawyers, doctors, clergymen, or engaged, like Cousin Jimmy, in the "tobacco business," and she supposed that "a stockbroker" must necessarily belong to a profession which was restricted to New York. The whole matter was hazy in her thoughts, but she hoped in time, by intelligent and tactful application, to overcome her ignorance as well as George's deeply rooted objection to her enlightenment.

"Well, you see, my income is uncertain, Gabriella. It depends a good deal upon the stock market and the sort of stuff we've been buying. Look here, darling, don't, for heaven sake, get the business bee in your bonnet. A mannish woman is worse than poison, and the less you know about stocks the more attractive you will be. Mother has lived for thirty years with father, and she doesn't know any more how he makes his money than you do at this minute."

This was as lucid, she suspected, as George was ever likely to be on the subject, and, since he was becoming visibly annoyed, she abandoned her fruitless search for information. After she was married there would be time and opportunity to find out all that she wanted to know; and even if he never told her anything more—well, she was quite accustomed to the masculine habit of never telling women anything more. Her mother and Jane were as ignorant of finance as they had been in their cradles; Cousin Pussy spoke of the "tobacco business" as if it were a sacred mystery superior to the delicate feminine faculties; and while Gabriella was engaged to Arthur, he had fallen into the habit of gently reminding her that she "knew nothing of law."

"Very well, dearest, I shan't bother you," she said cheerfully, "only, of course, I couldn't possibly leave mother with Jane and Charley. She doesn't realize it, but she would be perfectly miserable."

"She told me that leaving Richmond was like death to her."

"That's only because she knows she's going," answered Gabriella, but her endeavour to explain her mother's habit of mind appeared to her to be so hopeless that she added unconvincingly: "You can't imagine how dependent she is on me. Jane doesn't know how to manage her at all, though they are so much alike."

"Well, of course, if we live at home—"

"But you promised me we'd be to ourselves, George; you can't have forgotten it. We talked it over, every bit of it, and I told you in the beginning I couldn't leave mother."

"If you loved me enough to marry me, I should think you'd be willing to give up your family for me." He spoke doggedly; it was his way to speak doggedly when he was driving a point.

"It isn't that, dear, you know it isn't that."

Taking a letter from his pocket, he drew a sheet of blue note paper, closely interlined, from the envelope, and handed it to her.

"You can see for yourself how it is," he said in an aggrieved voice. By his tone he had managed to put her in the wrong as utterly as if she, not he, were trying to break her word. Yet she had told him in the very beginning that she could not leave her mother; she had refused to engage herself to him until he had offered Mrs. Carr a home with them. It had all been carefully arranged at the start, and now, within a month of their marriage, he had apparently forgotten that the matter was settled.

Leaning forward until the light fell on the paper, she read with trembling lips:

My Dear Son:

Your letter was a blow to me because you had said nothing of Gabriella's plan to bring her mother to New York to live with her, and, of course, this makes it out of the question that you should come straight to us. Now that Patty has gone—poor child, I am afraid she will live to repent her rashness—your father and I had quite looked forward to having you young people in the house; but we haven't room, even if I could bring myself to face the prospect of a rival mother-in-law under the same roof with me—and frankly I can't. And your father has simply put his foot down on the idea. As you know he hasn't been very well of late—the doctor says he is threatened with diabetes—so my one thought is to spare him every useless anxiety. He sleeps very badly and doesn't seem able, even at night, to detach his mind from his business worries. If he hadn't had such a bad summer, he might have been able to help you start housekeeping, but there have been a great many failures in the last few months, and he says he is obliged to cut down all his expenses in order to tide over the depression in the market. We are trying to retrench in every possible way, and, for this reason, I fear we shall hardly be able to go down to your wedding. This is a terrible disappointment to us both, and your father is particularly distressed because he will not be able to add to your income this year. Of course, if you should change your mind and decide to come to us, we can get Patty's old room ready for you at once, and turn yours into a sitting-room. Think this over and let me know as soon as you possibly can.

I see Patty occasionally. She is in high spirits, but looking a little thinner, I think. Billy has painted a portrait of Mrs. Pletheridge, but it isn't a bit flattering, and he wouldn't let her wear her pearls, so I'm afraid she won't buy it. I don't believe he will ever make anything of himself. What a waste when Patty might have been Duchess of Toxbridge. Though I am not a bit worldly, I can't help regretting all that she has lost.

Your loving mother,
EVELYN FOWLER.

When she had folded the letter and given it back to him, Gabriella dropped her hands in her lap and sat gazing thoughtfully at the square of sunlight by the window.

"If you cared as much as I do, you'd be willing to give up your family," he said suddenly, encouraged not only by her manner, which appeared yielding, but by his secret ineradicable conviction that her love was greater than his. Across the romantic screen of his features there flashed a swift change of expression, like the flicker of light on a coloured mask. If she could only have looked through the charming vacancy of his face, she would have been surprised to discover the directness and simplicity of his mental processes. He wanted his way, and he meant, provided it was humanly possible, to have whatever he wanted.

"It isn't that, George. Love has nothing to do with it. It is a question of right."

For a minute he surveyed her moodily; then, rising from her side on the sofa, he took two steps to the window and looked up at the boughs of the poplar tree. The gray squirrel was still there, and he watched it attentively while he pondered his answer. Yes, the whole trouble with Gabriella was too much conscience. This conscience of hers had got in his way before now, and he had suddenly an uneasy feeling, as if he had struck against the vein of iron which lay beneath the rich bloom of her passion. The thought of her opposition, of her secret hardness, bitterly angered him. He wanted her—no other woman could satisfy him—but he wanted her utterly different from what she was. He was seized with an indomitable desire to make her over, to change her entirely from that Gabriella with whom he had fallen in love. Of course, she was right as far as the mere facts of the case were concerned. He had promised that her mother should live with them; but he felt indignantly that it was an act of disloyalty for her to be right at his expense. She ought to have given in, and she ought to have given in gracefully, there was no question of that. When a woman loved a man as much as she loved him, it was unreasonable of her to let these innumerable little points of fact come between them; it was ungenerous of her to cling so stubbornly to her advantage. Her very quietness—that look of gentle obstinacy which refused either to fight back or to surrender—irritated him almost to desperation. His temper, always inflammable, suddenly burst out, and he felt that he wanted to shake her. He wanted, indeed, to do anything in the world except the sensible thing of walking out of the house and leaving her to reflection.

"I should think your first duty would be to your husband," he said, while the streak of cruelty which was at the heart of his love showed like a livid mark on the surface of his nature. His mind was conscious of but a single thought while he stood there in the wind which fluttered the curtains and filled the room with the roving scents of October, and this was the bitter longing to make Gabriella over into the girl that he wanted her to become. Though it cost him her love, he felt that he must punish her for being herself.

"Do you mean always to put your mother before me?" he asked passionately, after a minute.

Still she did not answer, and in the deep, earnest eyes that she turned on him he saw not anger, not sorrow even, but wonder. As he stretched out his hand, it fell on Mrs. Carr's window box, where a rose geranium remained bright green in the midst of the withered stems of the clove pinks, and the scent of the leaves, as he crushed them between his fingers, evoked a swift memory of Gabriella in one of her soft moods, saying over and over, "I love you! Oh, I do love you!" At the image his temper changed as if by magic, and crossing the room, he bent down and kissed her with a fierceness that bruised her lips.

"I adore you, Gabriella," he said.

Though she had seen these sudden changes in him before, she had never grown wholly used to them. Her deeper nature, with its tranquil brightness, untroubled by passing storms, was unprepared for the shallow violence which swept over him, leaving no visible trace of its passage. No, she could not understand him—she could only hope that after they were married the blindness would pass from her love, and she would attain that completer knowledge for which she was striving so patiently. The transforming miracle of marriage, she trusted, would reveal this mystery, with so many others.

"How can you hurt me so, George?" she asked with reproachful tenderness.

"It's because you are so stubborn, darling. If you weren't so stubborn I shouldn't do it. Do you know you get almost mulish at times," he added, laughing, while she moved nearer and rubbed her cheek softly against his sleeve.

"You frighten me," she whispered. "I was just beginning to believe that you really meant it."

"Oh, lovers always quarrel. There's nothing in that."

"But I hate to see you angry. It would almost kill me if it lasted longer than a minute. Never let it last, will you, George?"

"Of course not, Goosey. It never has lasted, has it?"

"Goosey" was one of his favourite names for her. He liked it because it gave him a merry feeling of superiority when he said it, and Gabriella liked it for perhaps the same reason. In the first ardour of her self-surrender she caught eagerly at any straw that she might cast on the flame of her passion.

"And I'm not really stubborn, dear. Tell me that I'm not really stubborn."

"You darling! I was only teasing you."

"I'll do anything on earth for you that I can, George."

"I know you will, dearest, and you don't honestly care more for your family, do you?"

"I love you better than all the rest of the world put together. There are times when I think it must be wrong to love any man as much as I love you. My grandmother used to say that when you loved like that you 'tempted Providence.' Isn't it dreadful to believe that you could tempt Providence by loving?"

He kissed her throat where a loosened strand of dark hair had fallen against the whiteness.

"Will you do what I ask, Gabriella?"

So it was all to begin over again! He had not really given in, he had not really yielded even while he was kissing her. She closed her eyes, leaning her head on his shoulder. For a moment she felt as if a physical pain were pressing into her forehead.

"Will you do it, Gabriella?" It was as if he put his soul into his voice, wooing her tenderly away from her better judgment. He was testing his power to dominate her; and never had she felt it so vividly, never had her will been so incapable of resisting him as at that instant. Moving slightly in his arms she looked at the clear red brown of his throat, at his sensitive mouth, with the faint dent in the lower lip, at his bright blue eyes, which had grown soft while he pleaded. His physical power over her was complete, and he knew it. Her flesh had become as soft as flowers in his arms, while her eyes, like dark flames, trembled and fell away from his look.

"It isn't only the thing itself, darling, but I don't like you to refuse me. It hurts me that you won't do what I ask of you."

"If it were anything else, George."

"But it isn't anything else. It is just that I want you to myself—all to myself, after we are married."

"Don't ask me, dearest. If you only knew how it makes me suffer."

Her voice was a caress when she answered, but, as he told himself passionately, she had not yielded an inch. Once again he had run against the iron hidden under the bloom.

"Then you refuse absolutely?" he asked, and though his voice quivered still, it was no longer from tenderness. He hated stubbornness, and, most of all, he hated it in the woman who was going to be his wife. A life of continual contradiction, he felt, would be intolerable. A strong will, which he had always admired in himself, became a positive failing in Gabriella. A woman's strength lay, after all, not in force of character, but in sweetness of nature. And yet how lovely she was! How soft, how sweet she looked as she gazed up at him with her radiant eyes. There was a fascination for him in her tall slenderness, in the graceful curve of her head, which drooped slightly like a dark flower on its stem. Everything about her charmed him, and yet he had never called her beautiful in his thoughts.

"I told you how it was, dear, when you first asked me to marry you," she said, with infinite patience. "I told you that it wasn't fair to ask you to take mother, but that I couldn't possibly leave her alone in her old age. Jane's home is wretchedly unhappy—she can never tell when Charley is to be counted on—and it would kill mother to be dependent on Charley even if he were willing. I see your side, George, indeed, indeed, I do, but I can't—I simply can't act differently. I have always known it was my duty to look after mother—nothing can change that, not even love. She worked for us while we were little, and it is trouble that has made her what she is to-day. You must see that I am right, George; you can't possibly help it."

But he couldn't see it. If the truth had been twice as evident, if Gabriella had been twice as reasonable, he could still have seen only his wishes.

"I am only asking you to do what is best for us both, Gabriella."

"But how can it be best for me to become an ungrateful child, George?"

Neither of them wanted to quarrel, yet in a minute the barbed words were flying between them; in a minute they faced each other as coldly as if they had been strangers instead of adoring lovers. At the last, he looked at her an instant in silence while she sat perfectly motionless with her deep eyes changing to gold in the sunlight; then, turning on his heel, without a word, he left the house, and walked rapidly over the coloured leaves on the pavement. As he passed under the poplar tree the gray squirrel darted gaily along a bough over his head, but he did not look up, and a minute later Gabriella saw him cross the street and vanish beyond the pointed yew tree in the yard at the corner.

"I wonder if this is the end?" she thought bitterly, and she knew that even if it were the end, that even if she died of it, she could never give way. Something stronger than herself—that vein of iron in her soul—would not bend, would not break though every fibre of her being struggled against it. All the happiness of her life vanished with George as he passed beyond the yew tree at the corner, yet she sat there with her hands still folded, her lips still firm, watching the tree long after its pointed dusk had hidden her lover's figure. Had she followed her desire as lightly as George followed his, she would have run after him as he disappeared, and bringing him back to the room he had left, dissolved in tears on his breast. She longed to do this, but the vein of iron held her firm in spite of herself. She could not move toward him, she could not even have put out her hand had he entered.

The bell rang, and her blood drummed in her ears; but it was only Cousin Jimmy bringing Mrs. Carr back from the cemetery. Hearty, deep-chested, meticulously brushed and groomed, he wore his Sunday frock with an unnatural stiffness, as if he were still hearing Pussy's parting warning to be "careful about his clothes." His dark hair, trained for twenty years from a side parting, shone with the lustre of satin, and his shining eyes, so like the eyes of adventurous youth, wore their accustomed Sabbath look of veiled and ashamed sleepiness.

"So you're going to take the old lady to New York with you, Gabriella?"

"I can't bear to think of it, Cousin Jimmy," remarked Mrs. Carr, while she adjusted her crape veil over the back of her chair. "I don't see how I can stand living in the North."

"Well, what about our friend Charley? Do you think you could get on any better with Charley for a son-in-law?"

"You oughtn't to joke about it, Cousin Jimmy. It is too serious for joking."

"I beg your pardon, Cousin Fanny—but where is George, Gabriella? I thought he was to meet you here."

"He had to go just before you came. Don't you think mother is looking well?"

"As well as I ever saw her. I was telling her so as we drove back from Hollywood. All she needs is to leave off moping for a while and she'd lose ten years of her age. Why, I tell you if it were I, I'd jump at the chance to go to New York for a few years. If there wasn't a single thing there except the theatres, I'd jump at it. You can go to a different show every night of your life, Cousin Fanny."

"I have never been inside of a theatre in my life. You ought to know me better than to think it," replied Mrs. Carr, while the corners of her mouth drooped. She had laid her bag of grosgrain silk on the table at her elbow, and untying the strings of her bonnet, she neatly rolled them into two tight little wads which she fastened with jet-headed pins.

"You make her go, honey, when you get hold of her," said Jimmy to Gabriella in a sympathetic aside "What she needs is bracing up—I was saying so to Pussy only this morning. 'If you could just brace up Cousin Fanny, she'd be as well as you or I,' was what I said to her Now I don't believe there's a better place on earth to brace a body up than old New York. I remember I took my poor old father there just a month or two before his last illness, when he was getting over a spell of lumbago, and it worked on him like magic. We stayed at the Fifth Avenue Hotel—you must be sure to get a dinner at the Fifth Avenue Hotel, Cousin Fanny—and went to a show every blessed night for a week. It made the old man young again, upon my word it did, and he was still talking about it when he came down with his last illness. Well, I must be going home to Pussy now. The boys and I went out squirrel hunting yesterday, and Pussy promised me Brunswick stew for dinner. Now, don't you forget to brace up, Cousin Fanny."

That's all on earth you need. The world ain't such a bad place, after all, when you sit down and think right hard about it."

He went out gaily, followed by Mrs. Carr's accusing eyes to the hatrack, where he stopped to take his glossy silk hat from a peg. Turning in the buggy as he drove off, he waved merrily back at them with the whip before he touched the fat flanks of his gray.

"Cousin Jimmy means well, but he has a most unfortunate manner at times," observed Mrs. Carr.

"What is the matter, Gabriella? Have you a headache?"

"Oh, no, but the sunshine is so strong."

"Then you'd better lower the shade. Why, what in the world has happened to my rose geranium? I was just going to pot it for the winter."

"I'm sure it isn't hurt, mother. George broke the leaves when he was looking out of the window."

"I thought he was going to stay for dinner. Did you make the jelly and syllabub?"

"I made it, but he wouldn't stay."

"Well, we'll send some upstairs to Miss Jemima. Do you know she had to have the doctor this morning? I met him as I was going out, and he said he was sorry to hear I was going to leave Richmond. I can't imagine where on earth he could have heard it, for I haven't mentioned it to a soul except Lydia Peyton. Yes, I believe I did speak of it to Bessie Spencer at the meeting of the Ladies' Aid Society the other day. Where are you going, Gabriella? Would you mind putting my bonnet in the bandbox?"

No, Gabriella wouldn't mind, and taking the folds of crape in her arms, she went to get the green paper bandbox out of the closet. Though she had sacrificed her happiness for her mother, she felt that it would be impossible for her to listen with a smiling face to her innocent prattle.

In the afternoon, when Mrs. Carr, with a small and inconspicuous basket in her hand, had set out on her Sunday visit to the Old Ladies' Home, and Marthy, attired in an apron with an embroidered bib, had taken the jelly and syllabub upstairs to Miss Jemima, Gabriella sat down in her mother's rocking-chair by the window, and tried desperately to be philosophical. The sound of the old maids from the floor above descending on their way to a funeral disturbed her for a minute, and she thought with an extraordinary clearness, "That is what my life will be if George never comes back. That is what it means to be old." And there was a morbid pleasure in pressing this thought, like a pointed weapon, into her heart. "That is all there will be for me—that will be my life," she went on after an instant of throbbing anguish. "I had no right to think of marriage with mother dependent on me, and the best thing for me to do is to start again with Mr. Brandywine. George was right in a way. Yes, it is hard on him, and I was wrong ever to think of it—ever to let him fall in love with me." The mere thought that George was right in a way gave her singular comfort, and while she dwelt on it, the discovery seemed to throw a vivid light on the cause of the quarrel. Of course, she had expected too much of him. It was natural that he should not want to be burdened with her family. What she had looked upon as selfishness was only the natural instinct of a man in love with a woman. He had said that he wanted her to himself, and to want her to himself appeared now to be the most reasonable desire in the world.

Yes, she had acquitted George; but, in acquitting him, it was characteristic of her that she should not have yielded an inch of her ground. She drew comfort from declaring him innocent, but it was the tragic comfort of one who blesses while she renounces. George's blamelessness did not alter in the least her determination to cling to her mother.

The afternoon wore on; the soft golden light on the pavement was dappled with shadows; and the wind, blowing over the iron urns in the yard, scattered the withered leaves of portulaca over the grass. Though the summer still lingered, and flowers were blooming behind the fences along the street, the faint violet haze of autumn was creeping slowly over the sunshine. Now and then an acquaintance, returning from afternoon service, looked up to bow to her, and while the daylight was still strong, Marthy, resplendent in Sunday raiment, came out of the little green gate at the side of the yard and passed, mincing, in the direction of the negro church. Then the door opened slowly, and the two old maids came in and stopped for a minute at the parlour door to see if Gabriella "had company."

"Such a lovely evening, my dear"—they never used the word afternoon— "we went all the way to the cemetery. She was buried in her grandfather's lot, you know, in the old part up on the hill. It was a beautiful drive, but Amelia and I couldn't help thinking of the poor young thing all the time."

It was Miss Jemima who had spoken, and her kind, plain face, all puffs and pleasant wrinkles, had not yet relaxed from the unnatural solemnity it had worn at the funeral. She was seldom grave, and never despondent, though to Gabriella she appeared to lead an unendurable life. Unlike Miss Amelia, she had not even a happy youth and a lover to look back upon; she had nothing, indeed, except her unfailing goodness and patience to support her.

"I don't like to see you alone, honey," she said, untying the strings of her black silk bonnet, which fitted her cheerful features like a frame. "If the doctor hadn't told me to go to bed as soon as I came in, we'd sit a while with you for company."

She felt that it was morbid and unnatural in Gabriella to sit alone in a dim room when there were so many young people out in the streets. "You mark my words, there's some reason back of Gabriella's moping all by herself," she remarked to Miss Amelia as she took off her "things" a few minutes later. "It wouldn't surprise me a bit to hear that she'd had a fuss with her sweetheart."

"I declare, sister Jemima, you are too sentimental to live," observed Miss Amelia as she filled the tea kettle on the fender "Anybody would think to hear you talk that there was nothing in life except making love."

"Well, there isn't anything else so interesting when you're young. You used to think so yourself, sister Amelia."

Standing gaunt and black, with the tea kettle held out stiffly before her, Miss Amelia turned her tragic face on her sister.

"Well, I reckon you don't know much about it," she responded with the unconscious cruelty of age. Having been once the victim of a great passion, she had developed at last into an uncompromising realist, wholly devoid of sentimentality, while Miss Jemima, lacking experience, had enveloped the unknown in a rosy veil of illusion.

"You don't have to know a thing to think about it, sister Amelia," replied the invalid timidly as she put on her flannel wrapper and fastened it with a safety pin at the throat.

"Well, I reckon it's all right for a girl like Gabriella," said Miss Amelia crushingly, "but when you look back on it from my age, you'll know it isn't worth a row of pins in a life."

And beside the window downstairs Gabriella was thinking passionately: "Shall I ever grow old? Is it possible that I shall ever grow old like that?"

With the bare question, terror seized her—the terror of growing old without George, the terror of dying before she had known the full beauty of life. Looking ahead of her at the years empty of love, she saw them like a gray road, leaf strewn, wind swept, deserted, and herself creeping through them, as bent, as wrinkled, as disillusioned, as Miss Amelia. The very image of a life without love was intolerable to her since she had known George—for love meant George, and only George, in her thoughts. That she could ever be happy again, ever take a natural pleasure in life if she lost him, was unimaginable to her at the instant. She loved him, she had loved him from the first moment she saw him, she would never, though she lived a million years, love any one else. It was as absurd to think that she could love again as that a flower could bloom afresh when its petals were withered. No, without George there was only loveless old age—there was only the future of Miss Amelia before her. And she clung to this idea with a horror which Miss Amelia, who seldom reflected that she was loveless and by no means considered herself an object of pity, would have despised.

"I have no right to marry George, and yet if I don't marry him I shall be miserable all my life," she told herself with a sensation of panic. It would be so long, the rest of her life, and without George it was as desolate as the gray road of her vision. All the beauties of the universe, all the miracles of hope, of youth, of spring; her health, her intellect, her capacity for work and for taking pleasure in little things—all these were as nothing to her if she lost George out of her life. "I oughtn't to marry him," she repeated, "but if I don't marry him I shall be miserable every minute until I die."

Then a terror more awful than any she had yet suffered clutched at her heart. Suppose he should never come back! Suppose he had really meant to leave her for good! Suppose he had ceased to love her since he went out of the house! The possibility was so agonizing that she rose blindly from her chair and turned from the window as if the quiet street, filled with the dreamy sunshine of October, had offered an appalling, an unbelievable sight to her eyes. If he had ceased to love her, she was helpless; and this sense of helplessness awoke a feeling of rage in her heart. If he did not come back, she could never go after him. She could only sit and wait until she grew as old and as ugly as Miss Amelia. While the minutes, which seemed hours, dragged away, she wept the bitterest tears of her life—tears not of wounded love, but of anger because she could do nothing but wait.

While she wept the bell rang. When she did not answer it, it rang again, and after an interminable pause the footsteps of Miss Amelia were heard descending the stairs. Then the door opened and shut, the footsteps began their slow ascent of the stairs, and after an eternity of silence, she knew that George had entered the room.

Wiping her eyes on the ruffle of the sofa pillow, she sat up and faced him, while her pride hardened again.

"Gabriella, I have come back."

"I see you have," she answered coldly, and choked over a sob.

"What are you crying about, Gabriella?"

"I—I have a headache."

"Have you thought about me at all to-day?"

"A little."

He laughed softly, the laugh of a conqueror.

"I'm glad at least that I didn't give you the headache."

"You didn't. I had it anyway."

He was radiant, he was as fresh as the wind. Never in his life had he looked so gay, so handsome, so kind. His blue eyes were brimming with light. The mere fact of being alive appeared to fill him with ecstasy. And she loved him for his gaiety, for his lightness, for the ease with which he took for granted her unchangeable love. She longed with all her soul and body to prove this love by a surrender more complete than any she had made in the past. She longed to say: "I am yours to do with as you please, and nothing in the universe matters but you and my love for you." The very core of her nature longed to say this to him; but her indomitable pride, which even passion could not overcome, kept her sitting there in silence while she felt that her heart was bursting with happiness.

"Have you thought it over, Gabriella?"

She nodded. To save her life, she felt, she could not utter a word without sobbing.

"And you have absolutely and finally decided to have your way?"

This time she shook her head, but the tears fell on her cheeks and she did not brush them away. From his voice she knew that she had triumphed, but there was no delight in the knowledge. She did not want to triumph; she wanted only to yield to him and to make him happy by yielding.

"O George!" she cried suddenly, and held out her arms to him.

As he looked down at her his expression changed suddenly to one of intense sadness. From his face, which had grown pale, he might have been contemplating the Eternal Verities, though, in reality, he was considering nothing more exalted than the dreary prospect of a lifetime spent in the society of Mrs. Carr.

Then, as Gabriella enfolded him, he laughed softly. He had given in, but he knew in the very instant of his defeat that he should some day turn it to victory.

# CHAPTER V

## THE NEW WORLD

Gabriella stood in front of the station, ecstatically watching George while he struggled for a cab. In the pale beams of the early sunshine her face looked young, flushed, and expectant, as if she had just awakened from sleep, and her eyes, following her husband, were the happy eyes of a bride. She wore a new dress of blue broadcloth, passionately overtrimmed by Miss Polly Hatch; on her head a blue velvet toque from Brandywine's millinery department rested as lightly as a benediction; and her hands clasped Arthur's wedding present, a bag of alligator skin bearing her initials in gold. One blissful month ago she and George had been married, and now, on the reluctant return from a camp in the Adirondacks, they were confronting the disillusioning actuality of the New York streets at eight o'clock in the morning. While Gabriella waited, shivering a a little, for the air was sharp and her broadcloth dress was not warm, she amused herself planning a future which appeared to consist of inexhaustible happiness. And mingling with her dreams there were divine memories of the last month and of her marriage. After that one quarrel George, she told herself, had been "simply perfect." His manner to her mother had been beautiful; he had been as eager as Gabriella to obliterate all memory of the difference between them, though, of course, after his yielding that supreme point she had felt that she must give up everything else—and the giving up had been rapture. He had shown not the faintest disposition to crow over her when at last, after consulting Mrs. Carr, she had told him that her mother really preferred to stay with Jane until summer, though he had remarked with evident relief: "Then we'll put off looking for an apartment. It's easier to find one in the summer anyway, and in the meantime you can talk it over with mother."

After this everything had gone so smoothly, so exquisitely, that it was more like a dream than like actual life when she looked back on it. She saw herself in the floating lace veil of her grandmother, holding white roses in her hand, and she saw George's face—the face of her dreams come true—looking at her out of a starry mist, while in the shining wilderness that surrounded them she heard an organ playing softly "The Voice That Breathed O'er Eden." Then the going away! The good-byes at the station in Richmond; her mother's face, pathetic and drawn against the folds of her crape veil; Cousin Jimmy, crimson and jovial; Florrie's violent waving as the train moved away; Miss Jemima, with her smiling, pain-tortured eyes, flinging a handful of rice; the last glimpse of them; the slowly vanishing streets, where the few pedestrians stopped to look after the cars; the park where she had played as a child; the brilliant flower-beds filled with an autumnal bloom of scarlet cannas; the white-aproned negro nurses and the gaily decorated perambulators; the clustering church spires against a sky of pure azure; the negro hovels, with frost-blighted sunflowers dropping brown seeds over the paling fences; the rosy haze of it all; and her heart saying over and over, "There is nothing but love in the world! There is nothing but love in the world!"

"I've got a cab—the last one," said George, pushing his way through the crowd, and laying his hand on her arm with a possessive and authoritative touch. "Let me put you in, and then I'll speak to the driver."

As he gave the address she watched him, still fascinated with the delicious strangeness of it all. It was like an adventure to have George whisk her so peremptorily into a cab, and then stand with his foot on the step while he curtly directed the driver. Nothing could surpass the romance—the supreme exciting romance of life. Every minute was an event; every act of George's was as thrilling as a moment in melodrama. And as they drove through the streets, over the pale bands of sunshine, she had a sense of lightness and wonder, as if she were driving in a world of magic toward ineffable happiness.

"Isn't it strange to be here together, George?" she said. "I can hardly believe it." But in her heart she was thinking: "I shall never want anything but love in my life. If I have George I shall never want anything else." The bedraggled, slatternly figures of the women sweeping the pavements in the cross-street through which they were driving filled her with a fugitive sadness, so faint, so pale that it hardly dimmed the serene brightness of her mood. "I wish they were all as happy as I am," she thought; "and they might be if they only knew the secret of happiness. If they only knew that nothing in the world matters when one has love in one's heart."

"You'll believe it soon enough when we turn into Fifth Avenue," replied George, glancing with disgust out of the window. A month of intimacy had increased the power of his smile over her senses, and when he turned to her again after a minute, she felt something of the faint delicious tremor of their first meeting. Already she was beginning to discover that beyond his expressive eyes he had really very little of importance to express, that his prolonged silences covered poverty of ideas rather than abundance of feeling, that his limited vocabulary was due less to reticence than to the simple inarticulateness of the primitive mind. Through the golden glamour of her honeymoon there had loomed suddenly the discovery that George was not clever—but cleverness mattered so little, she told herself, as long as he loved her.

"I hope your mother will like me," she said nervously after a minute.

"I'll be sorry for her if she doesn't."

"Do I look nice?"

"Of course you do. I never saw you when you didn't."

"I feel so dreadfully untidy. I never tried to dress in a sleeping-car before."

"It did rock, didn't it?"

"I'll never travel again at night if I can help it. There's a cinder in your eye; let me get it out for you." It thrilled her pleasantly to remove the cinder with the corner of her handkerchief, and to order him to sit still whenever the cab jolted. It was incredibly young, incredibly foolish, but it was all a part of the wonderful enchantment in which she moved. The cinder had made an agreeable episode, but when it had been removed there was nothing more for them to talk about. In four weeks of daily and hourly companionship they had said very easily, Gabriella had found, everything they had longed so passionately to say to each other. It was strange—it was positively astounding how soon they had talked themselves empty of ideas and fallen back upon repetition and ejaculation. Before her marriage she had thought that a lifetime would be too short to hold the full richness of their confidences; and yet now, after a month, though they still made love, they had ceased, almost with relief, to make conversation.

After turning into Fifth Avenue they drove for ages between depressing examples in brownstone of an architecture which, like George, was trying rather vaguely to express nothing; and then rolling heavily into Fifty-seventh Street stopped presently before one of the solemn houses which stood, in the dignity of utter ugliness, midway of a long block. "They are all so alike I don't see how I shall ever know where I live," thought Gabriella. Then, as George helped her out of the cab, the door opened as if by magic, and beyond the solemn manservant she saw the short, stout figure of a lady in a tightly fitting morning gown of black silk. Hurrying up the steps, she was pressed against a large smooth bosom which yielded as little as if it had been upholstered in leather.

"My dear daughter! my dear Gabriella!" exclaimed the lady in a charming voice; and looking down after the first kiss, Gabriella saw a handsome, slightly florid face, with the vivacious smile of a girl and a beautiful forehead under a stiffly crimped arch of gray hair which looked as hard and bright as silver.

"I've been up since seven o'clock waiting for you. You must be famished. Come straight in to breakfast. Your father is already at the table, George. Poor man, he has to start downtown so dreadfully early."

Bright, effusive, vivacious, and as emphatically Southern as if she had never left Franklin Street, Mrs. Fowler took off Gabriella's hat and coat, kissed her several times while she was doing so, and at last, still talking animatedly, led them into the dining-room.

"Archibald, here they are," she said in a tone of unaffected delight, while a thin, serious-looking man, with anxious eyes, pale, aristocratic features, and skin that had a curious parchment-like texture, put down the *Times*, and came forward to meet them. Though he did not speak as he kissed her, Gabriella felt that there was sincere, if detached, friendliness in his little pat on her shoulder. He led her almost tenderly to her chair; and as soon as she was comfortably seated and supplied with rolls and bacon, resigned her contentedly to his wife and the butler. His manner of gentle abstraction, which Gabriella attributed first to something he had just read in the newspaper, she presently discovered to be his habitual attitude toward all the world except Wall Street. He ate his breakfast as if his attention were somewhere else; he spoke to his son and his daughter-in-law kindly, but as if he were not thinking about them; he treated his wife, whom he adored, as if he had not clearly perceived her. In the profound abstraction in which he lived every impression appeared to have become blurred except the tremendous impression of whirling forces; every detail seemed to have been obscured except the gigantic details of "Business." His manner was perfectly well-bred, but it was the manner of a man who moves through life rehearsing a part of which he barely remembers the words. From the first minute it was evident to Gabriella that her father-in-law adored his wife as an ideal, though he seemed scarcely aware of her as a person. He had given her his love, but his interests, his energies, his attention were elsewhere.

"Is that the way George will treat me—as if I were only a dream woman?" thought Gabriella while she watched her father-in-law over the open sheet of the *Times*. Then, with her eyes on her husband, she realized that he was of his mother's blood, not his father's. Business could never absorb him. His restlessness, his instability, his love of pleasure, would prevent the sapping of his nature by one supreme interest.

The table, like everything else in the room, was solid, heavy, and expensive. On the floor a heavy and expensive carpet, with a pattern in squares, stretched to the heavy and expensive moulding which bordered a heavy and expensive paper. Mrs. Fowler's taste, like Jimmy's (he was her third cousin), leaned apparently toward embossment, for behind a massive repoussé silver service she sat, as handsome and substantial as the room, with her face flushing in splotches from the heat of her coffee.

Some twenty-odd years before the house had been furnished at great cost, according to the opulent taste of the early 'seventies, and, unchanged by severer and more frugal fashions, it remained a solid monument to the first great financial deal of Archibald Fowler. It was at the golden age, when, still young and energetic, luck had come to him in a day, that he had bought the brownstone house in Fifty-seventh Street, and his wife, also young and energetic, had gone out "to get whatever she liked." Trained in a simple school during the war, and brought up in the formal purity of high-ceiled rooms furnished in Chippendale and Sheraton, her natural tastes were, nevertheless, as ornate as the interiors of the New York shops. Though the blood of colonial heroes ran in her veins, she was still the child of her age, and her age prided itself upon being entirely modern in all things from religion to furniture.

As she sat there behind the mammoth coffee urn, from which a spiral of steam floated, her handsome face irradiated the spirit of kindness. Because of her rather short figure, she appeared at her best when she was sitting, and now, with her large, tightly laced hips hidden beneath the table and her firm, jet-plastered bosom appearing above it, she presented a picture of calm and matronly beauty. Not once did she seem to think of herself or her own breakfast. Even while she buttered her toast and drank her steaming coffee, her bright blue eyes travelled unceasingly over the table, first to her husband's plate, then to Gabriella's, then to her son's. It was easy to see that she was the dominant and vital force in the household. She ruled Archibald, less indirectly perhaps, but quite as consistently as Cousin Pussy ruled Cousin Jimmy.

"My dear, you must eat your breakfast," she said urgently to her daughter-in-law. "Archibald, let me give you your second cup of coffee. Remember what a trying day you have before you, and make a good breakfast. It is so hard to get him to eat," she explained to Gabriella; "I have to coax him to drink his two cups of coffee, for if he doesn't he is sure to come home with a headache."

"Well, give me a cup, Evelyn," replied Mr. Fowler, in his gentle voice, yielding apparently to please her. In his youth he must have been very handsome, Gabriella thought; but now, though he still retained a certain distinction, he had the look of a man who has been drained of his vitality. What surprised her—for she had heard him described as "a hard man in business"—was the suggestion of the scholar in his appearance. With his narrow, carefully brushed head, his dreamy and rather wistful blue eyes behind gold-rimmed glasses, his stooping, slender shoulders, and his long, delicate hands covered with prominent veins, he ought to have been either a poet or a philosopher.

"You must be happy with us, my dear," he had said to Gabriella, showing a minute later such gentle eagerness to return to a part of the newspaper which Gabriella had never read and did not understand, that his wife remarked pityingly: "Read your paper, Archibald, and don't let our chatter disturb you. There are a thousand things I want to say to the children."

"Well, it's time for me to be going, Evelyn," Mr. Fowler responded, reluctantly folding the pages; "I'll look into this on the way down."

"Remember, dear, that Judge Crowborough is coming to dinner."

"I'll remember. Is there any one else?"

"Mrs. Crowborough, of course, and Colonel Buffington, and one or two others. Nobody that you will care for except the judge and Patty and Billy."

"I shan't forget, but I may be a little late getting home. Good-bye, my dear, until evening."

Bending over her chair, he kissed her flushed cheek, while George remarked carelessly: "I'll see you later, father, when I've had a bath and a shave."

After the gentle tones of Mr. Fowler, the vitality of George's voice sounded almost brutal, and he added just as carelessly when the front door had shut softly: "The old man looks seedy, doesn't he, mother?"

A worried look brought out three startling lines in Mrs. Fowler's forehead, and Gabriella observed suddenly that there were tiny crow's feet around her blue eyes where the whites were flecked ever so faintly with yellow. Though she was well into the mid-fifties, her carefully preserved skin had kept the firmness and the texture of youth, and she still flushed easily and unbecomingly as she had done as a girl.

"He hasn't been a bit well, George. I am very anxious about him. You know when he worries over his business, he doesn't eat his meals, and as soon as he stops eating he begins to have nervous dyspepsia. He has just had a bad attack; that's why he looks so run down and haggard."

"Can't the doctor do anything for him?"

"He gave him some drops, but it is so hard to get your father to take medicine. Rest is what he needs, and, of course, that is out of the question while things are so unsettled. You must help him all you can, my boy, and Gabriella and I will manage with each other's company."

Her bright smile was still on her lips, but Gabriella noticed that she pushed her buttered roll away as if she were choking.

In the early afternoon, when George had gone to join his father in the office, and Gabriella, seated at a little white and gold desk in the room which had been Patty's, was just finishing a letter to her mother, Mrs. Fowler came in, and pushing a chintz-covered chair close to the desk, sank into it and laid her small nervous hand on the arm of her daughter-in-law. She was wearing a velvet bonnet, with strings, and a street gown of black broadcloth, which fitted her like a glove and accentuated, after the fashion of the 'nineties, her small, compact waist and the deep substantial curves of her bosom and hips. Her eyes, behind the little veil of spotted tulle which reached to the tip of her nose, were bright and wistful, and though her colour was too high, a smile of troubled sweetness lent it a peculiar charm of expression.

"How nice you look, my dear," she said, with her pleasant manner, which no anxiety, hardly any grief, could dispel. "Are you very busy, or may I talk to you a little while?"

Drawing closer to her, Gabriella raised the plump little hand to her lips. Beneath the surface pleasantness of Mrs. Fowler's life—that pleasantness which wrapped her like a religion—she was beginning to discern a deep disquietude.

"I want to talk to you, mamma," she said, and her manner was a caress.

"You love George very much, dear?" asked Mrs. Fowler so suddenly that Gabriella looked at her startled.

For a minute the girl could not speak. "Oh, yes; oh, yes," she answered presently, and choked over the words.

"We wanted so much to go to your wedding—we were afraid you would think it strange that we stayed away, but Archibald had his attack just then, and on top of it he was terribly worried about his affairs. We have had a very hard year, and we feel so sorry, both of us, that we can't do more for your pleasure. As it is, we are cutting down our expenses in every way, and I have even decided to give up my carriage the first of next year.

"I know, I know," said Gabriella, who had never had a carriage, and to whom the giving up of one seemed the smallest imaginable sacrifice. "We mustn't add to your cares," she went on after a minute. "Wouldn't it be better, really better, if we were to take an apartment at once instead of waiting until June?"

"Until June?" repeated Mrs. Fowler vaguely, and she added quickly: "It is the greatest pleasure to have you here. Since Patty went I get so terribly lonely, and I don't think it would be at all wise for you to go to yourselves. George has hardly anything except what his father is able to give him, you know. The poor boy hasn't the least head for business."

"But we shouldn't need much. I am sure I could manage just with what George makes—no matter how little it is."

For an instant Mrs. Fowler looked at her thoughtfully.

"You could, but George couldn't," she answered.

"You mean he is extravagant?"

"He has never had the slightest idea of the value of money—that is one of the things you must teach him. He is a dear boy, but he has never made a success of anything he has undertaken, and his father thinks he is too unpractical ever to do so. But you must try to get him to live within your means, my dear, or you will both be miserable. Try to keep him from borrowing."

"But he refuses to talk to me about his work. It bores him," said Gabriella; and her simple soul, trained to regard debt as a deeper disgrace than poverty, grew suddenly troubled. In her childhood they had gone without food rather than borrow, she remembered.

"The matter with dear George," pursued Mrs. Fowler—and from the sweetness of her manner she might have been paying him a compliment—"is that he has never been steady. He doesn't stick at anything long enough to make it a success. If he were left to himself he would speculate wildly, and this is why his father is obliged to overlook all that he does in the office. It is just here that you can be of such wonderful help to him, Gabriella, by your influence. This is why I am telling you."

But had she any influence over him? In spite of his passion for her had she ever turned him by so much as a hair's breadth from the direction of his impetuous desires? Once only she had withstood him—once only she had triumphed, and for that triumph she had paid by a complete surrender! She had been too glad to yield, too fearful of bringing a cloud over the sunny blue of his eyes.

"I want to help him—I want you to tell me how I can help him," she said earnestly. "While we are with you this winter, you must teach me how to do it. Before we begin housekeeping in the summer, I want to learn all I possibly can about George's affairs. He won't talk to me about practical matters, so you must do it."

"But where are you going, Gabriella? I thought you had decided to live with us?"

"But didn't George tell you? Surely he must have told you. We are to take an apartment in June so my mother can come to us. I felt, of course, that I couldn't leave mother, and George understands. He was perfectly lovely about it."

"I see, I see," murmured Mrs. Fowler, as if she were thinking of something else. "Well, that will all come right, dear, I hope."

Rising abruptly, she began to draw on her gloves. "If you only knew how I long to make you happy," she said softly; "as happy as I have been with George's father."

"They are so unlike," answered Gabriella, and the next day when she remembered the admission, she wondered how it had slipped from her.

"Yes, they are unlike," agreed Mrs. Fowler. "George takes after me, and I am a frivolous person. But there doesn't live a better man than my husband," she added, glowing. "I've been his wife for thirty years, and in all that time I don't believe he has ever thought first of himself. Yes, it was thirty years ago that I drove through the streets with my bridal veil on, and felt so sorry for all the girls I saw who were not going to be married. To-day I feel exactly the same way— sorry for all the women who couldn't have Archibald for a husband. I've lived with him thirty years, I've borne him children, and I'm still sorry for all the other women—even for you, Gabriella."

"He seems so kind," said Gabriella; "I felt that about him, and it's the best thing, after all, isn't it?" It was the best thing, and yet she knew that George was not kind—that he was not even good-tempered.

"Yes, it's the best thing, after all, in marriage," answered the older woman; "it's the thing that wears."

"I have always wanted the best of life," rejoined Gabriella thoughtfully; and she went on gravely after a moment: "I couldn't love George any more than I do, but I wish that in some ways he would grow like his father."

"The boy has a very sweet nature," replied George's mother, "and I hope marriage will steady him." It was a warning, Gabriella knew, and she wondered afterwards if her silent acquiescence in Mrs. Fowler's judgment had not been furtive disloyalty to George.

"A great deal will depend on you, dear, for he is very much in love," resumed Mrs. Fowler when Gabriella did not speak, and she repeated very solemnly, "I hope marriage will steady him."

In her heart Gabriella was hoping so, too, but all she said was, "I promise you that I will do all I can." She had given her word, and, looking into her eyes, Mrs. Fowler understood that her daughter-in-law was not one to give her word lightly. Gabriella would keep her promise. She would do her best, whatever happened.

The older woman, with her life's history behind her, watched the girl for a minute in silence. There was so much that she longed to say, so much that could never be spoken even between women. She herself was an optimist, but her optimism had been wrung from the bitter core of experience. Her faith was firm, though it held few illusions, for, if she was an optimist, she was also a realist. She believed in life, not because it had satisfied her, but because she had had the wisdom to understand that the supreme failure had been, not life's, but her own. If she could only have lived it again and lived it differently from the beginning! If she could only have used her deeper wisdom not to regret the past, but to create the future! Much as she had loved her husband, she knew now that she had sacrificed him to the world. Much as she had loved her children, she would have sacrificed them, also, had it been possible. To the tin gods she had offered her soul—to the things that did not matter she had yielded up the only things that mattered at all. And she knew now that, in spite of her clearness of vision, the worldliness which had ruined her life was still bound up in all that was essential and endurable in her nature. She still wanted the illusions as passionately as if she believed in their reality; she still winced as sharply at the thought of Patty's marriage and of all that Patty had given up. In the case of George, she admitted that it was her fault—that she had spoiled him—but how could she have helped it? She remembered how he had looked as a child, with his round flushed face, his chestnut curls, and his eager, questioning eyes. He had been a beautiful child, more beautiful even than Patty, and because of his beauty she had been able to refuse him nothing. Then she thought of his boyhood, of his reckless extravagance at college; of the tales of his wildness to which she had shut her ears; of his debts, and still of his debts, which she had paid out of the housekeeping money because she was afraid to let his father know of them. Yes, George, in spite of his sweet nature, had given them a great deal of trouble, so much trouble that she had been quite reconciled to his marriage with any respectable girl. The memory of a chorus girl with whom he had once entangled himself still gave her a shiver at the heart when she recalled it. Money, always more money, had gone into that; and at last, just as she had grown hopeless of saving him, he had met this fine, sensible Gabriella, who looked so strong, so competent, and there had come an end to the disturbing stories which reached her at intervals. Surely it was proof of her son's inborn fineness that from the pink perfection of girlhood he should have chosen the capable Gabriella! At first she had regretted his choice, hoping, as the worldly and the unworldly alike hope for their sons, that the object of George's disinterested affection would prove to be wealthy. Then at the sight of Gabriella she had surrendered completely. The girl was fine all through, this she could see as soon as she looked at her. She liked her noble though not beautiful face, with the broad clear forehead from which the soft dark hair was brushed back so simply, and, most of all, she liked the charm and sympathy in her voice. George had chosen well, and if she could trust his choice, why could she not trust him to be true to it?

"I wonder if you would like to put on your hat and come with me?" she asked, obeying an impulse. "I'm going to drive up to Patty's with some curtains for her bedroom."

"Oh, I'd love to," replied Gabriella with eagerness, for she hated inaction, and it was impossible to spend a whole afternoon merely thinking about one's happiness. "It won't take me a minute to get ready."

While she put on her hat and coat, Mrs. Fowler watched her thoughtfully, saying once: "It is quite cool, you'd better bring your furs, dear."

When Gabriella answered frankly, "I haven't any, I never had any furs in my life," a tender expression crept into the rather hard blue eyes of her mother-in-law, and she said quickly: "Well, I've a set of white fox that I am too old to wear, and you shall have it."

"But what of Patty?" asked Gabriella, for she had grown up thinking of other people and she couldn't break the habit of twenty years in a minute.

"Oh, Patty has all the furs she'll need for years. We spent every penny we had on Patty before she married," answered Mrs. Fowler, but she was saying to herself: "Yes, the girl is the right wife for him. I am sure she is the right wife for him."

The Park was brilliant with falling leaves, and as they drove beneath a perfect sky beside a lake which sparkled like sapphire, Gabriella, lifting her chin above the white furs, said rapturously, "Oh, I am so happy! Life is so beautiful!"

A shadow stole into the eyes with which Mrs. Fowler was watching the passing carriages, and the fixed sweetness about her mouth melted into an expression of yearning. Tears veiled the faces of the women who spoke to her in passing, for she was thinking of her first drive in the Park with her husband, and though her marriage had been a happy one, she felt a strange longing as if she wanted to weep.

"I never saw such wonderful horses," said Gabriella. "Cousin Jimmy would be wild about them;" and she added impetuously, "But the hats aren't in the least like the one I am wearing." A misgiving seized her as she realized that her dresses, copied by Miss Polly with ardent fidelity from a Paris fashion book, were all hopelessly wrong. She wondered if her green silk gown with the black velvet sleeves was different in style from the gowns the other women were wearing under their furs? Had sleeves of a different colour from the bodice, which Miss Polly considered the last touch of elegance, really gone out of fashion?

The carriage passed out of the Park, and turning into one of the streets on the upper West Side stopped presently before a small dingy apartment house, where a dozen ragged children were playing leapfrog on the pavement.

"Patty has the top floor—there's a studio." Drawing her skirts away from the children, for her generation feared contact with the lower classes, Mrs. Fowler walked briskly to the low brown steps, on which an ash can stood waiting for removal. Inside, where the hall smelled uninvitingly of stale cooking, they rang for the elevator under a dim yellow light which revealed a hundred secret lines in their faces.

"I can't imagine how Patty puts up with the place," remarked Patty's mother dejectedly. "You wouldn't believe the trouble we went to to start her well. She was the acknowledged beauty of her winter—everybody was crazy about her looks—and the very week before she ran off with Billy she had a proposal from the Duke of Toxbridge. Of course, if I'd ever dreamed she had a fancy for Billy, I'd have kept him out of her sight instead of allowing him to paint her portrait whenever she had any time she could spare. But who on earth would have suspected it? Billy King, whom she had known all her life, as poor as a church mouse, and the kind of painter whose work will never 'take' if he lives to be a thousand! His portraits may be good art—I don't pretend to know anything about that—but I do know pictures of pretty women when I see them, and his women are frights, every last one of them. If you're thin, he paints your skeleton, and if you're fat, he makes you as square as a house, and, thin or fat, he always gives you a blue and yellow complexion. He wouldn't even make Patty white, though I implored him to do it—and he made her look exactly ten years older than her age."

"I've never seen any portraits of living people—only of ancestors," said Gabriella, "and I am so much interested."

"Well, you mustn't judge them by Billy's, my dear, even if he did get all those prizes in Paris. But I always said the French were queer, and if they hadn't been, they would never have raved so over the things Billy painted. Now, Augustus Featherfield's are really charming. One can tell to look at his portraits that he paints only ladies, and he gives them all the most perfectly lovely hair, whether they have it or not. Some day I'll take you to his studio and let you see for yourself."

The elevator descended, creaking beneath the weight of a negro youth who seemed half asleep, and a little later, creaking more loudly, it bore them slowly upward to the top of the house.

"I feel as if I were taking my life in my hands whenever I come here," observed Mrs. Fowler, in the tone of dispassionate resignation with which she always discussed Patty and the surroundings amid which Patty lived. Marching resolutely, though disapprovingly, down a long hall, she pressed a small bell at the side of a door, and stood, holding tightly to the bundle of curtains, while her expression of unnatural pleasantness grew almost painful in its determination. Here, also, they waited some time, and when at last the door was opened by an agitated maid, without an apron, and they were led into a long, queerly furnished studio, with a balcony from which they had a distant cloudless view of the river, Gabriella felt for a minute that she must have fallen into a dream. Long afterwards she learned that Billy's studio was charming, with its blurred Italian tapestries, which had faded to an exquisite tone, with its broken torsos of old marble, warming to deep ivory in the sunlight, with its ecstatic haloed saints praying against dim Tuscan landscapes, with its odd and unexpected seats of carved stone on which the cushions made strange splotches and pools of colour. At the time, seen through provincial eyes, it seemed merely "queer" to her; and queerer still appeared the undraped figures of women, all lean lines and violet shadows, which, unframed and unhung, filled the dusty corners.

"The river is lovely, but it is so far away," she said, turning her abashed eyes from the nude figures, and thinking how terribly they would have shocked the innocence of Cousin Jimmy.

"I always look at the river when I come here," responded Mrs. Fowler, and her tone implied that the river at least was perfectly proper. "A month ago the colours were wonderful."

In the drive, which they could see from a corner view, a few old men, forgotten by time, warmed themselves in the sunlight. Far below, the river reflected the changeable blue of the sky, while the autumnal pageantry on the horizon was fading slowly, like a burned-out fire, to the colour of ashes.

"Mother, dear, I'm so glad," said a gay voice in the doorway, and turning quickly, Gabriella stared with wide eyes at the vision of Patty—of Patty in some soft tea-gown, which borrowed its tone from the old tapestries on the wall, with her honey-coloured hair hanging over her shoulders, and her eyes as fresh as blue flowers in the ivory pallor of her face.

"And this is Gabriella," she added, holding out her arms. "What a darling you are to come so soon, Gabriella."

She was a tall girl, so tall that she stooped to kiss Gabriella, whose height measured exactly five feet and seven inches, and she was beautiful with the faultless beauty which is seen only once or twice in a generation, but which, seen once, is never forgotten. For Patty's beauty, as a poet once wrote of a dead woman, was the beauty of destiny, the beauty that changes history and turns men into angels or into beasts. Though Gabriella had seen lovely skins on

Southern women—rose-leaf skins, magnolia skins, peach-blossom skins—she had seen nothing that resembled the exquisite colour and texture of Patty's face.

"The curtains were finished, so I brought them," said Mrs. Fowler, pointing to the bundle. "I wanted Gabriella to see the Park. You are coming to-night without fail, aren't you, Patty?"

"Without fail, even if we have to walk," answered Patty. "You can't imagine how much it costs to get about when one lives so far uptown. That's one reason we are anxious to move. Billy has been looking for a studio for weeks, and, do you know, he has really found one at last. Harry Allen is moving out of the Rubens Building, and we are going to take his studio on the top floor. We're awfully lucky, too, to get it, for it is the first vacancy there for years."

"But it's over a stable, isn't it?" asked Mrs. Fowler. "How could you possibly live there? And the East Side way down there is just as bad as up here"

"I believe there is a stable, but it won't bother us—we're too high," replied Patty.

"Well, we can't stop; Gabriella hasn't unpacked her trunks," returned Mrs. Fowler; "but be sure to come early, Patty. I want your father to see you."

"I wish there wasn't going to be anybody else. I want to talk to my sister. Isn't it lovely to have a sister, and mamma was too selfish to give me one. Do you call her 'mamma,' too, Gabriella?"

"Of course she calls me 'mamma,'" answered Mrs. Fowler before Gabriella could speak, "and she is a much better daughter already than you ever were."

"And a much better son, too, than George ever was?" asked Patty slyly.

"We aren't talking about George. George has settled down," said Mrs. Fowler quickly, too quickly it occurred to Gabriella, who was eager to hear all that the daring Patty would say. "Don't you think those white furs look well on Gabriella?"

"She looks like the snow queen in them. Does it matter what I wear to-night? Who is coming?"

"Nobody you will care about—only Judge and Mrs. Crowborough and Colonel Buffington."

"That old bore of a colonel! And why do you have to ask the judge again so soon? He looks like a turkey gobbler, Gabriella, and he has so much money that it is impossible to judge him by the standards of other people, everybody says that—even Billy."

"Hush, Patty. You mustn't corrupt Gabriella."

"If the judge doesn't, I shan't, mamma."

"Well, your father has the greatest respect for him, and as for asking him often to dinner, it isn't by any means so easy to get him as you think. I don't suppose there's another man in New York who is invited out so often and goes out so little."

"Papa is a sweet innocent," observed Patty maliciously, "but if you can stand the judge, mamma, dear, I am sure I can, especially as I shan't have to sit by him. That honour will be reserved for poor Gabriella. I wish you didn't have to go, but you really must, I suppose?"

"Yes, we must go. Come, Gabriella, or you won't have time to get into your trunks before dinner."

On the drive home Mrs. Fowler was grimly silent, while the sweetness about her mouth ebbed slowly away, leaving the faintest quiver of the muscles. For the first time Gabriella saw George's mother look as she must look in her sleep, when the artificial cheerfulness of her expression faded into the profound unconsciousness which drowns not only happiness, but the very pretence of happiness. So here, also, was insincerity, here, also, was the striving, not for realities, but for appearances! In a different form she saw her mother's struggle again—that struggle, without beginning and without end, which moved always in a circle and led nowhere. Was there no sincerity, no reality even in love? Was George, too, only a shadow? And the visible sadness of the November afternoon, with its faint haze like the haze of a dream landscape, seemed a part of this invisible sadness which had sprung from nothing and which would change and pass away in a breath. "If things would only last," she thought, looking with wistful eyes on the gold and purple around her. "If things would only last, how wonderful life would be!"

"To think that all Patty's beauty should have been thrown away," said Mrs. Fowler suddenly.

Though Gabriella had never seen Billy, she was inclined at the moment, in her mood of dissatisfaction with the universe, to sympathize with Mrs. Fowler's view of the matter. To her frugal mind, trained to economy of material, it seemed that Patty was altogether too much for a poor man—even though he could paint her in lean lines and violet shadows.

Upstairs she found her trunks in her bedroom, and after she had unpacked her wedding-gown of white satin, removed the tissue paper stuffing from the sleeves, and shaken out the creases with gentle hands, she sat down and pondered deeply the problem of dressing for dinner. By removing the lace yoke, she might make the gown sufficiently indecorous for the fashion of the period, and her only evening dress, the white muslin she had worn to dances in Richmond, she reflected gloomily, would appear absurd in New York.

"I wish I didn't look such a fright," she said aloud, as she ripped and sewed. Then, in a flash, her mind wandered from herself, and she thought: "I wonder why George didn't tell his mother that we are going to take an apartment? I wonder why he didn't tell her that mother is coming in June? When he comes I must ask him."

Looking at the clock, she saw that it was after seven, and hurriedly taking the last few stitches, she laid the gown on the bed, bathed her face in cold water, and then, sitting down before her dressing-table, drew the pins from her hair. In some obscure way she felt herself a different person from the bride who had watched George so ecstatically at the station that morning. She could not tell how she had altered, and yet she felt perfectly conscious that an alteration had taken place in her soul—that she was not the same Gabriella—that life could never be again exactly as it had been before. Nothing and yet everything seemed to have happened to her in a day. Her face, gazing gravely back at her from the mirror, looked young and wistful, the face of one who, like a bird flying suddenly out of darkness against a lamp, is bewildered by the first shock of the light.

When her hair was arranged in the simple way she had always worn it, she slipped her dress over her bare shoulders, and fastened it slowly—for Miss Polly had no patience with "back fastenings"—while she told herself again that George would not be satisfied. She knew that her gown was provincial, knew that she lacked the "dash" he admired in women; and from the first she had been mystified by a love which could, while still passionately desiring her, wish her different in so many ways. "I'd like him to be proud of me, but I suppose he never will be," she thought dejectedly, "and yet he fell in love with me just as I was, and he did not fall in love with any of the dashing women he knows," she added quickly, consoled by the reflection. "And of course in a few things I wish him different, too. I wish he wasn't so careless. He is so careless that I shall have to be twice as careful, I shall have to look after him all the time. Even to-night he has forgotten about the dinner, and he'll be obliged to dress in a hurry, which he hates."

Glancing at the clock again, she saw that it was a quarter of eight, and still George had not come.

# CHAPTER VI

## THE OLD SERPENT

At five minutes of eight o'clock he came in, with a lighted cigar in his mouth. For the first few days after her marriage there had been a pleasant excitement in the scent of George's cigars in her bedroom. Now, however, habit had dulled the excitement, and the smell of tobacco gave her a headache.

"Oh, George, you are late!" she exclaimed, sinking the lesser into the greater offence after the habit of wives. As if he had all night instead of five minutes before him in which to dress, he stood in the centre of the room, blandly looking her over.

"You're all right," he said after a pause. "I met a fellow at the club I hadn't seen for a year. He had been hunting big game in Africa, and he was telling me about it. By Jove, that is life!"

They had been married but a month; it was their first day at home, and he could linger at the club to talk of big game while she waited for him. Flushed, excited, he stood there on the white bearskin rug midway between the bed and the wood-fire, while she felt his charm stealing like a drug over her senses. Though she had begun to realize the thinness of his mental qualities, she was still as completely in the power of his physical charm as she had been on the day of her wedding. In the flickering light of the fire he appeared to diffuse the glamour of romance, of adventure; and she felt that this single day in New York had left a vital impression upon him. It was as if he had become suddenly more alive, more inexplicable in his simplicity; and, though she had grasped vaguely the fact that his personality was composed of innumerable reactions, she had never really understood before how entirely he was the creature of his environment. It was as if the very essence of his soul floated there, a variable and fluid quantity, forever changing form and colour beneath the shallow ripples of his personality. She had seen him in many moods, but never in this one. Did he possess a deeper subtlety than she had imagined or was it the sincerity of his nature that defied analysis?

"Did you enjoy yourself?" she asked cheerfully. Tell me about it."

"Oh, it was rather jolly," he replied, and she knew that this was as much as she should ever get out of him. Beyond a few stock phrases, words hardly existed for him at all, or existed only in foreign languages, for, having been educated abroad, he spoke French and German fluently, if without felicity. Already his inarticulateness was like an encumbering veil between them—a veil in which she struggled as helplessly as a moth in a net. And only a month ago she had believed that the very immensity of his nature rendered him dumb.

"Then you had better hurry, dear. Dinner is at eight, and you have only a minute."

"You go down and tell them not to wait. I was detained downtown, but it won't take me a second to dress."

As he passed under the electric light by the mirror, she saw his face with exaggerated distinctness, as if it were held under a microscope, and a heaviness, which she had never noticed before, marred the edge of his profile. If he hadn't been George, would she have said that he looked stupid at the moment? For a flashing instant of illumination she saw him with a vision that was not her own, but a stranger's, with a pitiless clearness unsoftened by any passion. Then the clearness faded rapidly before an impulse of tenderness, and she told herself that he was merely handsome, gay, and careless, as he had been on their honeymoon. If he would only talk to her, she felt that he would be perfect.

"Yes, I'm going. Come as soon as you can," she said; and catching up her satin train, she descended the oak staircase to the drawing-room, where a fire was burning and the lights were shaded in crimson.

Twenty minutes later, seated at the round table, which was bright with chrysanthemums in tall silver vases, she looked with a feeling of resentment at George's empty place. Why was he so careless? Time had for him, she realized, as little meaning as words had. Then, in the midst of her disquietude, she caught the serene blue eyes of George's mother fixed upon her. With her young face, her red lips, and her superb shoulders rising out of the rich black lace of her gown, Mrs. Fowler looked almost beautiful. Had Patty not been present, with her loveliness like a summer's day, her mother would have seemed hardly more than a girl; but who could shine while Patty, beside that long, lean man with the gray imperial, smiled with lips that were like a scarlet flower in her face?

There were only four guests, but these four, as Mrs. Fowler had said, "counted for something." The long, lean man beside Patty was one Colonel Buffington, a Virginia lawyer, who had wandered North in search of food in the barren years after the war. As his mind was active in a patient accumulative fashion, he had become in time a musty storehouse of war anecdotes, and achieving but moderate success in his law practice, his chief distinction, perhaps, was as a professional Southerner. Combining a genial charm of manner with as sterile an intellect as it is possible to attain, he was generally regarded as a perfect example of "the old school," and this picturesque reputation made him desirable as a guest at club dinners as well as at the larger gatherings of the various Southern societies. His conversation, which was entirely anecdotal, consisted of an elaborate endless chain of more or less historical "stories." Social movements and the development of civilization interested him as little as did art or science—for which he entertained a chronic suspicion due to the indiscretions of Darwin. Change of any kind was repugnant to his deeper instincts, and of all changes the ones relating to the habits of women appeared to him to interfere most unwarrantably with the Creator's original plan. For the rest he had the heart of a child, would strip the clothes from his back to give to a friend, or even to an enemy, and possessed an infallible gift for making a dinner successful.

On Colonel Buffington's right sat Mrs. Hamilton, a very pretty, very sprightly widow, with her hair coiled into the fashionable Psyche knot, and the short puffs of her sleeves emphasizing the hour-glass perfection of her figure. Next to Mrs. Hamilton there was Billy King, who wore a white flower in his buttonhole and looked like a soldier out of uniform, and beyond Billy sat Mrs. Crowborough, whom he was trying despairingly to entertain. She, renowned and estimable woman, was planning in her mind what she should say at a board meeting of one of her pet charities on the morrow, a charity which, like all of her favourite ones, concerned itself with the management and spiritual elevation of girl orphans. Tall, raw-boned, strung with jet, Mrs. Crowborough, who had been married for her money, looked as sympathetic as a moral principle or an organized charity. Unfortunately, for she was rather heavy in company, Judge Crowborough was obliged by custom to bring her to dinner; and she came willingly, inspired less by sociability than by the virtuous instinct which animated her being. Mr. Fowler had taken her in to dinner, and while he lent an inert attention to Billy's jests, he talked across Gabriella to Judge Crowborough, who was eating his soup with the complete absorption of a man to whom the smallest of his appetites is sacred. It was a grievance of Mrs. Fowler's that her husband would never, as she said, "pay any attention to women," and in order to feel assured of even so much as a cheerful noise at his end of the table, she was obliged to place within hearing distance of him somebody who could talk fluently, if not eloquently, of the stock market.

To Gabriella's surprise, her father-in-law, who had appeared inert and listless at breakfast, became, in the stimulating presence of the judge, not only awake, but mildly animated. She had felt before the charm in his scholarly face, with its look of detached spirituality so strangely out of keeping with the calling he pursued; and she recognized now the quality of controlled force which had enabled him to hold his own in the financial whirlpool of his country. Had the girl known more of life, she would have understood that in the American business world there were hundreds of such men winning their way and leaving their mark at that moment of history—men whose natures were redeemed from grossness by the peculiar idealism they infused into their material battles. Of Scotch-Irish inheritance, the direct descendant of one Gregory Truesdale, who had died a martyr for Presbyterianism, Archibald Fowler was inspired by something of the austere devotion which had fortified his religious ancestor. Since his college days his private life had been irreproachable. Though he was a stronger character than his wife, he regarded her with almost superstitious reverence, and made no decision above Wall Street without consulting her. His heart, and as much of his time as he could spare from business, were hers, and she made the most of them. Women, as women, did not attract him, and he avoided them except at his own table, where custom constrained him to be polite. After a few courteous words to Mrs. Crowborough, he had turned with relief to her husband.

"You've got a bright chap in your office, Stanley," he said; "that fellow Latham. I was talking to him this morning. He's from Colorado, isn't he?"

"Oh, yes, they're all from the West now," responded the judge—he had sat on the bench in his youth. "Ten years ago the bright ones were from the South, but you Southerners are outstripped to-day, and it's the men from the West who are doing it. There's a fundamental reason there, I suppose, if you go deep enough," he added, fingering the ends of his short gray moustache while he kept an eye on his champagne glass. "We've done with mere classifying and imitation, and we're waiting for a fresh explosion of raw energy. Now for pure constructive imagination the North and South don't hold a candle—they simply don't hold a candle—to the West. Mark my words, in twenty-five years there'll hardly be a big railroad man in the country who wasn't born in sight of the Rockies." Unlike Mr. Fowler, whose mind ran in a groove leading directly to business, the judge had a natural bent toward generalization, and when dining, preferred to discuss impersonal topics. He was a tall, florid man with an immense paunch flattened by artificial devices, and a vitality so excessive that it overflowed in numberless directions—in his hearty animal appetites, in his love of sports, in his delight in the theatre and literature, particularly in novels of the sentimental and romantic school, in his fondness for the lighter operas, and in his irrepressible admiration for pretty women. His face, large, ruddy, with a hooked nose, where the red was thickly veined with purple, and protruding lips over square yellow teeth that gripped like the teeth of a bulldog, aroused in Gabriella a quick repulsion which only the genial humour of his smile overcame. That he should have married his wife for her money was less amazing to the girl than that his wife should have married him for any reason whatsoever. Only a moral principle or a charitable institution, she felt, could have endured him and survived. But in spite of his repulsiveness he had evidently experienced the natural activities of humanity. He had taken a wife; he had begotten children; he had judged other men; he had dug into the bowels of the earth for mines, and had built railroads on its surface; he had made grass grow in deserts and had turned waste places into populous cities; he had read romances and heard music; he had attained a social position securely founded upon millions of dollars—and all these things he had achieved through his unconquerable colossal vitality. "I wonder why they put him by me," thought Gabriella. "I shall never get on with him."

Then he turned to her and said bluntly, between two mouthfuls of lobster: "So you're George's wife! Handsome chap George, but he hasn't much head for business. He lacks the grip of the old man. Where's he to-night?"

"He got home so late that he wasn't ready for dinner. He'll be down in a minute."

"It's a bad habit. He oughtn't to be late. Now, I haven't been late for dinner for twenty years."

"I'm afraid he doesn't pay much attention to time. I'll try to change him."

"You won't. No woman alive ever changed a man's habits. All you can do is to hide them."

That his blunt manner was an affectation, she was quick to discern. While he talked to her, he looked at her knowingly with his light fishy eyes, and by his look and his tone he seemed to establish an immediate intimacy between them—as if he and she were speaking a language which was foreign to the rest of the table. He appeared to be kind, she thought, and on his side he was thinking that she was a nice girl, with an attractive face and remarkable eyes. On the whole, he preferred brown eyes, though his wife's were the colour of slate. "Why the deuce did she marry that fool?" he questioned impatiently.

Across the table Billy King was working hopelessly but valiantly to engage Mrs. Crowborough's attention. What a splendid figure he had, and how clean and fine was the modelling of his features! He was just the man a girl like Patty would fall in love with, and Gabriella no longer felt that. Patty's beauty was wasted. Once or twice she caught fleeting glances passing between them, and these glances, so winged with happiness, spoke unutterable and ecstatic things.

A hush dropped suddenly on the table, and in this hush she heard the voice of Colonel Buffington telling a story in dialect. It was an immemorial anecdote of Cousin Jimmy's—she had heard him tell it a dozen times—and while she listened, it made her feel comfortably at home.

"'Uncle Amos,' I said to him, 'we've been together thirty years, but we've got to part. You're a drunkard and a thief and a worthless darky all round, and you've lived on my place ever since the war without doing a lick of work for your keep. I've stood it as long as I can, but there's an end to human endurance. Yes, Amos, the time has come for us to part.'

"Hi! Marse Beverly,' said the old rascal, 'whar you gwine?'"

"Capital!" ejaculated the judge softly. "Capital!" And he added for Gabriella's ear: "Buffington tells the best negro stories of any man I know. Ought to have heard him at the club the other night."

Gabriella did not answer; Cousin Jimmy's story had made her think of Cousin Jimmy, with his soft heart and his dark shining eyes like the eyes of a good and gentle dog. Then she thought of her mother, and reminded herself that she must ask George when they were to begin the hunt for an apartment. He had said they were very hard to find when you wanted them.

Another hush fell, and Colonel Buffington was just beginning a second story—one of Uncle Meriweather's this time—when George came in from the drawing-room, and after a murmured apology, took his seat between Patty and Mrs. Hamilton.

"That's a handsome boy," said the judge in a husky whisper to Gabriella, "but he hasn't much to say for himself, has he?"

His manner of playful intimacy conveyed the impression that the secret understanding between them did not include Gabriella's husband. George was an outsider, but this hideous old man, with his curious repelling suggestion of over-ripeness, as of fruit that is beginning to rot at the core, was the dominant personality in her mind at the moment. She wondered if he knew how repulsive he was, and while she wondered, the judge, unaware of his tragic plight, went on eating lobster with unimpaired relish. His importance, founded upon a more substantial basis than mere personal attraction, had risen superior not only to morality, but to the outward failings of the flesh. Had he been twice as repulsive, she realized that his millions would have commanded a respect denied to both beauty and virtue.

"I wonder how any woman can stand him," mused Gabriella. Then, glancing across the table at Mrs. Crowborough, she realized something of the amazing insensibility of the more ethereal sex. No man, not even in the last extremity, could have loved a woman as ugly as Judge Crowborough was. The roughest man would have had sufficient esthetic sense to have been shocked into revolt; yet a woman, a refined and intelligent woman, had married the judge and survived it. She appeared now, not only expressionless and unrevolted, but filled with a healthy zest for social reforms and the spiritual welfare of girl orphans.

"Well, I've learned something of life to-night," thought Gabriella while she watched her.

Later in the evening, when she passed into the drawing-room, with Mrs. Crowborough, bleak, unbending, and trailing her chains of jet, she comforted herself again with the reflection that what she was "seeing" might not be particularly exciting, "but it was life."

On a short, hard sofa near the fire, beside Fatty, who bloomed like a white rose under the red-shaded light, she listened to Mrs. Fowler's unflagging efforts to "get on" with the judge's wife. Never had the dauntless little woman revealed more surprising resourcefulness, never had she talked so vivaciously, never had she appeared so relentlessly pleasant. It was as if she said in the face of Mrs. Crowborough's insensibility, which was the insensibility not of mind, but of inanimate matter, "Whatever you do, you can't keep me from being sweet." And in this strained sweetness there was something touching, something wistful, a hint of inner weariness which showed now and then beneath the restless vivacity.

"Isn't it funny," said Patty suddenly, "how much mamma cares about things that don't matter at all? You wouldn't believe it to look at her, but she is in her heart the most worldly one of the family. Father wouldn't give a tallow candle for anything that isn't real."

A log broke in the centre, and fell, scattering a shower of golden embers over the hearth. Rising quickly, with one of her sprightly movements, Mrs. Fowler reached for a pair of small brass tongs and pushed the broken log back on the andirons. Then she threw some fresh wood on the flames, and resumed her seat with an animated gesture as if the incident had enlivened her.

"Now they are talking about the everlasting Pletheridges," whispered Patty. "I never understand how mother can take so much interest in those people just because they are rich."

But to Gabriella it was more inconceivable still that her mother-in-law, with the bluest blood of Virginia in her veins, should regard with such artless reverence the social activities of the granddaughter of a tavern-keeper. In her native State an impoverished branch of Mrs. Fowler's family still lived on land which, tradition said, had been granted one of her ancestors by Charles the Second in recognition of distinguished services to that dubious monarch; yet she could long enviously for a closer acquaintance with the plutocratic descendant of an Irish tavern-keeper—an honest man, doubtless, who had laid the foundations of his fortune in a string of halfway houses stretching from New York to Chicago.

"Yes, I dined with Mrs. Pletheridge once," she was saying in the tone in which her royalist ancestor might have acknowledged a command from his King.

"It always makes me angry, I can't help it," pursued Patty. "If dear mamma had only some other weakness—cards or wine or clothes or anything else. It's queer, with all her pride, how little social backbone she has. Now to hear her talk, you would imagine that that vulgar snob, whose father kept hotels and married one of his chambermaids, had conferred an honour by inviting her to dinner. And the funniest part is that, for all her good breeding, and her family portraits, and her titled ancestors, mother hasn't half so much respect for the genuine New Yorkers—I mean the New Yorkers whose names really mean something—as she has for these mushroom plutocrats. She had set her heart on George marrying one of them, you know, but it's a jolly good thing he didn't."

"That's the girl he told me about," said Gabriella. "Was he ever interested in her?"

"Not for a minute. We're awfully contrary about our love affairs. We will marry for love—even mother did though she may have forgotten it. We never marry the people—" She clipped off the sentence, but Gabriella caught it up with a laugh:

"I know," she said gaily, "you never marry the people your family pick out for you."

"Well, of course, Billy went dreadfully hard with them—at least with mother. She wanted the Duke of Somewhere so very badly. But it was Billy or nobody for me. I'd have married Billy," she added while her beautiful face grew stern, "if I'd had to walk all the way across the world to him."

"He looks as if he were worth it," admitted Gabriella.

"He is, but that probably wasn't my reason for marrying him. One never knows why one marries, I suppose, unless one marries for money and then it is so beautifully simple. Now, you and George don't seem a bit alike, but it all happened on the spur of the moment, didn't it?"

"It always seems that way when one looks back, doesn't it?" asked Gabriella. "But what I can't understand"—she brought it out with a frown—"is why marriage doesn't change one. I used to think I'd be different, but I'm not. And even love seems to leave people wanting everything else just as badly. Your mother has had a perfect love—she told me so—and yet it hasn't kept her from wanting all the other things in life, has it? I wish I could work it out," she finished, a little sadly, for she was thinking of her mother's cry on the night of Jane's attack: "I am tempted to hope Gabriella will never marry. The Carrs all marry so badly!" Why had those words come back to her to-night? She had not remembered them for months, she had even forgotten that she had heard them, and now they floated to her as clearly as if they had been spoken aloud.

In a little while Billy came in, and when, after a few moments of spasmodic affability, Mrs. Crowborough rose and pleaded an early board meeting on the morrow, Gabriella watched Patty wrap her honey-coloured head in a white scarf and then stand, waiting for a cab, in the doorway. Happiness, with so many people an invisible attribute, encircled Patty like a garment of light. It crowned her white brow under the glory of her hair; it shone in her eyes; it rippled in her smile; it lingered in a beam of sunshine on her lips. With her arm in Billy's she looked back laughing from the steps, and it seemed to Gabriella that all the brightness of life was going with them into the darkness. Beside the curbstone an old cab horse, dazzled by the light from the door, turned his head slowly toward them; and the look in his eyes, wistful, questioning, expectant, seemed to say, "This is not life, but a miracle." And from his box the red-cheeked, wheezy Irish driver gazed down on Patty with the same wistfulness, the same questioning, the same expectancy.

"I never see Patty go off in a cab that I don't feel she has thrown herself away," observed Mrs. Fowler, yawning, while she turned to the staircase. "Archibald, I hope you had a really good time with the judge. I must say it is like ploughing to talk to his wife."

Upstairs in her room a little later Gabriella said to George: "Patty was telling me about the girl your mother wanted you to marry."

He was pouring out a glass of water, and, absorbed in the act, he merely grunted for answer. It was his disagreeable habit to grunt when grunting saved effort.

"I wish you'd talk to me, George. It is so annoying to be grunted at."

"Well, what do you want?" he replied amiably enough. "Patty is a regular sieve, you know. Never tell her a secret."

"Did you ever like that girl—really?"

"The girl mother had in mind?" Having emptied the glass, he returned it to the tray and came over to her. "Yes, but if you want the truth, I preferred the girl in the chorus—the one the old lady got in a blue funk about, you know. She's still there, the last but one from the end, in the Golden Slipper. I'll take you to see it some night."

"Men are strange," observed Gabriella, with philosophic detachment. "Now I couldn't feel the slightest interest in a man in comic opera. Did she really attract you?"

"Um—humph," he was grunting again.

"Wasn't she terribly common?"

"Um—humph."

"Wasn't she vulgar?"

"Rather. They all are."

"And fast?"

"Regular streak of lightning."

Then it was that Gabriella arrived at an understanding of masculine nature. "You never can tell what men will like," she concluded.

While she spoke he winked at her from the mirror into which he was looking—mirrors always fascinated George and he could never keep away from them—and there was in his face the whimsical and appealing naughtiness of a child. Suddenly Gabriella felt that as far as character and experience counted, she was immeasurably older than George. Her superior common sense made her feel almost middle-aged when he was in one of his boyish moods. At the age of nine she had not been so utterly irresponsible as George was at twenty-six; as an infant in arms she had probably regarded the universe with a profounder philosophy. Though of course George was charming, he was without any sense of the deeper purpose of life. Like a child he must have what he wanted, and like a child he sulked when he was thwarted and grew angelic when his wishes were gratified. A single day had taught her that his father could not depend on him in business, that his mother could not trust him even to remember a dinner engagement. Gabriella loved him, she had chosen him, she told herself now, and she meant to abide by her choice; but she was not blind, she was not a fool, and she was deficient in the kind of loyalty which obliges one to lie even in the sanctity of one's own mind. She would be true to him, but she would be true with her eyes open, not shut.

"George," she said presently, while she loosened her hair, "your father told me you didn't stay more than an hour in the office." The question, "What were you doing?" rose to her lips, but she strangled the words before they escaped her. Her mind was quick to grasp facts, and she had learned already something of a man's instinctive dislike to being made to give an account of himself.

"You've been hearing too much gossip to-night," he rejoined gaily. "Take care what you listen to."

"Don't joke, dear. I wish you would tell me things."

"There isn't anything to tell, is there?"

"Is your father very rich?"

"Not very. Did you think you were marrying a millionaire?"

"I never thought about it, but everybody at home thinks he has a great deal of money, and yet your mother talks as if she were poor."

"Well, he made a pile of money in a big deal about ten years ago, and the papers had a lot about it. After that he lost it, or most of it, and the papers didn't tell. The fact is, he's always either making or losing, and now he's losing. That's why they wanted me to put off our marriage."

"They wanted you to put it off?"

"Mother did—the old man never interferes. She had got into her head, you see, that the only way for me to make a living was to marry one, so it was a little while before she could get used to the idea that I was going to marry because I wanted to, not because my family wanted me to. She was a brick though when she found out I was in earnest. Mother is true blue when you know how to take her."

"But you never told me."

"You bet I didn't. If I had, as likely as not, you would be Gabriella Mary Carr at this minute."

Drawing gently out of his grasp, which had grown possessive, she stood looking at him with a smile in which tenderness and irony mingled; and the tenderness was her own, while the irony seemed to belong to the vision of an impersonal spectator of life. The smile fascinated him. He could not withdraw his gaze from it, and yet it had the disturbing effect of placing her at an emotional distance.

"Your mother is very good to me," she said, "but I feel somehow as if I had taken an unfair advantage of her. And you hadn't even told her," she added, "that we are going to take an apartment in June."

"Oh, that's all right—there's plenty of time," he responded irritably. "Only you mustn't make mountains out of molehills."

Then, because she dreaded his anger, she gave up her point as she had given up many before. He was irresponsible, but he was hers and she loved him.

"I am so sleepy," she said, stifling a yawn, "that I feel as if I could cry."

Marriage, at the end of a month, had already disciplined the fearless directness of Gabriella. She had learned not to answer back when she knew she was right; she had learned to appear sweet when her inner spirit demanded a severe exterior; she had learned to hold her tongue when a veritable torrent of words rose to her lips. And these lessons, which George's temper and her own reason had taught her, remained with her in the future, long after she had forgotten George and the severity of her schooling.

There were many things for her to learn, and the lessons of that first day and night stretched through the winter and well into the beginning of spring. Accompanying Mrs. Fowler on her busy rounds, she discovered that here also, as in the house in Hill Street, the chief end of life was to keep up an appearance; here also the supreme effort, the best energies, were devoted to a sham—to a thing which had no actual existence. Though Mrs. Fowler was rich beside Mrs. Carr, Gabriella soon found out that she was not nearly so rich as her neighbours were, not nearly so rich as her position in society exacted that she should be. She was still not rich enough to be spared the sordid, nerve-racking effort to make two ends meet without a visible break. Her small economies, to Gabriella's surprise, were as rigid as Mrs. Carr's; and though she lived in surroundings which appeared luxurious to the girl, there was almost as little ready money to spend as there had been in Mrs. Carr's household. Bills were made recklessly, and dinner parties were given at regular intervals; for Mrs. Fowler, who denied herself a hundred small comforts of living, who gave up cream in her coffee and bought her butter from a grocer below Washington Square, took quite as a matter of course the fact that she must, as she put it, "pay off social scores." Though they ate the simplest food in the market for six days of the week, on the seventh, hothouse flowers bloomed profusely in the lower rooms and champagne flowed abundantly into the delicate Venetian glasses on the round table. To be sure, Mrs. Fowler's gown may have been two seasons old, but it was covered with rare laces, which she had picked up during her summers abroad; and her pearls—the string was short, but really good, for she had matched it in Paris—shone, rich and costly, around her still beautiful neck. After one of these dinners the family lived on scraps and looked at fading flowers for days, while Mrs. Fowler, with the air of one who has done her duty, sat upstairs before the little French writing-desk in her room, and patiently added accounts from morning till night. A strained look would come into her plump, firm face, three little wrinkles would appear between her eyebrows, and her blue eyes, circled by faint shadows, would grow dark and anxious. Then, when at last the accounts were finished and the unpaid bills laid away in a pigeonhole, she would remark with animation:

"I don't see how on earth I am ever to pay all these bills," and, after changing her dress, set out to bring her butcher or her grocer to reason. On one of these days she took Gabriella (they went in the stage because she had given up her carriage) on a hunt for bargains in underwear, and, to the girl's astonishment, her mother-in-law, who presented so opulent an appearance on the surface, purchased for herself a supply of cheap and badly made chemises and nightgowns. As she grew to know Mrs. Fowler better, she found that the expenditures of that redoubtable woman, in spite of her naturally delicate tastes, were governed by one of the most elementary principles of economy. Through long habit she had acquired a perception as unerring as instinct, and this perception enabled her to tell exactly where extravagance was useful and where it failed in its effect. She had learned to perfection never to spend money on things that did not show a result. An appearance was what she strove for, and one's chemises and nightgowns, however exquisite in themselves, could not very well contribute to one's external appearance. "Of course I like good underclothes," she remarked cheerfully to her daughter-in-law, "but, after all, nobody sees them."

This was so different from the poverty-stricken point of view of Gabriella's childhood, that the girl puzzled over it afterwards when she sat in her corner of the stage. Mrs. Carr had kept up an appearance, too, she reflected, but, like the old maids on the floor above, she had kept it up even to herself. Perhaps the difference lay in the immense gulf which divided the appearance of Hill Street from the appearance of the East Fifties. Mrs. Fowler was obliged by the public opinion she obeyed to appear affluent, while Mrs. Carr was merely constrained not to appear destitute. On the whole Gabriella felt that she preferred the safe middle distance between the two exacting standards of living.

But, though she might disapprove of her mother-in-law's philosophy, there was no question about her fervent admiration for her disposition. It was Mrs. Fowler's habit to appear "sweet," and never once did Gabriella see her lose her temper, never once, no matter how hard the day or how exasperating the accounts, did she show so much as a passing hint of irritability. Her temper was so angelic that it was the more surprising George should not have inherited a trace of it.

If George had not inherited his mother's nature, he revealed, as time went on, even less resemblance to the perfect reasonableness of his father's temperament. Ever since her first day in the house, Gabriella had been drawn to her father-in-law with an affection which his wife, for all her preoccupied kindness, had not inspired. She respected him for his calm strength, against which the boisterous moods of George reacted as harmlessly as the whims of a child, and she liked him for his unfailing courtesy, for his patience, for his gentleness, which made her feel that he was, in spite of the material nature of his occupation, the only member of the household who possessed even a glimmer of spirituality. All day long, and the greater part of the night, he thought about money, and yet he had escaped the spiritual corruption which the ceaseless pursuit of wealth had produced in the other rich men whom Gabriella met in his house. It was as if some subtle alchemy in his soul had transmuted the baser qualities into the pure gold of character; and sometimes the girl wondered if the fact that he worked not for himself but for others had preserved him from the grosser contamination of money. For he seemed to think of himself so little, that after three months in his house, Gabriella was still ignorant of his interests apart from his work, except, of course, his absorbing interest in the morning papers. From the time he got up at seven o'clock until he went to bed punctually on the stroke of ten, he appeared to order his life with the single purpose of giving as little trouble as was compatible with living at all. His tastes were the simplest; he drank only boiled water; he ate two eggs and a roll with his coffee at breakfast; he spent hardly a third as much on his clothes as George spent; and beyond an occasional visit to his club in the evening, he seemed to have absolutely no recreation. His life was in the stock market, and it was a life of almost monastic simplicity and self-sacrifice. If he had any pleasure, except the pleasure of providing his wife with the money for her dinner parties, which bored him excruciatingly, Gabriella had never discovered it. "He asks so little for himself that it is pathetic," she remarked to George one night, when Mr. Fowler had gone upstairs, carrying the evening papers to bed with him.

"Oh, well, he gets what he asks for," retorted George indifferently, "and that's more than the rest of us can say."

George was in a bad humour; he had been in a bad humour for weeks; and for this reason Gabriella had put off from day to day telling him that she expected a child in the autumn. All her efforts to soothe had merely exasperated him; and there were days when her presence worked him into a fit of nervous irritability. After four months of marriage prolonged boredom had replaced the passionate tenderness of their honeymoon. Why this should be so she was too well-balanced emotionally to understand. She saw only the outward evidences of change, of gradual disillusionment; and though at first she wept a little while she wondered, she ended by drying her tears and attributing his casual indifference and his explosive violence alike to some obscure disturbing condition of health. Every evening, except when there were guests, he spent at his club; he came to bed late, and his waking hour was filled with complaint about the number and the size of his bills. He treated these bills as if they had been gratuitous insults, as if they had leaped, without reason for being, out of a malign world to assail him. As yet Gabriella had bought nothing; and she dreaded the time when her clothes would wear out beyond the hope of repairing, and she should be obliged to add another bill to the growing pile under the silver paper weight on the little white and gold desk.

But in the last few weeks even this anxiety had faded from her mind, for the miracle of life which stirred in her body had diffused its golden halo around every trivial incident of her existence. After days of physical wretchedness, which she had hidden from George, she sat one evening, utterly at peace, in front of the fire in the room which had been Patty's before her marriage. It was past midnight, and she was waiting for George to come home because she felt that she could not sleep until she had told him. In the morning he had been unusually gentle, and as he left the house, she had said to herself a little sternly that he must know about the child before the day was over. A secret consultation with her mother-in-law had strengthened her resolution. "Don't keep it from him another day, Gabriella," Mrs. Fowler had urged. "It will make such a difference. I shall never forget Archibald's joy when I told him George was coming. Men are like that about children, you know."

"Yes, I'll tell him to-night," Gabriella had answered; and sitting now in the rocking-chair by the fire, she began to wonder if George would be exactly like other men about children.

The house was very still, but even in its stillness it exhaled the nervous apprehension which she felt to be its living character—as if George's parents, sleeping two doors away, had dropped their guard for the night, and allowed their anxious thoughts the freedom of the halls until daybreak. And these thoughts, which had become like invisible presences to the girl, wandered up and down the dim staircase, where the lowered lights awaited George's return, invaded the drawing-room, filled with stuffy red velvet chairs, so like crouching human beings in the darkness, and even thronged about her threshold, ready to spring inside at the instant when George should open the door. While her fire burned brightly on the andirons, and rosy shadows danced on the white rug beside her bed, on the lace coverlet turned back for the night, on the deep pillows with their azure lining showing through the delicate linen of the slips, on her simple nightdress, in which the buttonholes were so beautifully worked by her mother,—while she looked at these things it was easy for her to shut out the apprehensions of yesterday. But these apprehensions would come with George and they would not go until George left her again. The house with its heavy late-Victorian furniture, its velvet carpets which muffled footsteps, its thick curtains which hid doorways, its red walls, its bevelled mirrors, its substantial and costly ornaments, its solid paintings in solid frames—the house and all that it contained diffused for Gabriella an inescapable atmosphere, and this atmosphere was like the one in which she had waited expectantly in her childhood for the roof to be sold over her head. Now, as then, she waited for something to happen, and this something was a fact of dread, a shape of terror, which must be ignored as long as its impending presence was not directly before one's eyes. But with the look she was familiar, for she had seen it in her mother's face as far back as she could remember. It was associated in her mind with the need of money, with scant food, with scant fires, with a brooding and sinister hush in the house. With the knowledge of these things in her mind how could she hope that George would be glad of the child that was coming to them in the autumn?

And yet to Mrs. Fowler the news had appeared to bring no additional anxiety. She had seemed pleased rather than otherwise, mildly interested, animatedly sympathetic.

"I am afraid it will be very expensive," Gabriella had reminded her a little timidly, feeling frankly apologetic when she thought of all the trouble she must bring to the harassed and over-burdened little woman.

But into Mrs. Fowler's face there had come the look with which she was accustomed to receive the suggestion that her dinner parties were an extravagance. That economy which she practised so rigidly, which was so elastic to cover little pleasures and the minor comforts of life, broke like a cobweb when she tried to stretch it over larger needs and desires. The severity of her self-denial was directed entirely against the trivial and the unessential. With regard to the indispensable materials for happiness, she seemed to feel that she possessed an unquestionable right to enjoy them at any cost; and she had reassured Gabriella with an optimism which appeared perfectly genuine. After talking to her the girl had felt that she might allow herself to be happy if only George would change back into his old way.

Four months ago, at the beginning of her marriage, she had told herself that she needed only the daily intimacy of life to make her understand him. Now, after living with him, she felt that she was growing to understand him less every hour—that the relation which ought to have brought them spiritually closer, had ended by thrusting them to an incalculable distance from each other. Of the nervous reactions which he had suffered she knew nothing. All she saw clearly was that the widening breach between them would soon become impassable unless it could be filled by their new love for the child. The power to hold him must slip from her hands to the child's, and she was more than ready, she was even eager, to relinquish it. In the last few months her feeling for George had altered, and, though she was hardly conscious of the change in herself, her love for him had become less passionate and more maternal. The tenderness was there, but the yearning, the delight in his mere physical presence was gone. Like every other emotion that she had felt in the past, her love for her husband had become absorbed in the passion, the longing, the delight with which she enfolded the thought of her child.

"I wonder if mother felt like this about me," she would say to herself, and the wonder was like a cord drawing her back to her mother and to her own babyhood. Then George would become strangely vague, strangely remote in her thoughts; and her mother would seem nearer to her than everything except the child under her heart.

But since her talk with Mrs. Fowler, who had shown her photographs of George as a baby, some in long clothes, some in his first short frock, with a woolly lamb in his hands, some in a velvet suit, with his lustrous curls falling over a lace collar, Gabriella had felt that she possessed a new understanding of her husband and of the imperative needs of his nature. The child quality in him, the eternal boy that he betrayed sometimes by accident, appeared to her now to be the salient attribute of his character. After all, because of this quality, which was at once his charm and his weakness, she could not judge him as harshly as she might judge another man, she could not demand of him the gravity and the restraint of his father, who had never been young.

"I ought not to have kept it from him. His mother is right. She understands him better than I do," she thought, as she looked at the clock. "If I had told him sooner he might be with me now."

Through the muffled stillness of the house the sound of the opening front door stole up to her, and she heard George come in and stop for a minute to take off his hat and coat in the lower hail. Then she heard his footsteps move to the staircase; and while she listened she had a curious intuitive sense that it was not George at all, but a stranger who was coming to her, and that this stranger walked like a very old man. She heard him reach the bend in the stairs, and without stopping to put out the light, pass on to her door, which was the first on the landing. As he reached the top of the stairs, he stumbled once; then she heard his hand on the knob and a fumbling sound as if the knob would not turn. The door seemed to take an eternity to open, and while she sprang up with the clutch of terror at her heart, she felt again the sharp, agonizing premonition that a stranger was approaching her.

"George!" she called in a strangled voice, and waited, standing, for him to enter.

# CHAPTER VII

## MOTHERHOOD

At noon the next day Mrs. Fowler came into Gabriella's room and found her sewing beside the window which looked on a gray expanse of sky and street, where a few snowflakes were falling.

"Did you tell him, dear?" she asked, arranging a handful of red roses in a little alabaster vase on the desk.

No, Gabriella had not told him. She felt now that she should never be able to tell him, but all she said was:

"I didn't get a chance. How lovely those roses are."

Mrs. Fowler set the vase where the gray light fell on it, and then turning with empty hands from the desk, asked gently:

"Aren't you making a mistake, dear?" Her movements were like those of a character in a play who is made to fill in an awkward pause with some mechanical action.

"I couldn't tell him last night," replied Gabriella; "he was sick all night."

She was very pale, even her lips had lost their rich colour, and her eyes had a drawn and heavy look as if she had not slept. Without looking at her mother-in-law, she went on with her sewing, working buttonholes of exquisite fineness in a small white garment. In her lap there was a little wicker basket filled with spools of thread and odd bits of lace and cambric; and every now and then she stopped her work and gazed thoughtfully down on it as if she were trying to decide how she might use the jumble of scraps that it contained.

"Gabriella," said Mrs. Fowler suddenly, after she had watched her a moment, "did anything happen last night?"

"Happen? No, what could have happened?"

"At what time did George come in?"

"About one o'clock. I sat up for him."

"Was—was anything the matter with him? Was he in any way different?"

"He was sick. He was sick all night." A look of disgust crossed her face while she stopped to wipe away a drop of blood from her finger. "I don't remember pricking my finger since I was a child," she remarked.

"You are keeping something from me," said Mrs. Fowler; and sitting down in the small chair by the desk, she leaned her elbow, in her full sleeve of violet cashmere, on the edge of the blotting-pad. She was wearing a morning gown made, as all her house gowns were made, after the princess style, and Gabriella could see the tight expanse of her bosom rising and falling under a garniture of purple and silver passementerie. Her hair, fresh from the crimping pins, rose in stiff ridges from her forehead, and her bright red lips were so badly chapped from cold that they cracked a little when she smiled. She looked as hard as granite though in reality her heart was breaking with pity.

"I want to help you," she said, "and I can't if you keep things back."

"I told you George was sick. I was up all night with him." Again a look of disgust, which she could not control, flickered and died in her face.

"But you oughtn't to have let him keep you awake. You need all the sleep you can get. When he comes in late he must sleep in the spare room across the hall."

"His things are all in here and he would come in to get them; that would wake me."

For a moment Mrs. Fowler hesitated while the struggling breath grew more irregular under the passementerie on her bosom. The ripe colour faded from her cheeks and her lips looked blue in the harsh light from the window.

"I think I'd better speak to George," she said. "He is spoiled and he always thinks first of his own comfort. I suppose it's the way we brought him up—but when he understands, he will be more considerate."

For the first time Gabriella laid down her sewing and, leaning forward in her chair, fixed her eyes, with their look of deep stillness, of wistful expectancy, on the face of her mother-in-law.

"Would you mind telling me if George was ever—ever wild about women?" she asked, and though her voice was very low and quiet, her words seemed to echo loudly through the hushed suspense in her brain. It was as if every piece of furniture, every vacant wall, every picture, and every pane of glass, repeated the sound.

The pleasant smile on Mrs. Fowler's lips became suddenly painful. As if she were suffering a physical hurt, she put her handkerchief to her mouth while she answered:

"He was once—but that was before he fell in love with you. We hoped that you would be able to steady him—that marriage would make him settle down."

"Did he drink then?"

"A little—not enough to make him show it. I never saw him really show it but once, and then he was dreadfully sick. Was—was he like that last night?"

For a long minute, while she looked out of the window at the falling snowflakes, Gabriella did not reply. Then she spoke in a voice that was sternly accusing.

"You ought to have told me. I ought to have known." Her own wild passion for George was forgotten. She felt only a sense of outrage, of wounded and stunned resentment, They had treated her as if she were a child or a fool. That she had been a fool she was not prepared to admit at the instant—and yet it was less than a year ago, that June night when she had watched George over the clove pinks while her heart melted with happiness. She had had her way, and she was already regretting her madness. "Is this what love comes to?" she asked herself bitterly as she watched the white flakes whirling out of the gray sky. "Is this what it all comes to in the end, or am I different from other women?"

Moistening her dry lips with the tip of her tongue, Mrs. Fowler smiled bravely, though there were tears in her eyes. "Archibald wanted to, but I wouldn't let him," she replied; "I hoped that you would make everything different. He was so much in love with you. I thought you could do anything with him."

Though her reasoning failed to convince Gabriella, it was sufficiently forcible to justify her in her own judgment, and with an easier conscience, she settled comfortably behind the impregnable defences of the maternal instinct. After all, she had only done what she believed to be best for her boy. She had not been selfish, she had not even been thoughtless, she had been merely a mother.

"I wish you would tell me what really happened last night, Gabriella," she said, and her tone showed that she had recovered her shaken confidence in the righteousness of her cause.

"I can't tell you," answered Gabriella. "What good would it do? George was disgusting, that was all." She spoke sternly, for no lingering tenderness softened the judgment of her youth and her injured pride. How could she possibly have tenderness for a man who had tired of her in four months, who had become so lost to common decency that he could let her see him revoltingly drunk? And she had held her head so high, she had so despised Jane for her weakness and folly! At the moment she knew that she was helpless, but deep down within her she felt that this helplessness would not last—that the wings of her soul were still strong, still free, still untouched by the shame her body had suffered. With a single effort she could break the net of passion, and escape into the wonderful world which surrounded her. Like Jane, she had been a fool, but, unlike Jane, she would not stay a fool always.

"You seem so hard, Gabriella," said Mrs. Fowler. "Is it because you are young? Young people never make allowances."

The taste of bitterness rose to Gabriella's lips.

"I suppose I am hard," she answered, "and I am going to stay so. There is safety in hardness."

Remembering Jane, remembering the hereditary weakness of the Carrs, who had all married badly, she told herself that in hardness lay her solitary refuge from despair. After all, it was better to be hard than to break.

"You can't judge George quite as you would other men," began George's mother, and she was aware after a minute that the maternal instinct had in this instance led her to defeat.

"I am not judging other men," replied George's wife coldly; "I am judging George." Against men as men she had never even thought of cherishing a grievance. All her life she had looked to some man as to the saviour of the family fortunes, and her vision was still true enough to perceive that, as a human being, Archibald Fowler was finer and bigger than his wife, that Billy was finer and bigger than Patty. She had found men less the servants of mere instinct than she had found women, less the passive and unresisting vehicles of the elemental impulses. Then, too, they were so seldom the victims of life, and there was in her nature a fierce contempt for a victim. She despised people who submitted to circumstances, who resigned themselves to necessity, as if resignation were a virtue instead of a vice.

"Well, you must try not to worry, dear; worry is so bad for you. I am so sorry it happened. You won't mind my speaking to George, will you?"

Gabriella shook her head. "I don't care what you say to him."

"Do you feel able to come down to lunch?"

"Oh, yes, perfectly. I am simply dying for a cup of tea, and afterwards I think I'll go out for a walk. One gets so stuffy and dull when one stays in the house."

Her manner had changed as if by magic. In putting the thought of George out of her mind she seemed to have put aside her resentment and despondency.

In the evening George came home, looking a little yellow, with a box of gardenias in his hand; but the scent of the flowers sickened Gabriella, and she put them out of the room while she dressed for dinner. The attention, instead of pleasing her, brought an ironic twist to her lips, though she thanked George quite as courteously as if he had been a stranger to her. At dinner when Mr. Fowler abruptly asked his son why he had not been to the office, she kept her eyes fixed on her plate, in which she seemed to see palely reflected the anxious pleasantness of her mother-in-law's smile. It hardly occurred to her to wonder where George had spent his day, though, when she met Mr. Fowler's kind and tired look, a pang shot through her heart. She was sorrier for George's father than she was for herself. He looked so lonely, yet so patient. He so obviously needed help, and no one appeared to notice it, not even his wife, who began planning a dinner party in the futile effort to come to George's assistance. It was by coming to George's assistance in every difficulty, Gabriella surmised, that his mother had made George what he was; and the girl saw in imagination an endless line of subterfuges, of pitiful excuses and feeble justifications, all hidden in the tortuous labyrinthine windings of the maternal instinct. She saw, with the relentless vision of a Hebrew prophet, the inevitable ruin of the love that does not submit to wisdom as its law.

More than seven months afterwards, when she lay in her room with her child in the crook of her arm, she prayed passionately that some supreme Power would grant her the strength not of emotion, but of reason. All her life she had suffered from an unrestrained indulgence of the virtues—from love running to waste through excess, from the self-sacrifice that is capable of everything but self-discipline, from the intemperate devotion to duty that is as morbid as sin. Balance, moderation, restraint—these seemed to her, lying there with her child on her arm, to be the things most worth striving for. She saw her mother, worn to a shadow by the unnecessary deaths she had died, by the useless crucifixions she had endured; she saw Jane, haggard, wan, with her sweetness turning to bitterness because it was wasted; and again she found herself asking for balance, moderation, restraint. The child, a little girl, with George's eyes and hair like gauze, had liberated Gabriella from the last illusions of her girlhood.

And yet, though Gabriella prayed for moderation, she found after a few months that motherhood was absorbing the full strength of her nature. George hardly existed for her; he came and went like the passing of a shadow, and she began gradually to sink her life into the life of her child. Not until the winter was she brought back to a sharp realization of her neglected duty to her mother; and this came with a letter from Mrs. Carr during the last week in January. Mrs. Carr was still living with Jane, and though she had accepted mildly Gabriella's reasons for postponing her coming to New York, she was beginning somewhat plaintively to question. She had made little effort to hide her disappointment at not being with her daughter when her grandchild was born, for, in spite of the fact that she had tragically assisted at the entrance of Jane's six children into the world, she still possessed an insatiable appetite for the perpetually recurring scenes of birth and death. Then only did her natural bent of mind appear to be justified by universal phenomena.

And now on this morning in January, when Frances Evelyn, the baby, lay good and quiet in her crib, Gabriella read over again the disturbing letter she had just received from her mother.

MY DEAR DAUGHTER:

Jane wrote you that I had had a slight attack of pneumonia, so you understood why I was obliged to let so long a time go by without sending you a letter. Though I have been out of bed now for more than a fortnight, I still feel so weak and good for nothing that I am hardly equal to the exertion of writing. Then, too, I have had some trouble with my wrist—the right one—and this has made it really painful for me to hold a pen or even a fork. The doctor thinks it is a nervous affection and that it will pass away as soon as I get back my strength, and I am sure I hope and pray that it will. But sometimes I feel as if I should never get any stronger, and of course while my wrist is crippled I am unable to do any sewing. This has depressed me very much, for poor Jane has so many worries of her own that I dread being dependent on her, and Charley has not been at all well this winter, though kinder and more considerate than I have ever known him to be. He has his faults, but I have always felt that he was not entirely responsible and that we ought to pity rather than blame him. Women can never be too thankful that they are spared by a merciful Providence the temptations which seem to beset men. When we consider how much more sheltered our lives are, we ought to be lenient in our judgment, and I cannot help feeling that God meant us to be so when he gave us more spiritual natures than those of men. Dr. Preston gave a very instructive and impressive talk on that subject before the Ladies' Aid Society of our church the week before I was taken sick. Indeed, I am afraid I caught the cold that led to pneumonia sitting in Charley's pew, which gets a bad draught from the door of the Sunday-school room.

I must apologize for this dull letter, as I haven't been able to get out even to market. Before I was taken ill I used to do all of Jane's marketing, and you know what a place the market is for meeting people and hearing all the latest news. There are, however, two things to tell you, and you'll never be able to guess them. First, poor Miss Amelia Peterborough is dead. She was stricken with paralysis a week ago when she was all alone in the house—Miss Jemima was at a funeral—and she never regained consciousness until the end, which came at three o'clock Sunday night. Poor Miss Jemima, I feel so sorry for her. She keeps up beautifully and is very pious and resigned. They say she will go into the Old Ladies' Home as soon as the arrangements can be made.

The other piece of news is more cheerful, though, for my part, life seems so short and so uncertain that I can't see much cheerfulness anywhere. So many people are dying that you can't help wondering who will be next, and as Dr. Preston said when he called on me during my illness, our only substantial hope is in a blessed hereafter. My one regret will be leaving my children and grandchildren, and especially my precious little Frances Evelyn, whom I have never seen. I have no doubt that Mrs. Fowler was far more useful than I could have been at the time of your trial, but it was a great disappointment to me not to be able to receive the little darling into the world.

But I had entirely forgotten that I started to tell you about Florrie Spencer's marriage to Algernon Caperton. Of course I couldn't go, but Jane says the wedding was lovely and that Florrie looked really beautiful. Bessie had on rose-coloured brocade. Did you ever hear of such a thing at her age? She was just as gay and flirtatious as a girl, Charley said, and she sent me some of the cake and a bottle of champagne, which, of course, I didn't touch. It is a pity she is so loud, for there isn't a kinder heart in the world. Florrie and Algernon are going to New York on their wedding trip. Isn't it exactly like Florrie to want to go to all the theatres? They send you word, by the way, that they are certainly coming to see you and the baby.

And now that I have told all my news, I must write a little about myself, though I am afraid you will be upset by what I am obliged to tell you. I put it off as long as I could—for I do hate to worry you—but the doctor has just been to see me and he says I must go to Florida immediately to stay until the bad weather is over. I told him I couldn't possibly afford it—the trip would take a great deal of money—but he insisted that I should write and tell you exactly what he said. He said my lungs were very weak and that he ordered the change—you know they never seem to consider expense—and when he was leaving, he stopped in the hall to speak to Jane about it. Poor Jane, she is so worried that she has almost gone deranged over my health, but as far as I am concerned I feel that I would rather pass away than cause so much trouble and upset everybody. Jane, as you know, hasn't a cent to her name, and it is out of the question her asking Charley, because he has had a very bad winter financially. Even Cousin Jimmy stopped sending me the rent of the house since I moved to Jane's, and as for Uncle Meriweather, he has been obliged to give up his business and go to live with his niece in the country. So, much as I hate to ask you, my dear child, I feel that you would rather I did so—and that I ought to be perfectly frank about the situation, particularly since poor Jane feels so deeply her inability to help me. I am afraid I should need about four hundred dollars, as I have bought nothing to wear for years. Bessie Spencer has told me of a very reasonable place where I could board, and it is just possible that she will be going herself by the time I am ready. If for any reason you are unable to let me have the money, just destroy this letter and don't think about it again. I wouldn't cause you a moment's worry for anything in the world.

With love to George and a dozen kisses for my precious little grandchild,
Your devoted mother,
FANNY CARR.

Did I remember to tell you that Miss Polly Hatch has gone to New York to look after her nephew's children? He lost his wife a few months ago, and was left with four little children, the youngest only a year old.

So her punishment had come! As Gabriella dropped the letter into her lap, and looked at little Frances, so good and happy in her crib, she felt that she was punished not only for her reckless marriage, but for all the subterfuge, all the deceit which had followed it. She had not told her mother the truth, for she, also, had been chiefly concerned with "keeping up an appearance." For the purpose of shielding George, who was blandly indifferent to her shielding, she had lied to her mother, if not in words, yet in an evasion of the truth, and the result was that her lies and her evasions had recoiled not on George's head, but on her own. For George wouldn't care. So little value did he place upon Mrs. Carr's good opinion, that he would not care even if Gabriella were to tell her the truth. And if she had only been honest! If she had only refused to lie because custom exacted that a wife should be willing to lie in defense of her husband. Some obscure strain of dogmatic piety struggled in the convulsed depths of her being, as if she had been suddenly brought up against the vein of iron in her soul—against the moral law, stripped bare of clustering delusions, which her ancestors had known and fought for as "the Berkeley conscience." The Berkeley conscience, bred for centuries on a militant faith, told her now that she was punished because she had lied to her mother.

Then, as if this reversion to primitive theology had been merely an automatic reaction of certain nerve cells, she saw and condemned the childlike superstition. No, she was not punished so quickly; but she had been a fool, and she was paying the price of her incredible folly. How little, how pitifully little she knew of the world, after all! A year ago, on that horrible night, she had thought that her lesson was finished, but it was only beginning. Her immense, confiding ignorance would lead her into other abysses. And again, as on the morning after that night of revelation, she resolved passionately that she would not stay a fool always—that she would not become a victim of life.

The empty bottle had slipped to one side of the crib, and little Frances lay smiling at the friendly universe, with her wet mouth wide open and her blue eyes, so like George's, sparkling with laughter. The down on her head, as fine and soft as spun silk, made tiny rings over her pink skull, which was as clear and delicate as an eggshell; and these golden rings filled Gabriella with a tenderness so poignant that it brought tears to her eyes. Whatever her mother may have thought about the world, it was perfectly obvious that Frances Evelyn considered her part in it remarkably jolly. To be a well baby in an amiable universe was her ideal of felicity.

When George came up to luncheon, which he did sometimes now, he went straight to the nursery for a glimpse of his daughter. Ever since little Frances had lost her first hair and gained her golden down, he had taken an interest in the rapid stages of her development; and, though he never "wasted time," as he said, in the nursery, he liked to look in once a day and see whether or not she had changed in the night. On her side the baby treated her father as if he were an inexhaustible family joke, to be enjoyed not too seriously, but with a polite recognition of its humorous points. If she were sucking her bottle when he entered, she immediately stopped and laughed at him while the rubber nipple dropped from her toothless gums; if she awoke and discovered him at the side of her crib, she greeted him with subdued but inappeasable merriment; if he lifted her in his arms, her crocheted shoes could barely contain the kicks of her ecstatic feet. And because she was a jolly little beggar, George grew, after a time, to cherish a certain fondness for her. There was some use in a laughing baby, but he hated anything, child, woman, or animal, that cried.

On this particular day the baby happened to be asleep when he entered, so, without stopping, he went into Gabriella's bedroom, where the perfume of roses mingled with the scent of the burning logs on the andirons.

"That's a good fire," he observed, stopping on the hearth-rug. "I don't wonder you hate to go out."

"Yes, the room was a little chilly, so I lit the fire for the baby's bath. I don't usually have one," replied Gabriella, explaining her apparent extravagance.

"Has she been well?"

"She is always well. I haven't had a day's anxiety about her since she was born."

"But she isn't very old yet." Already little Frances was supplying conversational material to her parents.

"I wish you would sit down, George," said Gabriella, with a change of tone. "I want to read you a part of a letter from mother."

"Can't you tell me instead?"

"If you'd rather. You know I never told mother why we couldn't have her to live with us. I never told her anything. I simply made excuses."

"That was all right, wasn't it?" He was plainly nervous.

"At the time I thought I couldn't do differently, but now—"

She gave him the letter, and while he unfolded it awkwardly, she watched him anxiously and yet without interrupting his reading. Beyond the simple facts, she had told him nothing, and it was characteristic of her that she did not embellish these facts with picturesque phrases. She herself was so insensible to the appeal of rhetoric that she hardly thought of it as likely to influence anybody. Then, too, in moments of intense feeling she had always a sensation of dumbness.

"I'm awfully sorry about her illness," he said, "but when you think of it, the best thing that could have happened to her was not to come to New York. This climate would have been the end of her."

"Will you let me have the money, George? I will try to save in every way that I can. I've made all the baby's clothes, as it is, and I can easily make the few things I need, also. Since the baby came I have stopped calling with your mother."

A flush rose to his face. "I know you've been a regular brick about money, Gabriella. I never saw a woman buy as little as you do, and you always manage to look well dressed."

She smiled with faint irony. Her clothes were dowdy, for she had turned the broadcloth dress she had had at her marriage and was wearing it in the street; but if he thought her well dressed, it seemed hardly fair to undeceive him. Had she been any other woman, she reflected, he would probably have looked at her long enough to discover that she had grown decidedly shabby.

Since the baby's birth, as she told him, she had stopped calling with her mother-in-law, and a black net dress, given her by Mrs. Fowler because it had grown too small in the waist, was still presentable enough for the family dinners. But she never worried about her appearance, and it was a relief to find that George was quite as indifferent on the subject as she was. In the days of their honeymoon he had been so particular that she had spent hours each day before the mirror.

"Will you let me have the money, George?" she asked again. The form of the request had not changed, but there was a deeper note in her voice: the irony, which had been at first only a glancing edge to her smile, a subdued flash in her eyes, had passed now into her speech. George, looking sideways at the slightly austere charm of her profile, thought suddenly, "Gabriella is growing hard." He noticed, too, for the first time, that she looked older since the birth of the baby, that her bosom was fuller and that her figure, which had always been good, was now lovely in its long flowing lines. She was handsomer than she had been before her marriage, for her complexion had become clearer since she had lived in the North, and though she was still pale, her skin was losing its sallow tone.

Yet, though he thought her more attractive than she had been as a girl, she had ceased to make the faintest appeal to his senses. There were times even when he wondered how she had ever appealed to him, for she had not been beautiful, and beauty had always seemed to him to be essential in the women with whom one fell in love. But, however it had happened, still it had happened, and she was now his wife and the mother of the adorable Frances Evelyn.

"I'm awfully cut up about it, Gabriella," he said, "but honestly I am out of the money. I couldn't lay my hands on it just now to save my life."

His excuses convinced him while he uttered them, but he had barely paused before Gabriella demolished them with a single blow of her merciless logic.

"You were talking last night about buying a horse," she replied.

He frowned resentfully, and she immediately regretted her words. By speaking the truth she had defeated her purpose.

"It isn't as if I were buying a horse for pleasure," he answered doggedly; "I am dependent on exercise—you can see for yourself how I've gone off in the last two or three months. Of course if the horse were simply for enjoyment, like a carriage, it would be different. But mother has given up her carriage," he concluded triumphantly.

He was a spendthrift, she realized, but he was a spendthrift with a streak of stinginess in his nature. Though he enjoyed gratifying his own desires, which were many, it pained him inexpressibly to witness extravagance on the part of others, and by a curious twist of the imagination, all money spent by Gabriella appeared to him to be an extravagance. To be sure, he had just told her that she was a brick about money, but that had been intended as a warning to virtue rather than as an encouragement to weakness. There was, to be sure, a vague understanding that she might make bills when they were unavoidable; but so in want of spending money had she been since her marriage, that several times she had been obliged to borrow car fare from her mother-in-law. When she had asked George for an allowance, however small, he had put her off with the permission to charge whatever she bought in the shops. As the bills apparently never lessened, and her conscience revolted from debt, she had gone without things she needed rather than accept the barren generosity of his promises. At Christmas her father-in-law had given her fifty dollars in gold, and with this she had bought presents for her mother and Jane and the servants.

In the old days in Hill Street she had had little enough, but at least that little had really belonged to her; and since her marriage she had learned that when one is poor, it is better to live surrounded by want. To be poor in the midst of wealth—to be obliged to support a fictitious affluence on one's secret poverty— this was after all to know the supreme mortification of spirit. There were days when she almost prayed that the brooding suspense would assume a definite shape, that the blow would fall, the crash come, and ruin envelop them all. Any visible fact would be better than this impending horror of the imagination—this silent dread so much worse than any reality of failure—which encompassed them with the impalpable thickness and darkness of a cloud.

"Then I can't help my mother even if it's a matter of life and death?" she asked.

"I don't believe it's as bad as that, Gabriella. Ten chances to one the rest of the winter will be mild, and she would find Florida too depressing. You never can tell about doctors, you know. It's their business to make trouble. Now you mustn't let yourself worry—there's anxiety enough without that, heaven knows. Why, just look at father! He has lost almost all he ever had—he is simply staving off failure for I don't know how long, and yet from mother's manner who on earth would suspect that there is anything wrong? Now that's what I call pluck. By Jove—"

Again her impetuous spirit—dangerous gift!—flashed out recklessly in defence of the truth.

"Then why don't you try to help your father, George?" she asked. "He tells me that you rarely go down to the office." Her voice vibrated, but the stern lines of her mouth, which had lost its rich softness under the stress of her anger, hardly quivered.

His frown darkened to a scowl. The calm disdain in her manner made him feel that he hated her, and he told himself stubbornly that if she had been gentler, if she had been more womanly, he would have done what she asked of him, forgetting in his rage that, if she had been these things, he would have found even less difficulty in refusing her.

"You know as well as I do that I can't stand office work when I'm not fit," he returned sullenly. "It plays the devil with my nerves."

Her case was hopeless. If it had not been so in the beginning, she had ruined it by her irrefutable arguments, and while he rambled on moodily, making excuses for his neglect of business, she sat silently planning ways by which she might get the money for her mother. To ask her father-in-law was, of course, out of the question; and Mrs. Fowler, beyond a miraculously extended credit, due probably to the shining bubble of her husband's financial security, was as penniless as Gabriella. Unless she could find something to sell there seemed little likelihood of securing four hundred dollars in a day. It was imperative, then, that she should find something to sell; and remembering her mother's tragic visits to old Mr. Camberwell, she ran hastily over her few personal possessions. As her wedding gifts had been entirely in the form of clothes—the donors doubtless surmising that the wife of a rich man's son would have other gifts in abundance—there remained only the trinkets George and George's parents had given her. All through luncheon, while Mrs. Fowler, with an assumed frivolity which Gabriella found more than usually depressing, rippled on over the warmed-over salmon, the girl mentally arranged and sorted in their cases a diamond brooch, an amethyst necklace, a bracelet set with pearls, and a topaz heart she occasionally wore on a gold chain, which she valued because it had belonged to her grandmother. Once she stopped, and lifting her hand, looked appraisingly at her engagement ring for an instant, while Mrs. Fowler, observing her long gaze, remarked caressingly:

"I always thought it an unusually pretty stone, my dear. George knows a good deal about stones." Then, as if inspired by an impulse, she added quickly:

"Wasn't George upstairs before lunch? I thought I heard his voice."

"Yes, but he said he had an engagement at the club."

"I wonder if he knows I have asked the Capertons to dinner to-night? You know I got Florrie's card the other day. She is here on her wedding journey, but even then she doesn't like to be quiet, for she is her mother all over again. I used to know Bessie very well. Kind hearted, but a little vulgar."

"I didn't tell George. Perhaps you had better telephone him."

"Oh, well, he usually comes up to dinner because of the baby. I've asked one or two people to meet Florrie, for I remember that Bessie's one idea of enjoyment was to be in a crowd. The Crowboroughs are coming and the Thorntons and the Blantons."

"I'll be dressed in time," responded Gabriella, but she was thinking rapidly, "I can sell the diamond brooch and the bracelet and, if it is necessary, the amethyst necklace. The brooch must have cost at least three hundred dollars."

The meal was finished in silence, for even Mrs. Fowler's cheerfulness would flag now and then without a spur; and Gabriella made no effort to keep up the strained conversation. As soon as they had risen from the table, she ran upstairs to dress for the street, and then, before going out, she sat down at her desk, and wrapped up the brooch and the bracelet in tissue paper. For a minute she gazed, undecided, at the amethyst necklace. Mr. Fowler had given it to her, and she hated to part with it. George's gifts meant nothing to her now, but she felt a singular fondness for the amethyst necklace.

"I'd better take it with me," she thought; and wrapping it with the others, she put the package into her little bag, and went out of the room. It was her habit to stop for a last look at little Frances before she left the house, but to-day she hurried past the nursery, and ran downstairs and out of doors, where Mrs. Fowler was getting into a hansom with the assistance of Burrows, the English butler.

"May I drop you somewhere, Gabriella?" inquired Mrs. Fowler, while Burrows arranged the parcels on the seat of the hansom. In the strong sunshine all the little lines which were imperceptible in the shadow of the house—lines of sleeplessness, of anxiety, of prolonged aching suspense—appeared to start out as if by magic in her face. And over this underlying network of anxious thoughts there dropped suddenly, like a veil, that look of artificial pleasantness. She would have died sooner than lift it before one of the servants.

"No, thank you. I need the walk," answered Gabriella, stopping beside the hansom. "You will be tired if you do all those errands. May I help you?"

"No, no, dear, take your walk. I am so glad the storm is over. It will be a lovely afternoon."

Then the hansom drove off; Burrows, after a longing glance at the blue sky, slowly ascended the brownstone steps; and Gabriella, closing her furs at the throat, for the wind was high, hurried in the direction of Fifth Avenue.

The streets were still white after the storm; piles of new-fallen snow lay in the gutters; and when Gabriella crossed Madison Avenue, the wind was so strong that it almost lifted her from the ground. Above the shining whiteness of the streets there was a sky of spring; and spring was blossoming in the little cart of a flower vendor, which had stopped to let the traffic pass at the corner. There were few people out of doors, and these few appeared remote and strangely unreal between the wintry earth and the April sky. Beside the gutters, where the street cleaners were already at work, wagons drawn by large, heavy horses moved slowly from crossing to crossing. At Forty-second Street the traffic was blocked by one of these wagons; and from the windows of the stage, which had stopped by the sidewalk, the eyes of the passengers stared with moody resignation at the hurrying pedestrians. And it seemed to Gabriella that these faces wore, one and all, the look of secret anxiety, the faint network of lines which she had seen in the face of her mother-in-law. "I wonder if I have it, too," she thought, pausing before a shop window. But her reflection flashed back at her from the glass, smooth, stern, unsmiling, as if her features had been sculptured in marble.

Below Fortieth Street there was the shop of a jeweller she sometimes went to with Mrs. Fowler in that lady's despairing quest for suitable wedding presents at moderate prices; and something in the kindly, sympathetic face of the clerk who waited on them made Gabriella decide suddenly to trust him. As she unwrapped the tissue paper rather nervously, and keeping back the necklace, laid the brooch and the bracelet on the square of purple velvet he spread out on the counter, she raised her eyes to his with a look that was childlike in its appeal. Again she thought of the morning on which they had surreptitiously taken her silver mug, hidden in Mrs. Carr's gray and black shawl, to the shop of old Mr. Camberwell.

"How much might I get for these? I have worn them only a few times. They do not suit me," she said.

For a minute the clerk looked at her reflectively, but without curiosity; then lifting the trinkets from the square of velvet, he passed behind a green curtain into an adjoining room. After a short absence, in which she nervously examined an assortment of travelling clocks, he came back and told her that they would give her four hundred and fifty dollars for the two pieces.

"The stones alone are worth that," he added, "and, of course, they will have to be reset before we can sell them."

"May I have the check now?"

"Shall we send it to you by mail?"

"No, I must have it now. I want it this afternoon—immediately."

He yielded, still with his reflective but incurious manner; and when she left the shop a quarter of an hour later the check was in her little bag beside the amethyst necklace. "I am glad I didn't have to sell the necklace," she thought.

"Now I'll find a hotel and write to mother, and it will all be settled. It will all be settled," she repeated in a joyous tone; and this joyousness, overflowing her breast, showed in her eyes, in the little quivering smile on her lips, and in her light and buoyant step over the snow. A weight had been lifted from her heart, and she felt at peace with the world, at peace with the shivering passers-by, at peace even with George. The wind, hastening her walk, stung her face till it flushed through its pallor, and sent the warm blood bounding with happiness through her veins. Under the stainless blue of the sky, it seemed to her that the winter's earth was suddenly quickening with the seeds of the spring.

In the Waldorf she found a corner which was deserted, except for an elderly man with a dried face and a girl in a green hat, who appeared to be writing to her lover; and sitting down at a little desk behind a lamp, she wrote to her mother without mentioning George, without explaining anything, without even making excuses for her failure to keep her promise. She knew now that George had never meant that her mother should live with them, that he had never meant that they should take an apartment, that he had lied to her, without compunction, from the beginning. She knew this as surely as she knew that he was faithless and selfish, as surely as she knew that he had ceased to love her and would never love her again. And this knowledge, which had once caused her such poignant agony, seemed now as detached and remote as any tragedy in ancient history. She was barely twenty-two, and her love story had already dwindled to an impersonal biographical interest in her mind.

When she had finished her letter, she placed the check inside of it, and then sat for a minute pensively watching the girl in the green hat, whose face paled and reddened while she wrote to her lover.

"It seems a hundred years ago since I felt like that," she thought, "and now it is all over." Then because melancholy had no part in her nature, and she was too practical to waste time in useless regrets, she rose quickly from the desk, and went out, while the exhilaration of her mood was still proof against the dangerous weakness of self-pity. "It's life I'm living, not a fairy tale," she told herself sternly as she posted the letter and left the hotel. "It's life I'm living, and life is hard, however you take it." For a few blocks she walked on briskly, thinking of the shop windows and of the brightness and gaiety of the crowd in Fifth Avenue; but in spite of her efforts, her thoughts fluttered back presently to herself and her own problems. "After all, you can't become a victim unless you give in," she said grimly; "and I'll die rather than become a victim."

Her walk kept her out until five o'clock, and when she entered the house at that hour she found her mother-in-law in the front hall giving directions to Burrows. At sight of Gabriella she paused breathlessly, and said with undisguised nervousness:

"A very queer-looking person who says she was sent by your mother has just come to see you, dear—a seamstress of some kind, I fancy. As she looked quite clean, I let her go upstairs to the nursery to wait for you. I hope you don't mind. She was so eager to see the baby."

"Oh, it's Miss Polly!" cried Gabriella; and without stopping to explain, she ran upstairs and into the nursery, where little Frances was cooing with delight in Miss Polly's arms.

The seamstress' small birdlike face, framed by the silk quilling of her old lady's bonnet, broke into a hundred cheerful wrinkles at the sight of Gabriella. Even the grotesqueness of her appearance—of her fantastic mantle trimmed with bugles, made from her best wrap in the 'seventies, of her full alpaca skirt, with its wide hem stiffened by buckram, of her black cotton gloves, and her enormous black broadcloth bag—even these things could not extinguish the pleasure Gabriella felt in the meeting. If Miss Polly was ridiculous at home, she was twice as ridiculous in New York, but somehow it did not seem to matter. The sight of her brought happy tears to the girl's eyes, and in the attempt to hide them, she buried her face in the warm, flower-scented neck of little Frances.

"She's the peartest baby I ever saw," remarked Miss Polly with pride. "Wouldn't yo' ma dote on her?"

"Wouldn't she? But how did you leave mother and Jane and the children? The baby must be a big boy now."

"He's runnin' around all the time, and never out of mischief. I never saw such a child for mischief. I was tellin' yo' ma so last week. There's another baby on the way with Jane, you know."

"How in the world will she take care of it? I suppose Charley is just the same?"

"Well, if you ask me, Gabriella, I never was so dead set against Mr. Charley as the rest of you. I helped raise Jane from the time she was no higher than that—and I ain't sayin' nothin' against her except that Mr. Charley ain't half as bad to my mind as she makes him out. Some men respond to naggin' and some don't—that's what I said to her one day when she broke down and cried on my shoulder—and you've got to be mighty particular when you begin to nag that you're naggin' the right sort. But she won't listen, not she. 'If I don't tell Charley of his faults, who's goin' to?' she asks. You know Jane always did talk pretty free to me ever since she was a little girl. Well, there are some people that simply can't stand bein' told of their faults, and Mr. Charley is one of 'em. It ain't the kind of treatment that agrees with him, and if I'd been in Jane's place, I reckon I'd have found it out long ago. But it ain't her way to learn anything—you know that as well as I do. She's obliged to make the world over even if it drops to pieces in her hands."

"She doesn't seem to have done much with Charley."

"Well, you mark my words, Mr. Charley ain't bad, but he's full of natur', and Jane, is the kind of woman that's never happy unless she's gettin' the better of natur'. Whatever's natural is plum wrong, that's the way she looks at it; but mind you, I ain't sayin' she's all in the right. Naggin' ain't a virtue to my mind any mo' than drink is, but Jane, she can't see it that way, and there ain't a bit of use tryin' to make her. She's soft, but she's mulish, and the hardest thing on earth to push is a mule that looks soft."

"It's such a pity, but I suppose nothing will change her. Tell me about mother."

"Yo' ma looks downright po'ly. What with her sickness and her bother about Jane and the bad weather, she ain't managin' to keep as spry as I'd like to see her. From the stitch in her back she has most of the time it wouldn't surprise me any day to hear that she'd come down with kidney trouble, and she breathes so short that consumption has crossed my mind mo' than once when I was talkin' to her."

Miss Polly, having, as she expressed it, "an eye for symptoms," possessed an artistic rather than a scientific interest in disease; and the vivid realism of her descriptions had often, on her "sewing days" at home, reduced Gabriella to faintness, though Mrs. Carr, with her more delicate sensibilities, was able to listen with apparent enjoyment to the ghastly recitals. Not only had Miss Polly achieved in her youth a local fame as a "sick nurse," but, in the days when nursing was neither sanitary nor professional, she was often summoned hastily from her sewing machine to assist at a birth or a burial in one of the families for whom she worked. And happy always, as befits one whose life, stripped bare of ephemeral blessings, is centred upon the basic realities, she was never happier than when she put down her sewing, took off her spectacles, exchanged her apron for a mantle, and after carefully tying her bonnet strings, departed for a triumphant encounter with the Eternal Issues.

"I am so anxious about mother," said Gabriella. "Did she tell you she was going to Florida?"

"She cert'ny did. She was real full of it, and she talked a lot about you all up here—the baby and you and Mr. George. You know I ain't laid my eyes on Mr. George mo' than three times in my life. Well, I reckon I'd better be gettin' along back, or the children will miss me. I've got four children to do for now, and one of 'em ain't any bigger than Frances. It does seem funny—don't it, for an old maid to have her hands full of children? But, you know, I always did dote on children. There wouldn't be half so much fun in this world if it wan't for children and men, and there ain't a mite of difference between them under their skins. Yes, I can find my way back real easy. I always was good at finding my way about, and all I've got to do is to set out and walk in that direction till I come to a car over yonder by that high building, and as soon as I get on I'll ask the conductor to put me off right at my do'."

When she had gone, Gabriella went back into the nursery, and stood looking down at little Frances, who had fallen asleep, with the smile of an angel on her face. "I wonder if I can be the least bit like Jane?" she said aloud while she watched the sleeping child.

George did not come home to dinner; and the wonder was still in Gabriella's mind when she dressed herself in her black net gown, and went downstairs to meet Florrie, who looked younger and more brilliant than ever in a dress of white and silver brocade. Florrie's husband, a dreamy, quiet man,—the safe kind of man, Gabriella reflected, who inevitably marries a dangerous woman—regarded his noisy wife with a guileless admiration which was triumphantly surviving a complete submergence in the sparkling shallows of Florrie's personality. He was a man of sense and of breeding. He possessed the ordinary culture of a gentleman as well as the trained mind of a lawyer, yet he appeared impervious alike to the cheapness of Florrie's wit and the vulgarity of her taste. Her beauty had not only blinded him to her mental deficiencies; it had actually deluded him into a belief in her intelligence. He treated her slangy sallies as if they were an original species of humour; he accepted the sweeping comment of her ignorance as if it had been an inspired criticism of life. While she chattered, parrotlike, to the judge, who was obviously impressed by her appearance, Algernon listened to her ejaculatory conversation with a mixture of admiration and awe.

"How do you think Florrie is looking?" he asked in a low tone of Gabriella, while his wife's laugh, high, shrill, penetrating in its dry soprano quality, fluted loudly on the opposite side of the table. Beside Patty's patrician loveliness, as serene and flawless as that of a marble goddess, Florrie appeared cheap, common, and merely pretty to Gabriella. The hard brilliancy of her surface was like a shining polish which would wear off with sleep and have to be replenished each morning; and while she watched her, Gabriella saw, in imagination, a vaguely ominous outline surrounding her which might have been the uncertain edge of her mother's shadow. In twenty-five years Florrie would be the image of her mother—protuberant hips, pinched waist, mottled complexion, and hopelessly tarnished hair; yet, with this awful prospect before him, Algernon could appear not only tolerant, but positively adoring. He had seen Bessie—he had known her for years—and he could marry her daughter!

"I never saw her look handsomer," said Gabriella, "that white and silver gown is very becoming."

"That's what I told her, but she wouldn't believe me. She thought it was too plain for her style. Your sister-in-law is something of Florrie's type, isn't she? Not quite so striking a figure, perhaps, but the same sort of colouring."

Was it possible that for the first time in his life the simple Algernon was speaking in irony? Turning in her chair, she looked questioningly into his kind, grave face, so empty of humour, into his serious gray eyes, which followed each movement of his wife's with admiring attention. No, he was not ironic; he was perfectly solemn. It was a miracle—a miracle not of piety, but of passion—that she was witnessing.

"Yes, Patty is lovely," she answered, thinking, as she reflected upon the eccentricities of love, how much too good he was for his wife.

Across the table Florrie's voice was heard exclaiming: "Now, you don't mean it! Well, I'm just as flattered as I can be!" and Gabriella surmised that she was completing her conquest of the judge.

"It's wonderful how well she gets on with everybody," observed Algernon. "She's never at a loss for a word, and I tell her if I had her ready wit, I'd be the greatest lawyer in Virginia to-day. Have you noticed the way she is managing Judge Crowborough?"

"She always gets on well with men," acquiesced Gabriella, though without the enthusiasm of Algernon. "Do you remember what a belle she always was at the germans?" Though she was willing to admit that love was the ruling principle of life, it occurred to her that Algernon would be more amusing if he were less abundantly supplied with that virtue.

They talked of nothing but Florrie until the women went into the drawing-room; and there, from the safe haven of a window, Gabriella listened to Florrie's ceaseless prattle about herself. She was as egotistical, as effervescent, as she had been as a schoolgirl; and it seemed to Gabriella that she was hardly a day older. Her eyes, of a grayish blue, like pale periwinkles, were as bold, as careless, as conquering in their glances; her hair was still as dazzling; her face, with its curious resemblance in shape to the face of a pretty cat, was still as frank, as naïve, as confiding in its innocence. If she had changed at all, it was that, since her marriage to the silent Algernon, she had become even more talkative than she had been in her girlhood. Her vivacity was as disturbing as the incessant buzzing of a June beetle.

"Well, you need never tell me again that you wouldn't rather live in New York, Gabriella," she fluted at parting, "because I shan't believe a single word of it. Why, we've been to the theatre every night for a fortnight, and we haven't seen half the good plays that are going on. Algy wanted to stay at Niagara Falls—you know we went to Niagara Falls first—but it was so deadly quiet I couldn't stand it. 'I don't care if I am married,' I said to Algy, 'what I want is the theatre.'"

After she had gone, adoringly wrapped up by Algernon, Patty turned to her mother with a little malicious grimace:

"I know it's horrid to say she's dreadful, mamma, but she really is."

"Don't, Patty, it isn't kind, and, besides, she's a friend of Gabriella's. What I can't understand," she added, "is how Bessie ever came out of Virginia, yet there were always a few like her. You don't remember Pussy Prime, do you? Of course you don't, she died long before your day, but she was just that loud, boisterous kind, and all the men were in love with her."

"Well, if I'm ever born again," remarked Gabriella, as she kissed Patty good-night, "I hope I'll be born a fat blonde. They always get taken care of."

She ascended the stairs wearily to her room. Yes, she was barely twenty-two and love was over forever. "I couldn't hold a man six months," she thought dejectedly, "and yet Florrie, who is a fool and vulgar, will be adored all her life."

BOOK SECOND

THE AGE OF KNOWLEDGE

CHAPTER I

DISENCHANTMENT

In July Gabriella joined her mother in the mountains of Virginia, and when she returned in the autumn, she found that the character of her home had changed perceptibly during her absence. Brightness had followed gloom; the fog of suspense had dissolved, and the hazy sunshine of an ambiguous optimism flooded the house. What the change implied she could not immediately discover; but before the first day was over she surmised that the financial prospects of her father-in-law had improved since the spring. If she had had any doubt of his rising fortunes, the sight of the diminished pile of bills on Mrs. Fowler's desk would have quickly dispelled it.

And even George had apparently altered for the better. His improved finances had sweetened his temper and cast the shining gloss of prosperity over his appearance; and, in a measure at least, time had revived in him the ardent, if fluctuating, emotions of the lover. For three months after her return, he evinced a fervent sentiment for Gabriella, which she, who was staunchly paying the price of her folly, received with an inner shrinking but an outward complaisance. Her feeling for George was quite dead—so dead that it was impossible for any artificial stimulus to revive it—but she had learned that marriage is founded upon a more substantial basis than the romantic emotions of either a wife or a husband. Though she had ceased to love George, she could still be amiable to him; and it occurred to her at times that if one had to choose between the two not necessarily inseparable qualities of love and amiability, George was not losing greatly by the exchange. When, however, at the end of three months, George's capricious symptoms disappeared as suddenly as they had come, and his attentions lapsed into casual expressions of a nonchalant kindness, she drew a breath of relief, and devoted her happiest days to the nursery. There at least she had found a stable refuge amid the turmoil of selfish human desires.

In the house, which like George, began presently to show the gloss of prosperity, the winter brought a continuous flashing stream of gaiety, in which Mrs. Fowler darted joyously about like some bright hungry minnow beneath the iridescent ripples of a brook. There were new rugs, new curtains, new gowns, new bonnets; and Gabriella was led compliantly from dressmaker to milliner, until she lost in the process her look of shabbiness and developed into the fashionable curving figure of the period. She had always liked clothes; her taste was naturally good; and as she followed eagerly from shop to shop, she recalled the three months she had spent in Brandywine's millinery department, and the rudiments of a trade she had learned there. "I'd rather design my next gown myself," she said one day to Mrs. Fowler, while they were looking at French models in the establishment of Madame Dinard, who had been born an

O'Grady. "I know I can do better than these, and besides I shan't meet duplicates of myself every time I go out." That night she dreamed of hats and gowns, and the next morning she drew pictures of them in coloured chalk. "It's the only talent I ever had," she remarked gaily to her mother-in-law, "and it is running to waste."

Madame, who regarded the sketches with uncompromising disdain, showed great interest in the practical application of Gabriella's ideas to the dressing of Mrs. Fowler.

"Yes, you have undoubtedly ideas," she said, discarding in her enthusiasm the accent she had spent twenty years in acquiring, "and there is nothing so rare in any department—in any walk of life—as ideas. You have style, too," she pursued admiringly, turning her eyes on Gabriella's figure in one of her Parisian models. "It is very rare—such chic. You wear your clothes with a grace."

"That, also, is a marketable asset in a dressmaker," laughed Gabriella. "Do you know I ought to have been a dressmaker, Madame. Only I hate the very sight of a needle."

"But I never sew! I haven't had a needle in my hand for twenty years—no, not for thirty," protested Madame.

"Then I mustn't give up hope. If I ever have to earn my living, I'll come to you, Madame."

Then Madame bowed and smiled and shrugged as if at a gracious jest, and Mrs. Fowler observed in her crisp, matter-of-fact manner: "Yes, my daughter has a genuine instinct for dress, and, as you say, that is very rare. She carries her clothes well, doesn't she? It's such a blessing to be tall—though my husband insists that the women who have ruled the world have always been small ones. But I do love a fine figure, and she looks so distinguished in that cherry-coloured cloth, doesn't she?"

To all of which Madame agreed, as she bowed them out, with her ingratiating professional manner.

"It's so lovely to have clothes," said Gabriella, sinking back in the victoria, "money is one of the best gifts of the gods, isn't it?"

"It's hard to do without it," replied Mrs. Fowler, brisk and perfectly businesslike even in her generalizations. "I expect the worst suffering in the world comes from poverty."

Then, after a thoughtful pause, she added with the practical air of one who scorns to be abstract: "But do you know I sometimes think Archibald and I'd both be happier if we had never made any money at all—I mean, of course, except just enough to live simply somewhere in the South. When once you begin, you can't stop, and I wish sometimes we had never begun." Above the narrow black velvet strings of her bonnet, her round florid face, from which the fine tracery of lines had vanished, assumed the intent and preoccupied expression which Gabriella associated with the pile of unpaid bills on the little French desk. "I believe Archibald feels that way, too," she concluded after a minute, while her firm and unemotional lips closed together over the words.

"But you enjoy it so much when you have it."

"That's just the trouble. You have to enjoy it as quickly as you can because you never know when you are going to lose every bit of it without warning. It's been that way ever since I married—rich one year, poor the next, or poor for two years and then rich for three. Life has been a seesaw with prosperity at one end of the plank and poverty at the other. Of course I know," she pursued, with characteristic lucidity, "that you think me dreadfully extravagant, but we'd just as well spend it as lose it, and it's sure to be one thing or the other."

"But couldn't you save something? Couldn't you put by something for the future?" Saving for the future was one of the habits of Gabriella's frugal past which still clung to her.

"That would go, too. If we ever come to ruin—and heaven knows we've been on the brink of it before this—Archibald would not keep back a penny. That's his way, and that's one of the reasons I spend all we have—up to the very margin of his income."

The logic of this was so confusing that Gabriella was obliged to stop and puzzle it out. At the end she could only admit that Mrs. Fowler's reasoning processes, which were by nature singularly lucid and exact, showed at times a remarkable subtlety—as if some extraneous hybrid faculty had been grafted on the simple parent stock of her mind.

"I can't help feeling, though," resumed the practical little lady before Gabriella had reached the end of her analysis, "that I'd be a great deal happier at this minute if we'd been poor all our lives."

"It wouldn't have suited George," observed George's wife with an inflection of irony.

"He mightn't have liked it, but I believe it would have been a great deal better for him," replied Mrs. Fowler, while she bowed gravely to a woman in a passing victoria. "There are many things George can't be blamed for, and the way he was brought up is one of them. Of course, he's no good whatever as a business man—his father hardly ever sees him in the office—but it's useless to scold him about it, for it only exasperates him. But he might have been a sensible, steady boy, if he had been brought up in some small place in the South where there was nothing to tempt him."

That there was any place in the South small enough not to afford temptation to George seemed improbable to Gabriella; but she felt that Mrs. Fowler's earnest belief, supported as it was by the unshakable prop of maternal feeling, hardly justified the effort she must make to dispel it; and she had still no answer ready when the carriage turned into Fifty-seventh Street, and stopped beside the pavement where little Frances—they had already begun to call her Fanny—sat in a perambulator. Flushed and smiling, with her red mouth gurgling delightedly, and a white wool lamb clasped in her arms, the adorable child was certainly worth any seesaw of destiny, any disillusioning experience of marriage.

Before the beginning of the next winter Gabriella's second child was born— a brown, sturdy boy, who came into the world with a frowning forehead and crying lustily from rage (so the nurse said) not from fright. He was named Archibald after his grandfather, who developed immediately a passionate fondness for him. His eyes were brown like the eyes of the Carrs, though by the time he was two years old, he was discovered to be painfully near-sighted, a weakness which Mrs. Carr, when she heard of it, insisted he must have inherited from his father's side of the family. He was not nearly so beautiful a baby as little Fanny had been; but he was from the very beginning a child of much character, strong, mutinous, utterly uncompromising in his attitude toward life. When he was first put into shoes he fought with desperation, and surrendered at last, neither to persuasion nor to punishment, but to an exhaustion so profound that he slept for hours with his small protesting feet doubled under him and sobs of fury still bursting from his swollen lips. The next day the struggle began again, and Mrs. Fowler remarked sympathetically:

"You'll never be able to break his will, Gabriella. He is unmanageable."

"I don't want to break his will, mamma," replied Gabriella, for she belonged to a less Scriptural generation, "but he must be disciplined, if it kills me." Pale, gentle, resolute, she waited for Archibald to surrender. In the end she carried her point and won the adoring obedience of Archibald. There was a magnanimous strain in him even at that age, Gabriella used to say, and though he fought to the bitter end, he bore no malice after he was once soundly defeated.

Long afterwards, when Gabriella looked back on the next few years of her life, she could remember nothing of them except the tremendous difference that the children had made. All the rest was blotted out, a drab blur of what Mrs. Fowler described with dignity as "social duties," moving always against the variable atmosphere of the house, which was gay or sombre, light or gloomy, according to the fluctuating financial conditions in Wall Street. There were extravagant winters and frugal winters; winters of large entertainments and winters of "women's luncheons"; but always the summers shimmered green and peaceful against the blue background of the Virginia mountains. The summers she loved even in memory; but of the winters she could recall but one glowing vision, and that was of Patty. Though she had lost George, she had gained Patty, and it was impossible to deny that Patty might be compensation for almost any lack.

For the rest she made few friends, partly from reserve, partly from the shyness she always felt in the presence of strangers. It was difficult to establish fundamental relations at dinners or even at women's luncheons; social reforms were scarcely beginning to be fashionable; and apart from the reading which she did in order, as she said, "to keep her mind open," her life narrowed down gradually to a single vivid centre of activity. She lived in her children and in the few books she obtained from the library—(since the purchase of books, even in extravagant years, represented gross prodigality to Mrs. Fowler)—in Patty's friendship, and in the weekly gossiping letters she received from her mother.

Mrs. Carr had long ago given up her plan to live with Gabriella and George; and a failure of circumstances, which fitted so perfectly into the general scheme of her philosophy, had done much to fortify the natural melancholy of her soul. Since even so gentle a pessimist was not devoid of a saving trace of spiritual arrogance, she found consoling balm in the thought that she had refrained from reminding Gabriella how very badly the Carrs had all married. There was, for example, poor Gabriel's brother Tom, whose wife had "gone deranged" six months after her wedding, and poor Gabriel's sister Johanna, who had died (it was common gossip) of a broken heart; and besides these instances, nobody could possibly maintain that Jane had not made a disastrous choice when she had persisted, against the urgent advice of her mother, in marrying Charley. Yes, the Carrs had all married badly, reflected Mrs. Carr, with the grief of a mother and the pride of a philosopher whose favourite theory has been substantially verified—every one of them, with, of course, the solitary exception of poor Gabriel himself.

Her weekly letters, pious, gossipy, flowing, reached Gabriella regularly every Monday morning, and were read at breakfast while Mr. Fowler studied the financial columns of the newspaper, and his wife opened her invitations in the intervals between pouring out cups of coffee and inquiring solicitously if any one wanted cream and sugar.

"What's the news?" George would sometimes ask carelessly; and Gabriella would glance down the pages covered with the formless characters of Mrs. Carr's fine Italian handwriting (the ladylike hand of the 'sixties), and read out carefully selected bits of provincial gossip, to which a cosmopolitan dash was usually contributed by the adventures, matrimonial or merely amorous, of Florrie Caperton. Hard, dashing, brilliant on the surface at least, a frank hedonist by inclination, if not by philosophy, Florrie had triumphantly smashed her way through the conventions and the traditions of centuries.

"It's really dreadfully sad about Florrie," wrote Mrs. Carr. "I am so sorry for poor Bessie, who must feel it more than she lets any one see. While Algernon was alive we always hoped he would keep Florrie straight (you remember how everybody used to talk about her when she was a girl), but now he has been, dead only a year and a half, and she has already married again and gotten a divorce from her second husband. You know she ran away with a man named Tom Westcott—nobody ever heard of him, but she met him at the White Sulphur Springs, where he had something to do with the horses, I believe—and the marriage turned out very badly, though for my part I don't believe he was the least bit to blame. Florrie is so reckless that she would make any man unhappy, and two weeks after the wedding she was separated from him and was back here with Bessie, looking as well and pretty as I ever saw her. You know black was so becoming to her that she didn't take it off even when she eloped, and now after her divorce she always wears it, just as if she were still in mourning for poor Algernon. Nobody would believe, unless they had seen her in it, how very loud black can be. I used to think widows ought to wear it because it kept them from being noticed, but on Florrie it is the most conspicuous thing you ever imagined—as Cousin Jimmy says it simply makes her blaze, and you know how striking she always was anyway. I am sure I should think it would be embarrassing for her to go in the street in New York where nobody knows that she is really a lady—or at least that she was born a lady on her father's side—and this reminds me—(I declare I ramble on so I can never remember what I started to say)—but this reminds me that she has just been in to tell Jane that she is going to New York to take an apartment somewhere downtown; she told me the street and the number, but I have forgotten both of them. Jane says she looks more beautiful than ever after her last tragic experience (though she doesn't seem to think it tragic at all), but I was brought up to believe that a divorced woman, even if she is in the right, ought to live in a retired way and show that she feels her position. Now, I saw Florrie for a minute as she was going out and she ran on like a girl of sixteen—you would think from her talk that she is not a bit sensitive about the unfortunate situation she is in. She had on a huge bunch of violets, and Cousin Pussy tells me another man is paying her the most devoted attention. Please don't mention this to a soul—I hate so to spread gossip—but I felt that you ought to be prepared, for Florrie will certainly come to see you, and you must be kind and polite to her, though I do not think you ought ever to be intimate again. It is not as if she were merely unfortunate—many divorced women are that, and we sympathize with them because they show that they realize their position—but I cannot believe that Florrie is unfortunate if she allows another man to pay her such marked attention, and even accepts handsome presents from him. So do be careful, my child, and if you find yourself in an embarrassing situation, consult Mrs. Fowler and be guided by her advice."

"Florrie Spencer is coming to New York," said Gabriella on the morning she received Mrs. Carr's letter. "You know she has just been divorced from her second husband—somebody she met at the White Sulphur Springs."

George looked up interested, from his breakfast.

"Florrie coming, is she?" he remarked. "Well, she's great fun. I wonder if she has her eye on anybody now?"

"Not on you, I hope," observed his father, who joked mildly on the mornings when the news was good; "but she's a beautiful woman, and she'll doubtless be able to get whatever she has set either her heart or her eye on."

"She'll marry again within six months," prophesied Mrs. Fowler, with an anxious glance in the direction of her husband's coffee cup. "Poor Algy, I always thought he was a hundred times too good for her," she added, while she abstractedly buttered her toast. It was one of their extravagant years, and the butter was delicious.

"He adored her," said Gabriella. "I shall never forget the evening they spent here. He couldn't keep his eyes away from her. If she had been the most admirable character on earth he couldn't have loved her better."

"As if a man ever loved a woman because of her character!" remarked Mrs. Fowler, from the security of her experience.

Several months later Florrie arrived, gay, brilliant, and beautiful, with her waxlike complexion as unlined by care as if it had been on the face of a doll. Though she had lightened her mourning since Mrs. Carr had described her to Gabriella, she still wore black, and her flaring skirt, her inflexible collar, and her lace sleeves, narrow at the shoulder and full at the wrists, resembled a fashion plate. Perched at a daring angle above her wheaten-red pompadour, with its exaggerated Marcel wave, she wore a curiously distorted hat of black velvet, lavishly overtrimmed with ostrich feathers; and before this miracle of style, Gabriella became at once oppressively aware of her own lack of the quality which Florrie would have described as "dash." Already Florrie's figure was becoming slightly too protuberant for the style of the new century, and after kissing Gabriella effusively, she stood for a minute struggling for breath, in the attitude of her mother, with her hands pressed to the palpitating sides of her waist.

"I told mother I was certainly coming to see you right straight," began Florrie, while, with her recovered breath, her figure curved as suddenly as if it were moved by a spring into the fashionable bend of the period. "I've been perfectly crazy to come, but between dressmakers and theatres and I don't know what else, I simply haven't had a minute in which I could sit down and breathe. Mother says I ought to be downright ashamed of myself for being so frivolous when I've just got out of such a scrape—did you ever hear before of anybody getting married for two weeks, Gabriella? But I know you never did—you needn't trouble to tell me so. Well, mother says I oughtn't to look so pleased, and I tell her there might be some sense in that if I'd stayed in the scrape, but if I haven't a right to look pleased at getting out, I'd like to know who has. It was all too funny for words, now, wasn't it? Of course, I shouldn't dream of talking to everybody like this—even if I am a big talker, I reckon I know when to hold my tongue and when not to—but I've always told you everything, Gabriella, and I don't mind the least bit in the world telling you about this. It always relieves my mind to talk to somebody I can trust, and I know I can trust you. Don't you remember the way I used to run in on rainy afternoons when you lived way over in Hill Street, and tell you all about Fred Dudley and Barbour Willis? And then I used to come and talk about poor Algy by the hour. Wasn't it too distressing about poor Algy? I don't believe I'll ever get over it if I live to be a hundred, and even if I do run on like this, it doesn't mean that my heart isn't broken—simply broken—because it is. Mother used to say, after father died, that you couldn't measure a widow's grief by the length of her veil; and that's just exactly the way I feel about Algy. I know you'll understand, Gabriella, because you always understand everything—"

"He was so deeply in love with you," observed Gabriella sympathetically, while Florrie, diving amid the foam of her laces, brought out a tiny handkerchief, and delicately pecked at the corner of her eye, not near enough to redden the lid and not far enough away to disturb the rice powder on the side of her nose.

"He was crazy about me to the very last, you never saw anything like it. Of course we weren't a bit alike, I don't mind telling you so, Gabriella, because I know you'll never repeat it. We weren't really congenial, for Algy was just wrapped up in his law books, and there were whole days together when he wouldn't open his mouth, but that didn't seem to make any difference because, as he used to say, one of us had to listen sometimes. But, you know, mother says a pair of opposites makes the happiest marriage, and after being married to Algy,

I feel how true that is. I got into the habit of talking so much when I used to run on about nothing to cheer him up—he was always so grave and glum even as a boy, you remember—and during his last illness—you know he died of Bright's disease, poor darling, and it came on just like that!—he used to make me talk to him for hours and hours just to keep him from thinking. Well, well, that's all over now, and I don't care what anybody says, my heart's buried with Algy. I don't believe you were ever in love but once either, were you, Gabriella?" she inquired cheerfully.

"Well, what about Mr. Westcott? Is that his name?" asked Gabriella, without malice. As a study Florrie had always interested her, for she regarded her less as an individual than as an awful example of the utter futility of moral maxims. Florrie was without intelligence, without feeling, without imagination, virtue, breeding, or good taste, yet possessing none of these qualities, she had by sheer beauty and "dash" achieved all the ends for which these qualities usually strive. Good humour she had as long as one did not get in her way; but, beyond this single redeeming grace, she was as empty of substance as a tinted shell filled with sea foam. If power and efficiency are the two supreme attributes of success, then by all the laws and principles of logic, Florrie ought to have been a failure. But she was not a failure. She was a fool whose incomparable foolishness had conferred not only prosperity, but happiness upon her. She shone, she scintillated, she diffused the glow of success. Though she was undeserving of admiration, she had been surfeited on it from her childhood; though she was devoid of the moral excellence which should command love, by a flashing glance or a waving curl, she could bring the most exalted love down from the heavens. There was no question that Algernon had really loved her to distraction, and Algernon was a man of sense, of breeding, of distinction. As for Florrie, she had, of course, as little capacity for loving as she had for thinking.

"Tom Westcott! I declare, Gabriella, I am almost ashamed to tell you about him. You've never been to a Virginia summer resort, so you couldn't understand that there is something about a Virginia summer resort that just seems to make any man better than none at all. You get so bored, you know, that you'd flirt with a lamp-post if there wasn't anything human around; and when you haven't laid eyes on a real sure enough man for several months, it's surprising how easy it is to take up with the imitation ones. Of course, I don't mean that Tom wasn't all right as far as family and all that goes; but he was simply no earthly account— he was just mean all through, and as soon as I found it out, I packed right straight up and left him. After Algy I couldn't have stood one of that sort, and there was no sense in my trying to. Life is too short, I always say, for experiments. There's no use sticking to a bad job when you can get away from it. That's the trouble with so many women, you know; they try and try to stand the wrong man when they know all the time that it isn't a particle of use, and that they are just bringing wrinkles into their faces; and then by the time they give up, they're all worn out and it's too late to look about for another chance. Now, I've seen too much of that kind of thing, and so I thought two weeks weren't long enough to bring wrinkles in my face, but they were plenty long for me to find out whether or not I could stand any man on earth. So here I am in little old New York instead of being stuck away in some God-forsaken Virginia town, where there isn't even a theatre, darning stockings for a family of children. But there's no use talking about that—" And Florrie, who had been born a lady on her father's side, adjusted her pompadour under the high bandeau of her hat, and rose with a dashing air from the sofa.

"I'd love to see the babies, darling," she said; "I'm just crazy about babies."

"They are out in the Park. I'm so sorry. Perhaps they are coming in now, I hear the door-bell."

But it was George instead of the children; and he entered presently with a moody look, which vanished quickly before the brilliant vision of Florrie.

"I thought I heard you," he observed with the casual intimacy of an old playmate, "so I came in. Have you got fixed yet? What about the apartment? You'd better let me help you hunt for it?"

"Oh, I'm not sure about the apartment. I may take a house—a teeny weeny one, you know," said Florrie, as she bent softly toward him, scented and blooming. If one didn't know there wasn't really a bit of harm in her, one would be puzzled just what to think of her, Gabriella reflected. Amid the perfect order of Gabriella's inner life, the controlled emotion, the serene efficiency, the balanced power, Florrie's noisy beauty produced a disturbing effect. She liked her because she had known her from childhood, and it was impossible to think any harm of a girl one had played with at school; but she could not deny that Florrie was vulgar. As a matter of fact, Florrie's mother had been vulgar before her, and the thin strain of refinement inherited from her father's stock had obviously been overborne by the torrential vulgarity of the maternal blood.

"A house? Well, that's even better," replied George. "I've no use for apartments, have I, Gabriella?"

His effrontery was incredible! That he should joke about his broken promise before Florrie amazed Gabriella even after her disillusioning experience with him.

"Then I'll get you to help me. Will you lend him to me, darling?" trilled Florrie piercingly from the door, where she stood in a striking pose which revealed her "fine figure" to the best advantage. The request was directed to Gabriella, but her blue eyes mocked a challenge to George while she spoke.

"Oh, I'll give him," answered Gabriella pleasantly. There was no harm in it, she told herself innocently again; but it was a pity that Florrie, with her remarkable beauty, should be quite so ill bred.

Five minutes later when George came back from putting Florrie into her hansom, he remarked carelessly:

"She's got a figure all right."

"Yes, she looks beautiful in black. No wonder she won't leave it off."

"By Jove, to think it's little Florrie! Why, I don't believe there's a finer figure in New York. When she passed by the club yesterday the men were breaking their necks to look out of the window." Then, as if struck by a sudden suspicion, he added quickly: "Where did she get her money from? I thought Algy died rather hard up."

"I never heard much about it. Mrs. Spencer must give her something."

"I don't believe the old lady has a penny over three thousand a year, and that won't do in New York. This Westcott didn't have anything, did he?"

"It never occurred to me to ask," replied Gabriella indifferently. What did it matter to George where Florrie got her money? But, then, George was always like that, and though he never made a penny himself, he was possessed of an insatiable curiosity about the amount and the sources of other people's incomes.

"Well, it looks queer," he observed with intense interest after a prolonged pause. "That short pearl necklace she had on couldn't have cost a cent under ten thousand dollars."

"It was lovely. I noticed how well the pearls matched," replied his wife. She was not in the least excited about the methods by which Florrie had obtained the necklace—all that was a part of the miraculous way she got everything she wanted in life—but she liked the pearls and she had envied Florrie while she looked at them.

A deep furrow had appeared between George's eyebrows, and his mouth sagged suddenly at the corners, giving his face the ugly look Gabriella distrusted and dreaded. While she watched him she recalled vaguely that she had once thought the latent brutality in his face an expression of power. How young she had been when she married him! How inconceivably ignorant! Yet at twenty years she had imagined herself wise enough to judge a man. She had deluded herself with the sanctified fallacy that mere instinct would guide her aright—that her marriage would be protected from disaster by the infallible impulse which she had mistaken for love.

"I wonder," said George with a suddenness that startled her out of her musing—"I wonder if it can be Winston Camp!"

And Gabriella, who had forgotten Florrie, looked up to remark absentmindedly: "Winston Camp? You mean the man who dined here last winter and couldn't eat anything but nuts?"

In the months that followed George did not mention Florrie again, and if he pursued his investigations into the obscure sources of her livelihood, his researches did not lead him back in the direction of Gabriella. But, from the day of Florrie's visit, it seemed to Gabriella, when she thought of it afterwards, his casual indifference began to develop into brutal neglect. Not that she regretted his affection, or even his politeness, not that she cared in the least what his manner was—this she made quite plain to herself—but her passion to see life clearly, to test experience, to weigh events, brought her almost breathlessly round again to the question, "What does it mean? Is there something hidden? Am I still the poor abject fool that Jane was or am I beginning really to be myself?"

"You aren't looking well, Gabriella," said Mrs. Fowler at breakfast one morning when George, as she confided afterwards to Patty, had behaved unspeakably to his wife before his father came down. "I want you to go about with me more, as you used to do before the children took up all your time."

Gabriella had just crossed George's will about something—a mere trifle, something about calling on Florrie—and he had turned to her with a look of hatred in his eyes, a kind of nervous, excitable hatred which she had never seen until then. "Why does he look at me like that?" she had thought quite coldly; "and why should he have begun all of a sudden to hate me? Why should my words, my voice, my gestures even, exasperate him so profoundly? Of course he has stopped loving me, but why should that make him hate me? I stopped loving him, too, long ago, yet there is only indifference, not hate, in my heart."

"You must go about with me more, dear," repeated Mrs. Fowler, in obedience to a vague but amiable instinct, which prompted her to shield George, to deceive Gabriella, to deny the truth of facts, to do anything on earth except acknowledge the actual situation in which she found herself. "Don't you think she ought to go about more, George?"

"I don't care what she does," returned George brutally, while his blue eyes squinted in the old charming way from which all charm had departed. "I don't care—I don't care—" He checked himself, snapping his words in two with a virulent outburst of temper, and then, rising hurriedly, as his father entered the room, he left the table with his breakfast uneaten.

"He's so nervous. I can't imagine what's the matter. I hope Burrows wasn't in the pantry. Did you say anything to hurt his feelings before you came down, Gabriella?" asked Mrs. Fowler, distractedly, with one eye on her daughter-in-law and the other on the pantry door, through which the discreet Burrows had disappeared at the opportune instant.

"No, I haven't said anything that I can remember," answered Gabriella with calmness. It occurred to her that George's behaviour was hardly that of a man whose "feelings" had been wounded, but she made no audible record of her reflection; "and of course I'll go out with you if you want me to," she added, for she felt sincerely sorry for her mother-in-law, even though she had ruined George in his infancy. "I am going to the library to return a book, and we might pay some calls afterwards."

"That's just what I was thinking," responded Mrs. Fowler, embarrassed, bewildered. Was it possible, she asked herself, that Gabriella had not noticed George's outrageous behaviour?

But Gabriella did not "go about" with her mother-in-law that season, for a higher will than Mrs. Fowler's frustrated that lady's benevolent intentions. To a casual glance it would have seemed the merest accident which disturbed these felicitous plans, but such accidents, when Gabriella looked back on them afterwards, appeared to her to be woven into the very web and pattern of life. It was plainly incredible that her whole existence should be changed merely because Archibald was naughty, as incredible as the idea that Destiny should have used so small a medium for the accomplishment of its tragic designs.

But Archibald had hardly reached the Park before he was brought home, resisting with all his strength, because he had given his shoes and stockings away; and the next ten minutes, while Gabriella gently reasoned with him on the pavement, were pregnant with consequences.

"He's fierce, that's what he is," declared the nurse, who was Irish and militant. "He kicked me so I'm black and blue, ma'am, all over the shins, and every bit because I wouldn't let him pull off his shoes and socks and give 'em to a barefooted boy in the Park. You tell her, darlin'"—to Frances, who stood, bright-eyed and indignant, in her white fur coat and little fur cap which she wore drawn down tight over her curls—"you tell your mamma, darlin', you tell her how fierce and bold he was, and how he kicked me about the shins because I wouldn't let him take off his shoes and socks."

"The poor boy wanted 'em! I won't wear 'em! I will give 'em to the poor boy!" screamed Archibald, furious, scowling, struggling in the restraining hold of his nurse. He was a robust, thick-set child of four years, with a thatch of dark-brown hair, and strange near-sighted brown eyes, behind spectacles which he had worn from the time he could walk.

"What is it, Archibald? Tell me about it. Tell mother," pleaded Gabriella while he struggled desperately to escape from her tender grasp. "Who was the poor boy and where did you see him?"

"He oughtn't to have been in the Park, ought he, mamma?" inquired Frances, who was guiltless of democratic tendencies. "Ragged people have no right to be in the Park, have they?"

"Hush, darling, I want to hear what Archibald has to say. Tell me about him, Archibald. Shall you and I go out to look for him?"

"If you do, he'll pull his shoes and socks right off again," insisted Frances emphatically. "He had got one quite off and had given it to the boy before we saw him, and Nanny was obliged to go and take it back, and I had to hold Archibald while she put it on him. He screamed very loud and everybody stopped to ask what was the matter, and one old gentleman with a long beard, like Moses in the Bible, gave Archibald a little box of candy—he took it out of his pocket—but Archibald threw it away, and kept on hollerin' louder than ever—"

"That's right, darlin', you tell her," urged nurse, a stout woman with a red face and three gold teeth in the front of her mouth.

"I understand now. Don't tell any more, Fanny," said Gabriella. "Now, Archibald dear, will you stop crying and be good?"

"Am," replied Archibald sullenly, twisting out of her hands.

"Am what, darling?"

"Am good."

"Well, will you stop crying?"

"Have."

"Then what do you want? Shall we go back and look for the poor boy?"

"Hadn't any shoes. Feet were red. Wanted to give him shoes, 'cause I had plenty more at home. Nanny jerked him back. Hated Nanny. Hoped she would die. Hoped bears would eat her. Hoped tigers would eat her. Hoped lions would eat her. Hoped robins would cover her with leaves in the Park—"

While he sobbed out his accusations against nurse, Gabriella, holding his hand tightly in hers, turned toward Fifth Avenue, and by the time he was pacified, they had walked several blocks together, with nurse and Fanny sedately bringing up the rear. Then, at last, having reasoned him alike out of his temper and his generosity, Gabriella retraced her steps, and entering the house with her latchkey, ran quickly up the stairs to the closed door of Mrs. Fowler's room. As she raised her hand to knock the sound of her own name reached her, and almost involuntarily she hesitated for an instant.

"Yes, Gabriella is out. I saw her a minute ago on her way to the Park with the children."

"Well, somebody ought to tell her, mother. I think it is perfectly outrageous to keep her in ignorance. Everybody is talking about it."

"Oh, Patty, you couldn't! How on earth could you tell her a thing like that?" wailed George's mother, and she went on with a plaintive sigh as Gabriella opened the door: "George was always so mad about beauty, and though Gabriella has a fine face, she isn't exactly—"

Then, at the startling apparition of Gabriella, with her face paling slowly above her black furs and her large indignant eyes fixed on them both, Mrs. Fowler wavered and broke off with a pathetic clutch at the pleasantness which had entirely departed from her manner. "Why, Gabriella, I didn't know you had come in! I was just saying to Patty—" It was, as she said afterwards to her husband, exactly as if her mind had become suddenly blank. She couldn't to save her life think of a single word to add to her sentence, and all the time Gabriella was standing there, as white as a ghost, with her accusing eyes turning slowly from one to the other of them. "Somehow I just couldn't lie to her when she looked like that, and the truth seemed too dreadful," Mrs. Fowler added that night to Archibald. "Damn George!" was Mr. Fowler's fervent retort. "And it took me so by surprise I almost fainted, for I'd never in my life heard him swear before," his wife had commented later. "But aren't men strange? To think he knew how all the time and kept it to himself! I declare they are entirely too secretive for anything!"

"I heard what you were saying when I knocked," began Gabriella, with perfect composure. "I don't quite know what it was about, but I think—I think—"

"It was nothing, dear; Patty and I were gossiping," replied Mrs. Fowler, with an eagerness that was almost violent. "Oh, Patty, you wouldn't!"—for Patty had broken in, conquering and merciless, with the declaration: "If you don't tell Gabriella, mamma, I'm going to. It's outrageous, anyhow, I've always said so, the way people keep things from women. Gabriella has a right to know what everybody is saying."

"Of course I've a right to know," rejoined Gabriella, with a firmness before which Mrs. Fowler felt herself gradually dissolving—"melting away" was the description she gave of her feeling. "If anybody has a right to know, I suppose I have. Of course, it's about George. I know that much, anyhow," she added quietly.

"I don't believe it's half so bad as they say," protested Mrs. Fowler feverishly. "I don't believe he really keeps her. His father says he couldn't possibly do it on the allowance he gives him, and, you know, George doesn't make a cent himself—not a cent. He never supported himself in his life—"

She paused breathlessly, with a bright and confident glance as if she had made a point—a minor one perhaps, but still a point—in George's favour. The jet fringe on her bosom, which had rattled furiously with her excited palpitations, became gradually quiet, and as she pressed her lips firmly with her handkerchief, which she had rolled into a ball, she appeared to be pressing her customary smile back into place.

"It won't last, Gabriella," she began again very suddenly with renewed assurance. "These things never last, and I think Patty is quite wrong to insist upon telling you. Of course it is humiliating for a time, but—but"—she hesitated, and then brought out triumphantly—"he married very young, you know, and men aren't like women—there's no use pretending they are. Now when a woman loves a man—"

"But, you see, I don't love George," answered Gabriella, and her awful words seemed to reverberate through the horrified silence that surrounded her.

"Not love him? O Gabriella! Of course, it's natural that you should feel angry and wounded, and that your pride should resent what looks like an affront to you; but you can't mean in your heart that you've got over caring. Women don't change so easily. Why, you're his wife—poor foolish boy that he is—and Florrie—"

"So it's Florrie?" observed Gabriella, with a strangely dispassionate interest. It was queer, she reflected afterwards, that she had not felt the faintest curiosity about the woman.

"I always suspected that there was something wrong about her," pursued Mrs. Fowler, reassured by the knowledge that she was placing the blame where it belonged according to all the laws of custom and tradition. "I must say I never liked her manner and her way of dressing, and she made eyes at every man she was introduced to—even at Archibald—"

"Well, I didn't believe there was any real harm in her," said Gabriella, in a tone she might have used at one of her mother-in-law's luncheons. She was still standing near the door, in the very spot where she had paused at her entrance, with her head held high above the black fur at her throat, and one gloved hand playing with a bit of cord on the end of her muff. She could not possibly have taken it better. Bad as the situation was, it might have been a hundred times worse except for Gabriella's composure, thought Mrs. Fowler discreetly, adding with an inexplicable regret, that in her youth women were different. Yes, they had shown more feeling then, though they had behaved perhaps less well in a crisis. In spite of her gratitude—and she was sincerely grateful to her daughter-in-law for not making a scene—she became conscious presently that she was beginning to cherish an emotion not unlike resentment on George's account. That the discovery of George's faithlessness should be received so coolly by George's wife appeared almost an affront to him. Mrs. Fowler liked Gabriella, she was fond of her—and nobody could look in the girl's face and not see that she was a fine woman—but there were times, and this was one of them, when she thought her a little hard. Had Gabriella wept, had she raged, had she threatened Florrie's life or happiness, it might have been painful, but at least it would have been human; and above all things Mrs. Fowler felt that she liked women to be human.

"Nothing that anybody says or does can excuse George," said Patty sternly. "He has behaved abominably, and if I were Gabriella, I'd simply wash my hands of him. I don't care if he is my brother, that doesn't make me blind, does it? If he were my husband," she concluded passionately, "I'd feel just the same way about it."

"Oh, you mustn't! Oh, Patty, hush, it's wicked! It's sinful!" moaned Mrs. Fowler, shutting her eyes, as if the sight of Patty's indignant loveliness gave her a headache. "Don't try to harden Gabriella's heart against him. Don't try to make her think she's really stopped loving him."

Gabriella's answer to this outburst was a look which, as poor Mrs. Fowler said afterwards, "cut her to the heart." Backing weakly to a chair, the valiant little lady sat down suddenly, because she felt that her legs were giving way beneath the weight of her body. And, though she was unaware of its significance, her action was deeply symbolical of the failure of the old order to withstand the devastating advance of the new spirit. She felt vaguely that she wished women and things were both what they used to be; but this, since she had little imagination, was as far as she penetrated into the psychology of Gabriella's behaviour.

"But, you see, you're making the mistake of thinking that I love George," said Gabriella, with a reasonableness which made Mrs. Fowler feel that she wanted to scream, "and I don't love him—I don't love him at all. I haven't loved him for a long time—not since the night I saw him drunk. How could I love a man I've seen drunk—disgustingly drunk—a man I couldn't respect? I'm not made that way, and I can't help it. Some women may be like that, but I'm not. I couldn't, even if I wanted to, love a man who has treated me as George has done. I don't see how any woman could—any woman with a particle of pride and self-respect. Of course I had to live with him after I married him," she finished abruptly. "Marriage isn't made for love. I used to think it was—but it isn't—"

"But, Gabriella, you don't mean—you can't—" Mrs. Fowler was really pitiable, for, after all, George was her son, and the ties of blood would not break so easily as the ties of marriage. In the depths of her humiliation she had almost convinced herself that she had never respected George, that she had never believed in him, forgetting the pride and adoration of her young motherhood. Whatever George did she could not change his relation to her—she could not shatter the one indissoluble bond that holds mankind together.

"Gabriella, you don't—you can't—" she repeated wildly.

Then, as Gabriella turned quickly and left the room, a scene—she became conscious presently that she was beginning to cherish an emotion not unlike resentment on George's account. That the discovery of George's faithlessness should be received so coolly by George's wife appeared almost an affront to him. Mrs. Fowler liked Gabriella, she was fond of her—and nobody could look in the girl's face and not see that she was a fine woman—but there were times, and this was one of them, when she thought her a little hard. Had Gabriella wept, had she raged, had she threatened Florrie's life or happiness, it might have been painful, but at least it would have been human; and above all things Mrs. Fowler felt that she liked women to be human.

"Nothing that anybody says or does can excuse George," said Patty sternly. "He has behaved abominably, and if I were Gabriella, I'd simply wash my hands of him. I don't care if he is my brother, that doesn't make me blind, does it? If he were my husband," she concluded passionately, "I'd feel just the same way about it."

"Oh, you mustn't! Oh, Patty, hush, it's wicked! It's sinful!" moaned Mrs. Fowler, shutting her eyes, as if the sight of Patty's indignant loveliness gave her a headache. "Don't try to harden Gabriella's heart against him. Don't try to make her think she's really stopped loving him."

Gabriella's answer to this outburst was a look which, as poor Mrs. Fowler said afterwards, "cut her to the heart." Backing weakly to a chair, the valiant little lady sat down suddenly, because she felt that her legs were giving way beneath the weight of her body. And, though she was unaware of its significance, her action was deeply symbolical of the failure of the old order to withstand the devastating advance of the new spirit. She felt vaguely that she wished women and things were both what they used to be; but this, since she had little imagination, was as far as she penetrated into the psychology of Gabriella's behaviour.

"But, you see, you're making the mistake of thinking that I love George," said Gabriella, with a reasonableness which made Mrs. Fowler feel that she wanted to scream, "and I don't love him—I don't love him at all. I haven't loved him for a long time—not since the night I saw him drunk. How could I love a man I've seen drunk—disgustingly drunk—a man I couldn't respect? I'm not made that way, and I can't help it. Some women may be like that, but I'm not. I couldn't, even if I wanted to, love a man who has treated me as George has done. I don't see how any woman could—any woman with a particle of pride and self-respect. Of course I had to live with him after I married him," she finished abruptly. "Marriage isn't made for love. I used to think it was—but it isn't—"

"But, Gabriella, you don't mean—you can't—" Mrs. Fowler was really pitiable, for, after all, George was her son, and the ties of blood would not break so easily as the ties of marriage. In the depths of her humiliation she had almost convinced herself that she had never respected George, that she had never believed in him, forgetting the pride and adoration of her young motherhood. Whatever George did she could not change his relation to her—she could not shatter the one indissoluble bond that holds mankind together.

"Gabriella, you don't—you can't—" she repeated wildly.

Then, as Gabriella turned quickly and left the room, Mrs. Fowler rose stoically to her feet, adjusted her belt with a tremulous movement of her hands, and smiled bravely as she went to the mirror to put on her hat. Heartbroken and distraught of mind though she was, she submitted instinctively to the lifelong tyranny of appearances.

# CHAPTER II

## A SECOND START IN LIFE

With deliberation Gabriella walked the length of the hall to her room, turned and locked the door after she had entered, and took off her hat and wraps and put them away in the closet. Her head was still carried high and her eyes were defiant and dark in the marble-like pallor of her face. Except for her burning eyes and the scarlet line of her tightly closed lips, she looked as still and as cold as a statue.

"I'd rather die than have them know that it made any difference," she thought. "I'd rather die than have them know that I cared." Then sinking into a chair by the dressing-table, she laid her head on her arm and wept tears, not of wounded love, but of deep and passionate anger.

She had spoiled her life! Because of her mad and headstrong folly, she had spoiled her life, and she was barely twenty-seven! Had she been the veriest fool she couldn't have done worse—she who had thought herself so sensible, so strong, so efficient! Jane couldn't have done worse, and yet she had always despised Jane for her weakness. But she had been as weak as Jane, she had been as unreasonable, she had been as incredibly sentimental and silly. And even in her folly she had irretrievably failed. She had made her choice, and yet she had not been able to keep the thing she had chosen. George had tired of her—here was the sharpest sting—a man had tired of her after a few months—had tired of her while she was still deeply in love with him. Her humiliation, while she sat there strangling her sobs, was so intense that it ran in little flames over her body. At the moment she was not angry with George, she was not even angry with Florrie. It was as if all the slumbering violence of her nature was aroused to a burning and relentless hatred of her own weakness. This emotion, which was so profound, so torrential, in its force that it seemed to shake the depths of her being, left room for no other feeling—for no other thought in her consciousness. She had but one life to live, and by her own fault, she had ruined it in its beginning.

Then her mood changed, and she sat up, straight and stern, while she wiped her reddened eyelids with an impetuous and resolute gesture. No, she was not crushed; she would not allow herself even to be hurt. Her lot might be as sordid as Jane's, but she would make it different by the strength and the effectiveness of her resistance. She would never submit as Jane submitted; she would never become, through sheer inertia, a part of the ugliness that enveloped her. Thanks to the vein of iron in her soul she would never—no, not if she died fighting—become one of the victims of life.

Going into the dressing-room, she bathed her eyes with cold water; and she was still drying them before the mirror when the children came in, flushed and blooming, with their hands in Miss Polly Hatch's. What splendid children they were, she thought, looking wistfully at their eager faces. Any father, any mother in the world, might be proud of them. Fanny, the elder, was like an angel in her white fur coat and pert little cap, with her short golden curls like bunches of yellow silk on her shoulders, and her blue eyes, as grave as a philosopher's, beaming softly under her thick jet-black lashes. She was not particularly bright; she was, for her age, an unconscionable snob; but no one could deny that she was as beautiful as an angel to look at.

"Miss Polly wanted to kiss me, mamma, but I wouldn't," she said coolly as she examined a little bundle of sewing the seamstress had put down on the table. "I needn't kiss people if I don't want to, need I? Archibald doesn't like to kiss either. He's naughty about it sometimes when ladies ask him to. He doesn't like scratchin'. Isn't it funny to call kissing, 'scratchin'? He told me Miss Polly scratched him and he didn't like it. He is afraid of her because she is so ugly. Why are you ugly, Miss Polly? Couldn't you help it? Did God make you ugly just for fun? Why doesn't he make everybody pretty? I would if I were God. What is God's last name? Archibald says it is Walker. Is it Walker, mamma, and how does Archibald know? Who told him—"

When at last she was suppressed and sent out of the room with the nurse, she went at a dancing step, turning to make faces at Archibald, who stood stolidly at his mother's knee, biting deep bites into a red apple Miss Polly had given him. He was not a handsome child, even Gabriella admitted that his spectacles spoiled his appearance; but he was remarkably intelligent for his four years, and he was so strong and sturdy that he had never had a day's illness in his life. His face was unusually thoughtful and expressive, and his eyes, in spite of the disfiguring glasses, were large, brown, and beautiful, with something of the luminous softness of Cousin Jimmy's. Though she could not remember her father, it pleased Gabriella to think that Archibald was like him, and Miss Polly declared, with conviction, that he was "already his living image." Of the two children, for some obscure reason which she could not define and which was probably rooted in instinct, Gabriella had the greater tenderness for her son; and though she denied this preference to herself, Mrs. Fowler and Miss Polly had both commented upon it. Even his temper, which was uncontrollable at times, endeared him to her, and the streak of savage in his nature seemed to awaken some dim ancestral memories in her brain.

"Thank Miss Polly for the apple and run away to Fanny," said his mother, after she had held him pressed closely to her breast for a minute. While she did so, she felt, with profound sadness, that her whole universe had dwindled down to her children. Of all her happiness only her children remained to her.

"Don't want to run," replied Archibald with beaming good humour. In his passion for brevity he eliminated pronouns whenever it was possible.

"But Fanny is waiting for you."

"Would rather stay with mother than go with Fanny and Mutton." That was another of his eccentricities. Just as he had insisted that God's "last name was Walker," so he had begun of his own accord, and for no visible reason, to call nurse "Mutton." He was always fitting names of his own invention to persons; and in his selection he was guided by a principle so obscure that Gabriella had never been able to discover its origin. Thus his grandmother from the first had been "Budd," and he had immediately started to call Miss Polly "Pang."

"Don't you want to go back to the Park, Archibald? You must finish your walk."

"Will the poor boy be there?" He never forgot anything. It was quite probable that he would inquire for "the poor boy" a year hence.

"Perhaps. You might take him an apple and a penny."

He stood gravely considering the plan, with one hand in his mother's and one on Miss Polly's knee.

"I'll take Pang to nurse him," he said when he had decided against the suggestion of the apple and the penny. "He hasn't any nurse, and Fanny wouldn't like him to have hers. I'll take Pang."

"But Pang isn't a nurse, dear. There, now, run to Fanny. Miss Polly lives so far away she can't stay very long."

He went obediently, for he was usually amenable to his mother's commands, stopping only once at the door to ask if "Pang lived as far away as God and could she manage to get a message to Him about the poor boy needing shoes?"

"I declare I can't make out that child to save my soul," remarked Miss Polly as he shut the door carefully and ran down the hall to the nursery. "The more I study him the curiouser he seems to me. If he wan't so quick about some things you might think his wits were sort of addled—but they ain't, are they? Now, whatever do you reckon put the notion in his head to call me 'Pang?'"

All the smiling, circular wrinkles in her face were working with amusement while her little black eyes twinkled like jet beads above the ruddy creases in her cheeks.

"I can't imagine, for he must have made up the word for himself. But don't you think he is like father, Miss Polly? I love to hear you say so."

"That child? Why, he's the very spit of yo' pa, Gabriella, and there ain't any two ideas about it. I thought so the very first time I ever saw him, and now that I come to think of it, it is exactly like yo' pa to be makin' up all kinds of foolish names out of nothin'. Yo' pa used to call me Poll Parrot, that he did."

"Mother thinks Archibald is going to be very much like him. She saw him in the mountains last summer."

"So she told me when I was down home. You ain't looking a bit well, Gabriella. You've got exactly the look Miss Letty Marshall had before she came down with heart complaint. The doctors were fussin' over her for weeks before they could find out what the trouble was, but I said all along it wan't nothin' in the world but a bruised heart, and sure enough that was just what they found out was the matter. You ain't had a feelin' of heart burn after you eat, have you? Sometimes it don't take you that way, though; you just begin to have palpitations when you go up and down stairs and then you start to wakin' up in the night with shortness of breath. That's the way my Aunt Lydy had it. You know I nursed her till she died, and I've seen her get right black in the face when she stooped to pick up a pin. It's her daughter Lydy that's waiting on old Mrs. Peyton now. You know Mrs. Peyton was feelin' kind of run down so her son

Arthur—I call him Arthur to his face because I used to sew there when he wan't more'n knee high—well, Arthur said she'd have to have somebody to wait on her every minute and she thought she'd rather have Lydy than anybody else because Lydy was always so handy in a sickroom. That was six months ago, and Lydy's been stayin' on there ever since. She says there ain't anybody on earth like Mr. Arthur, and she never could make out why you didn't marry him. He ain't ever had an eye for anybody but you, and he's got yo' picture—the one in the white dress—on his bureau and he keeps a rose in a vase before it all the time. That ain't much like a man, but then there always was a heap of a girl in Arthur in little ways, wan't there?"

"I wonder why I didn't marry him?" said Gabriella softly; and not until Miss Polly answered her, was she aware that she had spoken aloud. In her spiritual reaction from the grosser reality of passion, the delicacy and remoteness of Arthur's love borrowed the pious and mystic qualities of religious worship. She had seen the sordid and ugly sides of sex; and she felt now a profound disgust for the emotion which drew men and women together—for the light in the eyes, the touch of the lips, the clinging of the hands. Once she had idealized these things into love itself; now the very memory of them filled her with repulsion. She still wanted love, but a love so pure, so disembodied, so ethereal that it was liberated from the dominion of flesh. In the beginning, as a girl, she had accepted love as the supreme good, as the essential reality; now, utterly disillusioned, she asked herself: "What is there left in life? What is the thing that really counts, after all? What is the possession that makes all the striving worth while in the end? At twenty-seven love is over for me, and if love is over, what remains to fill the rest of my life? There must be something else—there must be a reality somewhere which is truer, which is profounder, than love." This, she knew, was the question which neither tradition nor custom could answer. Religion, perhaps, might have helped her; but it was characteristic of her generation that she should give religion hardly a thought as a possible solution of the problem of life. She wanted substance, facts, experience; she wanted to examine, to analyze, to discover; and it was just here that religion hopelessly failed her as a guide. Faith she had had in her cradle—faith in life, faith in love, faith in herself; and it was faith that had brought her to this bleak disenchantment of spirit. No, she wanted knowledge now, not faith; she wanted truth, not illusion.

"Well, you never can tell about a thing like that," Miss Polly was saying in her sprightly way, quite as if she were discussing the pattern of a dress or the stitching of a seam. "It was feelin', I reckon, and feelin' is one of the things nobody can count on. But you did mighty well, even if you didn't marry Arthur. I saw Mr. George downtown yesterday, when I went around to Stern's to match the edging for a baby dress, and I thought to myself I'd seldom seen a handsomer piece of flesh than he was. He was walkin' along up Fifth Avenue with Florrie Spencer—I'll always call her Florrie Spencer I don't care how many times she marries—and everybody in the street turned right plumb round to look at 'em. She's prettier than she ever was, ain't she? And such a fit as her dress was! One of them trailin' black things that fit as tight as wax over the hips and flares out all round the feet. She was holdin' up her skirts to show her feet, I reckon, and her collar was so high behind her ears, she could hardly turn her head to look at Mr. George. But I never saw anybody with more style—no, not if it was that Mrs. Pletheridge who is everlastingly in the Sunday papers. I declare Florrie's waist didn't look much bigger round than the leg of that table— honestly it didn't—and her hat was perched on a bandeau so high that you could see the new sort of way she'd gone and had her hair crimped—they call it Marcellin' up here, don't they?"

"Was she with George?" asked Gabriella indifferently.

"They were goin' to some restaurant or another for tea, I reckon, and they certainly were a fine-lookin' pair. I wish you could have seen 'em. Not that you wouldn't have been a match for 'em," she added consolingly. "You and Mr. George look mighty well when you're together. You're just on a level, and if you could manage to tighten yo' corset a little mite at the waist, and hold yo'self with that bend out at the back the way Florrie does, you'd have pretty near as fine a figure as she has. Ain't it funny," she added irrelevantly, "but I was just studyin' last night about the way yo' ma used to say that all yo' folks married badly. I reckon she got that idea along of yo' pa's kin. You don't recollect much about 'em, but one of yo' pa's brothers married a woman who went clean deranged inside of a year and tried to kill him. Then there was yo' Cousin Nelly Harrison—she married badly, or only middlin' well anyway. There certainly was a lot of 'em when you come to think—not countin' Jane and Mr. Charley, and I can't help what happens," she concluded sentimentally, "I ain't ever goin' back on Mr. Charley—not after the way he sent me two loads of coal the winter I was laid up with rheumatism and couldn't work. Well, it's about time for me to be goin', Gabriella. If you want me for anything, you just drop me a line to say so. William's children are gettin' so big, I can come out for the day 'most any time now, and if William's courtin' goes on all right, I reckon he won't be wantin' me much longer. He's been waitin' on a young woman right steady for more'n six months, and it wouldn't surprise me a bit if something was to come of it befo' summer."

"Then you'd go South again, wouldn't you?" There was a wistful sound in Gabriella's voice as she put the question. Miss Polly was a tiresome person, but at least she was faithful, and long habit had established a bond of tolerance, if not of affection, between them. In the last few months Gabriella had grown to look upon her as the one living association with her childhood, and she was so lonely that she dreaded to sever the single tie with the past that still remained to her. "I believe she'd work her fingers to the bone for me, and, of course, she can't help being so garrulous," she thought.

"I reckon I will, if it comes to that, but I'd hate like anything to leave you and the children," answered Miss Polly. "I feel somehow as if I belonged up here with you all, and I've grown real fond of Archibald."

"Yes, I'd hate to give you up," said Gabriella, as she let her go and turned back again into the room. Her brain had worked quickly while Miss Polly was talking, and the undercurrent of gossip had helped, rather than retarded, the clearness and rapidity of her thoughts. All her weakness, all her anger had passed. She saw the situation without exaggeration and without illusion, for she had made her decision in the few minutes between the entrance and the departure of the seamstress. The embittering memories of her life with George were submerged in the invigorating waves of energy that flooded her being. Her inert body responded to the miraculous restoration of her spirit; and, while she walked swiftly from the door to the window, she had a sensation of lightness and ease as if she had just awakened from a refreshing sleep. For seven years all the strength of her character had been drained by the supreme function of motherhood; but now her children had ceased to need the whole of her life, and she was free to belong at least in part to herself—free to enter unrestricted into the broader human activities. And, above all, she was free from George. She had escaped from the humiliating bondage of her marriage; for, since he had broken the tie between them, she realized with a strange, an almost unnatural, exhilaration, how little except duty—how little except the bare legal husk of the marriage contract—still held her to him. She had loved him once, but she loved him no longer, and she resolved passionately that she would not allow her life to be spoiled because of a single mistake. Seven years were lost out of her youth, it was true, but those years had given her her children, and so they were not wasted in spite of the mistakes she had made, of the shame she had suffered. Judged simply as a machine she was of greater value at twenty-seven than she had been at twenty, and a part of this value lay in her deeper knowledge of life. She had had her adventure, and she was cured forever of adventurous desires. Her imagination, as well as her body, was firmer, harder, more disciplined than it had been in her girlhood; and if her vision of the universe was less sympathetic, it was also less sentimental. The bluest eyes in the world, she told herself sternly, could not trouble her fancy to-day, nor could the wildest romance quicken her pulses.

A wagon, filled with blue and white hyacinths, passed by in the street, and while she watched it, there flashed into her mind, with the swiftness of light, a memory of the evening when she had broken her engagement to Arthur. All her life he had loved her, and, but for an accident, she might have married him. If she had not seen George at Florrie's party—if she had not seen him under a yellow lantern, with the glow in his eyes, and a dreamy waltz floating from the arbour of roses at the end of the garden—if this had not happened, she would have married Arthur instead of George, and her whole life would have been different. Because of a single instant, because of a chance meeting, she had wrecked the happiness of three lives. Now, when the bloom had dropped from her love, it was impossible for her to gather the withered leaves and bare stems in her hands and find any fragrance about them; it was impossible for her to understand how or why she had followed so fleeting an impulse. People had told her that love lasted forever, yet she knew that her emotion for George was so utterly dead that there was no warmth left in the ashes. It had all been so vivid once, and now it was as dull and colourless as the dust drifting after the blue and white hyacinths.

From the trail of dust and the fragrance of the hyacinths, Arthur's face floated up to her, grave, gentle, and thin-featured, with its look of detached culture, of nameless distinction. She recalled the colour of his eyes, as clear and cool as running water, his sensitive lips under the thin, brown moustache, and his slender, aristocratic hands, with their touch as soft and as tender as a woman's. "He had intellect—he had culture—I suppose these are the things that really matter," she thought, for George, she knew, possessed neither of these qualities. And, as she remembered Arthur, she was stirred, not by tenderness, but by a passionate gratitude. He had loved her, and by loving her, he had saved her pride from defeat. In the hour of her deepest humiliation, she found comfort in the knowledge of his bleeding heart, of his tragic and beautiful loyalty; for though she was strong enough to live without love, she was not strong enough to live with the thought that no man had ever loved her.

For a few minutes she allowed her fancy to play with the comforting memory of Arthur's devotion—with the image of her photograph on his bureau and the single rose in the vase he kept always before it. "But for an accident I might have loved him," she said, and the thought of this love which might have been sent a wave of sweetness to her heart. "I might have loved him and been happy." The vision was so dangerously beautiful that she put it resolutely away from her, and told herself, with an effort to be philosophical, that there was no use whatever in regretting the past, and since love was over for her, she must set her mind to solve the problem of work. "I've got my life to live," she said with stoical calmness, "and however bad it is I've nobody to blame for it but myself."

Then, because she had only one talent, however small, she changed her dress, and went out to ask for a position as designer, saleswoman, or milliner in the house of Dinard.

The Irish woman, voluble, painted, powdered, bewigged, and with the remains of her handsome figure laced into a black satin gown, nodded her false golden locks and smiled an ambiguous smile when she heard the explanation of young Mrs. Fowler's afternoon call.

"But, no, it ees impossible," she protested, forgetting her foreign shrug and preserving with difficulty the trace of an accent. Then, becoming suddenly natural as she realized that no immediate profit was to be derived from affectation, she added decisively, "you have no training, and I have quite as many salesladies as I need at this season. Not that you are not chic," she hastened to conclude, "not that you would not in appearance be an adornment to any establishment."

"I am willing to do anything," said Gabriella, pressing her point with characteristic tenacity. "I want to learn, you know, I want to learn everything I possibly can. You yourself told me that I had a natural gift for designing, and I am anxious to turn it to some account. I believe I can make a very good milliner, and I want to try."

"But what would Madame Fowler, your mother-in-law, say to this? Surely no one would want to earn her living unless she was obliged to."

For Madame had known life, as she often remarked, and the knowledge so patiently acquired had gone far to confirm her natural suspicion of human nature. She had got on, as she observed in confidential moments, by believing in nobody; and this skepticism, which was fundamental and rooted in principle, had inspired her behaviour not only to her patrons, but to her husband, her children, her domestic servants, her tradespeople, and the policeman at the corner. Thirty years ago she had suspected the entire masculine world of amorous designs upon her person; to-day, secretly numbering her years at sixty-two, and publicly acknowledging forty-five of them, she suspected the same world of equally active, if less romantic, intentions regarding her purse. And if she distrusted men, she both distrusted and despised women. She distrusted and despised them because they were poor workers, because they were idlers by nature, because they allowed themselves to be cheated, slighted, underpaid, underfed, and oppressed, and, most of all, she despised them because they were the victims of their own emotions. Love was all very well, she was accustomed to observe, as a pleasurable pursuit, but, as with any other pursuit, when it began to impair the appetite and to affect the quality and the quantity of one's work, then a serious person would at once contrive to get rid of the passion. And Madame prided herself with reason upon being a strictly serious person. She had been through the experience of love innumerable times; she had lost four husbands, and, as she pointed out with complacency, she was still living.

In the dubious splendour of her showrooms, which were curtained and carpeted in velvet, and decorated with artificial rose-bushes flowering magnificently from white and gold jardinières, six arrogant young women, in marvellously fitting gowns of black satin, strolled back and forth all day long, or stood gracefully, with the exaggerated curve of the period, awaiting possible customers. Though they were as human within as Madame Dinard—and beneath her make-up she was very human indeed—nothing so variable as an expression ever crossed the waxlike immobility of their faces; and while they trailed their black satin trains over the rich carpets, amid the lustrous piles of silks and velvets which covered the white and gold tables, they appeared to float through an atmosphere of eternal enchantment. Watching them, Gabriella wondered idly if they could ever unbend at the waist, if they could ever let down those elaborate and intricate piles of hair. Then she overheard the tallest and most arrogant of them remark, "I'm just crazy about him, but he's dead broke," and she realized that they also belonged to the unsatisfied world of humanity.

Madame, who had slipped away to answer the telephone, came rustling back, and sank, wheezing, into a white and gilt chair, which was too small to contain the whole of her ample person. Though she had spoken quite sharply at the telephone, her voice was mellifluous when she attuned it to Gabriella.

"That gown is perfect on you," she remarked in honied accents. "It was one of my best models last season, and as I said before, Madame, you are so fortunate as to wear your clothes with a grace." She was urbane, but she was anxious to be rid of her, this young Mrs. Fowler could see at a glance. "Your head is well set on your shoulders, and that is rare—very rare! It would surprise you to know how few women have heads that are well set on their shoulders. Yes, I understand. You wish to learn, but not to make a living. That is very good, for the only comfortable way for a woman to make her living is to marry one—a man is the only perfectly satisfactory means of livelihood. I tell this to my daughter, who wishes to go on the stage. If you are looking for pleasure, that is different, but when you talk of a living—well, there is but one way to insure it, and that is to marry a man who is able to provide it—either as allowance or as alimony. The best that a woman can do gives her only bread and meat—an existence, not a living. Only a man can provide one with the essential things— with clothes and jewels and carriages and trips to Europe. These are the important things in life, and what woman was ever able to procure these except from a man?"

Her face, so thickly covered with rouge and liquid powder that it was as expressionless as a mask, turned its hollow eyes on a funeral which was slowly passing in the street; and though her creed was hardly the kind to fortify one's spiritual part against the contemplation of death, she surveyed the solemn procession as tranquilly as any devoted adherent of either religion or philosophy could have done. Not a shadow passed over her fantastic mockery of youth as she glanced back at her visitor.

"But you have worked—you have supported yourself," insisted Gabriella with firmness.

"Myself and six children, to say nothing of three husbands. Yes, I supported three of my four husbands, but what did I get out of it?" replied Madame, shrugging her ample shoulders. "What was there in it for me? Since we are talking freely, I may say that I have worked hard all my life, and I got nothing out of it that I couldn't have got with much less trouble by a suitable marriage. Of course this is not for my girls to hear. I don't tell them this, but it is true nevertheless. Men should do the work of the world, and they should support women; that is how God intended it, that is according to both nature and religion; any priest will say as much to you." And she, who had defied both God and Nature, wagged her false golden head toward the funeral procession.

"Yet you have been successful. You have built up a good business. The work has repaid you."

"A woman's work!" She snapped her gouty fingers with a playful gesture. "Does a woman's work ever repay her? Think of the pleasures I have missed in my life—the excursions, the theatres, the shows. All these I might have had if I hadn't shut myself up every day until dark. And now you wish to do this! You with your youth, with your style, with your husband!"

She protested, she pleaded, she reasoned, but in the end Gabriella won her point by the stubborn force of her will. Madame would take her for a few weeks, a few months, a few years, as long as she cared to stay and gave satisfaction. Madame would have her taught what she could learn, would discover by degrees the natural gifts and the amount of training already possessed by young Mrs.

Fowler. Young Mrs. Fowler, on the other hand, must "stand around" when required in the showrooms (it was just here that Gabriella won her victory); she must assist at the ordering of gowns, at the selections, and while Madame's patrons were fitted, young Mrs. Fowler must be prepared to assume graceful attitudes in the background and to offer her suggestions with a persuasive air. Suggestions, even futile ones, offered in a charming voice from a distinguished figure in black satin had borne wonderful results in Madame's experience.

"I began that way myself, Mrs. Fowler. You may not believe it, but I was once slenderer than you are—my waist measured only nineteen inches and my bust thirty-six—just the figure a man most admires. The result was, you see, that I have had four husbands, though it is true that I supported three of them, and it is always easy to marry if one provides the support. Men are like that. It is their nature. Yes, I began that way with little training, but much natural talent, and a head full of ideas. If one has ideas it is always possible to become a success, but they are rarer even than waists measuring nineteen inches. And I had charm, though you might not believe it now, for charm does not wear. But I made my way up from the bottom, first as errand girl, at the age of ten, and I made it, not by work, for I could never handle a needle, but by ideas. They were once plentiful, and now they are so scarce," she broke off with a sigh of resignation which seemed to accept every fact of experience except the fact of age. "It was a hard life, but it was life, after all. One is not put here to be contented, or one would dread death too much for the purpose of God." In spite of her uncompromising materialism, she was not without an ineradicable streak of superstition which she would probably have called piety.

"I am ready to begin at once—to-morrow," said Gabriella, and she added without explanation, obeying, perhaps, an intuitive feeling that to explain a statement is to weaken it, "and I should like to be called by my maiden name while I am here—just Mrs. Carr, if you don't mind."

To this request Madame agreed with effusion, if not with sincerity. For her own part she would have preferred to speak of her saleswoman as young Mrs. Fowler; but she reflected comfortably that many of her patrons would know young Mrs. Fowler by sight at least, and to the others she might conveniently drop a word or two in due season. To drop a word or two would provide entertainment throughout the length of a fitting; and, for the rest, the mystery of the situation had its charm for the romantic Irish strain in her blood. The prospect of securing both entertainment and mystery at the modest expenditure of fifteen dollars a week impressed her as very good business, for she combined in the superlative degree the opposite qualities of romance and economy. To be sure, except for the advertisement she afforded and the gossip she provided, young Mrs. Fowler might not prove to be worth even her modest salary; but there was, on the other hand, a remote possibility that she might turn out to be gifted, and Madame would then be able to use her inventiveness to some purpose before the gifted one discovered her value. In any case, Madame was at liberty to discharge her with a day's notice, and her salary would hardly be increased for three months even should she persist in her eccentricity and develop a positive talent for dressmaking. And if young Mrs. Fowler could do nothing else, Madame reflected as they parted, she could at least receive customers and display models with an imposing, even an aristocratic, demeanour.

To receive Madame's customers and display Madame's models were the last occupations Gabriella would have chosen had she been able to penetrate Madame's frivolous wig to her busy brain and detect her prudent schemes for the future; but the girl was sick of her dependence on George's father, and, in the revolt of her pride, she would have accepted any honest work which would have enabled her to escape from the insecurity of her position. Of her competence to earn a living, of her ability to excel in any work that she undertook, of the sufficiency and soundness of her resources, she was as absolutely assured as she had been when she entered the millinery department of Brandywine & Plummer. If Madame, starting penniless, had nevertheless contrived, through her native abilities, to support three husbands and six children, surely the capable and industrious Gabriella might assume smaller burdens with the certainty of moderate success. It was not, when one considered it, the life which one would have chosen, but who, since the world began, had ever lived exactly the life of his choice? Many women, she reflected stoically, were far worse off than she, since she started not only with a modicum of business experience (for surely the three months with Brandywine & Plummer might weigh as that) but with a knowledge of the world and a social position which she had found to be fairly marketable. That Madame Dinard would have accepted an unknown and undistinguished applicant for work at a salary of fifteen dollars a week she did not for an instant imagine. This inadequate sum, she concluded with a touch of ironic humour, represented the exact value in open market of her marriage to George.

In the front room, where a sparse mid-winter collection of hats ornamented the scattered stands, she stopped for a few minutes to inspect, with a critical eye, the dingy array. "I wonder what makes them buy so many they can't sell?" she said half aloud to the model at which she was gazing. "Nobody would wear these hats—certainly nobody who could afford to buy Parisian models. I could design far better hats than these, I myself, and if I were the head of the house I should never have accepted any of them, no matter who bought them. I suppose, after all, it's the fault of the buyer, but it's a waste—it's not economy."

Lifting a green velvet toque trimmed with a skinny white ostrich feather from the peg before which she was standing, she surveyed the august French name emblazoned in gold on the lining. "Everything isn't good that comes from Paris," she thought, with a shrug which was worthy of Madame at her best. "Why, I wonder, can't Americans produce 'ideas' themselves? Why do we always have to depend on the things the French send over to us? Half the hats and gowns Madame has aren't really good, and yet she makes people pay tremendous prices for things she knows are bad and undistinguished. All that ought to be changed, and if I ever succeed, if I ever catch on, I am going to change it." An idea, a whole flock of ideas, came to her while she stood there with her rapt gaze on the green velvet toque, which nobody had bought, and which she knew would shortly be "marked down," august French name included, from forty to fifteen and from fifteen to five dollars. Her constructive imagination was at work recreating the business, and she saw it in fancy made over and made right from the bottom—she saw Madame's duplicity succeeded by something of Brandywine & Plummer's inflexible honesty, and the flimsy base of the structure supplanted by a solid foundation of credit. For she had come often enough to Dinard's to discern the slipshod and unsystematic methods beneath the ornate and extravagant surface. Her naturally quick powers of observation had detected at a glance conditions of which the elder Mrs. Fowler was never aware. To sell gowns and hats at treble their actual value, to cajole her customers into buying what they did not want and what did not suit them, to give inferior goods, inferior workmanship, inferior style wherever they would be accepted, and to get always the most money for the least possible expenditure of ability, industry, and honesty—these were the fundamental principles, Gabriella had already discovered, beneath Madame's flourishing, but shallow-rooted, prosperity. Brandywine & Plummer did not carry Parisian models; their shop was not fashionable in the way that the establishment of a New York dressmaker and milliner must be fashionable; but the standard of excellence in all things excepting style was far higher in the old Broad Street house in the middle 'nineties than it was at Madame Dinard's during the early years of the new century. Quality had been essential in every hat that went from Brandywine & Plummer's millinery department; and Gabriella, deriving from a mother who worked only in fine linen, rejected instinctively the cheap, the tawdry, and the inferior. She had heard a customer complain one day of the quality of the velvet on a hat Madame had made to order; and pausing to look at the material as she went out, she had decided that the most prosperous house in New York could not survive many incidents of that deplorable sort. To be sure, such material would not have been supplied to Mrs. Pletheridge, or even to the elder Mrs. Fowler, who, though Southern, was always particular and very often severe; but here again, since this cheap hat had been sold at a high price, was a vital weakness in Madame's business philosophy.

On the whole, there were many of Madame's methods which might be improved; and when Gabriella passed through the ivory and gold doorway into the street, she had convinced herself that she was preëminently designed by Nature to undertake the necessary work of improvement. The tawdriness she particularly disliked—the trashy gold and ivory of the decorations, the artificial rose-bushes from which the dust was never removed, the sumptuous velvet carpets which were not taken up in the summer.

While she was crossing the street a man joined her; and glancing up as soon as she was clear of the traffic, she saw that it was Judge Crowborough. In the last seven years her dislike for him had gradually disappeared, and though she had never found him attractive, she had grown to accept the general estimate of his character and ability. A man so gifted ought not to be judged as severely as poorer or less actively intelligent mortals; and as long as other men did not judge him, she felt no inclination to usurp so unfeminine a prerogative. He had always been kind to her, and she understood now from his manner that he meant to be still kinder. It occurred to her at once that he knew of George's infatuation for Florrie, and that he was chivalrously extending to George's wife a sympathy which he would probably have withheld in such circumstances from his own. Had it been possible she would have liked to explain to him that in her case his sympathy was not needed; but she realized, with resentment, that one of her most galling burdens would be the wasted pity which her unfortunate situation would inspire in the friends of the family. Social conventions made it impossible for her to tell the world, including Judge Crowborough, that George's infidelity was a matter of slight importance to her, since it struck only at her pride, not at her heart. Her pride, it is true, had suffered sharply for an hour; but so superficial was the wound that the distraction of seeking work had been almost sufficient to heal it.

"A most extraordinary day for January," remarked the judge as they reached a corner. "You hardly need your furs, the air is so mild."

Overhead small, birdlike clouds drifted in flocks across a sky of changeable brightness, and the wind, blowing past the tray of a flower vendor at the corner, was faintly scented with violets. It was one of those rare days when happiness seems as natural as the wind or the sunlight, when the wildest dreams appear not too wild to come true in reality, when one hopes by instinct and believes, not with the reason, but with the blood. To Gabriella, forgetting her humiliation, it was a day when life for the sake of the mere act of living—when life, in spite of disappointment and loss and treachery and shame, was enough to set the heart bounding with happiness. For she was one of those who loved life, not for what it brought to her of pleasure, but for what it was in itself.

"Yes, it is a lovely afternoon," she answered, and added impulsively: "It is good to be alive, isn't it?" She had forgotten George, but even if she had remembered him, it would have made little difference. For six years, not for a few hours, George had been lost to her; and in six years one has time to forget almost anything.

The judge's answer to this was a look which penetrated like a flash of light into her brain. By this light she read all that he thought of her, and she saw that he was divided between admiration of her spirit and an uneasy suspicion of its perfect propriety. Tier offence, she knew, was that, being by all the logic of facts an unhappy wife, she should persist so stubbornly in denying the visible evidence of her unhappiness. Had her denial been merely a pretence, it would, according to his code, have appeared both natural and womanly; but the conviction that she was sincere, that she was not lying, that she was not even tragically "keeping up an appearance," increased the amazement and suspicion with which he had begun to regard her. He walked on thoughtfully at her side, fingering the end of his long yellowish-gray moustache, and bending his sleepy gaze on the pavement. When he was thinking, he always looked as if he were falling asleep, and he seldom made a remark, even to a woman, without thinking it over. Into his small steel-gray eyes, surrounded by purplish and wrinkled puffs of skin, there crept the cautious and secretive look he wore at directors' meetings, while a furtive smile flickered for an instant across his loose mouth under the drooping ends of his moustache. His ungainly body, with its curious suggestion of over-ripeness, of waning power, straightened suddenly as if in reaction from certain destructive processes within his soul. Though he was only just passing his prime, he had lived so rapidly that he bore already the marks of age in his face and figure.

"Yes, it's good to be alive," he assented, for there was nothing in either his philosophy or his experience to contradict this simple statement. "I've always maintained, by the way, that happiness is the chief of the virtues."

For an instant Gabriella looked at the sky; then turning her candid eyes to his, she answered: "Happiness and courage. I put courage first—before everything."

Her gaze dropped, but not until she had seen his look change and the slightly cynical smile—the smile of one who has examined everything and believes in nothing—fade from his lips. She had touched some chord deep down within him of which he had long ago forgotten even the existence—some echoed harmony of what had been perhaps the living faith of his youth.

"You're a gallant soul," he said briefly, and she wondered what it was that he knew, what it was that he was keeping back.

At the corner where they parted, he stood for a few moments, holding her hand in his big, soft grasp while he looked down on her. The suspicion and the cynicism had gone from his face, and she understood all at once why people still trusted him, still liked him, notwithstanding his reputation, notwithstanding even his repulsiveness. He was all that—he was immoral, he was repulsive—but he was something else also—he was human.

When she entered the house her first feeling was that the old atmosphere had returned, the old suspense, the old waiting, the old horror of impending calamity. A nervous dread made her hesitate to mount the steps, to go to her room, to inquire in a natural voice for the children. It was imaginary, of course, she assured herself, but it was very vivid as long as it lasted. Then she noticed that the usual order of the hall was disturbed, and when she rang, Burrows came, with a hurried, apologetic manner, after keeping her waiting. Mrs. Fowler's fur scarf hung on the massive oak post of the staircase; the cards in the little tray on the hall table were scattered about; and the petals of a yellow chrysanthemum were strewn over the carpet.

Burrows, instead of explaining the confusion, appeared embarrassed when she questioned him, and spurred by a sharp foreboding, she ran up the stairs to her mother-in-law's sitting-room. At her entrance a trembling voice wailed in a tone of remonstrance:

"Oh, Gabriella, have you been out?"

"Yes, I've been out. Mamma, what is the matter?"

"I looked for you everywhere. Archibald has been here, but he has just gone out again. I have never seen him so deeply moved—so—so indignant—" Mrs. Fowler broke off, bit her lip nervously, and paused while she tried to swallow her sobs. Her hat lay on a chair at her side, and in her hands she held a pair of half-soiled white gloves, which she smoothed out on her knee, as if she were hardly aware of what she was doing. In her blue eyes, so like George's, there was an agonizing terror and suspense. Her usually florid face was pale to the lips; and this pallor appeared to accentuate the dark, faintly lined shadows beneath her eyes and the grayness of her rigidly waved hair.

"Courage!" said Gabriella in a whisper to herself, and aloud she asked gently: "Dear mamma, what is it? Don't be afraid. I can bear it."

"Archibald has ordered George out of the house. He—George, I mean—had given him his promise not to see Florrie again, and it seems that he—he broke it. There has been a dreadful scene. I never imagined that Archibald could be so angry. He was terrible—and he is ill anyway and in great trouble about his financial affairs. I have been worried to death about him for weeks. He says things are going so badly downtown that he can't stave off the crash any longer, and now—this—this—" She broke down utterly, burying her convulsed face in her hands, which even in the instant of horror and tragedy, Gabriella noticed, had been manicured since the morning. "George has gone—we think he has gone off with Florrie," she cried, "and he—he will never come back as long as Archibald lives."

She was not thinking of Gabriella. True to the deepest instincts of her nature, she thought first of her son, then of her husband. It was not that she did not care for her daughter-in-law, did not sympathize; but the fact remained that Gabriella was only George's wife to her, while George was flesh of her flesh, bone of her bone, soul of her soul. Though her choice was not deliberate, though it was unconscious and instinctive—nevertheless, she had chosen. At the crucial moment instinct had risen superior to reason, and she had chosen, not with her judgment, but with every quivering nerve and fibre of her being. Gabriella was right, but George was her son; and had it been possible to secure George's happiness by sacrificing the right to the wrong, she would have made that sacrifice without hesitation, without scruple, and without regret.

"There's his father now," she whispered, lifting her disfigured face. "Oh, Gabriella, I believe it will kill me!"

While Gabriella stood there waiting for George's father to enter, and listening to his slow, deliberate tread on the stairs, the heavy, laborious tread of a man who is uncertain of his strength, she remembered vividly, as if she were living it over again, the night she had waited by her fire to tell George that his first child was to be born. Many thoughts passed through her mind, and at last these thoughts resolved themselves into a multitude of crowding images—all distinct and vivid images of George's face. She saw his face as she had first seen and loved it, with its rich colouring, its blue-gray eyes, like wells of romance she had once thought, its look of poetry and emotion which had covered so much that was merely commonplace and gross. She saw him as he had looked at their marriage, as he had looked, bending over her after her first child was born, and then she saw him as he had parted from her that morning—flushed, sneering, a little coarsened, but still boyish, still charming. Well, it was all over now. It had been over so long that she had even ceased to regret it—for she was not by nature one of the women who could wear mourning for a lifetime.

The door opened: Archibald Fowler came in very slowly; and the first sight of his face brought home to her with a shock the discovery that he was the one of them who had suffered most. He looked an old man; his gentle scholar's face had taken an ashen hue; and his eyes were the eyes of one who has only partially recovered from the blow that has prostrated him.

"My dear child," he said; "my dear daughter," and laid his hand on her shoulder.

She clung to him, feeling a passionate pity, not for herself, but for him. "You have too much to bear," she murmured caressingly. "You mustn't take it like this. You must try to get over it. For all our sakes you must try to get over it." The irony of it all—that she should be consoling her husband's father for her husband's desertion of her—did not appear to her until long afterwards. At the time she thought only that she—that somebody—must make the tragedy easier for him to bear.

"Come and sit down, Archibald," said Mrs. Fowler pleadingly. "Let me give you a glass of sherry and a biscuit; you are too tired to talk."

There was the old devotion in her manner, but there was also a new deference. For the first time in thirty years of marriage he had shown his strength to her, not his gentleness; for the first time he had opposed his will to hers in the cause of justice, and he had conquered her. In spite of her anguish, something of the romantic expectancy of her first love had returned to her heart and it showed in her softened voice, in her timid caresses, in her wistful eyes, which held a pathetic and startled brightness. He had triumphed in honour; and if her defeat had not involved George, she could almost have gloried in the completeness of her surrender.

He sat down with the air of a man who is not entirely awake to his surroundings; and his wife, after ordering the sherry, hovered over him with the touching solicitude of one who is living for the moment in the shadow of memory. While he sipped the wine, he waited until Burrows' footsteps had passed down the staircase, and then said with his usual quietness:

"There is something else, Evelyn, that I kept back. I couldn't tell you while you were so worried about George, but there is something else—"

She caught the words from him eagerly, with a gesture almost of relief.

"You mean it has come at last. I suspected it, and, oh, Archibald, I don't care—I don't care!"

"There were several failures to-day in Wall Street, and—" He broke off as if he were too tired to go on, and added slowly after a moment: "I am too old to begin again. I'd like to go back home—to go back to the South for my old age. Yes, I'm old."

But his wife was on her knees beside him, with her arms about his neck and her face hidden on his breast. "I don't care, I never cared," she said in a voice that was almost exultant. "We can be happy on so little—happier than we've ever been in our lives—just you and I to grow old together. We can go home to Virginia—to some small place and be happy. Happiness costs so little."

Slipping away, Gabriella went into the hall, and passing her room, noiselessly pushed open the door of the nursery, where the children were sleeping. A night lamp was burning in one corner under a dark shade, and the nurse's knitting, a pile of white yarn, was lying on the table in the circle of green light, which was as soft as the glimmer of a glow-worm in a thicket. In their two little beds, separated by a strip of white rug, the children were sleeping quietly, with a wonderful freshness, like the dew of innocence, on their faces. Frances lay on her back, very straight and prim even in sleep, with the sheet folded neatly under her dimpled chin, her hands clasped on her breast, and her golden curls spread in perfect order over the lace-trimmed pillow. Her miniature features, framed in the dim gold of her hair, had the trite prettiness of an angel on a Christmas card; and beside her ethereal loveliness there was something gnome-like in the dark sturdiness of Archibald, who slept on his side, with his fists pressed tightly under the pillow, and the frown produced by near-sightedness still wrinkling his forehead. Though he was not beautiful, he showed already the promise of character in his face, and his personality, which was remarkably developed for a child of his age, possessed a singular charm. He was the kind of child people describe as "unlike other children." His temperament was made up of surprises, and this quality of unexpectedness inspired in his mother a devotion that was almost tragic in its intensity. Never had she loved the normal Frances Evelyn as she loved Archibald.

As she looked down on them, sleeping so peacefully in the green light, a wave of sadness swept over her, and she thought of them suddenly as fatherless, impoverished, and unprotected, dependent on her untried labour for their lives and their happiness. Then, before the anxiety could take possession of her mind, she put it from her, and whispered, "Courage!" as she turned away and went out of the room.

# CHAPTER III

## WORK

They had planned the future so carefully that there was a pitiless irony in the next turn of the screw—for when they tried to awaken Archibald Fowler in the morning, he did not stir, and they realized presently, with the rebellious shock such tragedies always bring, that he had died in the night—that all that he had stood for, the more than thirty years of work and struggle, had collapsed in an hour. When the first grief, the first excitement, was over, and life began to flow quietly again in its familiar currents, it was discovered that the crash of his fortune had occurred on the day of his son's flight and disgrace, and that the two shocks, coming together, had killed him. While they sat in the darkened house, surrounded by the funereal smell of crape, the practical details of living seemed to matter so little that they scarcely gave them a thought. Not until weeks afterwards, when Patty and Billy had sailed for France, and Mrs. Fowler, shrouded in widow's weeds, had gone South to her old home, did Gabriella find strength to tear aside the veil of mourning and confront the sordid actuality. Then she found that the crash had buried everything under the ruins of Archibald Fowler's prosperity—that nothing remained except a bare pittance which would insure his widow only a scant living on the impoverished family acres. For the rest there was nothing, and she herself was as poor as she had been in Hill Street before her marriage.

Walking back from the station after bidding her mother-in-law a tearful and tender good-bye, she tried despairingly to gather her scattered thoughts and summon all her failing resources; but in front of her plans there floated always the pathetic brightness of Mrs. Fowler's eyes gazing up at her from the heavy shadow of the crape veil she had lifted. So that was the end—a little love, a little hope, a little happiness, and then separation and death. Effort appeared not only futile, but fantastic, and yet effort, she knew, must be made if she were to ward off destitution. She must recover her cheerfulness, she must be strong, she must be confident. Alone, penniless, with two children to support, she could not afford to waste her time and her energy in useless regret. Whatever it cost her, she must keep alive her fighting courage and her belief in life. She had youth, health, strength, intelligence, resourcefulness on her side; and she told herself again that there were thousands of women living and fighting around her who were far worse off than she. "What others have done, I can do also, and do better," she murmured aloud as she walked rapidly back to Dinard's.

In the long front room the crowded mid-winter sale was in progress, and the six arrogant young women, goaded into a fleeting semblance of activity, were displaying dilapidated "left over" millinery to a throng of unfashionable casual customers. Madame, herself, scorned these casual customers, but her scorn was as water unto wine compared with the burning disdain of the six arrogant young women. They sauntered to and fro with their satin trains trailing elegantly over the carpet, with their fashionable curves accentuated as much as it was possible for pride to accentuate them, with their condescending heads turning haughtily above the high points of their collars. As Gabriella entered she saw the tallest and the most scornful of them, whose name was Murphy, insolently posing in the green velvet toque before a jaded hunter of reduced millinery, who shook her plain, sensible head at the hat as if she wished it to understand that she heartily disapproved of it.

Madame was not visible, but Gabriella found her a little later in the workroom, where she was volubly elucidating obscure points in business morality to the forewoman. Of all the women employed in the house, this particular forewoman was the only one who appeared to Gabriella to be without pretence or affectation. She was an honest, blunt, capable creature, with a face and figure which permanently debarred her from the showrooms, and a painstaking method of work. There was no haughtiness, no condescension, about her. She had the manner of one who, being without fortuitous aids to happiness, is willing to give good measure of ability and industry in return for the bare necessaries of existence. "She is the only genuine thing in the whole establishment," thought Gabriella while she watched her.

If Miss Smith, the forewoman, had been in ignorance of the failure and death of Archibald Fowler, she would probably have read the announcement in Madame's face as she watched her welcome the wife of his son. There was nothing offensive, nothing unkind, nothing curt; but, in some subtle way, the difference was emphasized between the eccentric daughter-in-law of a millionaire and an inexperienced young woman who must work for her living. For the welcome revealed at once to the observant eyes of Miss Smith the significant detail that Madame's role had changed from the benefited to the benefactor. And, as if this were not enough for one morning's developments, it revealed also that Gabriella's fictitious value as a saleswoman was beginning to decline; for Madame was disposed to scorn the sort of sensational advertisement which the newspapers had devoted of late to the unfortunate Fowlers. At one moment there had been grave doubt in Madame's mind as to whether or not she should employ young Mrs. Fowler in her respectable house; then, after a brief hesitation, she had shrewdly decided that ideas were worth something even when lacking the support of social position and financial security. There were undoubtedly possibilities in Gabriella; and disgrace, Madame concluded cheerfully, could not take away either one's natural talent or one's aristocratic appearance. That the girl had distinction, even rare distinction, Madame admitted while she nodded approvingly at the severe black cloth gown with its collar and cuffs of fine white crape. The simple arrangement of her hair, which would have ruined many a pretty face, suited the ivory pallor of Gabriella's features. Mourning was becoming to her, Madame decided, and though she was not beautiful, she was unusually charming.

"She has few good points except her figure, and yet the whole is decidedly picturesque," thought Madame as impersonally as if she were criticising a fashion plate. "Very young men would hardly care for her—for very young men demand fine complexions and straight noses—but with older men who like an air, who admire grace, she would be taking, and women, yes, women would undoubtedly find her imposing. But she is not the sort to have followers," she concluded complacently.

"Shall I go to the workroom?" asked Gabriella in a businesslike voice when she had taken off her hat, "or do you wish me at the sale?"

Her soul shrank from the showrooms, but she had determined courageously that she would not allow her soul to interfere with her material purpose, and her purpose was to learn all that she could and to make herself indispensable to Madame. Only by acquiring a thorough knowledge of the business and making herself indispensable could she hope to succeed. And success was not merely desirable to her; it was vital. It meant the difference between food and hunger for her children.

"Miss Smith will find something for you to do this morning," replied Madame, politely, but without enthusiasm. "If there is a rush later on in the millinery, I will send for you to help out."

In the old days, when Dinard's was a small and exclusive house in one of the blocks just off Fifth Avenue, Madame would have scorned to combine the making of gowns and hats in a single establishment; but as she advanced in years and in worldly experience, she discovered that millinery drew the unwary passer-by even more successfully than dressmaking did. Then, too, hats were easy to handle; they sold for at least four or five times as much as they actually cost; and so, gradually, while she was still unaware of the disintegrating processes within, Madame's principles had crumbled before the temptation of increasing profits. A lapse of virtue, perhaps, but Madame, who had been born an O'Grady, was not the first to discover that one's virtuous principles are apt to modify with one's years. The time was when she had despised false hair, having a natural wealth of her own, and now, with a few thin gray strands hidden under her golden wig, she had become morally reconciled to necessity. "It is a hard world, and one lives as one must," was her favourite maxim.

On the whole, however, having a philosophic bent of mind, she endeavoured to preserve, with rosy cheeks and golden hair, several other cheerful fictions of her youth. The chief of these, the artless delusion that, in spite of her obesity, her wig and her rouge, she still had power to charm the masculine eye, offered to her lively nature a more effective support than any virtuous principle could have supplied. A perennial, if ridiculous, coquetry sweetened her days and added sprightliness to the gay decline of her life. Being frankly material, she had confined her energies to the two unending pursuits of men and money, and having captured four husbands and acquired a comfortable bank account, she might have been content, had she been as discreet as she was provident, to rest on her substantial achievements. But the trouble with both men and money, when considered solely as rewards to enterprise, is that the quest of them is inexhaustible. One's income, however large, may reasonably become larger, and there is no limit to the number of husbands a prudent and fortunate woman may collect. And so age, which is, after all, a state of mind, not a term of years, was rendered harmless to Madame by her simple plan of refusing to acknowledge that it existed. This came of keeping one's head, she sometimes thought, though she never put her thought into words—this and all things else, including financial security and the perpetual pursuit of the elusive and lawless male. For at sixty-two she still felt young and she believed herself to be fascinating.

But Gabriella, patiently stitching bias velvet bands on the brim of a straw hat for the early spring trade, felt that she was sustained neither by the pleasures of vanity nor by the sounder consolations of virtue. Her philosophy was quite as simple, if not so material, as Madame's. Human nature was divided between the victors and the victims, and the chief thing was not to let oneself become a victim. Her theory, like those of greater philosophers, was rooted not in reason, but in character, and she believed in life with all the sanguine richness of her blood. Of course it was a struggle, but she was one of those vital women who enjoy a struggle—who choose any aspect of life in preference to the condition of vegetative serenity. Unhappiness, which is so largely a point of view, an attitude of mind, had passed over her at a time when many women would have been consecrated to inconsolable misery. She was penniless, she was unloved, she was deserted by her husband, she had lost, in a few weeks, her friends, her home, and her family, and she faced the future alone, except for her dependent and helpless children—yet in spite of these things, though she was thoughtful, worried, and often anxious, she realized that deep down in her the essential core of her being was not unhappy. When she had tried and failed, and lost her health and her children—if such sorrows ever came to her, then there would be time enough for unhappiness. Now, she was only twenty-seven; the rich, wonderful world surrounded her; and this world, even if she put love out of her life, was brimming over with beauty. It was good to be alive; it was good to watch the crowd in the street, to see the sunlight on the pavement, to taste the air, to feel the murmurous currents of the city flow around her as she walked home in the twilight. It was good to earn her bread and to go back in the evening to the joyful shouts of two well and happy children. She saw it all as an adventure—the whole of life—and the imperative necessity was to keep to the last the ardent heart of the true adventurer. While she stitched with flying fingers, there passed before her the pale sad line of the victims—of those who had resigned themselves to unhappiness. She saw her mother, anxious, pensive, ineffectual, with her widow's veil, her drooping eyelids, and her look of mournful acquiescence, as of one who had grown old expecting the worst of life; she saw poor Jane, tragic, martyred, with the feeble virtue and the cloying sweetness of all the poor Janes of this world; and she saw Uncle Meriweather wearing his expression of worried and resentful helplessness, as if he had been swept onward against his will by forces which he did not understand. All these people were victims, and from these people she had sprung. Their blood was her blood; their traditions were her traditions; their religion was her religion; even their memories were her memories. But something else, which was not theirs, was in her nature, and this something else had been born in the instant when she revolted against them. Perhaps the fighting spirit of her father—of that father who had gone out like a flame in his youth had battled on her side when she had turned against the inertia and decay which had walled in her girlhood.

In the afternoon Madame summoned her into the showrooms, and she assisted the exhausted young women at the sale of slightly damaged French hats to the unfashionable purchasers who preferred to pay reasonable prices. While she served them, which she did with a cheerfulness, an interest, and an amiability that distinguished her from the other saleswomen, she wondered how they could have so little common sense as to allow themselves to be deluded by the French labels on the soiled linings? She could have made a better hat in two hours than any one of those she sold at the reduced price of ten dollars; yet even the dingiest of them at last found a purchaser, and she saw the green velvet toque, which had been rejected by the sensible middle-aged woman in the morning, finally pass into the possession of a hard-featured spinster. What amazed her, for she had a natural talent for dress, was the infallible instinct which guided the vast majority of these customers to the selection of the inappropriate. A few of them had taste, or had learned from experience what they could not wear; but by far the larger number displayed an ignorance of the most elementary principles of dress which shocked and astonished Gabriella. The obese and middle-aged winged straight as a bird toward the coquettish in millinery; the lean and haggard intuitively yearned for the picturesque; the harsh and simple aspired to the severely smart. Yet beneath the vain misdirection of impulses there was some obscure principle of attraction which ruled the absurdity of the decisions. Each woman, Gabriella discovered after an attentive hour at the sale, was dressing not her actual substance, but some passionately cherished ideal of herself which she had stored in a remote and inaccessible chamber of her brain.

In all of the tedious selections Gabriella assisted with the pleasant voice, the ready sympathy, and the quick understanding which had made her so popular when she had worked for the old shop in Broad Street. The truth was that human nature interested her even in its errors, and her pleasant manners were simply the outward manifestation of an unaffected benevolence.

"I shouldn't mind going there if they were all like that one," remarked a customer, who had bought three hats, in the hearing of Madame as she went out; "but some of them are so disagreeable you feel like slapping their faces. Once last winter I had that tall girl with red hair—the handsome, stuck-up one, you know—and I declare she was so downright impertinent that I got straight up and walked out without buying a thing. Then I was so angry that I went down to Paula's and paid seventy-five dollars for this hat I've got on. It was a dreadful price, of course, but you'll do anything when you're in a rage."

"Do you know the name of this one? I'd like to remember it."

"Yes, it's Carr. I asked for her card. C-a-r-r. I think she's a widow."

From her retreat behind one of the velvet curtains Madame overheard this conversation, and a few minutes later she stopped Gabriella on her way out, and said amiably that it would not be necessary for her to leave the showroom to-morrow.

"I believe you can do better there than in the workroom," she added, "and, after all, that is really very important—to tell people what they want. It is astounding how few of them have the slightest idea what they are looking for."

"But I want to get that hat right. I left it unfinished, and I don't like to give up while it is wrong," replied Gabriella, not wholly pleased by the command.

But Madame, of a flightier substance notwithstanding her business talents, waved aside the remark as insignificant and without bearing upon her immediate purpose.

"I am going to try you with the gowns," she said resolutely; "I want to see if you catch on there as quickly as you did with the hats—I mean with the sale, of course, for your work, I'm sorry to say, has been rather poor so far. But I'll try you with the next customer who comes to place a large order. They are always so eager for new suggestions, and you have suggestions of a sort to make, I am sure. I can't quite tell," she concluded uncertainly, "whether or not your ideas have any practical value, but they sound well as you describe them, and to talk attractively helps; there is no doubt of that."

It was closing time, and Miss Fisher, one of the skirt fitters, came up, in her black alpaca apron with a pair of scissors suspended by red tape from her waist, to ask Madame a question. As Mrs. Bydington had not kept her appointment, was it not impossible to send her gown home as they had promised?

"Oh, it makes no difference," replied Madame blandly, for she was in a good humour. "She'll come back when she is ready. The next time she is here, by the way, I want her to see Mrs. Fowler—I mean Mrs. Carr. She has worn out every one else in the place, and yet she is never satisfied; but I'd like her to take that pink velvet from Gautier, because nobody else is likely to give the price." The day was over and Madame's blandness was convincing evidence of her satisfaction.

As Gabriella passed through the last showroom, where the disorder of the sale was still visible, she saw Miss Murphy, the handsomest and the haughtiest of the young women, wearily returning the few rejected hats to the ivory-tinted cases.

"You are glad it is over, I know," she remarked sympathetically, less from any active interest in Miss Murphy's state of feeling than from an impulsive desire to establish human relations with her fellow saleswoman. If Miss Murphy would have it so, she preferred to be friendly.

"I am so tired I can hardly stand on my feet," replied Miss Murphy, piteously. Her pretty rose-leaf skin had faded to a dull pallor; there were heavy shadows under her eyes; her helmet of wheaten-red hair had slipped down over her forehead, and even her firmly corseted figure appeared to have grown limp and yielding. Without her offensive elegance she was merely a pathetic and rather silly young thing.

"I'll help you," said Gabriella, taking up several hats from a chair. "The others have gone, haven't they?"

"They got out before I'd finished waiting on that middle-aged frump who doesn't know what she wants any more than the policeman out there at the corner does. She's made me show her all we've got left, and after she'd tried them all on, she said they're too high, and she's going to think over them before she decides. She's still waiting for something, and my head's splitting so I can hardly see what I'm doing." With a final surrender of her arrogance, she grew suddenly confidential and childish. "I'm sick enough to die," she finished despairingly, "and I've got a friend coming to take me to the theatre at eight o'clock."

"Well, run away. I'll attend to this. But I'd try to rest before I went out if I were you."

"You're a perfect peach," responded Miss Murphy gratefully. "I said all along I didn't believe you were stuck up and snobbish."

Then she ran out, and Gabriella, after surveying the customer for a minute, selected the most unpromising hat in the case, and presented it with a winning smile for the woman's inspection.

"Perhaps something like this is what you are looking for?" she remarked politely, but firmly.

The customer, an acidulous, sharp-featured, showily dressed person—the sort, Gabriella decided, who would enjoy haggling over a bargain—regarded the offered hat with a supercilious and guarded manner, the true manner of the haggler.

"No, that is not bad," she observed dryly, "but I don't care to give more than ten dollars."

"It was marked down from thirty," replied Gabriella, and her manner was as supercilious and as guarded as the other's. There were women, she had found, who were impressed only by insolence, and, when the need arose, she could be quite as insolent as Miss Murphy. Unlike Miss Murphy, however, she was able to distinguish between those you must encourage and those you must crush; and this ability to draw reasonable distinctions was, perhaps, her most valuable quality as a woman of business.

"I don't care to pay more than ten dollars," reiterated the customer in a scolding voice. Rising from her chair, she fastened her furs, which were cheap and showy, with a defiant and jerky movement, and flounced out of the shop.

That disposed of, Gabriella put on her coat, which she had taken off again for the occasion, and went out into the street, where the night had already fallen. After her long hours in the overheated air of the showrooms, she felt refreshed and invigorated by the cold wind, which stung her face as it blew singing over the crossings. Straight ahead through the grayish-violet mist the lights were blooming like flowers, and above them a few stars shone faintly over the obscure frowning outlines of the buildings. Fifth Avenue was thronged, and to her anxious mind there seemed to be hollowness and insincerity in the laughter of the crowd.

At the house in East Fifty-seventh Street, from which she would be moving the next day, she found Judge Crowborough awaiting her in the dismantled drawing-room, where packing-cases of furniture and pictures lay scattered about in confusion. In the dreadful days after Archibald Fowler's death, the judge had been very kind, and she had turned to him instinctively as the one man in New York who was both able and willing to be of use to her. Though he had never attracted her, she had been obliged to admit that he possessed a power superior to superficial attractions.

"I dropped in to ask what I might do for you now?" he remarked with the dignity of one who possesses an income of half a million dollars a year. "It's a pity you have to leave this house. I remember when Archibald bought it— somewhere back in the 'seventies—but I suppose there's no help for it, is there?"

"No, there's no help." She sat down on a packing-case, and he stood gazing benevolently down on her with his big, soft hands clasped on the head of his walking-stick and his overcoat on his arm. "I've rented three rooms in one of the apartments of the old Carolina over on the West Side near Columbus Avenue. The rest of the apartment is rented to art students, I believe, and we must all use the same kitchen and the same bath-tub," she added with a laugh. "Of course it isn't luxury, but we shan't mind very much as soon as we get used to it. I couldn't be much poorer than I was before my marriage."

"But the children? You've got to have the children looked after."

"I've been so fortunate about that," her voice was quite cheerful again. "There's a seamstress from my old home—Miss Polly Hatch—who has known me all my life, and she is coming to sleep in a little bed in my room until we can afford to rent an extra bedroom. As long as she has to work at home anyhow, she can very easily look after the children while I am away. They are good children, and as soon as they are big enough I'll have to send them to school— to the public school, I'm afraid." This, because of Fanny's violent opposition, was a delicate point with her. She felt that she should like to start the children at a private school, but it was clearly impossible.

"The boy won't be big enough for a year or two, will he?" He was interested, she saw, and this unaffected interest in her small affairs moved her almost to tears.

"I wanted him to go to kindergarten, but, of course, I cannot afford it. He is only four and a half, and I'm teaching him myself in the evenings. Already he can read very well in the first reader," she finished proudly.

For a minute the judge stared moodily down on her. His sagging cheeks took a pale purplish flush, and he bit his lower lip with his large yellow teeth, which reminded Gabriella of the tusks of a beast of prey. Then he laid his overcoat and his stick carefully down on a packing-case, and held out his hand.

"I'm going now, and there's one thing I want to ask you—have you any money?"

It was out at last, and she looked up composedly, smiling a little roguishly at his embarrassment.

"I have six hundred dollars in bank for a rainy day, and I am making exactly fifteen dollars a week."

"But you can't live on it. Nobody could live on it even without two children to bring up."

She shook her head. "Oh, Judge Crowborough, how little you rich men really know! I've got to live on it until I can do better, and I hope that will be very soon. If I am worth anything now, in three months I ought to be worth certainly as much as twenty-five dollars a week. In a little while—as soon as I've caught on to the business—I'm going to ask for a larger salary, and I think I shall get it. Twenty-five dollars a week won't go very far, but you don't know how little some people can live on even in New York."

"As soon as the six hundred dollars go you'll be headed straight for starvation," he protested, sincerely worried.

"Perhaps, but I doubt it."

"How much do you have to pay for your rooms?"

"Twenty-five dollars a month. It isn't much of a place, you see, as far as appearances go. Fortunately, I have a little furniture of my own which Mrs. Fowler had given me."

His embarrassment had passed away, and he was smiling now at the recollection of it.

"Well, you're a brick, little girl," he said, "and I like your spirit, but, after all, why can't you put your pride in your pocket, and let me lend you a few thousands? You needn't borrow much—not enough to keep a carriage—but you might at least take a little just to show you aren't proud—just to show you'll be friends. It seems a downright shame that I should have money to throw away, and you should be starting out to pinch and scrape on fifteen dollars a week. Fifteen dollars a week! Good Lord, what are we coming to?"

She was not proud, and she wanted to be friends, but she shook her head obstinately, though she was still smiling. "Not now—not while I can help it—but if I ever get in trouble—in real trouble—I'll remember your offer. If the children fall ill or I lose my place, I'll come to you in a minute."

"Honour bright? It's a promise?"

"It's a promise."

"And you'll let me keep an eye on you?"

She laughed with the natural gaiety which he found so delightful. "You may keep two eyes on me if you will!"

He had already reached the door when, turning suddenly, he said with heavy gravity: "You don't mind my asking what you're going to do about George, do you?"

"No, I don't mind. As soon as I can afford it, I shall get my freedom, but everything costs, you know, even justice."

"I could help you there, couldn't I?"

From the gratitude in her eyes he read her horror of the marriage which still bound her. "You could—and, oh, if you would, I'd never, never forget it," she answered.

Then they parted, and he went out into the cold, with a strange warmth like the fire of youth at his heart, while she ran eagerly up the uncarpeted stairs to the nursery.

The trunks were packed, the boxes were nailed down, and the two children were playing shipwreck while they ate a supper of bread and milk at a table made from the bare top of a packing-case. Several days before the nurse had left without warning, and Miss Polly sat now, in hat and mantle, on one of the little beds which would be taken down the next day and sent over to the apartment on the West Side.

"I've been to the Carolina and unpacked the things that had come," she said at Gabriella's entrance. "Those rooms ain't so bad as New York rooms go; but it does seem funny, don't it, to cook in the same kitchen with a lot of strangers you never laid eyes on befo'? I br'iled some chops for the children right alongside of an old maid who had come all the way up from New Orleans to study music—imagine, at her age! Why, she couldn't be a day under fifty! And on the other side there was the mother of a girl who's at the art school, or whatever you call it, where they teach you paintin'. They are from somewhere up yonder in New England and their home folks had sent 'em a pumpkin pie. She gave me a slice of it, but I never did think much of pumpkin. It can't hold a candle to sweet potato pudding, and I wouldn't let the children touch it for fear it might set too heavy in the night. I ain't got much use for Yankee food, nohow."

"I hope the place is perfectly sanitary," was Gabriella's anxious rejoinder. "The front room gets some sunshine in the afternoon, doesn't it?"

"It's a horrid street. I don't want to live there," wailed Fanny, who had rebelled from the beginning against her fallen fortunes. "I got my white shoes dirty, and there were banana peels all about. A man has a fruit-stand in the bottom of our house. Don't let's go there to live, mother."

"You'll have to wear black shoes now, darling, and you mustn't mind the fruit-stand. It will be a good place to buy oranges."

"I like it," said Archibald stoutly. "I like to slide on banana peels, and I like the man. He has black eyes and a red handkerchief in his pocket. Will you buy me a red handkerchief, mamma? He has a boy, too. I saw him. He can skate on roller skates, and the boy has a dog and the dog has a black ear. May I have roller skates for my birthday, and a dog—a small one—and may I ask the boy up to play with me?"

"But the boy is ugly and so is the dog. I hate ugly people," complained Fanny.

"I like ugly people," retorted Archibald, glowering, not from anger, but from earnestness. "Ugly people are nicer than pretty ones, aren't they, mamma? Pang is nicer than Fanny."

He was always like that even as a baby, always on the side of the unfortunate, always fighting valiantly for the under dog. With his large head, his grotesque spectacles, and his pouting lips, he bore a curious resemblance to a brownie, yet when one observed him closely, one saw that there was a remarkable blending of strength and sweetness in his expression.

The next day Miss Polly finished the moving, and at six o'clock Gabriella went home in the Harlem elevated train to the grim, weather-beaten apartment house on the upper West Side. The pavements, as Fanny had scornfully observed, were not particularly clean; the air, in spite of the sharp wind which blew from the river, had a curiously stagnant quality; and the rumble of the elevated road, at the opposite side of the house, reached her in a vibrating undercurrent which was punctuated now and then by the staccato cries of the street. The house, which had been built in a benighted and spacious period, stood now as an enduring refuge for the poor in purse but proud in spirit. A few studios on the roof were still occupied by artists, while the hospitable basement sheltered a vegetable market, a corner drug-store, a fruit-stand, and an Italian bootblack. Within the bleak walls, from which the stucco had peeled in splotches, the life of the city had ebbed and flowed for almost half a century, like some deep wreck-strewn current which bore the seeds of the future as well as the driftwood of the past on its bosom. One might never have set foot outside those gloomy doors and yet have seen the whole of life pass as in a vivid dream through the dim halls, lighted by flickering gas and carpeted in worn strips of brown carpet. And once inside the apartments one might have found, sometimes, cheerfulness, beauty of line and colour, and a certain spaciousness which the modern apartment house, with its rooms like closets, its startling electricity, and its more hygienic conditions of living, could not provide. It was because she could find space there that Gabriella, guided by Miss Polly, had rented the rooms.

She passed the drug-store and the fruit-stand, entered the narrow hall, where a single gas-jet flickered dimly beside the door of the elevator, and after touching the bell, stood patiently waiting. After a time she rang again, and presently, with deliberate ease and geniality, the negro who worked the elevator descended slowly, with a newspaper in his hand, and opened the door for her.

"Good evening, Robert," she said pleasantly, for he also was from Virginia, and the discovery of the bond between them had given Gabriella a feeling of confidence. Like Miss Folly, she had never become entirely accustomed to white servants.

The ropes moved again, the elevator ascended perilously to the fifth floor, and Gabriella walked quickly along the hall, and slipped her latchkey into the keyhole of the last apartment. As the door opened, a woman in worn black came out and spoke to her in passing. She was the old maid of Miss Folly's narrative, and her face, ardent, haggard, with the famished look which comes from a starved soul, gazed back at Gabriella with a touching expression of admiration and envy. There were spots of vivid colour in her cheeks, and this brightness, combined with her gray hair, gave her a theatrical and artificial appearance.

"I have been playing to your little boy, Mrs. Carr," she said with the manner which Miss Polly had described as "flighty." "He came into my room when he heard the piano, and it was a real pleasure to play for him."

"You are very good," returned Gabriella, wondering vaguely who she was, for she was obviously the kind of woman people wondered about. "I hope Archibald didn't make himself troublesome."

"Oh, no, I enjoyed him. My name is Danton. I am Miss Danton," she added effusively, "and I'm so glad you have come into this apartment. My room is the one next to yours."

Then she fluttered off, with her look of spiritual hunger, and Gabriella closed the door and went on to her rooms, which were at the opposite end of the hall from the kitchen. On the way she passed the pretty art student, who was coming from the bathroom, with a freshly powdered face and a pitcher of water in her hand, and again she was obliged to stop to hear news of the children.

"I'm so glad to have your little girl here. I want to paint her. I'm just crazy about her face," said the girl, whose name she learned afterwards was Rosy Plover. Though she was undeniably pretty, and had just powdered her face with scented powder, she had a slovenly, unkempt appearance which Gabriella, from that moment, associated with art students. "If she'd only dress herself properly, she'd be a beauty," she thought, with the aversion of one who is an artist in clothes. She herself, after her long, hard day, was as neat and trim as she had been in the morning. Her severe black suit was worn with grace, and hung perfectly; her crape collar was immaculately fresh; her mourning veil fell in charming folds over her hat brim. "It's a pity some one can't tell her," she mused, as she smiled and hurried on to the doubtful seclusion of her own end of the apartment.

With the opening of the door, the children fell rapturously into her arms, and while she took off her hat and coat, Miss Polly laid the table for supper in front of the ruddy glow of the fire. On the fender a plate of buttered toast was keeping warm, a delicious aroma of coffee scented the air, and a handful of red carnations made a cheerful bit of colour in the centre of the white tablecloth. It was a pleasant picture for a tired woman to gaze on, and the ruddy glow of the fire was reflected in Gabriella's heart while she enfolded her children. After a day in Madame's hothouse atmosphere, it was delightful to return to this little centre of peace and love, and to feel that its very existence depended upon the work of her brain and hands. The children, she realized, had never loved her so dearly. In better days, when she was rarely separated from them for more than a few hours at a time, they had seemed rather to take her care and her presence for granted; but now, after an absence of nine hours, she had become a delight and an enchantment, something to be looked forward to and longingly talked about through the whole afternoon.

"Mother, you've been away forever," said Fanny, folding her veil for her and putting away her furs.

"Are you going every day just like this for ever and ever?"

"Every day, darling, but I'm here every night. Shall I run back to the kitchen and broil the chops, Miss Polly?"

But the chops were already broiled, for Miss Polly had finished her sewing early, and she had beaten up two tiny cups of custard for the children.

"It's nicer than nursery suppers, isn't it, Fanny?" asked Archibald a little later while he ate his bread and milk from a blue bowl. "Mother, I like being poor. Let's stay poor always."

A phrase of Mrs. Fowler's, "happiness costs so little," floated through Gabriella's mind as she poured Miss Folly's coffee out of the tin coffee pot. She was so tired that her body ached; her feet were smarting and throbbing from the long standing; and her eyes stung from the cold wind and the glare of the elevated train; but she knew that in spite of these discomforts she was not unhappy—that she was, indeed, far happier than she had been for the past six years in the hushed suspense of her father-in-law's house. When she had carried the supper things back to the sink in the kitchen, had taught the children their lessons, heard their prayers, and put them to bed, she repeated the words to herself while she sat sewing beside the lamp in front of the comforting glow of the fire, "After all, happiness costs so little."

The next morning, and on every morning throughout the winter, she was up by six o'clock, and had taken in the baker's rolls and the bottle of milk from the outer door before Miss Polly or the children were stirring. Then, having dressed quickly, she ran back to the kitchen and made the coffee and boiled the eggs while the other lodgers were still sleeping. Sometimes the mother of one of the art students would join her over the gas range, but usually her neighbours slept late and then darted through the hall in kimonos, with tumbled hair, to a hurried breakfast at the kitchen table.

Her life was so busy that there was little time for anxiety, and less for futile and painful dwelling upon the past. To get through the day as best she could, to start the children well and in a good humour, to make herself useful, if not indispensable, to Madame, to return with a mind clear and fresh enough to give Fanny and Archibald intelligent lessons, to sew on their clothes or her own until midnight, and then to drop into bed, with aching limbs and a peaceful brain, too tired even to dream—these things made the life that she looked forward to, week after week, month after month, year after year. It was a hard life, as Miss Polly often remarked, but hard or soft, her strength was equal to it, her health was good, her interest in her work and in her children never flagged for a minute. Only on soft spring days, coming home in the dusk, she would sometimes pass carts filled with hyacinths, and in a wave the memory of Arthur and of her first love would rush over her. Then she would see Arthur's face, gentle, protective, tender, as it had looked on that last evening, and for an instant her lost girlhood and her girlhood's dream would envelop her like the fragrance of flowers. At such moments she thought of this love as tenderly as a mother might have thought of the exquisite dead face of an infant who had lived only an hour. Though it was over, though it bore no part, with its elusive loveliness, in her practical plans for the future, this dream became gradually, as the years passed, the most radiant and vital thing in her life. Though it was so vague as to be without warmth, it was as vivid and as real as light. The knowledge that in the past she had known perfect love, even though in her blindness she had thrust it aside, was a balm which healed her wounds and gave her courage to go on, friendless and alone, into the loveless stretch of the future. There was hardly a minute of her day for the next three years which was not sweetened by this hyacinth-scented dream of the past, there was hardly an hour of her drudgery which was not ennobled and irradiated by the splendour of this love that she had lost.

Of George—even of George as the father of her children—she rarely thought. He had dropped out of her life like any other mistake, like any other illusion, and she was too sanguine by nature, too buoyant, too full of happiness and of energy, to waste herself on either mistakes or illusions. During the months when she had waited for her freedom she had resolutely put the thought of him out of her mind, and when at last her divorce was granted, she dismissed the fact as completely as if it had not changed the entire course of her life. The past was over, and only that part of it should live which contributed sweetness and beauty to the present—only that part of it which she could use in the better and stronger structure of the future. Whatever living meant in the end, she told herself each morning as she started out to her work, it must mean, not resignation, not inertia, but endeavour, enterprise, and courage.

# CHAPTER IV

## THE DREAM AND THE YEARS

In one of the small fitting-rooms, divided by red velvet curtains on gilt rods from the long showrooms of Madame Dinard, a nervous group, comprising the head skirt fitter, the head waist fitter, Miss Bellman, the head saleswoman, and Madame herself, stood disconsolately around the indignant figure of Mrs. Weederman Pletheridge, who, attired in one of Madame's costliest French models, was gesticulating excitedly in the centre of four standing mirrors. For three years Mrs. Pletheridge had lived in Paris, and her return to New York, and to the dressmaking establishments of Fifth Avenue, was an event which had shaken Dinard's, if not the fashionable street in which it stood, to its foundations.

"I don't know what is the matter with it," she said fussily, "but it doesn't suit me, and yet it looked so well in the hand. I wonder if I could wear it if you were to take out some of this fulness, and change the set of the sleeves? The fashions this spring are perfectly hopeless."

"Why, it suits you to perfection, Madame. Just a stitch or two like this—and this—and it will look as if it were designed for you by Worth. Is it not so, Miss Bellman? Don't you think it is wonderful on Madame?"

Miss Bellman, having learned her part, agreed effusively, and then each of the fitters, as she was appealed to in turn, contributed an enraptured assent to the discussion. The price of the gown was a thousand dollars, and Mrs. Pletheridge's favourable decision was worth exactly that much in terms of money to Dinard's. As the season had been scarcely a brisk one, Madame was particularly anxious to have her more extreme models taken off her hands. "It was unpacked only yesterday," she lied suavely, "and no one else has had so much as a glimpse of it."

"I can't imagine what is the matter with it," Mrs. Pletheridge sighed dejectedly, while she regarded her ample form with a resentful and critical gaze. As long as one had nothing else to worry about, Madame reflected without sympathy, one might find cause for positive distress in the fact that a gown appeared to better advantage in the hand than on one's person. The truth—and the truth, as sometimes happens, was the last thing Mrs. Pletheridge cared to admit—was that she had grown too stout to wear pronounced fashions.

"Nothing could be more charming," insisted Madame with increased effusion, "but if you are in doubt, let us ask the opinion of Mrs. Carr. She has the true eye of the artist—a wonderful eye. I don't know whether you remember Mrs. Archibald Fowler or not?" she added as the skirt fitter sped in search of Gabriella; "this is her daughter-in-law. Her husband ran away with another woman about three years ago. It made a great sensation at the time, and his wife got a divorce from him afterwards. Ever since then she has been in my establishment."

No, Mrs. Pletheridge did not remember Mrs. Fowler; but, having had a notorious amount of trouble with her own husbands, she was amiably disposed toward the unfortunate daughter-in-law of the lady she couldn't remember. Thirty years ago, as a pretty, vulgar, kind-hearted girl, she had captured with a glance the eldest son of the newly rich Pletheridge, who had, perhaps, inherited his grandfather's genial admiration for chambermaids; but, to-day, after a generation of self-indulgence, her prettiness had coarsened, her vulgarity had hardened, and her kind heart had withered, through lack of cultivation, to the size of a cherry. And, from having had everything she wanted for so long, she had at last reached that melancholy state of mind when she could think of nothing more to want.

A brisk step crossed the room outside, the curtains were parted with a commanding movement, and Gabriella joined the anxious group surrounded by the four mirrors.

"Did you send for me, Madame?" she asked, and waited, grave, attentive, and perfectly composed, with her hand, the small, strong hand of the Carrs, on the curtain. Her hair was brushed severely back from her candid forehead, and though her figure had grown somewhat heavier and less girlish in line, she still wore her plain black dress and white collar with an incomparable distinction. Through all the hardship and suffering of the last three years she had kept her look of bright intelligence, of radiant energy. In dress and manner she was the successful woman of business, but she was the woman of business with something added. Though she spoke in a matter-of-fact tone, her voice had a vibrating quality; though she wore only the plainest clothes, her grace, her good-breeding, her indefinable charm, softened the severity.

"Mrs. Pletheridge is uncertain about this gown," explained Madame, "but I tell her that it suits her to perfection, as well as if it had been designed for her by Worth. Do you not agree with me, Mrs. Carr? You have, as I said to her, the true eye of the artist."

Without changing her position or moving a step into the room, Gabriella attentively regarded the gown and the wearer. From the mirror Mrs. Pletheridge stared back at her ill-humouredly, with a spiteful gleam in her small black eyes between the carefully darkened lids.

"I can't imagine what is the matter with it," she reiterated, as if she were repeating a sad refrain, and her manner was as insolent as Miss Murphy's had been to the casual customer.

For an instant Gabriella returned her look with the steady gaze of one who, having achieved the full courage of living, has attained also a calm insensibility to the shafts of arrogance. Three years ago she would have flinched before Mrs. Pletheridge's disdain, but in those three years she had passed beyond the variegated tissue of appearances to the bare structure of life—she had worked and wept and starved and suffered—and to-day her soul was invulnerable against even more destructive weapons than the contempt of a plutocrat. Perhaps, too, though she assured herself that she was without snobbishness, there was a secret satisfaction in the knowledge that one of her ancestors had been a general under Washington while the early Pletheridges were planting potatoes in a peasant's patch in Ireland. Her dignity was more assured than Madame's; for she was perfectly aware of a fact to which Madame was blind, and this was, that, in spite of her position in the social columns of the newspapers and her multitudinous possessions, Mrs. Pletheridge was not, and could never be, a lady. While Gabriella stood there these thoughts flashed recklessly through her mind; yet she answered Madame's question as frankly and honestly as if the woman they were staring at with such intentness had not been the tragic vulgarian she was.

"I think the gown doesn't suit her at all," she said quietly to Madame, who made a horrified face at her over the sumptuous shoulder of Mrs. Pletheridge. "There is too much of it, too much billowy lace everywhere." She did not add that the coral and silver brocade gave Mrs. Pletheridge a curious resemblance to an overblown prize hollyhock.

Madame's horrified face changed, as if under a spell, to one of abject despair; and a menacing frown convulsed the puffy features of Mrs. Pletheridge, while she burst out of her gorgeous sheath with a petulant haste which expressed her inward perturbation better than words could have done. For a minute one could have heard a flower drop in the fitting-room; then the offended customer spoke, and her words, when she found them, were not lacking in either force or effectiveness. "No, there's no use trying on anything else, I have an appointment at Cambon's." Cambon was Dinard's hated and wholly incompetent rival; and until this illuminating instant Madame had never suspected that her particular Mrs. Pletheridge had ever entered the high white doors of Cambon's establishment.

"But, surely, we have something else. There is a lovely Doucet model—in white and silver—"

But no, Mrs. Pletheridge would have none of the lovely model. "Give me my skirt at once," she commanded haughtily, bending her opulent bosom and holding the lacy frills of her petticoat together while Agnes, the youngest and the gentlest of the assistants, knelt at her feet with her dress skirt held invitingly open on the floor. As she inserted the toe of her exquisitely shod foot into the opening, she remarked maliciously: "It is impossible to find decent clothes in New York—one might as well give up trying. Paris dressmakers send you only their failures." And, having crushed Madame to silence, she finished her dressing, fastened her black lace veil with a flying swallow in diamonds, flung her feather boa over her shoulders, and taking up her gold chain bag, studded with rubies, marched out of the establishment with all the pomp and impressiveness of a military parade.

"I've lost her. She will never come back," moaned Madame, and burst into tears.

"But she couldn't possibly have worn that gown. She would have found it out as soon as she got home," replied Gabriella reassuringly, though her heart was almost as heavy as Madame's.

It was all her fault, of course, as Madame, recovering her voice as she lost her temper, began immediately to tell her. It was all her fault, and yet how could she have stood there and lied to the woman in cold blood because Madame expected it of her as a part of her work? That she had infuriated Madame and imperilled her position she realized perfectly; but, realizing this, she still felt that she could not have told Mrs. Pletheridge that the gown was becoming to her. "There are times when one has to be honest no matter what happens," she thought rebelliously, while she went back to the workroom. Had Madame discharged her on the spot she would not have been surprised, and it was with a sensation of relief that she presently saw the forewoman measuring a dose of aromatic spirits of ammonia, and heard that the crisis was passing. A little later, when she went into the showroom with a hat for Miss Bellman, she encountered Madame bonneted, cloaked, panting, with moist eyes and raddled cheeks, preparing to take a slow airing in a hansom. As she was assisted into the vehicle by Miss Murphy and the driver, Madame pressed her beringed hand to her forehead with a despairing gesture; then the driver cracked his whip, the horse started, and the hansom disappeared up Fifth Avenue.

"What under the sun did you do to her?" inquired Miss Murphy, holding her wheaten-red pompadour down in the wind. "I declare I thought at first it was murder!"

"I told her the truth, when she asked me, that was all."

"Well, I never! Now what, in the name of goodness, possessed you?"

"I had to. I don't see how I could have kept from it."

"Good gracious! There're always ways, but what sort of truth was it? You see, it's been so long since I've met one," she explained airily, "that I don't even know what they're like."

"It was about Mrs. Pletheridge's gown—the one she wanted her to buy, you know. I told her it didn't suit her. And it didn't—you know it didn't," she concluded emphatically.

"Of course it didn't, but I don't see why you had to go and tell her."

"She asked me. They both asked me, and if I'd lied she wouldn't have believed me. You can't fool people so outrageously, and I wouldn't if I could. It isn't honest, and it isn't good business."

"Anything is good business that gets by," remarked Miss Murphy, who had a philosophy. "I must go indoors or this wind will blow all my puffs away."

She departed breezily; and Gabriella, returning to the workroom, spent her afternoon patiently stitching flat garlands of flowers on the brim of a hat. When she left the house at six o'clock the April weather was so lovely that she decided to walk all the way home; and while she moved rapidly with the crowd in Fifth Avenue, she considered anxiously the possible disastrous results of Madame's anger. Between her and absolute want there stood only her salary, and she had deliberately—she realized now how deliberate her reply had been—undermined that thin and insecure protection. Though she was now earning as much as thirty dollars a week, an illness of a year ago, when she had been obliged to stop work for several months, had exhausted the remains of the modest nest egg with which she had started; and to lose her place, she knew, would mean either starvation or beggary. There was no one, with the exception of Cousin Jimmy, of whom she could beg, and to beg of him would be a tacit confession that she had failed as a breadwinner. In Mrs. Carr's last letter Charley had appeared in a new light as a reformed character, a devoted attendant at church, and an enthusiastic convert to the prohibition party; and Gabriella had gathered from her mother's pious rambling that, like other sinners who have outlived temptation, he was devoting his middle years to a violent crusade against the moderate indulgences of the abstemious. But Charley, she felt, was out of the question. She would die before she would stoop to ask help of a man she had despised as heartily as she had once despised Charley. She must sink or swim by her own strength, not by another's.

"I wonder why I did it?" she asked herself again, and again she could not answer the question. She felt that she might have lied had it been merely a lie and not a test of courage before her; but she could not lie simply because she was afraid of speaking the truth. In every character there is one supreme vice or virtue which strikes the deepest root and blossoms most luxuriantly, and in the character of Gabriella this virtue was courage. At the crucial moments of life some primordial instinct prompted her to fight, not to yield. "I ought to have been evasive, I suppose," she thought regretfully. "But how could I have been?" There were instants, she had discovered, when wisdom surrendered to the more militant virtues.

When she reached home she found Fanny, who was fretfully recovering from influenza, lying on the sofa in the living-room, with Miss Polly busily stitching at her side, while Archibald, excited by a strenuous afternoon with the son of the Italian fruit dealer, was kneeling before the window, making mysterious signs to a group of yellow-haired German children in the apartment house on the opposite side of the street. Both children were eagerly expecting their mother, and as soon as she entered they grew animated and cheerful.

She kissed and cuddled them, and listened sympathetically to their excited stories of the day, and of Dr. French, who had been to see Fanny, and who had waited as long as he could.

"He's going to take us for a drive to-morrow, mother, and we're to sit in the carriage while he goes in to pay his calls, and then he's to show us the river and we're to stop somewhere to have tea."

"Did he stay long?" asked Gabriella of Miss Folly.

"For more than an hour," replied Miss Folly, and commented shrewdly after a minute: "It looks to me as if there was more in that young man than you can see on the surface, Gabriella."

A blush tinged Gabriella's cheek, but she shook her head almost indignantly. "Oh, there's nothing of that kind," she answered emphatically, and rose to take off her hat and prepare supper.

Since her illness of a year ago, when she had summoned the strange young doctor who had once been the assistant of the Fowlers' family physician, she had grown to feel a certain dependence upon Dr. French as the only useful friend who was left to her. He was a thin, gray-eyed, fair-haired young man, who practised largely among the poor, from choice rather than from necessity, since Dr. Morton had given him an excellent start in life. His pale, ascetic face had attracted Gabriella from their first meeting; there was the flamelike enthusiasm of the visionary in his eyes; and he had, she thought, the most beautiful and sympathetic hands she had ever seen. Even Fanny, who was usually impervious to sensitive impressions, felt the charm of his touch when he stroked her forehead or placed his long, delicate fingers on her wrist. From that first visit he had been a source of comfort and strength to Gabriella; but of late she had felt moments of uneasiness when she was with him. Was it possible, she asked herself now, as she went back to the kitchen to stew the oysters Miss Polly had bought for supper, that the kindly doctor was misinterpreting the simple and unaffected nature of her friendship? For herself she felt that she had put the reality of love out of her life, and that if the emotion existed for her at all, it existed only as a dream and a regret. She enshrined the memory of Arthur in something of the sentimental worship which Mrs. Carr had consecrated to Gabriel after she had lost him. It was an exquisite consolation to her to feel that if things had been otherwise, she might have loved a man with the whole of her nature—with both body and spirit; there were even moments in the spring of the year, when, softened by the caressing air and the scent of hyacinths, she felt that she did so love a memory; but beyond this her feeling was as bodiless and ethereal as the vague image to which it was dedicated. And yet this gentle regret was all that she wanted of love.

In the kitchen she found Miss Danton, the musical spinster, making her scant supper of tea and toast on the gas-range. Though the hectic flush still burned in Miss Danton's cheeks, the famished look in her eyes seemed to have devoured all the strength of her body, and she moved like one who has run to the point of exhaustion and is about to drop to the ground. Long ago Gabriella had heard her story, and she understood now that the yearning in her face was the yearning for life, which she had rejected in her youth, and which, in middle-age, had eluded her. As a young girl, aflame with temperament, she had sacrificed herself to a widowed father and a family of little brothers and sisters in a small town in the South. For thirty years she had fought down her dreams and her impulses; for thirty years she had cooked, washed, ironed, and sewed, until the children had all grown up and married, and her father, after a long illness, had died in her arms. On her fifty-second birthday her freedom had come— freedom not only from cares and responsibilities, but from love, from duty, from the constant daily thought that she was necessary to some one who depended on her. At fifty-three, with broken health and a few thousand dollars brought from the sale of the old home, she had come to New York to study music as she had dreamed of doing when she was young. And the tragedy of it was that she had a gift, she had temperament, she had genuine artistic feeling.

"When I remember the way I used to cook for the children," she remarked while she measured a teaspoonful of green tea into a little Japanese tea-pot, "why, I'd think nothing of roasting a turkey when we had one at Christmas or

Thanksgiving, and now, I declare, it seems too much trouble to do more than make a pot of tea. Sometimes I don't even take the trouble to toast my bread."

"You ought to eat," replied Gabriella, briskly. "When one gets run down, one never looks at life fairly." True to her fundamental common sense, she had never underestimated the importance of food as a prop for philosophy.

"I'd never eat if I could help it," rejoined Miss Danton, with the abhorrence of the aesthetic temperament for material details. "It's queer the thoughts I have sometimes," she added irrelevantly as she sat down before the kitchen table, and poured out a cup of tea. "I don't know what's come over me, but I'd give anything on earth—if it wasn't wicked I'd almost give my soul—to be your age and to be starting to live my life. I never had any life. It wasn't fair. I never had any," she repeated bitterly, dropping a lump of sugar into her cup.

"Well, I've had my troubles, too," observed Gabriella, busily stirring the oysters.

"You've had them and you'll have others. It doesn't matter—nothing really matters as long as you're young. It's all a part of the game, trouble and everything else—everything except old age and death. I'm getting old—I'm getting old, and I began too late, and that's the worst that can happen to a woman. Do you know I never had a love affair in my life," she pursued bitterly after a moment. "I never had love, or pleasure, or anything but work and duty— and now it's too late. It's too late for it all," she finished, rising to take her toast from the oven.

"Poor thing, she exaggerates so dreadfully," thought Gabriella. "I believe it comes from drinking too much green tea"; and she resolved that she would never touch green tea as long as she lived. Like most women whose love had ended not in unfulfilment, but in satiety and bitterness, she was inclined to deny the supreme importance of the passion in the scheme of life. As a deserted wife and the mother of two children, she felt that she could live for years without the desire, without even the thought of romantic love in her mind. "I wonder why I, who have known and lost love, should be so much freer from that obsession than poor Miss Danton, who has never been loved in her life?" she asked herself while she carried the supper tray down the long hall and into the living-room.

Some hours later, when the children were asleep, and Gabriella sat darning Archibald's stockings beside the kerosene lamp, she described to Miss Polly the scene with Madame and Mrs. Pletheridge.

"I don't know how it will end. She may discharge me to-morrow," she deliberated, as she cut off a length of black darning cotton, and bent over to thread her needle. "I wonder what I ought to do?"

"Well, now, ain't that exactly like you, Gabriella," scolded Miss Polly; "but when you come to think of it," she conceded after a minute or two, "I reckon we're all made like that in the beginning. Why, I remember way back yonder in the 'seventies how I was always tryin' to persuade a woman with a skinny figure not to wear a cuirass basque and a woman with a stout figure not to put on a draped polonaise. I got to know better presently, and you will, too, before you've been at it much longer. They all think they can look like fashion plates—the skinniest and the stoutest alike—and there ain't a bit of use tryin' to undeceive 'em. The last thing a woman ever sees straight is her figure."

"I can't help feeling," demurred Gabriella, forsaking the moral issue for the argument of mere expediency, "that honesty is good business."

"Well, it ain't," retorted Miss Polly sharply. "It may be good religion and good behaviour, but there's one thing it certainly ain't, and that is good business. How many of these rich men we read about in the papers do you reckon spend their time settin' around and bein' honest? Mind you I ain't sayin' I'd lie or steal myself, Gabriella, but I'm poor, and what I'm sayin' is that when you feel that way about it, you're as likely to stay poor as not."

But the next day, life, with one of those startling surprises which defy philosophy and make drama, confirmed the most illogical of Gabriella's assumptions. Madame, coming in late, with a blotched face and puffy eyelids, had dispatched her to the workroom, and she was sitting before one of the long tables, embroidering azure beads on a black collar, when Agnes darted through the door and jerked the needle out of her hand.

"Madame is asking for you. Come as quick as you can!" she cried excitedly, and sped back again to the shelter of the artificial rose-bushes at the end of the hall.

Rising hurriedly, and brushing the scraps of silk from her cloth skirt as she walked, Gabriella followed the sound of Madame's wheedling voice, and found herself, as she parted the curtains of a fitting-room, in the opulent presence of Mrs. Pletheridge.

"Yes, as I told you, we trust implicitly to Mrs. Carr's eye. She has the true eye of the artist," Madame simpered fawningly as she entered. "Did you send for me?" asked Gabriella, business-like and alert on the threshold.

"Good morning, Mrs. Carr! I told Madame Dinard that I wanted you to wait on me. I want some one who tells me the truth," explained Mrs. Pletheridge so graciously that Gabriella would hardly have recognized her. Something—sleep, pleasure, or pious meditation—had altered overnight not only her temper but even the fleshly vehicle of its uncertain manifestations. Her features appeared to have adjusted themselves to the size of her face, and she spoke quite affably, though still with her manner of addressing an inferior.

"I want you to show me something that will really suit me," she said. "I think the grayish-green cloth from Blandin might be copied in silver, but I should like you to see it on me. I know you will tell me what you really think." Her voice faltered and deepened to a note of pathos.

"Poor woman," thought Gabriella, "it must be hard for her to get people to tell her what they really think," and she added exultantly while she went for the gowns: "If I satisfy her now, I am saved with Madame!"

When she returned, with the green cloth in one hand and a charming lavender crêpe tea-gown in the other, she approached Mrs. Pletheridge with the manner of intelligent sympathy, of serene and smiling competence, which had made her so valuable to Madame as a saleswoman. She had the air not only of seeking to please, but of knowing just how to go about the difficult matter of pleasing. With the eye of an artist in dress, she analyzed Mrs. Pletheridge's possibilities; and softening here and there her pronounced features, succeeded presently in producing a charming and harmonious whole. By the time a dozen gowns were tried on and their available points discussed and criticised in detail, Mrs. Pletheridge had given the largest order ever received by the house, and was throwing out enthusiastic hints of an even greater munificence in the future. She left at last in a thoroughly good humour not only with Dinard's, but with her own rejuvenated attractions; and Gabriella, exhausted but triumphant, watched Agnes gather up the French models from chairs and sofas and carry them back to the obscurity of the closets. In her heart there was both peace and rejoicing because her belief in life had been justified. In spite of Madame, in spite of Miss Polly, in spite of experience, the day had proved that it was, after all, "good business" to be honest. Though she was still in debt, though she was still compelled to scrimp and save over market bills, nevertheless she felt that her work had progressed beyond the experimental stages, and that her place at Dinard's was secured until some better opening appeared. For that morning at least she had made herself indispensable to Madame. For years, she knew, Madame had striven fawningly for the exclusive patronage of Mrs. Pletheridge, and she, Gabriella, had attained it, without loss of pride or self-respect, by a few words of honest and sensible criticism. She had applied her intelligence to the situation, and her intelligence had served Dinard's more successfully than Madame's duplicity had done.

At home she found Dr. French, who had just brought the delighted children back from their drive. When she thanked him, she saw that there was a glow of pleasure in his rather delicate face, and that this glow lent an expression of ecstasy to his dark-gray eyes—the eyes of a mystic and a dreamer. "I wonder how he ever became a physician," she thought. "He is more like a priest—like a priest of the Middle Ages." But aloud she only said: "You have done them a world of good. Fanny has got some of her colour back already, and that means an appetite for supper."

"We had tea," broke in Archibald, with enthusiasm, "but it was really milk, and we had cake, but it was really bread and butter." He looked so well and vigorous that Gabriella called the doctor's attention to the animation in his face. "If only he didn't have to wear glasses," she said. "I'm so afraid it will interfere with his love of sports. His ambition is to be captain of a football team and to write poetry."

"It's a queer combination," responded the doctor, smiling his slightly whimsical smile. He was rather short, with an almost imperceptible limp, and he had, as he put it, "never gone in for sports." "There's so much else when one comes to think of it," he added, pausing, with his hat in his hand, at the door; "there are plenty of ways of having fun even without football." Then he turned away from the children, and said directly to Gabriella:

"Will you come out with me to-morrow? It is Sunday."

"And leave the children?" she asked a little blankly.

"And leave the children!" He was laughing, but it occurred to her suddenly, for the first time, that her maternal raptures were beginning to bore him. For a year she had believed that his interest in her was mainly a professional interest in the children; and now she was confronted with the disturbing fact that he wanted to be rid of the children for a few hours at least, that he evidently saw in her something besides the overwhelming force of her motherhood.

"But I never leave them on Sunday. It is the only day I have with them," she answered.

"Don't go, mother! You mustn't go!" cried Fanny, and clung to her.

"Oh, very well," returned Dr. French, dismissing the subject with irritation. "But you look pale, and I thought the air might do you good."

He went away rather abruptly, while Gabriella stood looking at Miss Polly in regret and perplexity. "I hope I didn't hurt his feelings by declining," she said; and then, as the children raced into the nursery to take off their coats, she added slowly, "He couldn't expect me to go without them."

"If you want to know what I think," replied Miss Polly flatly, "it is that he's just sick to death of the children. You've stuck them down his throat until he's had as much of them as he can swallow."

For a moment Gabriella considered this ruefully.

"You don't honestly believe that he's interested in me in that way?" she demanded in a horrified whisper.

"I don't know but one way in which a man's ever interested in a woman," retorted Miss Polly. "It's either that way or it's none at all, as far as I can see. But if I was you, honey, I'd drop him a little encouragement now and then, just to keep up his spirits. Men ain't no mo' than flesh and blood, after all" and it's natural that he shouldn't be as crazy about the children as you are."

"But why should I encourage him? Even if you are right, I couldn't marry him. I could never marry again."

"I'd like to know why not, if you get a chance? You're free enough, ain't you?"

"Yes, it isn't that—but I couldn't."

"You ain't hankerin' after George, are you, Gabriella?"

"After George? No!" responded Gabriella with so sincere an accent that Miss Polly jumped.

"Well, I'm glad you ain't," observed the seamstress soothingly as she stooped to pick up her sewing. "I shouldn't think he was worth hankerin' after, myself, but you've looked kind of peaked and thin this spring, so I've just been wonderin'."

"I never loved George. It was madness, nothing else," returned Gabriella, and she really believed it.

"Well, your thinkin' it madness now don't mean it wan't love ten years ago," commented Miss Polly, with the shrewdness of a detached and observant spinster.

"I suppose you're right," admitted Gabriella thoughtfully. Though she had not mentioned Arthur, her mind was full of him, and she was perfectly convinced that she had loved him all her life—even during her brief period of "madness." It was a higher love, she felt, so much higher, indeed, that it had been too spiritual, too ethereal, to take root in the earthly soil from which her passion for George had sprung. But, if it were not love, why was it that every faint stirring of her emotions revived the memory so poignantly? Why was it that Miss Polly's sentimental interpretation of the doctor's interest evoked the image of Arthur?

"No, I never think of George—never," she repeated, and her fine, pure features assumed an expression of sternness. "But I shan't marry again," she went on after a pause in which Miss Polly's sewing-machine buzzed cheerfully over its work. "I've had enough of marriage to last me for one lifetime."

The machine stopped, and Miss Polly, snipping the thread as she came to the end of a seam, turned squarely to answer. "Don't you be too sure about that, honey. You may have had enough to last you for ten years or so, but wait till you've turned forty, and if the hankerin' for love don't catch you at forty, you may begin to expect it somewhere around fifty. Why, just look at that poor piano-playin' old maid in there. Wouldn't you think she'd have done with it? Well, she ain't—she ain't, and you ain't either, for that matter, I don't care how hard you argue!"

"There are ten happy years ahead of me anyhow!" rejoined Gabriella, with a ringing laugh—the laugh, as Dr. French had once remarked, of a woman who is sound to the core. She had triumphed over the past, and was not afraid, she told herself valiantly, of the future.

At the beginning of July the children went with Miss Polly to the country, and Gabriella, after seeing them off, turned back alone to begin a long summer of economy and drudgery. In order to keep Fanny and Archibald out of town she was obliged to deny herself every unnecessary comfort—luxuries she had given up long ago—and to stay at Dinard's, in Madame's place, through the worst weeks of the year, when the showroom was deserted except for an occasional stray Southerner, and even the six arrogant young women were away on vacations. Even if she had had the chance, the money for a trip would have been lacking, and to fill Madame's conspicuous place gave her, she realized, a certain importance and authority in the house. There was opportunity, in a small way, to work out some of her ideas of system and order, and there was sufficient time to think out a definite and practical plan for the future. Her aim from the first had been, not only to catch on, but to master the details of the business, and she knew that, in spite of Madame's sporadic attempts to keep her in her place, she was gradually making herself felt—she was slowly impressing her individual methods upon the establishment. Madame was no longer what she once was, and the business was showing it. She was getting old, she was growing tired, and her naturally careless methods of work were fastening upon her. In the last years she had offered less and less resistance to her tendency to let go, to leave loose ends ungathered, to allow opportunities to slip out of her grasp, to be inexact and unsystematic. There was urgent need of a strong hand at Dinard's, if the business was to be kept from running gradually downhill, and

Gabriella became convinced, as the days passed, that hers was the only hand in the house strong enough to check the perilous descent to failure. Her plans were made, her scheme arranged, but, as Madame was both jealous and suspicious, she saw that she must move very cautiously.

There were times—since this is history, not romance—when her spirits flagged and her strength failed her. The heat of the summer was intense, and the breathless days dragged on interminably into the breathless nights. When her work was over she would wait until the last of her fellow-workers had gone home, and then walk across to Sixth Avenue and take the Harlem elevated train for her deserted rooms, which appeared more desolate, more ugly than ever because the children were absent. In the lonely kitchen—for Miss Danton and the art students were all away—she would eat her supper of bread and tea, which she drank without cream because it was more economical; and then, lighting her lamp, she would sew or read until midnight. Sometimes, when it was too hot for the lamp, and she found it impossible to work by the flickering gas, she would sit by her window and look down on the panting humanity in the street below—on the small shopkeepers seated in chairs on the sidewalk, on the little son of the Italian fruiterer playing with his dog, on the three babies of the Jewish tobacco merchant, sprawling in the door of the tiny shop which was pressed like a sardine between a bakery and a dairy. She was alone in the apartment, and there were late afternoons when the grim emptiness of the rooms seemed haunted, when she shrank back in apprehensive foreboding as she turned her key in the lock, when the profound silence within preyed on her nerves like an obsession. On these days she dreaded to go down the long hail to the kitchen, where the fluttering clothes-lines on fire-escapes at the back of the next apartment house offered the only suggestion of human companionship in the unfriendly wilderness of the city. The sight of the children's toys, of Fanny's story books, of Archibald's roller skates, moved her to tears once or twice; and when this happened she caught herself up sharply and struggled with the vague, malignant demon of melancholy.

"Whatever comes, I must not lose my courage," she told herself at such times. "If I lose my courage I shall have nothing left."

Then she would put on her hat, and go down into the street, where the unwashed children swarmed like insects over the pavements, and the air was as hot and parched as the air of a desert. If the mother of the Jewish babies sat on her doorstep, she would stop for a little talk with her about the heat and the health of the children, and the increasing price of whatever one happened to buy in the market, or, perhaps, if the fruit stall still kept open, she would ask after the Italian's little boy, and stop to pat Archibald's friend, the white mongrel with the black ear. She had left her acquaintances when she left Fifty-seventh Street, and, with the exception of Judge Crowborough, who telephoned occasionally to inquire if she needed assistance, she was without friends in New York. Patty wrote often from Paris, but Billy was happy with his work, and they said nothing of returning to America. In the whole city, outside of Dinard's, she knew only Dr. French, and from him she had had no word or sign for several months.

It was on one of these depressing evenings, while she was boiling an egg in the kitchen, that the ringing of the door-bell reverberated with an uncanny sound through the empty apartment. Spurred by an instinctive fear of a telegram, she ran to open the door, and found Dr. French standing in the dimly lighted hall, with the negro Robert grinning cheerfully at his back.

"I am so glad," she said, "so glad," and her voice shook in spite of the effort she made.

"I've been thinking about you all summer," he explained, "and the other day I passed you in the street as you were coming from work. You are not looking well. Is it the heat?"

"No, it isn't the heat. I think it is the loneliness. You see it is so different not having the children to come back to in the afternoon, and when I get lonely I see things in false proportions. This apartment has been like a grave to me all summer."

She led the way into the living-room, where her sewing, a blue cambric frock she was scalloping for Fanny, was lying on the chair by the window. "Things are all upset. I hope you won't mind," she added apologetically while she folded the dress and laid it aside, "but nothing seems to matter when I sit here all by myself."

"What are you doing?"

"Oh, I work all day. There is really very little to do except plan for the autumn, and I like that. Madame is in Paris, and I am in charge of the place."

"And in the evenings?"

She laughed with recovered spirit. "In the evening I sew and read and mope."

"Well, we must change all that," he said, with a tenderness which brought tears to her eyes. "Why can't you come out with me somewhere to dinner?"

Three years ago, when she was first separated from George, she would have evaded the suggestion; but to-night, at the end of the long summer, she caught eagerly at the small crumb of pleasure.

"Oh, I'd love to! Only wait until I put out the stove and tidy my hair."

"I want to see what you have to eat," he remarked in his whimsical tone, as he followed her back into the kitchen. "Only an egg!"

"It is so hot. I wasn't hungry, but I am now," she replied gaily, her thin face flushing to beauty. After her loneliness there was a delight in being cared for, in being scolded. "But for the mistake I made this might happen to me always," she thought, and her mind went back to Arthur.

When she came out of her room, wearing a fresh linen blouse, with her hair smoothly brushed, and her eyes sparkling with pleasure, he was gazing abstractedly down into the street, and she was obliged to speak twice to him before he heard her and turned. At last he broke away, almost with an effort, from his meditation, and when he looked at her she saw that there was the mystic gleam in his eyes—the light as of a star shining through clouds—which attracted her so strongly. The thought flashed through her vague impressions, "He loves me. I may win him by a smile, by a word, by a look," and, for a minute, she rested on the certainty with an ineffable sense of peace, of ease, of deep inward rejoicing. "Love is everything. There is nothing worth while except love," she thought; and love meant to her then, not passion, not even romance, but comfort, tenderness, and the companionship that sweetens the flat monotony of daily living. Then, beneath the beauty and sweetness of the vision, she felt the vein of iron in her soul as she had felt it whenever she struggled to escape the sterner issues of life. The face of Arthur rose in her memory, tender, wistful, protecting, and young with the eternal youth of desire. No, love was not for her again. Not for the second time would she betray the faith of her Dream.

They dined at a little French restaurant, where the green-shaded lights, festooned with grape leaves, shed a romantic pallor over their faces, and the haunting refrains of an Italian love song stirred the buried ghosts in their hearts. The doctor made her drink a glass of champagne; and after her frugal meals and the weakening effect of the heat and the loneliness, the sparkle of the wine, mingling with the music and the lights, sent a sudden rush of joy through her veins. Her courage came back to her, not in slow drops, but in a radiant flood, which pervaded her being. After the lonely months there was delight in the clasp of a friend's hand, in the glance of a friend's eye, in the sound of a friend's voice speaking her name. Life appeared divinely precious at the instant; and by life she meant not happiness, not even fulfilment, but the very web, the very texture and pattern of experience.

"You're better already," he said, with a solicitude that was more intoxicating than wine to her. "How I wish I'd known all summer that you were here. I might have done something to make you happy, and now I've missed my chance."

"I don't think I've ever been so happy as I am to-night," she answered simply, and then after a pause she let fall word by word, "After all, it takes so little to make me happy."

"One can tell that to look at you. You have the air of happiness. I noticed it the first moment I saw you. And yet you have not had an easy life. There must have been terrible hours for you in the past."

"No, I haven't had an easy life, but I love it. I mean I love living."

"I know, I understand," he said softly. "It is the true American spirit— optimism springing out of a struggle. Do you know you have always made me think of the American spirit at its best—of its unquenchable youth, its gallantry, its self-reliance—"

They walked back slowly through the hot, close streets, and sat for an hour beside her window-sill on which a rose geranium was blooming in an earthen pot. Now and then a breeze entered warily, stealing the fragrance from the rose geranium, and rippling the dark, straying tendrils of Gabriella's hair. By the dim light she saw the wistful pallor of his face, and his blue eyes, with their exalted look, which moved her heart to an inexpressible tenderness.

"You are so different from other physicians," she said in perplexity, "I can't think of you as one, no matter how hard I try. All the others I have known, even old Dr. Walker, were materialists."

"Well, I got in some way. There are fools in every school, I suppose. But if it's any comfort to you, they've done their best to get rid of me. They don't like my theories." When he talked of his work he seemed all at once another man to her, and she discerned presently, while she listened to his earnest voice, that he was one of the men whose emotional natures are nourished by an abstract and impersonal passion—by the passion for science, for truth in its concrete form. After all, he was a mystic only in his eyes. Beneath his dreamer's face he was a scientist to the last drop of his blood, to the last fibre of his being. "He can't be hurt deeply through the heart," she thought; "only through the mind."

"I've wondered about you all summer," he repeated presently, "and yet I kept away—partly, I suppose, because I was thinking too much of you."

At his change of tone from the impersonal to the tender all the frozen self-pity in her heart seemed to melt suddenly, threatening in its overflow the very foundations of her philosophy. The temptation to yield utterly, to rest for a while not on her strength, but on his, assailed her with the swiftness and the violence of a spiritual revulsion. For an instant she surrendered to the uncontrollable force of this desire; then she drew quickly back while the world about her—the room, the window, the bare skeleton of the elevated road, the street, and even the rose geranium blooming on the sill—became as remote and impalpable as a phantom.

"It has been a long summer," she heard herself saying from a distance in a thin and colourless voice.

"And you suffered?"

"Sometimes, but I'm interested in my work, and I've been thinking and planning all summer."

For a moment he was silent, and though she did not look at him, she could feel his intense gaze on her face. The breeze, scented with rose geranium, touched her forehead like the healing and delicate stroke of his fingers.

"You are still so young, so vital, not to have something else in your life," he went on presently in a voice so charged with feeling that her eyes filled while she listened to it.

"I have had love, and I have my children."

"But you will love again? You will marry again some day?"

She shook her head, hearing, above the street cries and the muffled rumble of the elevated train, a voice that said: "I shall never give you up, Gabriella!" To her weakened nerves there appeared, with the vividness of an hallucination, the memory of Arthur as he had looked in her school-days when she had first loved him; and in this hallucination she saw him, not as he was in reality, but divinely glorified and enkindled by the light her imagination had created around him.

"No, I shall never love again, I shall never love again," she answered at last, while a feeling of exultation surged through her.

"You mean," his voice shook a little, "that your husband still holds you?"

"My husband? No, I never think of my husband."

"Is there some one else?"

Before answering she looked up at him, and by his face she knew that her reply would cost her his friendship. She wanted his friendship—at the moment she felt that she would gladly give a year of her life for it. It meant companionship instead of loneliness, it meant plenty instead of famine. Yet only for an instant, only while she stopped to draw breath, did she hesitate. "Women must learn to be honourable," she found herself thinking suddenly with an extraordinary intensity.

"Yes, there is some one else—there has always been some one else," she said, driven on by an impulsive desire for full confession, for absolute candour. "When I met George I was engaged to another man, and I have loved that man all my life."

She had confessed all, she told herself; and the remarkable part was that she really believed her confession—she was honestly convinced that she had spoken only the truth. Her soul, like the soul of Cousin Jimmy, sheltered a romantic strain which demanded that one supreme illusion should endure amid a world of disillusionment. Because she was obliged to believe in something or die, she had built her imperishable Dream on the flame-swept ruins of her happiness.

"He must be a big man if he can fill a life like yours," said Dr. French.

"I don't know why I told you," she faltered; "I have never told any one else. It is my secret."

"Well, it is safe with me. Don't be afraid."

For the few minutes before he rose to go they talked indifferently of other things. She had lost him, she knew, and while she held his hand at parting, she felt a sharp regret for what was passing out of her life—for the one chance of love, of peace, of a tranquil and commonplace happiness. But beneath the regret there was a hidden spring of joy in her heart. At the instant of trial she had found strength to be true to her Dream.

# CHAPTER V

## SUCCESS

"I declare you're real pretty to-night, honey," remarked Miss Polly from the floor, where she knelt pinning up the hem of a black serge skirt she was making for Gabriella. "Some days you're downright plain, and then you flame out just like a lamp. Nobody would ever think to look at you that you'd be thirty-seven years old to-morrow." For it was the evening before Gabriella's birthday, and she was at the end of her thirty-sixth year.

"I feel young," she answered brightly, "and I feel happy. The children are well, and I've had all the success I could ask. Some day I'm going to own Madame's business, Miss Polly."

"I reckon she's gettin' mighty old, ain't she?"

"She gave up the work years ago, and I believe she'd be glad to sell out to me to-morrow if I had the money.

"I wish you had. It would be nice for you to be at the head, now wouldn't it?" rejoined Miss Polly, speaking with difficulty through a mouthful of pins.

"Yes, I wish I had, but I've thought and thought, and I don't see how I could borrow enough. I've sometimes thought of asking Judge Crowborough to invest some money in the business. It would be investing, the returns are so good."

"He'd do it in a minute, I expect. He always set a lot of store by you, didn't he?"

"He used to, but somehow I hate to ask favours."

"You were always a heap too proud. Don't you remember how you'd never eat the other children's cake when you were a child unless you had some of your own to offer 'em?"

Gabriella laughed. "No, I don't remember, but it sounds like me. I was horrid."

"There was always a hard streak somewhere down in you, and you don't mind my sayin' that you ain't gettin' any softer, Gabriella. There are times now when your mouth gets a set look like your Aunt Becky Bollingbroke's. You don't recollect her, I 'spose, but she never married."

"Well, I married," Gabriella flippantly reminded her; "so it can't be that."

Though the hard work of the last ten years had left its visible mark upon her, and she looked a little older, a little tired, a little worn, experience had added a rare spiritual beauty to her face, and she was far handsomer than she had been at twenty. The rich sprinkling of silver in the heavy waves of hair over her ears framed the firm pale oval of her face with a poetic and mysterious darkness, and gave depth and softness to her brilliant eyes. For the struggle, which had stolen her first freshness and left faintly perceptible lines in her expressive face, had not robbed her of the eyes and the heart of a girl.

"I don't count George, somehow," retorted Miss Polly. "That wan't like marryin' a real man, you know, and, when all's said and done, a lone woman gets mighty hard and dried up."

"But I can't marry when there's nobody to marry me," laughed Gabriella. "I haven't seen a man for seven years except in the street or occasionally in the shop. Men have either passed me by without seeing me or they have wanted to sell me something."

At the sound of the children's voices she slipped out of the serge skirt, and began hurriedly fastening the old black silk gown she wore at dinner. Through all the years of toil and self-denial she had preserved a certain formality of living, a gracious ease of manner, which she kept for the evenings with her children. Cares were thrust away then, to be taken up again as soon as Fanny and Archibald were in bed, and no matter how hard the day had been, she was always cheerful, always gay and light-hearted for the dinner hour by the fireside. Not often had she been too poor to buy a handful of flowers for the table, and never once, except during her illness, had she come home too tired to change to the black silk gown, which she had turned and made from bishop sleeves to small ones, and from "dropped" shoulders to high ones, for the last six or seven years. The damask on the table was darned and mended, but it was always spotlessly fresh. In winter the fire was made up brightly in the evenings; in summer the room was deliciously scented with rose geranium and heliotrope from the box in the window. For ten years she had not had a holiday; she had worked harder than a man, harder than any servant, for she had worked from dawn until midnight; but into her hard life she had instilled a quality of soul which had enabled her to endure the strain without breaking. "No life is so hard that you can't make it easier by the way you take it," she had said to herself in the beginning; and remembering always that courage is one of the eternal virtues, she had disciplined her mind as well as her body to firmness and elasticity of fibre. "Nobody, except myself, is ever going to make me happy," she would repeat over and over again when the day was wearying and the work heavy. "I want to be happy. I have a right to be happy, but it depends on myself."

This indestructible belief in her "right to happiness" supported her through the hardest hours of her life, and diffused an invigorating atmosphere not only in her home, but even in her long working hours at Dinard's. The children grew and strengthened in its bracing air; Miss Polly quickly responded to it; the women in the workroom breathed it in as if it were the secret of health, and even Madame showed occasional signs that she was not entirely impervious to its vital and joyous influence. It was not always easy for Gabriella to keep the light in her eyes and the faith in her heart. There were days when both seemed to fail her, when, with aching body and depressed mind, she felt that she could not look beyond the immediate suffering minute, when she told herself despairingly that she had lost everything in losing her courage. But bad days passed as irrevocably as good ones; and left her, when they were over, with her strong soul unshaken, and her philosophy of happiness still undestroyed. Like other human beings, she found that her moods were largely controlled by her physical health.

"Oh, mother dear, I went down to meet you, and I missed you by just five minutes," said Fanny, kissing her cheek. "I wanted you to go with me to look at the house in London Terrace. Miss Polly and I are crazy about it."

"I know," said Gabriella tenderly, while she feasted her eyes on her daughter.

The old apartment house in which they had spent the last ten years would be torn down in the summer, and Fanny and Miss Folly had devoted the past week to an exhaustive hunt for a home.

"Then you'll look at it to-morrow, won't you, mother?" urged Fanny. "We can get the upper rooms and they are larger than these. There is a little yard in front, with an elm tree and a rose-bush, and plenty of space for flowers."

"I can't recall the house exactly," said Gabriella thoughtfully. "It must be in a row, isn't it? I have a vague recollection of some old houses, with fronts of stuccoed pilasters, and rather nice yards. But West Twenty-third Street is too far away, dear. I don't like the neighbourhood. Wouldn't you rather be in Park Avenue?" Her ignorance of New York, though she had lived there seventeen years, amazed Fanny, who was a true child of the city.

"Carlie Herndon lives in that row, mother"—Carlie Herndon, the daughter of a distinguished and unpopular novelist, was Fanny's best friend for the moment—"and I could always go out with her in the evening."

"It isn't the location I should have liked, Fanny," said Gabriella, weakly yielding, as she always yielded to her daughter; "but if you really fancy the house, I'll try to look at it on my way home to-morrow. One has to be very careful about the plumbing in these old houses. I insist upon good plumbing. After that, you may have what you want."

"Oh, it has brand new bathrooms, Mrs. Mallon told me so, and she's lived there until a year ago. And if you had only seen the new apartments we looked at, mother, nothing on the East Side that would have held us under twenty-five hundred a year, and even at that the bedrooms were no bigger than closets, and you'd have to have electric light all day in the bathroom. We searched everywhere, didn't we, Miss Polly?"

"West Twenty-third Street is mighty far out of the way, honey," observed Miss Polly cautiously.

"Oh, but I'd have Carlie, and she's my best friend," persisted Fanny, with caressing obstinacy.

"Well, we'll see, precious," said Gabriella, while she assured herself that if Fanny cost her every penny she had, at least the child was worth what she spent on her. To a superficial observer, Fanny would probably have appeared merely an attractive girl, of Jane's willowy type, with something of Jane's trite prettiness of feature; but to Gabriella, who suffered from a maternal obliquity of vision, she seemed both brilliant and beautiful. Of course she was selfish, but this selfishness, as long as it was clothed in her youth and loveliness, was as inoffensive as the playfulness of a kitten. Her face was round and shallow, with exquisite colouring which veiled the flatness and lack of character in her features. Above her azure eyes her hair, which was not plentiful, but fine and soft, and as yellow as ripe corn, broke in a shining mist over her forehead. All her life, by being what she was, she had got, without effort, everything that she wanted. She had got dolls when she wanted dolls; she had got Miss Ludwell's expensive school when she wanted an expensive private school; she would get the house in West Twenty-third Street to-morrow, and when she began to want love, she would get it as easily and as undeservedly as she got everything else. She was very expensive, but, like the flowers on the table and the spotless damask and the lace in Gabriella's sleeves, she was one of her mother's luxuries to be paid for by additional hours of work and thought.

"Wasn't Archibald with you?" inquired Gabriella, while she pushed the chairs into place and tidied the room.

"He stopped at the library. There's his ring now. I'll open the door."

She ran out, and Gabriella, with the tablecloth in her hand, stood waiting for Archibald to enter. In her eager expectancy, in the wistful brightness of her eyes, in the tender quivering of her lips, she was like a girl who is awaiting a lover. Every evening, after her day's work, she greeted her son with the same passionate tenderness. Never had it lessened, never, even when she was most discouraged, had she failed to summon her strength and her sweetness for this beatific end to the day. For Archibald was more than a son to her. As he grew older their characters became more perfectly adjusted, and the rare bond of a deep mental sympathy held them together. Fanny loved her as a spoiled child loves the dispenser of its happiness; but in Archibald's devotion there was something of the worship of a man for an ideal.

Flushed and hungry, the boy came in, and after kissing her hurriedly, ran off to wash his face and hands before dinner. When he came back the table was laid, with a bunch of lilacs in a cut glass vase over the darned spot in the tablecloth, and Miss Polly was bringing in the old-fashioned soup tureen, which had belonged to Gabriella's maternal grandmother.

"If you don't sit right straight down everything will be cold," said Miss Polly severely, for this was her customary manner of announcing dinner. Every night for ten years she had threatened them with a cold dinner while she served them a hot one.

With a child on either side of her, Gabriella sat down, and ladled the soup out of the old china tureen. It was her consecrated hour—the single hour of her toiling day that she dedicated to personal happiness; and because it was her hour, her life had gradually centred about it as if it were the divine point of her universe—the pivot upon which her whole world revolved. Nothing harsh, nothing sordid, nothing sad, ever touched the sacred precincts of her twilight hour with her children.

"I can beat any boy at school running, mother," said Archibald, watching his plate of soup hungrily as it travelled toward him. "If my eyes won't let me be captain of a football team, I'm going to become the champion runner in America. I bet I can, if I try."

"I shouldn't wonder, dear. It's good for you, too. I never saw you look better."

He was a tall, thin boy, with a muscular figure, and thick brown hair, which was always rumpled. Through his ugly spectacles his eyes showed large, dark, and as beautifully soft as a girl's. His mind was remarkably keen and active, and there was in his carriage something of Gabriella's capable and commanding air, as if, like her, he embodied those qualities which compel acknowledgment. Though she had never admitted it even to herself, he was her favourite child.

When dinner was over she had the children to herself—to the gracious, unhurried self she gave them—until ten o'clock. Then their books were put away, and after she had kissed them good-night, and tucked the covers about them, she came back to the living-room, and sat down to her sewing with Miss Polly. The ease and cheerfulness dropped from her at the approach of midnight, and while the two women bent over their needles they talked of their anxieties, and planned innumerable and intricate ways of economy.

"Fanny's school costs so much, and, of course, she must have clothes. All the other girls dress so expensively."

"You spend three times as much on her as you do on Archibald."

"I know," her voice melted to the mother note, "but Archibald is different. He is a man, and he will make his way in the world. Then, too, his expenses will be trebled next year when he goes off to school, and after that, of course, will come college. I don't believe anything or anybody can keep Archibald back," she went on proudly. "Do you know he talks already of going to work in a shipping office in order to help me?"

"It's a pity about his eyes."

"There's nothing wrong except near-sightedness, but he'll have to wear glasses all his life."

For a minute Miss Polly stitched almost furiously, while her small weatherbeaten face, with its grotesque features, was visited by an illumination that softened and ennobled its ugliness. From living entirely in the lives of others, she had attained the spiritual serenity and detachment of a saint as well as the saint's immunity from the intenser personal forms of suffering. Long habit had accustomed her to think of herself only in connection with somebody's need of her, and beyond this she hardly appeared as an individual existence even in her own secret reflections. As far as it is possible to achieve absolute unselfishness in a world planned upon egoistic principles Miss Polly had achieved it; and the result was that she was almost perfectly happy.

"Fanny seems right set on goin' down to Twenty-third Street, don't she?" she inquired, after an interval of musing.

"It's all because Carlie lives in the row, and by next year, after we've had all the trouble of moving, she'll find another bosom friend and want to go to Park Avenue."

"It's a real comfortable sort of house, more like Richmond than New York, and I reckon we could get flowers to grow there just about as well as they did in Hill Street."

"I don't like having those O'Haras on the lower floor. If they are loud and common, it might be very disagreeable."

"There ain't but one, a man, and he's hardly ever there, the caretaker's wife told me. She said he was almost always in the West, and anyway his lease is up next year, and he thinks he'll give up his rooms. She says he has made piles of money in mines somewhere out West, and he only keeps those rooms because they used to belong to a man who picked him out of the street when he was a little boy selling newspapers. That caretaker's wife seems to be a mighty kind-hearted creature, but she talks as if she was never goin' to stop."

"I think I could afford to take an apartment in Park Avenue," returned Gabriella, dismissing the name of O'Hara; "but, of course, I want to save as much as I can in order to invest in the business. If it wasn't for that, I could stop scraping and pinching. I can't bear, though, to think of leaving nothing for the children when I die."

"Go away from here, honey. The idea of your talkin' about dyin'! You look healthier than you ever did in your life, only you're gettin' that set look again about your mouth."

"I wonder if I'm growing hard," said Gabriella, stopping to glance in the mirror. "I suppose that's the problem of life for the working woman—not to grow hard." In some ways, she realized, Miss Polly was right. She was a handsome woman, as Madame occasionally informed her; but she was no longer shrinking, she was no longer alluringly feminine. To dress smartly for Dinard's was a part of her work, and she had grown quite indifferent to having men turn and stare after her in the street or when she entered a restaurant. But the men who stared never spoke to her as they did to Fanny when she was alone. They regarded her admiringly, but she aroused neither disrespect nor the protective instinct in their minds. Only when she smiled her face grew as young as her eyes, and with the powdering of silver on her hair, gave her a look of radiance and charm; but at other times, when she was grave or preoccupied with the management of Dinard's, the "set look" that Miss Polly dreaded hardened her mouth.

"I wish you could go easier now for a while," resumed the little seamstress, after a pause which she had filled with vague speculations about Gabriella's sentimental prospects. "I just hate like anything to see you wearing yourself out. Of course I'd like you to own part of the business, and I can't help thinkin' that the judge could get you the money as easy as not. It ain't as if you couldn't pay him the interest regular, is it?" she pursued with the financial helplessness of a woman who has never thought in terms of figures. "You couldn't be doin' any better, could you? There ain't anybody can run the business as well as you do, I don't care who 'tis."

"I sometimes think," returned Gabriella deliberately, while she draped a lace bertha on a white silk frock she was making for Fanny, "that I will try to borrow the money."

"It couldn't hurt, could it?"

"No, I don't suppose it could hurt."

Her eyes were on the lace, which she was adjusting over the shoulder, and Miss Polly followed her gaze with a look which was not entirely approving.

"There ain't a bit of sense in your wearin' yourself out over that child," said the seamstress presently, with so sharp an accent that Gabriella glanced up quickly from her work. "It was just the way Mrs. Spencer started Florrie, and it ain't right."

"Florrie!" exclaimed Gabriella, startled, and she added slowly, "I wonder what has become of her? I haven't thought of her for years."

"It was a mean trick she played you, Gabriella. I'd never have believed it of Florrie if I hadn't been there to see it with my own eyes."

"Yes, it was mean," assented Gabriella, but there was no anger in her voice. She had left the past so far behind her that its disappointments and its cruelties had become as dim and shadowy to her imagination as if they had been phantoms of the mind instead of actual events through which she had lived.

"Well, I'm glad she didn't spoil your life for you, honey."

"No, she didn't spoil my life. Don't I look happy? And Madame told me to-day that my figure was distinguished. Now, when a woman's life is spoiled her figure and her complexion are the first things to show it."

"Of course you ain't gettin' slouchy, I don't mean anything like that. But I hate to see you workin' your fingers to the bone and bringin' lines around your eyes when you ought to be taken care of. I don't hold with women workin' unless they're obliged to."

"But I'm obliged to. How on earth could I take care of the children if I didn't work?"

For a minute there was an austere silence while Miss Polly reflected grimly that Gabriella Mary—she thought of her as "Gabriella Mary" in moments of disapprobation"—was gettin' almost as set as her ma."

"You could marry," she said flatly at last, stopping to press down the hem she had turned with the blunted nail of her thumb. "Of course your ma would be dead against it, but there ain't any reason in the world why you shouldn't go back home and marry Arthur Peyton, as you ought to have done seventeen years ago."

Though Gabriella laughed in reply, there was no merriment in the sound, and a look of sadness crept into the eyes she turned away from the sharp gaze of the little seamstress.

"You've forgotten that I haven't seen him for seventeen years," she answered.

"That don't make any difference in his sort, and you know it. He ain't ever married anybody else, and he ain't goin' to. The faithfulness that ought to be spread over the whole sex gets stored up in a few, and he's one of 'em."

"He has never written to me. No, he must have got over it," responded Gabriella, with an impassioned emphasis, "and, besides, even if he cared, I don't want to marry again. My children are enough for me."

"It won't look that way next year when both the children are away at school, and when they once break away from your apron strings they're the sort that will go the way they want to and look out for their own happiness. You won't have much of Archibald while he's at school and college, and Fanny will marry befo' she's twenty just as sure as you live. Why, she's already got her head full of beaux. Have you noticed that picture of an actor she keeps on her bureau?"

"Yes" admitted Gabriella anxiously, "I've noticed it, but when I asked her about it, she only laughed."

After this the conversation dropped, and the two women put away their work for the might; but hours later, while Miss Polly lay in her hard little bed wondering if it would be possible to "fix" things between Gabriella and Arthur, the stern heroine of her romance wept a few tender tears on her pillow.

In the morning, with the tears still ready to spring at a touch, Gabriella read a letter from her mother, which he had found, beside the baker's rolls, at the door.

*Richmond, Thursday.*
DEAR CHILD:

As the others are all out to-night, and I have finished the mat I was crocheting, I thought I would send you a letter to reach you on your birthday instead of the telegram from the family. I am so thankful to hear that you keep well and happy and that Fanny has quite recovered from her cold. It was thoughtful of you to send the check, and I shall find it very useful, though Jane refuses to let me pay any board since Charley has inherited such a large income from his brother Tom. I sent you all the papers about the dreadful accident on the River road in which poor Tom and his wife were killed, but you haven't heard yet that Tom left his new house in Monument Avenue—they had only just moved into it—and almost all of his property to Charley. Of course, this will make a great difference in our manner of living; but just now none of us can think of anything except poor Tom and Gertrude, to whom we were all so deeply attached. No amount of money could in any way soften the blow of their loss, and the accident has given me such a horror of automobiles, though both Charley and Jane tell me this is very foolish.

To turn to more cheerful subjects, I can't begin to tell you how much the last photograph of Fanny has been admired. She is such a lovely girl, almost as pretty, we think, as Jane used to be when she first grew up, and I'm sure there could be no higher praise than that. You pleased me by saying that Archibald is like his grandfather, even if he isn't so handsome, and that he has a strong character. Good looks aren't nearly so important in a man as they are in a woman, and, you know, I don't think that men are as handsome to-day as they used to be when I was a girl. They have lost something—I can't make out just what it is.

Charley and Jane are at the Prohibition meeting. It is the first
time they have gone anywhere since the accident, but we all felt
that Tom and Gertrude would have wanted them to go for the sake of
the cause. I don't suppose you, would recognize Charley now if you
were to meet him. He is entirely changed, and I believe our new
minister is the reason for it, though Jane likes to think that her
influence reclaimed him. But, you remember, neither you nor I ever
thought that Jane went about reforming Charley in the right way;
and even now, though I wouldn't hurt dear Jane's feelings for
anything in the world, I am afraid she nags Charley and the
children too much. Of course, she means it for the best. No one
could look at the dear child without realizing what a beautiful
character she is.

But the change in Charley is really remarkable, and he won't allow
a drop of alcohol to come into the house—not even as medicine. I
can't help feeling sorry for poor old Uncle Meriweather, who
despises grape juice and misses his mint julep when he comes to
dine on Sunday; but Charley forbids Jane to make him a julep; and I
suppose he is right since he says it is a matter of principle. Even
Jane, however, thinks dear Charley is going a little too far when
he refuses to let me have the sherry and egg the doctor ordered.
However, I tell Jane that, since Charley feels so strongly about my
taking it, she must not try to persuade him against his
convictions. Dr. Darrow doesn't know that I stopped the sherry when
Charley found out I was buying it. Perhaps the plain eggs will do
me quite as much good. Anyhow, I wouldn't let my health stand in
the way of Charley's salvation.

Margaret has gone out to a concert, and you would never guess who
came to take her. I said to her when she was starting, "Well, I'm
going to sit straight down and write your Aunt Gabriella that
you've gone out with her old sweetheart." But doesn't it make you
realize how time flies when you think of Arthur Peyton's paying
attention to Jane's daughter? Of course, it isn't anything
serious—everybody knows that he has never recovered from his
feeling for you—but last winter he took Margaret to two germans
and to any number of plays. I believe Jane would be really pleased
if he were to take a fancy to Margaret, but I don't think there is
the faintest chance of it, for his Cousin Lizzie told me last
winter that she couldn't mention your name in his presence. She
says his faithfulness is perfectly beautiful, and she ought to know
for she has lived with him ever since his mother's death. Of

course, he has never accomplished very much in his profession. Chancy says all the men downtown look upon him as a failure; but, then, he is such a perfect gentleman, and, as I tell Charley and Jane, one can't have everything. How different your life would have been, my dear daughter, if you had listened to the prayers of your mother, and married a gentle Christian character like Arthur Peyton.

But I mustn't let my thoughts run away with me. Of course, even if your heart had not been broken, it would be impossible for you to think of another man as long as your husband is living. No pure woman could do that, and when people tell me about divorced women who remarry, I always maintain that they are not what my mother and I would call "pure women." I would rather think of you nursing your broken heart forever in solitude than that you should put such a blot upon your character and the name of the Carrs. Of course, you were right to divorce George after he forsook you for Florrie—even his mother tells everybody that you were right—but the thought of a second marriage would, I know, be intolerable to your refined and sensitive nature. After all, he is still your husband in the sight of God, and I said this to Miss Lizzie Peyton when we were talking of Arthur.

It is almost eleven o'clock, and I must stop and undress. Kiss the dear children, and remember me kindly to Miss Polly.
Your loving MOTHER.

As she refolded the letter Gabriella stood for an instant with her dreaming gaze on the delicate Italian handwriting on the envelope.
"It's amazing how wide the gulf is between the generations," she thought, not without humour. "I believe mother thinks of George oftener than I do, and I'd marry Arthur to-morrow if he wanted me to—except for the children."
Then, as Archibald rushed into the room, she caught him in her arms, and held him hungrily to her bosom.
"My darling, you want to keep your mother, don't you?"
"I jolly well do. What's the trouble, mother? I believe it's all that sitting up over Fanny's old dresses. Why don't you make something pretty for yourself?"
"She has to have things, and you love me just as well without them, don't you?"
"But I want you to have them, too. I like you to look pretty, and you are pretty."
"Then I can look pretty in plain clothes, can't I?"
"I tell you what I am going to do," he hesitated a minute, knitting his heavy brows over his spectacles, which looked so odd on a boy. "Next summer when school is over I'm going to work and make some money so you can have a

velvet dress in the autumn—a black velvet dress with lace on it—lots of lace—and a hat with feathers."

"You foolish boy!" laughed Gabriella. "Do you think for an instant I'd let you?" Her voice was gay, but when he had broken away from her clasp, and was racing along the hail for his school books, she turned aside to wipe the tears from her eyes.

"It's wrong, but I love, him more than I love Fanny," she said. "I love him more than all the rest of the world.".

An hour later, sitting beside an Italian labourer in an elevated train, she tried hard to keep her mind on the day's work and on the morning paper, which she held open before her—for in adopting a business life she had adopted instinctively a man's businesslike habits. A subtle distinction divided her from the over-dressed shopgirls around her as completely as her sex separated her from the portly masculine breadwinner in the opposite seat. Her tailored suit of black serge, with its immaculate white collar and cuffs, had an air of charming simplicity, and the cameolike outline of her features against the luminous background of the window-pane was the aristocratic racial outline of the Carrs. In the whirlpool of modern business she still preserved the finer attributes which Nature had bred in her race. The bitter sweetness of the mother's inheritance, grafted on the hardy stock of the Carr character, had flavoured without weakening the daughter's spirit, and, though few of the men in the train glanced in the direction of Gabriella, the few who noticed her in her corner surmised by intuition that she possessed not only the manner, but the heart of a lady. She was not particularly handsome, not particularly young, and her charm was scarcely the kind to flash like a lantern before the eye of the beholder. To the portly breadwinner she was probably a nice-looking American business woman, nothing more; to the Italian labourer she was, doubtless, a lady with a pleasant face, who would be polite if you asked her a question; and to the other passengers she must have appeared merely a woman reading her newspaper on her way down to work. Her primal qualities of force, restraint, and capability were the last things these superficial observers would have thought of; and yet it was by these qualities that she must succeed or fail in her struggle for life.

When she reached Dinard's she found Miss Smith, the only woman in Madame's employ who was ever punctual, ill-humouredly poking the spring hats out of the cases. Miss Smith, who excelled in the cardinal virtues, manifested at times a few of those minor frailties by which the cardinal virtues are not infrequently attended. Her one pronounced fault was a bad temper, and on this particular morning that fault was conspicuous. As she carried the hats from the cases to the window, which she was decorating with the festive millinery of the spring, she looked as if she were resisting an impulse to throw Madame's choicest confections at the jovial figure of the traffic policeman. Gabriella, who was used to what she called the "peculiarities" of the forewoman, said "good morning" with her bright amiability, and hurried back to the dim regions where she changed from her street suit to the picturesque French gown which she wore in the showroom. When she came out again Miss Smith had finished ornamenting the white pegs in the window, and was vigorously upbraiding a messenger boy who had delivered a parcel at the wrong door.

"You are always so prompt," remarked Gabriella cheerfully, as she arranged the hats in the front room. Her rule of business conduct was simple, and consisted chiefly of the precept that whatever happened she must keep her temper. Never once, never even in Madame's most trying moments, had she permitted herself to appear angry, and her strict adherence to this resolution had established her in an enviable position of authority. Obeying unconsciously some inherited strain of prudence in her nature, she had sacrificed her temper on the solid altar of business expediency.

"Somebody has to be on time, I guess," replied Miss Smith snappishly. "I'd like to know who would be here if I wasn't?"

She was a thin, soured, ugly little woman, with an extraordinary capacity for work, and an excess of nervous vitality bordering on hysteria. Gabriella, who knew something of her story, was aware of the self-sacrificing goodness of her private life, and secure in her own unclouded cheerfulness, could afford to smile tolerantly at the waspish sting.

"It's a pity we can't get more system here," she observed, for Miss Smith, she knew, was no tale-bearer. "The waste of time and misdirected energy are appalling. The business would be worth three times as much to anybody who could give her whole attention to it, but, as Madame is forever telling us, her health keeps her from really overlooking things."

"I wonder why she doesn't sell out?" asked Miss Smith, suddenly good-humoured and interested. "There's a lot in it for the right person, and it isn't in nature that she can hold on much longer. If I could find the money, I'd buy it and cut down expenses until I made a big profit. It would be easy enough." Then she added, while she slammed the ivory-tinted door of a case: "I wish you could run the house, Mrs. Carr. You are so pleasant to work with. Nothing ever seems to depress you."

"It would be nice, wouldn't it?" responded Gabriella promptly, and as she said the words, she decided that she would try to borrow the money from Judge Crowborough. For three months she had been struggling to bring herself to the point of asking his help—or at least his advice—and now, in a flash, without argument or discussion, she had settled the question. "It's a simple business proposition—a promising investment," she thought. "I'll ask him to get the money for me at a fair interest—to get me enough anyhow to give me control of the business. The worst he can do is to refuse," she concluded, with a kind of forlorn optimism; "at least he can't kill me."

Making a hurried excuse, she went back to the telephone, and calling up the judge, asked for an appointment in his office at five o'clock. From his surprised response she inferred his curiosity, and from his hearty acquiescence, she gathered that his surprise was not an unpleasant one. "At five o'clock, then. It is so good of you. There is a little matter of business. Yes, I know how kind you are, and of course your advice is invaluable. I can't think of anybody else on earth I can ask. Oh, thank you. Yes, at five o'clock. I shan't be late and I promise to keep you but a minute. Good-bye. What? Oh, yes, I'll come straight from Dinard's."

His voice, eager and friendly over the telephone, had given her confidence, and when she went back to the showroom, where the saleswomen were assembling, she was already planning the interview.

At eleven o'clock Madame, who never arrived earlier, was seen descending from a hansom, and a few minutes later she waddled, wheezing, asthmatic, and infirm of joints, through the ivory and gold doorway. Like some fantastically garlanded Oriental goddess of death, her rouged and powdered face nodded grotesquely beneath the flowery wreath on her hat. The indestructible youth of her spirit, struggling valiantly against the inert weight of the flesh, had squeezed her enormous figure into the curveless stays of the period, and had painted into some ghastly semblance of health the wrinkled skin of her cheeks. For underneath the decaying mockery of Madame's body, the indomitable soul of Madame still fought the everlasting battle of mind against matter, of the immaterial against the material elements.

"There was no use my trying to get here any sooner," she began in an apologetic tone when she was face to face with Gabriella behind the red velvet curtains of her private office. "My asthma was so bad all night, I had to doze sitting up, and I didn't get any sound sleep until daybreak. If I don't begin to mend before long I'll have to give up, that's all there is to it. There ain't any use my trying to hold on much longer. I'm too sick to think about fighting, and sometimes I don't care what becomes of the business. I want to go to some high place in Europe where I can get my breath, and I'm going to stay there, I don't care what happens. There ain't any use my trying to hold on," she repeated disconsolately.

Gabriella's opportunity had come, and she grasped it with the quickness of judgment which had enabled her to achieve her moderate success.

"I believe I could carry on this business," she said, and her quiet assurance impressed Madame's turbulent temper. With a brief return of her mental alertness, the old woman studied her carefully.

"I don't want any responsibility. I want to be rid of the whole thing," she said after a pause.

Gabriella nodded comprehendingly. "I believe I could carry it on successfully," she repeated. "Your customers like me. I think I understand how the business ought to be run. I have been here ten years, and I feel perfectly confident that I could make it successful."

"I've had offers—good offers," observed Madame warily, for she was incapable of liberating herself at the age of seventy-two from the lifelong suspicion that some one was taking advantage of her, that something was being got from her for nothing, "and, of course, I was only joking about having to stop work," she added, "I am retiring from choice, not from necessity."

"I understand," agreed Gabriella quietly.

"But I should like you to have the name," pursued Madame "A little money would be necessary, of course—perhaps you might buy a half interest—that would be simple. You could make a big success of it with your social position and your wealthy acquaintances. Surely you can find some one who is ready to make such a splendid investment?"

"Perhaps," admitted Gabriella, as quietly as before. Unlike Madame, who, being an incurable idealist, had won her victories not by accepting but by evading facts, Gabriella was frankly skeptical about the practical value of either her social position or her wealthy acquaintances. Neither possession impressed her at the moment as marketable, except in the vivid imagination of Madame, and her social position, at least, was constructed of a very thin and unsubstantial fabric. Guided by the prudent streak in her character, she rested her hope not upon incorporeal possessions, but upon the solid bodies of her patrons that must be clothed. Her imposing acquaintances would avail her scarcely more, she suspected, than would the noble ghost of that ancestor who was a general in the Revolution. What she relied on was the certainty that she knew her work, and that Madame's customers from the greatest to the least, from Mrs. Pletheridge to poor Miss Peterson, who bought only one good gown a year, admitted the thoroughness of her knowledge. She had got on by learning all that there was to learn about the details of the work, and she stood now, secure and unassailable, on the foundation of her achievement. In ten years she had fulfilled her resolution—she had made herself indispensable. By patience, by hard work, by self-control, by ceaseless thought, and by innumerable sacrifices, she had made herself indispensable; and the result was that, as Madame weakened, she had grown steadily stronger. Without her Dinard's would have dropped long ago to the position of a second-rate house, and she was aware that Madame understood this quite as clearly as she did. For whatever Madame's executive ability may have been in the past, it had dwindled now to the capricious endeavours of a chronic invalid—of an aging invalid, notwithstanding her desperate struggle for youth. Half as much energy as Madame had spent resisting Nature might have won for her a sanctified memory had it been directed toward the practice of piety, or a tablet of imperishable granite had it been devoted to as tireless a pursuit of art or science. To her battle against age she had brought the ambition of a conqueror and the devotion of a martyr; and at the last, even to-day, there was a superb defiance in her refusal to acknowledge defeat, in her demand that her surrender should be regarded as a capitulation.

"In a day or two I hope to be able to discuss my plan with you," said Gabriella, and she could not keep the softness of pity out of her voice. So this was what life came to, after all? For an instant she felt the overwhelming discouragement which is the portion of those who approach life not through vision, but through outward events, who seek a solution not in the deeper consciousness of the spirit, but in the changing surface of experience. Then, even before her glance had left Madame's golden head, her natural optimism regained control of her mind, and she told herself stoutly that if this was Madame's present, then it followed logically that Madame must have had a past, and that past must have been an agreeable one. It was inconceivable that she should defy the laws of God for the sake of a prolongation of tragedy.

"It is a splendid investment," croaked the old woman in the midst of Gabriella's painful reflections. "The house was never more flourishing."

The ruling principle which decreed that Gabriella should keep her temper had disciplined her not less thoroughly in the habit of holding her tongue. The house was in a flourishing condition; but she remembered how fragile and thinly rooted had been its showy prosperity, when she had entered it; and had she cared to confound Madame utterly, she might have reminded her of that unwritten history of the past ten years in which the secret episode of Mrs. Pletheridge occurred. For Gabriella was not inclined to underrate her own efficiency, and her confidence was supported by the knowledge that if she left Dinard's the most fashionable of Madame's clientele would follow her.

"You'll never have such another opportunity—not if you live to be a hundred. At your age I should have jumped at the idea," persisted Madame.

"So should I," responded Gabriella merrily, "if I were sure of landing on my feet."

"You'll always land on your feet—you're that sort. You've got push, and it's push that counts most in business. A woman may have all the brains in the world, but without push she might as well give up the struggle. That was what brought me up in spite of four husbands and six children," pursued Madame, while she took out a small flask from one of the drawers of her desk and measured out, as she remarked in parenthesis, "a little stimulant." "Yes, I had a great success in my line, and if I could only have kept clear of men, I might have saved a fortune to retire on in my old age. But I had a natural taste for men, and they were the ruin of me. As soon as I lost one husband and managed to get on a bit, another would come, and I couldn't resist him. I never could resist marriage; that was the undoing of me as a woman of business."

"Four husbands, and yet you were remarkably successful," observed Gabriella, because it was the only thing with a cheerful sound she could think of to utter, and an intermittent cheerful sound was all that Madame required from a listener when she was under the enlivening influence of brandy.

"But think what I might have done with my talent if I had remained a widow, as you have done. It was my misfortune to attract men whether I wanted to or not," wheezed Madame, wiping her eyes; "some women are like that."

"So I have heard," murmured Gabriella, seeing that Madame paused for the note of encouragement.

"I don't suppose that has been your trouble, for there's a stand-offishness about you that puts men at a distance, and they don't like to be put at a distance. Then, though your figure is very fine for showing off models, it isn't exactly the kind that men lean to. If you'd fatten up it might be different, but that would spoil you for the clothes, and that, after all, is more important. It's strange, isn't it?" she croaked, with an alcoholic chuckle, "how partial men are to full figures even after they have gone out of fashion?"

And with this wonder still ringing in her ears, Gabriella turned away, to attend a customer, who demanded, in cool defiance of man and nature, to be transformed into a straight silhouette.

Gabriella had not seen Judge Crowborough for several years, and her first impression, when she entered his office at five o'clock, was one of surprise at his ugliness. Though he had changed but little since their first meeting at Mrs. Fowler's dinner, the years had softened her memory of his appearance, and she had skilfully persuaded herself that one should not judge a man by a repelling exterior, which, after all, might cover a great deal of goodness. After George's flight and Archibald Fowler's death he had been very kind to her. "I don't know what I should have done without him at that time," she thought now, as she stood with his big, soft hand clasping hers and his admiring fishy eyes on her face. "No, it is impossible to judge by appearances, and all men think well of him, all men respect him," she concluded, feeling suddenly reassured.

"It's been a long time—it must be nearly' three years—since I saw you," he remarked, with flattering geniality, "and you look younger than ever."

"Hard work keeps me young, then. I work very hard." Her charming smile flashed like an edge of light on her lips, and lent glow and fervor to her pale face beneath the silver-brightened cloud of her hair. She read his admiration in the bold gaze he fastened upon her, and though she was without coquetry, she was conscious that her vanity was agreeably soothed.

"What is it? Dressmaking?" He was obviously interested.

"Yes—dresses and hats. Hats are rather my specialty. I manage things now almost entirely at Dinard's. Have you ever heard of the house?"

He nodded. "I remember. That's where you went after Archibald died, wasn't it?" His memory amazed her. What a mind for trifles he had! What a wonderful man he was for his years!

"Yes, I've been there ever since. I've done well as things go, but, of course, it has been hard. It has been a hard life."

"And you never came to me. I wanted to help you. I'd have done anything I could to make it easier for you, but you were so proud. You'd have got on twice as well if you had given up your pride."

The telephone rang, and while he answered it, she watched his broad, slouching back, his swelling paunch overflowing now above the stays he wore to reduce it, the coarsened flesh of his neck, bulging above the edge of his collar, and the shining, baldness on the top of his head, which gave an appearance of commanding intellect to his empurpled forehead. How hideous he was, how revolting, and yet what a power! A face like his on a woman would have condemned her to isolation and misery, but, so far as one could judge, it had scarcely interfered with his happiness. His mental force had risen superior to his face, to his paunch, to his whole repulsive appearance. Greater than Madame because of his sex, he had achieved a triumph over the corporeal mass of his body which she, fortified and abetted by a hundred cosmetics and manipulations, could never attain. Where Madame relied on futile artificial aids in her battle against decay, he hurled the tremendous power of his personality, and ugliness became at once as insignificant as immorality in his life. "One can't judge him by the standards of other men," thought Gabriella, using a remembered phrase of Fifty-seventh Street.

Judge Crowborough was still talking earnestly into the telephone, and she gathered vaguely that his earnestness related to a donation he had promised his church. "Raise two hundred thousand, and I'll double it," he said abruptly, and hung up the receiver. "We want a new organ—something really fine, you know," he observed casually as he turned back to Gabriella. "We are moving—everything is moving up, and the church has to keep step with the age. You can't keep progress out of religion any more than you can out of business—not that I'm in favour of modernism or any of that stuff—but we've got to keep moving." He spoke with conviction, and there was no doubt that he sincerely believed himself to be an important factor in the religious movement of his country. Then his tone changed to one of intimate friendliness and he asked: "Have you heard any music this winter? If I'd only known about you, I'd have sent you tickets to the opera."

"The children go sometimes," she answered. That he should imagine her buying opera tickets for herself, with the children needing every penny she made, seemed to her ridiculous; but rich men were always like that, she reflected a little scornfully.

"If I'd only remembered about you," he murmured, and turning heavily in his chair, he added authoritatively: "Now tell me about it. Tell me the whole thing straight through. I am going to help you."

She told him rapidly, and while she talked a sense of perfect peace and security enveloped her. It was so long since she had been able to ask advice of a man; it was so long since anybody bigger and stronger than she had undertaken to adjust her perplexities. The past returned to her as a dream, and she felt again that absolute reliance on the masculine ability to control events, to ease burdens, to remove difficulties, which had visited her in her childhood when Cousin Jimmy appeared in the front parlour in Hill Street. "It's wonderful how men manage things," she thought. "It's wonderful being a man. Everything is so simple for men."

"Well, don't worry a minute longer. It's all as easy as—as possible," observed the great man serenely when she had finished. "From what you tell me it looks as if it were a pretty good investment to begin with, and there are plenty of people around looking for ways to invest money. I'm looking for ways myself, when it comes to that," he proclaimed, with a paternal smile as he sank back on the luxurious leather cushions of his chair.

"You are so good," she responded gratefully, "so good"; and she was speaking sincerely.

With his casual gaze, which seemed to turn inward, fixed on the ceiling above her head, he invited her confidence by a few perfectly chosen expressions of comprehension and sympathy. The acuteness and activity of his mental processes delighted her while he questioned her. After the slovenly methods of Madame, after the loose reasoning and the muddled thinking of all the women she met in the course of her work, there was a positive pleasure in following the exactness and inflexibility of his logic. His reasoning was orderly, neat, elastic, without loose ends or tangled skeins to unravel, and she felt again, while she listened to him, the confidence which had come to her as soon as she entered his office. He was efficiency incarnate, and from her childhood up she had respected efficiency. In an hour, in less time than it had taken her to tell her story, he had lifted the weight from her shoulders, had mastered the details of Madame's intricate problems, and had outlined the terms by which Gabriella could accept the old woman's offer without placing herself under financial obligations. Her pride, he had discerned at a glance, shrank from obligation, and he was as alert to save her pride as he was to make a good bargain with Madame.

"It's a good thing. It's good business. Don't think I'm losing for a minute," he said as she rose to go, and she felt that some secret delicacy, the last feeling she would have attributed to him, was prompting his words.

"I can't tell you what a relief it is to talk to you," she said, holding out her hand while she hesitated between the desk and the door. "I can't even begin to tell you how grateful I am. I haven't had any one to advise me since I left Richmond, and it is such a comfort"

"Well, I'll give you the best advice in my power. I'll give you the very best," he replied as frankly as if he were discussing his gift to the church. "What's more, I'll think it over a bit while I'm at the Hot Springs, and talk to you about it when I come back. I suppose I can always get you on the telephone, can't I?"

His manner was still casual and business-like, and it did not change by so much as a shade when he moved a step nearer and put his arm about her waist. If he had taken down his hat or lighted a cigar, he would probably have performed either action with the same air of automatic efficiency; and she realized, in the very instant of her amazement, that his manner was merely an authoritative expression of his power. What astonished her most in the incident, after all, was not the judge's share in it, but the vividness and coolness of her own mental impressions. She was not frightened, she was not even disturbed, she was merely disgusted. Never before had she understood so clearly the immeasurable distance that divided the Gabriella of seventeen years ago from the Gabriella who released herself calmly from the appalling clasp of the casual and business-like old man. To the Gabriella who had loved George such an episode would have appeared as an inconceivable horror. Now, with her worldly wisdom and her bitter knowledge of love, she found herself regarding the situation with sardonic humour. The stupendous, the incredible vanity of man!—she reflected disdainfully. Was there ever a man too ugly, too repulsive, or too old to delude himself with the belief that he might still become the object of passion?

"Now you've spoiled it," she said shortly, but without embarrassment. "Now you've spoiled it." She put the case to him plainly, the Gabriella who would have blushed and trembled and wept seventeen years ago.

"But I meant nothing," he said, genuinely disturbed. "I assure you I am truly sorry if I have offended you. It was nothing—a mere matter of—" the word "habit," she knew, hovered on his lips, though he did not utter it, and broke off inconclusively.

So there had not been even the excuse of emotion about it. He had embraced her as instinctively, as methodically, as he might have switched on the electric light over his desk. Here again she was brought to a stop before an overwhelming realization of the fundamental differences between man and woman. To think of woman behaving like that merely because it had become a matter of habit!

"I always liked you, you know," he said abruptly, with a sincere emphasis.

"Well, there are different ways of liking," she rejoined coldly, "and I happen not to care for this way."

"If you don't like it, I'll never do it again," he promised, almost humbly. "I'll be a good friend to you, honestly I will. I'll treat you as if you were—you were—"

"A gentleman," finished Gabriella, and smiled in spite of herself. After all, what was the use of resenting the facts of life? What was the use of reproaching the mud that spattered over one's clothes?

"Well, that's a bargain. I'll treat you as a gentleman." There was a fine quality about the man; she could not deny it.

"I'll forgive you then and forget it." It was the tolerant Gabriella who spoke—the Gabriella of disillusioning experience and a clear vision of life—not the impassioned idealist of the 'nineties. When all was said, you had to take men and things as you found them. That was philosophy, and that was also "good business." It was foolish to apply romantic theories to the positive actuality.

"Well, you *are* a gentleman," exclaimed the judge, with facetiousness. "That's why I always liked you, I suppose. You're straight and you're honest and there's no nonsense about you."

If he had only known! She thought of the romantic girl of the 'nineties, of her buoyant optimism, her childlike ignorance, her violent certainties, and of her triumphant, "I can manage my life!" If he had only known how she had "muddled things" at the beginning, would he have said that she had "no nonsense about her?"

In the subway, a little later, clinging to a dirty strap, with a blackened mechanic in the seat before her, a box of tools at her feet, and a garlic-scented charwoman jolting against her shoulder, she was overcome by a sudden cloud of despondency. Her courage, her hopefulness, her philosophy, seemed to melt like frost in her thoughts, leaving behind only a sodden sense of loss, of emptiness, of defeat. "I've had a mean life," she said to herself resentfully. "I've had a mean life. What has ever happened to me that was worth while? What have I ever had except hard work and disappointment? I am thirty-seven years old. My youth is going, and I have nothing to show for it but ten years of dressmaking. The best of my life is over, and when I look back on it, it is only a blank." It was as if the interview with the great man she had just left had completed the desolating retrospect of a lifetime. Was there nothing but disenchantment ahead of her? Was life merely the dropping of illusion after illusion, the falling of petals at the first touch from a flower that is beginning to fade? "Yes, nothing has ever happened to me that was worth while," she repeated, forgetting her children for the moment. Then, because the heavy air stifled her, she left the car and turned into West Twenty-third Street where the lights were coming out softly in the spring twilight. Though it was too late to go over the house Fanny wanted, it occurred to her that she might look at the outside of it before she took the Harlem elevated train at one of the West Side stations. The walk would do her good and perhaps blow away the disquieting recollections of her encounter with Judge Crowborough. Not until her mood changed, she determined, would she go back to the children.

At the corner she bought a bunch of lilacs because a man held them out to her temptingly when she approached, and as she buried her face in the blossoms, she said resolutely: "No, I haven't had a mean life. It can't be mean unless I think it so, and I won't—I won't. After all, it isn't the kind of life you have, but the way you think about it that matters."

The air was deliciously mild; streaks of pale gold lingered above the grim outlines of the buildings; and the wild, sweet spirit of spring fluttered like an imprisoned creature in the gray streets of the city. It was May again, and the pipes of Pan were fluting the ancient songs in the ancient racial fields of the memory. There was a spring softness in the fleecy white of the clouds, in the flowing gold of the sunset, in the languorous kiss of the breeze, in the gentle rippling waves of the dust on the pavement. For years she had been so tranquil, and now suddenly, at the flitting touch of the spirit of spring, she knew that youth was slipping, slipping, and that with youth, went romance, enchantment, adventure. It was slipping from her, and she had never really held it. She had had only the second-rate; she had missed the best always—the best of life, the best of love, the best of endeavour and achievement. She had missed the finer reality. From somewhere, from the past or the present, from the dream or the actuality, her young illusions and her young longings rushed over her, driven by the fragrance of the lilacs, which was stinging her blood into revolt. Only an instant the revolt lasted, but in that instant of vision nothing mattered in life except romance, enchantment, adventure.

"Yes, I've missed life," she thought, and the regret was still in her mind when one of those miracles which in our ignorance we call accidents occurred. Out of the lilac-scented twilight, out of the wild, sweet spirit of spring, a voice said in her ear, "Alice, you waited!"

Turning quickly, she had a vivid impression of height, breadth, bigness, of roughened dark red hair, of gray eyes so clean that they looked 'as if they had been washed by the sea. Then the voice spoke again: "I beg your pardon. It was a mistake." And the next instant she was alone in the street.

# CHAPTER VI

## DISCOVERIES

"Who is Alice?" she wondered on her way home, "and for whom was she waiting?" A shopgirl perhaps, and he was, probably—not a clerk in a shop—he looked more like a mechanic—but hardly a gentleman. Not, at any rate, what her mother or Jane would call a gentleman—not the kind of gentleman that George was, or Charley Gracey, for instance. He was doubtless devoid of those noble traditions by and through which, her mother had always told her, a gentleman was made out of a man—the traditions which had created Arthur and Cousin Jimmy as surely as they had created George and Charley. "I wonder what tradition really amounts to?" she thought, while she stood on the rear platform of a Harlem train, grasping the handle of the door as the car swung round a curve. "All my life, I have been getting farther away from it—a woman has to, I suppose, when she works—and if I get away from it myself how can I honestly hold to it for men, who, according to mother, can't be gentlemen without it?" Then reverting to her first question, she resumed musingly: "Who *is* Alice? It would be rather amusing to be Alice for one evening, and to find out what it means to be loved by a man like that, even if he isn't a gentleman. He was, I think, the cleanest creature I ever saw, and it wasn't just the cleanness of soap and water—it went deeper than that. It was the cleanness of the winds and the sea—as if his eyes had been washed by the sea. I wonder who Alice is? A common little shopgirl probably from Sixth Avenue, with padded hair and painted lips, and smelling of cheap powder. That's just the kind of girl to fascinate a big, strong, simple creature like that Yes, of course, Alice is cheap and tawdry and vulgar, with no substance to her mind." She tried to think of Arthur, but her mental image of him had become as thin and unsubstantial as a shadow.

When she reached the apartment, Fanny rushed into her arms, and inquired breathlessly if she had taken the house?

"We went down again to look at it, mother, and we like it even better than ever. It will be so lovely to live next door to Carlie. We can tango every evening, and Carlie knows a lot of boys who come in to dance because the floor is so good."

Her cheeks flushed while she talked, and, for the moment, she lost entirely her resemblance to Jane, who was never animated, though she made a perpetual murmurous sound. Unlike Jane, Fanny was vivacious, pert, and, for her years, extraordinarily sophisticated. Already she dressed with extreme smartness; already she was thinking of men as of possible lovers; and already she was beginning, in her mother's phrase, "to manage her life." Her trite little face, in its mist of golden hair, which she took hours to arrange, still reminded one of the insipid angel on a Christmas card; but in spite of the engaging innocence of her look, she was prodigiously experienced in the beguiling arts of her sex. Almost from the cradle she had had "a way" with men; and her "way" was as far superior in finesse to the simple coquetry of Cousin Pussy as the worldliness of Broadway was superior to the worldliness of Hill Street. From her yellow hair, which she wore very low over her forehead and ears, to her silk stockings of the gray called "London smoke," which showed coquettishly below her "hobble" skirt, and above the flashing silver buckles on her little pointed shoes of; patent leather, Fanny was as uncompromisingly modern in her appearance as she was in her tastes or her philosophy. Her mind, which was small and trite like her face, was of a curiously speculative bent, though its speculations were directed mainly toward the by-paths of knowledge which Gabriella, in her busy life, had had neither the time nor the inclination to explore. For Fanny was frankly interested in vice with the cool and dispassionate interest of the inquiring spectator. She was perfectly aware of the social evil; and unknown to Gabriella she had investigated, through the ample medium of the theatre and fiction, every dramatic phase of the traffic in white slaves. Her coolness never deserted her, for she was as temperamental as a fish, and, for all the sunny white and gold of her surface, she had the shallow restlessness of a meadow brook. At twelve years of age she had devoted herself to music and had planned an operatic career; at fourteen, she had turned to literature, and was writing a novel; and a year later, encouraged by her practical mother, she had plunged into the movement for woman suffrage, and had marched, in a white dress and carrying a purple banner, through an admiring crowd in Fifth Avenue. To-day, after a variable period, when she had dabbled in kindergarten, wood engraving, the tango, and settlement work, she was studying for the stage, and had fallen in love with a matinée idol. Gabriella, who had welcomed the wood engraving and the kindergartening and had been sympathetically, though impersonally, aware of the suffrage movement, just as she had been aware many years before of the Spanish War, was deeply disturbed by her daughter's recent effervescence of emotion.

"I suppose she'll get over it. She gets over everything," she had said to Miss Polly, drawing painful comfort from the shallowness and insincerity of Fanny's nature, "but something dreadful might happen while she is in one of her moods."

"Not with Fanny," Miss Polly had replied reassuringly. "Fanny knows more already than you and I put together, and she's got about as much red blood as a lemon. She ain't the sort that things happen to, so don't you begin to worry about her. She's got mighty little sense, that's the gospel truth, but the little she's got has been sharpened down to a p'int."

"I can't help feeling that she hasn't been well brought up. I did what I could, but she needed more time and care than I could give her. It wasn't, of course, as if I'd chosen to neglect her. I have been obliged to work or she would have starved."

"Oh, well, I wouldn't bother about that. It's like wishing chickens back in the shell after they're hatched—there ain't a particle of use in it. If you ask me what I think—then, I'd say that Fanny would be just exactly what she is if you'd raised her down yonder in Virginia. Her father's in her as well as you, and it seems to me that she grows more like him every day that she lives. Now, Archibald is your child, anybody can tell that at a glance. It's queer, ain't it how the boys almost always seem to take after the mother?"

"But Charley has a splendid daughter. Think of his Margaret."

"Of course, there ain't any rule that works out every time; but you know, I'll always take up for Mr. Charley if it's with the last breath I draw. It ain't always the woman that gets the worst of marriage, though to hear some people talk you'd think it was nothin' but turkey and plum puddin' for men. But it ain't, I don't care who says so, and if anybody but a saint could have married Jane without takin' to drink, I'd like to have seen him try it, that's all."

That was three weeks ago, and to-night, while Fanny rattled on about the house in West Twenty-third Street, her mother watched her with a tolerant affection in which there was neither admiration nor pride. She was not deluded about Fanny's character, though the maternal mote in her eye obscured her critical vision of her appearance. But, notwithstanding the fact that she thought Fanny beautiful, she was clearly aware that the girl had never been, since she left the cradle, anything but a source of anxiety; and for the last week or two Gabriella had been more than usually worried about her infatuation for the matinée idol. In spite of Miss Polly's assurances that Fanny was too calculating for rash adventures, Gabriella had spent several sleepless nights over the remote possibility of an entanglement, and her anxiety was heightened by the fact that the child told her nothing. They were so different that there was little real sympathy between them, and confidences from daughter to mother must spring, she knew, from fulness of sympathy. "I wonder if she ever realizes how hard I have worked for her?" she thought. "How completely I've given up my life?" And there rose in her thoughts the wish that her children could have stayed children forever. "As long as they were little, they filled my life, but as soon as they get big enough for other things, they break away from me—even Archibald will change when he goes away to school, next year, and I shall never have him again as he is now." At the very time, she knew, when she needed them most—when middle-age was approaching—her children were failing her not only as companions, but as a supreme and vital reason for living. If they could have stayed babies, she felt that she should have been satisfied to go on forever with nothing else in her life; but in a little while they would grow up and begin to lead their own intense personal lives, while she, having outlived her usefulness, would be left with only her work, with only dressmaking and millinery for a life interest. "Something is wrong with me," she thought sternly; "the visit to the judge must have upset me. I don't usually have such wretched thoughts in the evening."

"Did you bring me your school report, darling?" she asked.

Yes, Fanny had brought it, and she drew it forth reluctantly from the pages of a novel. It was impossible to make her study. She was as incapable of application as a butterfly. "I thought you were going to do better this month, Fanny," said Gabriella reproachfully.

"Oh, mother dear, I want to leave school. I hate it! Please let me begin to study for the stage. You know you always said the study of Shakespeare was improving."

They were in the midst of the argument when Archibald came in, and he showed little sympathy with Fanny's dramatic ambition.

"The stage? Nonsense! What you want is to get safely married," he remarked scornfully, and Gabriella agreed with him. There was no doubt in her mind that for some women, and Fanny promised to be one of these, marriage was the only safeguard. Then she looked at Archibald, strong, sturdy, self-reliant, and clever; and she realized, with a pang, that some day he also would marry—that she must lose him as well as Fanny.

"I've had a letter from Pelham Forest, dear," she said—Pelham Forest was a school in Virginia—"and I am making up my mind to let you go there next autumn."

"And then to the University of Virginia where Grandfather went?"

"Yes, and then to the University of Virginia."

Though she tried to speak lightly, the thought of the coming separation brought a pang to her heart.

"Well, I'd rather work," said Archibald stoutly. "I don't want to go away to school. I'd a long sight rather start in with a railroad or a steamship company and make my way up."

"But, darling, I couldn't bear that. You must have an education. It's what I've worked for from the beginning, and when you've finished at the university, I want to send you abroad to study. If only Fanny would go to college, too, I'd be so happy."

"Don't you waste any money on Fanny's education," retorted Archibald, "because it isn't worth it. What we ought to do is to get to work and let you take a rest. The first money I make, I'm going to spend on giving you pretty clothes and a rest."

"I don't want to rest, dear," replied Gabriella, with a laugh. "I'm not an old lady yet, you silly boy." How ridiculous it was that he always spoke of her work as if it were a hardship—a burden from which she must be released at the first opportunity. That was so like Cousin Jimmy, a survival, she supposed, from the tradition of the South. Unlike Fanny, whose horizon was bounded by her personal inclinations, Archibald seemed never to think of himself, never to put either his comfort or his career before his love for his mother. To attempt to shape Fanny's character was like working in tissue paper, but there was stout substance in Archibald. Gabriella had tried hard—she told herself over and over again that she had tried as hard as she could—with both of her children; and with one of them at least she felt that she had succeeded. There was, she knew, the making of a splendid man in her son; and his very ugliness, which had been so noticeable when he was a child, was developing now into attractiveness. For it was the ugliness of strength, not of weakness, and there was no trace in his nature of the self-indulgence which had ruined his father.

"But I don't want to go to college, mother dear," protested Fanny, who always addressed Gabriella as "dear" when she was about to become intractable; "I want to go on the stage."

"You are not to see another play, except when I take you, for a whole year. Remember what I tell you, Fanny!" replied Gabriella sternly. Not Mrs. Carr herself, not Cousin Becky Bollingbroke, of sanctified memory, could have regarded an actress's career with greater horror than did the advanced and independent Gabriella. Any career, indeed, appeared to her to be out of the question for Fanny (a girl who couldn't even get on a street car without being spoken to), and of all careers the one the stage afforded was certainly the last she would have selected for her daughter.

"I'll remember," responded Fanny coolly, and Gabriella knew in her heart that the girl would disobey her at the first opportunity. It was impossible to chaperon her every minute, and Fanny, unchaperoned, was, in the realistic phrase of her brother, "looking for trouble."

"I'll send her to boarding-school next year," Gabriella determined; and she reflected gloomily that with Fanny and, Archibald both away, she might as well be a bachelor woman.

"Well, children, you're both going away next winter," she said positively. "I can't look after you, Fanny, and make your living at the same time, so I shall send you to boarding-school. What do you say to Miss Bradfordine's?"

"That's up on the Hudson, mother. I don't want to go out of New York." Fanny was genuinely alarmed at last.

"The farther away from New York the better, my daughter."

"What will you do here all alone with Miss Polly?

"Oh, we'll do very well," answered Gabriella with cheerful promptness; "you need not worry about me."

"If I'm good this summer, will you change your mind, mother?"

"Try being good, and see." Though Gabriella spoke sweetly, it was with the obstinate sweetness of Mrs. Carr. One thing she had resolved firmly in the last quarter of an hour: Fanny should go away to boarding-school next September.

"Ain't you goin' to walk in the suffrage parade this year, Fanny?" inquired Miss Polly, who always thought it necessary to interrupt an argument between Gabriella and her daughter.

"I haven't anything to wear," replied Fanny pettishly. Her brief interest in "votes for women" had evaporated with the entrance of the matinée idol into her life.

"There's a lovely white gown just in from Paris I'll get for you," said Gabriella pleasantly. She was tired, for she had had a trying day; but long ago, when her children were babies, she had determined that she would never permit herself to speak sharply to them. In Fanny's most exasperating humours, Gabriella tried to remember her own youthful mistakes, tried to be lenient to George's faults which she recognized in the girl's character.

"As if anybody needed to be dressed up to march!" exclaimed Archibald scornfully, and he added: "She's always acting, isn't she, mother?"

"Hush, dear, you mustn't tease your sister," Gabriella admonished the boy, though her voice when she spoke to him was attuned to a deeper and softer note.

"If you make me go to boarding-school next year, I don't care whether you take the rooms in Twenty-third Street or not," said Fanny sullenly, for, in spite of her fickle temperament, there was a remarkable tenacity in her thwarted inclinations.

"Very well. I'll look at the house and decide to-morrow." As the servant came in to lay the table, Gabriella dismissed the subject of Fanny's school, and opened the book—it chanced to be a volume of Browning—which she was reading aloud to the children.

"I am really worried about Fanny," she said to Miss Folly at midnight, while she lingered in the living-room before going to bed. "I honestly don't know what to make of her, and I feel, somehow, that she is one of my failures."

"Well, you can't expect everything to go the way you want it. Did you see the judge?"

"Yes, I saw him, but it was no use." Her visit to Judge Crowborough appeared to her perturbed mind as a piece of headstrong and extravagant folly, and she dismissed it from her thoughts as she had dismissed heavier burdens in the past. "Men simply won't treat Women in business as they treat men, and I don't see unless human nature changes, how it is to be helped. But what about the house in Twenty-third Street? Do you think I ought to look at it?"

"It was the most homelike place we saw, by a long way. There ain't many places in New York where you can have a flower-bed in the front yard."

"Do you think Fanny will be happy there? A year before this stage mania seized her, you know, she was wild to move to Park Avenue."

"Well, you know I've got a suspicion," Miss Folly dropped her voice to a whisper. "Of course it ain't nothin' but a suspicion, for she never opens her mouth about it to me, but I've got a right smart suspicion that that young actor she is so crazy about lives somewhere down there in that neighbourhood, and she thinks she could watch him go by in the street. I don't believe, you know, that she's ever so much as spoken to him in her life."

"It's impossible!" exclaimed Gabriella, for this revelation of Miss Polly's discernment was astonishing to her; "but if that's the case," she added gravely, "I oughtn't to think of moving into the house."

"Oh, well, I don't know that he's anywhere very near, and Fanny's goin' to be at boarding-school for a year or two and away with Jane at the White Sulphur in the summers. She won't be there much anyhow, will she?"

"Not much, but how I shall miss her—and, of course, if I miss her, I'll miss Archibald even more, because he gives me no anxiety. It's odd," she finished abruptly, "but I've been depressed all day. I suppose my birthday has something to do with it."

"You ain't often like that, Gabriella. I never saw anybody keep in better spirits than you do."

"I'm happy, but the spring makes me restless. I feel as if I'd missed something I ought to have had."

"All of us feel that way at times, I reckon, but it don't last, and we settle down comfortably after a while to doin' without what we haven't got. And you've been mighty successful, honey. You've succeeded in everything you undertook except marriage."

"Yes, except my marriage."

"Well, I reckon things happen and you can't do 'em over again," observed the little seamstress, with the natural fatalism of the "poor white" of the South.

As she undressed and got into bed, Gabriella told herself cheerfully that there was, indeed, no need to worry over things that you couldn't change after they happened. From the open window a shaft of light fell on her mirror, and while she watched it, she tried to convince her rebellious imagination that she was perfectly satisfied, that life had given her all that she had ever desired. "I have more than most women anyhow," she insisted, weakening a little. "I've accomplished what I undertook, and by the time I'm fifty, if things go well, I may become a rich woman. I'll be able to give Fanny everything that she wants, and if she hasn't married, we can go abroad every summer, and Archibald can join us in Switzerland or the Tyrol. About Archibald, at least, I can feel perfectly easy. He is the kind of boy to succeed. He is strong, he hasn't a weakness, and I am sure there isn't a brighter boy in the world." Around the shaft of light in the mirror a stream of sparks, like tiny comets, began to form and quiver back and forth as if they were flying. "It's a pity the judge can't help me, but it wouldn't do. I'd never forget what happened to-day, and you can never tell when trouble like that is coming. I'll either make Madame give me half the profits for managing the business or I'll go to Blakeley & Grymn at a salary of ten thousand a year. She won't let me go, of course, because she knows I'd take two thirds of her customers with the. Then I'll invest all I can save in the business until finally I am able to buy it entirely—" An elevated train passed the corner, and while the rumble died slowly in the distance, she found herself thinking of Arthur. "How different my life might have been if I had only stayed true to him. That's the happiest lot that could fall to a woman, to be loved by a man as faithful and tender as Arthur." For a few minutes she lay, without thought, watching the lights quiver and dance in the mirror, and listening to the faint rumble of the elevated train far up the street. Then, just as she was falling asleep, a question flashed out of the flickering lights into her mind, and she started awake again. "I wonder who Alice is?" she said aloud to the night.

Several weeks, later, at the end of a busy day, Gabriella stood in front of the house in London Terrace, watching her furniture as it passed across the pavement and up the flagged walk into the hail. The yard was neglected and overgrown with dandelions and wire-grass; but an old rose-bush by the steps was in full bloom, and already Miss Polly was surveying the tangled weeds with the eye of a destroyer.

"I declare I'm just hungerin' for flowers," she said wistfully, following the dining-room table as far as the foot of the steps where Gabriella stood. "The very first thing in the morning before I get breakfast, I'm goin' to sow some mignonette and nasturtium seeds in that border along the wall, and fix some window boxes with clove pinks and sweet alyssum in 'em like your ma used to have in summer. I reckon that's why I was so set on this place from the first. It looks more like Richmond in old times than it does like New York."

Beyond the grass and weeds, over which Gabriella was gazing, the street was so quiet for the moment that it might have been one of those forgotten squares in Richmond (she had never called them blocks) where needy gentlewomen still practised "light housekeeping" in the social twilight of the last century. Now and then a tired man or woman slouched by from work; once a newsboy stopped at the gate to shout the name of his paper in belligerent accents; and a few wagons or a clanging car passed rapidly in the direction of Broadway. From the corner of Ninth Avenue the elevated road, which seemed to her at times the only permanent thing in her surroundings, still roared and rumbled its disturbing undercurrent in her life.

"I think we shall be quite comfortable here," she said, watching the last piece of furniture pass through the door. "Where are the children?" The air had the rich softness of summer, and the roving fragrance from the old garden rose-bush by the steps awakened a strange homesickness in her heart—that mysterious homesickness which the spring gives us for places we have never seen.

"The children are upstairs fixing their rooms," replied Miss. Polly, stooping to pluck up a weed by the roots. "I reckon I'd better go and tell Minnie to begin gettin' dinner, hadn't I?"

"Yes, I'll come in presently. I hate to leave the air and the roses."

"I wish we had the whole house, Gabriella."

"It would be ever so much nicer, because I'm afraid the man on the first floor is dreadfully common. I don't like the look of that golden-oak hatrack in the hail."

"Well, men never did have much taste. Think of the things your Cousin Jimmy would admire if Miss Pussy didn't tell him not to. Do you recollect that paper in your parlour at home? Now Mr. Jimmy thought that paper downright handsome. I've heard him say so."

"It was dreadful, but, do you know, I designed a gown last winter in peacock blue like that paper, and it was a tremendous success. Poor mother, I wish she could have seen it—peacock blue with an embossed border."

"You may laugh about it now, but I don't believe your mother minded it much. People in old times didn't let things get on their nerves the way they do to-day."

She went indoors to attend to the dinner table; and as Gabriella turned back to the steps, she heard the gate slam and a man's voice exclaim heartily: "I'll see you about it to-morrow." Then a figure came rapidly up the walk—a large, free figure, with a buoyant swing, which awoke a trivial and fleeting association in her memory. Without noticing her, the man stooped for an instant beside the rose-bush, plucked a bud, and held it to his nostrils as he turned to the steps. His voice, singing a snatch of ragtime which she recognized without recalling the name of it, rang out, gay and powerful, as he approached her.

"I've seen him somewhere. Who can he be?" she thought, and then swiftly, as in a blaze of light, she remembered the May afternoon in West Twenty-third Street, and "Alice," whom she had wondered about and forgotten. She had again a vivid impression of bigness, of freshness, and of gray eyes that, reminded her vaguely of the colour of a storm on the sea.

"Good evening!" he remarked with impersonal friendliness as he passed her; and from the quality of his voice she inferred, as she had done on that May afternoon, that he was without culture, probably without education.

He went inside; the door of his front room opened and shut, and after a minute or two the snatch of ragtime floated merrily through his window. If there was anything on earth she disliked, she reflected impatiently, it was a comic song.

"He isn't a gentleman. I was right, he is common," she thought disdainfully, as she went indoors and ascended the stairs. "And he may make it very disagreeable for us if he insists on bringing common people into the houses" There was a vague impression in her mind that the males of the lower classes were invariably noisy.

"I saw the man on the first floor as I came up," she remarked to Miss Folly. "I hope he isn't going to be an annoyance."

"Mrs. Squires says he's never in evenings. He gets all his meals out except breakfast, and she fixes that for him. She told me he was hardly ever here unless he was eatin' or sleepin', so I don't reckon he'll bother us?"

"Well, I'm glad of that, because he isn't the kind of person I'd like the children to see anything of. You can tell that he is quite common."

"What does he look like? Is he rough?"

"Oh, no, he is good looking enough—a fine animal. I suppose he's handsome in a way, and he was dressed very carefully, but, of course, he isn't a gentleman." For the second time this stranger had made her feel that she had missed something in life, and she felt almost that she hated him.

"Oh, well, I don't reckon it will hurt us to pass him in the hall," replied Miss Polly soothingly, "as long as he don't bring in any diseases."

The next day they settled comfortably in the upper rooms and, as far as sound or movement went, the floor below might have been tenanted by the dead. When she went out Gabriella passed the dreadful hatrack of golden-oak in the lower hail; and after a day or two she noticed that it held a collection of soft felt hats, two overcoats of good cut and material, and an assortment of gold-headed walking-sticks, which appeared never to be used. Though she tried to ignore the presence of the hatrack, there was an aggressive masculinity about it which revived in her the almost forgotten feeling of having "a man in the house." The mere existence of a man—of an unknown man—on the first floor, altered the character not only of the lower hail, but of the entire house; it was, she felt instinctively, a different place from a house occupied by women alone. She had seen so little of men in the last ten years that she had almost forgotten their distinguishing characteristics, and the scent of tobacco stealing through the closed door of the front room downstairs came as a fresh surprise when she passed Out in the morning. "I suppose I'm getting old maidish," she thought. "That comes of leading a one-sided life. Yes, I am getting into a groove." And she determined that she would go out more in the evenings and try to take an interest in the theatre and the new dances. But even while she was in the act of resolving, she realized that when her hard day's work was over, and she came home at six o'clock, she was too tired; too utterly worn out, for anything except dinner and bed. There was still the cheerful hour with the children (that she had kept up in the busiest seasons); but when the question of going out was discussed at dinner, she usually ended by sending the children to a lecture or a harmless play with Miss Polly. "When you work as hard as I do, there isn't much else for you in life," she concluded regretfully, and there swept over her, as on that May afternoon, a sense of failure, of dissatisfaction, of disappointment. Youth was slipping, slipping, and she had missed something.

At such moments she thought sadly of her life, of its possibilities and its significance. It ought in the nature of things, she felt, to mean so much more than it had meant; it ought to have been so much more vital, so much more satisfying and complete. As it was, she could remember of it only scattered ends, frayed places, useless beginnings, and broken promises. With how many beliefs had she started, and now not one of them remained with her—well, hardly one of them! The dropping of illusion after illusion—that was what the years had brought to her as they passed; for she saw that she had always been growing farther and farther away from tradition, from accepted opinions, from the dogmas and the ideals of the ages. The experience and the wisdom of others had failed her at the very beginning.

At the end of the week, when she and Miss Polly were watering seeds in the yard one afternoon at sunset, the man from the first floor came leisurely up the walk, and removing a big black cigar from his mouth, wished them "good evening" as he passed.

"Good evening," responded Gabriella coolly. She had resolved that there should be no interchange of unnecessary civilities between the first floor and the upper storeys. "One can never tell how far men of that class will presume," she thought sternly.

"Don't you think he's good lookin', honey?" inquired Miss Polly in a whisper when O'Hara had entered the house with his latchkey and closed the door after him.

"Is he? I didn't look at him."

"You wouldn't think he'd ever had a day's sickness in his life. I reckon he's as big as your Cousin Micajah Berkeley was. You don't recollect, him, do you?"

"He died before I was born. Are those wisps of gray green, in the border, pinks, Miss Polly?"

"Clove pinks like your ma used to raise. It ain't the right time to set 'em out, but I sent all the way down to Richmond for 'em. I'm goin' to get a microphylla rose, too, in the fall. Do you reckon it would grow up North, Gabriella?"

"Well, we might try, anyhow. Where are the children?"

"Fanny's over at Carlie's, an' Archibald said he was goin' to the gymnasium befo' dinner. He's just crazy about gettin' as strong as the man on the first floor. He was punching a ball this mornin', and Archibald saw him. I never knew the boy to take such a sudden fancy."

"When did he speak to him?" asked Gabriella, and her tone had a touch of asperity so unusual that Miss Polly exclaimed in astonishment: "For goodness sake, Gabriella, what has come over you? Do you feel any sort of palpitations? Shall I run after the harts-horn?"

"No, I'm not ill, but I don't like Archibald to pick up acquaintances I know nothing about."

"I reckon if you're goin' to sample all Archibald's acquaintances, you'll have a job on your hands. You ain't gone an' taken a dislike to Mr. O'Hara for nothin', have you?"

"Oh, no, but I have to be careful about the children. Suppose he should begin speaking to Fanny?" She had been vividly aware of the man as he passed, and the sensation had provoked her. "If it wasn't for Alice, I shouldn't have given him another thought," she told herself savagely. "Imagine me at my age blushing because a strange man spoke to me in the street!"

"You needn't worry about his admirin' Fanny," replied Miss Polly, in her matter-of-fact manner, while she lifted the green watering-pot. "He was on the steps when she set out for school this mornin', an' he didn't notice her any more than he did me. Fanny ain't the sort he takes notice of, I could see that in a minute."

"Then he must be blind." There was a resentful sound in Gabriella's voice. "It embarrasses me when I get on a street car with her because the men stare so."

"Well, he didn't stare. But it's a mighty good thing that all men haven't got the same kind of eyes, ain't it? What I could never make out was why men ever marry women who haven't got curly hair, an' yet they do it every day—they go right straight out an' do it with their wits about 'em."

The front door opened suddenly, and the man came out again, and, descended the walk with the springy step Gabriella had noticed at their first meeting. Notwithstanding his size, he moved with the lightness and agility of a boy, and without looking at him she could see, as she bent over the flower-bed, that he had the look of exuberant vitality which accompanies perfect physical condition. Without meaning to, without knowing why she did it, she glanced up quickly and met his eyes.

"So you are making a garden?" he remarked, and stopped beside the freshly turned flower-bed. Against the gray twilight the red of his hair was like a dark flame, and the vivid colour appeared to intensify the sanguine glow in his face, the steady gaze of his eyes, and the cheerful heartiness of his voice.

"He is cyclonic," she said to herself. "Yes, that is the word—he is cyclonic—but he isn't a gentleman."

"It's a pity to let the yard run to waste," she responded, with an imperiousness which took Miss Polly's breath away, though it left the irrepressible O'Hara still buoyantly gay and kind.

"Now it takes a woman to think of that," he observed with an off-hand geniality which she felt was directed less toward herself than toward an impersonal universe. "I like to look at that old rose-bush when it is in bloom, but the idea"—(he pronounced it idee)—"of planting anything would never have occurred to me."

Gabriella's lips closed firmly, while she sprinkled the earth with an air of patient finality which made Miss Polly think of Mrs. Carr on one of her neuralgic days.

"What's that stringy looking grass over there?" pursued the man, undismayed by her manner.

"Clove pinks." Nothing, she told herself indignantly, could persuade her to encourage the acquaintance of a man who mispronounced his words so outrageously.

"And here?" He pointed to the flower-bed she was watering.

"Mignonette and nasturtium seeds."

"When will they come up?"

"Very soon if they're watered."

"And they'll bloom about July, I guess?"

"They ought to bloom all summer. In the autumn, if we have room, we're going to plant some dahlias, and a row of hollyhocks against the house. By next summer the yard will look much better."

"By George!" he exclaimed abruptly, and after a minute or two: "Do you know, I can remember the first time I ever saw a flower—or the first time I took notice of one, anyway. It was red—a red geranium. There was a whole cart of 'em, and that's why I noticed 'em, I expect. But a red geranium is a Jim-dandy flower, ain't it?"

To this outburst Gabriella made no reply. Her will had hardened with the determination not to be drawn into conversation, and while he waited with his eager gray eyes—so like the alert, wistful eyes of a great dog—on her profile, she began carelessly plucking up spears of grass from the flower-bed.

For a minute he waited expectantly; then, as she did not look up, he remarked, "So long!" in a voice of serene friendliness, and went on to the gate. He had actually said "So long" to her, Gabriella, and he had said it with a manner of established intimacy!

"Well, what do you think of that?" she demanded scornfully of Miss Polly when he had disappeared up the street.

"I reckon he don't know any better, honey. You don't learn much about manners in a mine, I 'spose, and when he ain't down in a mine, Mrs. Squires says he's building railroads across deserts. She says he ain't ever had anything, education or money, that he didn't pick up for himself, and you oughtn't to judge him as you do some others you've known. Anyway, she says he's made a big pile of money."

"I believe you're taking up for him, Miss Polly. Has he bewitched you?"

"I don't like to see you hard, Gabriella. You're almost always so tolerant. It ain't like you to sit in judgment."

"I am not sitting in judgment, but I don't see why I'm obliged to be friendly with a strange man who says 'idee.' It would be bad for the children."

"Mrs. Squires has known him for thirty years—he's forty-five now—and she says it's a miracle the way he's come up. He was born in a cellar."

"I dare say he has a great deal of force, but you must admit that blood tells, Miss Polly."

"I never said it didn't, Gabriella—only that there's much more credit to a man that comes up without it."

"Oh, I'll admire him all you please," retorted Gabriella, "if you'll promise to keep him away from the children."

Though she spoke sharply, the sharpness was directed not to Miss Polly, but to herself—to her own incomprehensible childishness. The man interested her; already she had thought of him daily since she first came to the house; already she had begun to wonder about him, and she realized that she should wonder still more because of what Miss Polly had told her. When he had approached her in the yard, she had been vaguely disturbed, vaguely thrilled by the strangeness and the mystery surrounding him; she had been subtly aware of his nearness before she heard his step, and turning, found his eyes fixed upon her. Her own weakness in not controlling her curiosity, in recurring, in spite of her determined resolve to that first meeting, in allowing a coarse, rough stranger—yes, a coarse, rough, uneducated stranger, she insisted desperately—to hold her attention for a minute—the incredible weakness of these things goaded her into a feeling of positive anger. For ten years there had been no men in her life, and now at thirty-seven, when she was almost middle-aged, she was beginning to feel curious about the history of the first good-looking man she encountered—about a mere robust, boisterous embodiment of masculinity. "What difference can it make to me who Alice is?" she demanded indignantly. "What possible difference?" She forced herself to think tenderly of Arthur; but during the last few months the image of Arthur had receded an immeasurable distance from her life. His remoteness and his unreality distressed her; but try as she would, she could not recall him from the gauzy fabric of dreams to the tangible substance of flesh.

"It isn't that I care for myself," she said to Miss Polly abruptly, as if she were defending herself against an unspoken accusation. "I am a working woman, and a working woman can't afford to be snobbish—certainly a dressmaker can't— but I must look after my children. That is an imperative duty. I must see that they form friendships in their own class."

But life, as she had already discovered, has a sardonic manner of its own in such crises. That night she planned carefully, lying awake in the darkness, the subterfuges and excuses by which she would keep Archibald away from O'Hara, and the very next afternoon when she came home from work she found confusion in the street, a fire engine at the corner, and, on the steps of her home, the boy clinging rapturously to the hand of the man.

"You ought to have been here, mother," cried Archibald in tones of ecstatic excitement. "We had a fire down the street in that apartment house—and before the firemen came Mr. O'Hara went in and got out a woman and some children who had been overcome by smoke. He had to lower them from a fire-escape, and he got every one of them out before the engine could get here. I saw it all. I was on the corner and saw it all."

"I hope Mr. O'Hara wasn't hurt," remarked Gabriella, but her voice was not enthusiastic.

"To hear the kid run on," responded O'Hara, overpowered by embarrassment, "you'd think I'd really done something, wouldn't you? Well, it wasn't anything. It was as easy as—as eating. Now, I was caught down in a mine once in Arizona—"

"Tell me about it. Mother, ask him to tell you about it," entreated Archibald. The boy was obviously consumed with curiosity and delight. Gabriella had never seen him so enthusiastic, so swept away by emotion. Already, she suspected, he had fallen a victim to the passion of hero worship, and O'Hara—the man who spoke of "idees"—was his hero! "I shall have to be careful," she thought. "I shall have to be very careful or Archibald will come under his influence."

"Well, I guess I must be going along," remarked O'Hara, a little nervously, for he was evidently confused by her imperious manner. "A fellow is expecting me to dinner over at the club."

"But I want to hear about the mine. Mother, make him tell us about the mine!" cried Archibald insistently.

"I'll tell you another time, sonny. We'll get together some day when your mother don't want you, and we'll start off on a regular bat. How would you like that?"

"When?" demanded the boy eagerly. His fear of losing O'Hara showed in the fervour with which he spoke, in the frantic grasp with which he still clung to his hand. It occurred to Gabriella suddenly that she ought to have thrown Archibald more in the companionship of men, that she had kept him too much with women, that 'she had smothered him in her love. This was the result of her selfish devotion—that he should turn from her to the first male creature that came into his life!

Her heart was sore, but she said merely: "That is very kind of you, Mr. O'Hara, but I'm afraid I mustn't let my boy go off on a regular bat without me."

"Oh, yes, I may, mother. Say I may," interrupted Archibald with rebellious determination.

"Well, we'll see about it when the time comes." She turned her head, meeting O'Hara's gaze, and for an instant they looked unflinchingly into each other's eyes. In her look there was surprise, indignation, and a suspicion of fear—why should he, a stranger, come between her and her son?—and in his steady gaze there was surprise, also, but it was mingled, not with indignation and fear, but with careless and tolerant amusement. She knew from his smile that he was perfectly indifferent to her resentment, that he was even momentarily entertained by it, and the knowledge enraged her. The glance he gave her was as impersonal as the glance he gave Miss Polly or the rose-bush or the street with its casual stream of pedestrians. It was the glance of a man who had lived deeply, and to whom living meant action and achievement rather than criticism or philosophy. He would not judge her, she understood, simply because his mind was not in the habit of judging. His interest in her was merely a part of his intense, zestful interest in life. She shared with Miss Polly and Archibald, and any chance object that attracted his attention for an instant, the redundant vitality of his inquiring spirit. "No wonder he has worked his way up with all that energy," she reflected. "No wonder he has made money." His face, with its clear ruddiness, was the face of a man who has breathed strong winds and tasted the sharp tang of sage and pine; and she noticed again that his deep gray eyes had the unwavering look of eyes that have watched wide horizons of sea or desert. There was no suggestion of the city about him, though his clothes were well cut, and she was quick to observe, followed the latest styles of Fifth Avenue. "Yes, he is good looking," she admitted reluctantly. "There is no question about that, and he has personality, too—of a kind." His hat was in his hand—a soft hat of greenish-gray felt—and her eye rested for a moment on his uncovered head with its thick waves of red hair, a little disordered as if a high wind had roughened them. "If he only had breeding or education, he might be really worth while," she added, almost approvingly.

When he spoke again O'Hara ignored Gabriella, and turned his alert questioning glance on the little seamstress. Fanny had sauntered up the walk to join the group—Fanny in all the glory of her yellow curls, and her "debutante slouch "—and he bowed gravely to her without the faintest change of expression. If he admired Fanny's beauty and pitied Miss Polly's plainness, there was no hint of it in the indifferent look he turned from the girl to the old woman.

"The next time you're planting things," he said earnestly, "I wish you'd set out a red geranium. I saw a cart of 'em go by in the street this morning and I had half a mind to buy a pot or two for the yard. If I get some, will you put 'em out?"

"Why, of course, I will. I'll be real glad to," responded Miss Polly, agreeably flattered by his request. "Is there any special place you want me to plant them?"

"Anywhere I can see 'em from the window. I'd like to look at 'em while I eat my breakfast. And while we are about it, wouldn't it be just as well to set out a whole bed of 'em?" he asked with a munificent gesture which included in one comprehensive sweep the weeds, the walk, the elm tree, the blossoming rose-bush, and the freshly turned flower-borders. The large free movement of his arm expressed a splendid scorn of small things, of little makeshifts, of subterfuges and evasions.

"Don't you think it would cut up the yard too much to make another bed?" asked Gabriella, inspired by the whimsical demon of opposition. It was true that she had no particular fondness for red geraniums; but if Miss Polly had expressed, on her own account, a desire to plant the street with them, she would never have thought of objecting.

"Well, the yard ain't much to brag of anyhow," replied Miss Polly with that careful penetration which never sees below the surface of things. "To tell the truth I've always had a sort of leanin' toward geraniums myself—especially rose geraniums. I don't know why on earth," she concluded with animated wonder, "I never thought of putting rose geraniums in that window box along with the sweet alyssum. They would have been the very things and they don't take so much watering."

"That's a bargain, then," said O'Hara, with his ringing laugh which made Gabriella smile in spite of herself. Then, after shaking hands with each one of the group, he went down the walk and passed with his vigorous stride in the direction of Broadway.

When the gate had closed, and his large figure had vanished in the distance, Gabriella said sternly: "Archibald, you must not lose your head over strangers. We know nothing on earth about Mr. O'Hara except that he lives in this house."

"Oh, but, mother, he was splendid at the fire! You ought to have seen him holding a girl by one arm out of the window. He was as brave as a fireman, everybody said so, didn't they, Miss Polly?"

"Men of that sort always have courage," observed Gabriella contemptuously, and despised herself for the remark. What was the matter with her this afternoon? Why did this man arouse in her the instinct of combativeness, the fever of opposition? Was it all because she suspected him of a vulgar intrigue with a shopgirl? And why had she decided so positively that Alice was vulgar? Certainly, she, a dressmaker, should be the last to condemn shopgirls as vulgar.

"I declare, I can't begin to make you out, Gabriella," said Miss Polly uneasily. "I never heard you talk about folks bein' common before. It don't sound like you."

"Well, he is common, you know," protested Gabriella, with a strange, almost tearful violence. "Why did he have to shake hands with us all—with each one of us, even Fanny, when he went away? We'd hardly spoken to him."

"I don't know what's come over you," observed the seamstress gloomily. "I reckon I'm common, too, so I don't notice it. But I must say I like the way he spoke about geraniums. He showed a real nice feelin'."

The words were hardly out of her mouth before Gabriella had caught her in her arms. "I know I'm horrid, dear Miss Polly," she said penitently, "but I don't like Mr. O'Hara."

"Then I shouldn't see any more of him than I was obliged to, honey, and there ain't a bit of use in Archibald's goin' with him if you don't want him to."

"I don't like to forbid him. Of course, I know nothing against the man—it is only a feeling."

"Well, feelin's are mighty queer things sometimes," remarked Miss Polly, scoring a triumph which left the indignant Gabriella at her mercy; "and when I come to think of it; I don't recollect that yours have always been such good judges of folks."

The geraniums arrived in a small cart the next morning, but O'Hara did not appear, and for several weeks, though Gabriella glanced suspiciously at the hatrack each morning when she passed through the hall, there was no sign of life in his rooms. Then one afternoon he reappeared as suddenly as he had vanished, and she found Archibald with him in the yard when she came home at six o'clock. That the boy would be her difficulty, she knew by instinct, for he had been seized by one of those unaccountable romantic fancies to which the young of the race are disposed. Though the sentiment was certainly far less dangerous than Fanny's passion for the, matinée idol, since it revealed itself principally as a robust and wholly masculine ambition to follow in the footsteps of adventure, Gabriella fought it almost as fiercely as she had fought Fanny's incipient love affair.

"He is making Archibald rough," she said to Miss Polly, after a fortnight of unavailing opposition to the new influence in Archibald's life. "Until we came here," she added despondently, "Archibald loved me better than anything in the world, and now he seems to think of nothing but this man."

"It looks to me as if it was mighty good for the child, honey. You can't keep a boy tied to your apron-strings all the time. Archibald needs a father the same as other boys, and if he hasn't got one, he's either goin' to break loose or he's goin' to become a mollycoddle. You don't want to make a mollycoddle of him, do you?"

"Of course not," answered Gabriella honestly, for, in spite of her strange fits of unreasonableness, she was still sensible enough in theory. "I've tried hard to keep him manly—not to spoil him, you know that as well as I do. And it isn't that I object to his making friends. I'd give anything in the world if he could know Arthur. If it had been Arthur," she went on gently, "I should have been glad to have him come first. I shouldn't have cared a bit if he had loved Arthur better than me."

"You oughtn't to talk like that, Gabriella, for you know just as well as can be that Archibald don't love anybody better than he loves you. As far as I can make out though, Mr. O'Hara sets him a real good example. I don't see that he's doin' the child a particle of harm, and I don't believe you see it either. To be sure you don't think much of football, but it's a long ways better than loafin' round with nothin' to do, and this boy scout business that Archibald talks so much about sounds all right to me. Now, he never would have thought a thing about that except for Mr. O'Hara."

"Yes, that's all right. I approve of that, but I can't help hating to see a stranger get so strong an influence over my son. It isn't fair of him."

"Then why don't you tell him to stop it. I believe he'd be sensible about it, and if I was you, I'd have it every bit out with him."

"If it doesn't stop, I'll find some way of showing him that I object to the friendship. But, after all, it may be only a fancy of Archibald's. Anyhow, I'll wait a while before I take any step."

At the beginning of August Gabriella sent the children to the country with Miss Polly, and sailed, on a fast boat, for a brief visit to the great dress designers of Paris. Ever since Madame's age and infirmities had forced her to relinquish this annual trip, Gabriella had taken her place, and all through the year she looked forward to it as to the last of her youthful adventures. On her last visit, Billy and Patty had been in Switzerland; but this summer they met her at Cherbourg; and she spent several brilliant days with them before they flitted off again, and left her to the doubtful consideration of dressmakers and milliners. Patty, who appeared to grow younger and lovelier with each passing year, came to her room the evening before they parted, and asked her in a whisper if she had heard of George or Florrie in the ten years since their elopement?

"Not a word—not a single word, darling. I haven't heard his name mentioned since I got my divorce."

"You didn't know, then, that Florrie left him six months after they ran away?"

"No, I didn't know. Does he ever write to you?"

"Not to me, but mother hears from him every now and then when he wants money badly. Of course she doesn't have much to send him, but she gives him every penny she can spare. A year ago she had a letter from some doctor in New Jersey telling her that he was treating George for the drink habit, and that he needed to be kept somewhere for treatment for several months. We sent her the money she needed, Billy and I, but in her next letter she said that George had escaped from the hospital and that she hadn't heard of him since. That must have been about six months ago."

"It's dreadful for his mother," observed Gabriella, with vague compassion, for she felt as if Patty were speaking of a stranger whose face she was incapable of visualizing in her memory. In the last ten years she had not only forgotten George, but she had forgotten as completely the Gabriella who had once loved him. Though it was still possible for her to revoke the hollow images of the past, she could not restore to these images even the remotest semblance of reality and passion. It was as if some nerve—the sentimental nerve—had atrophied. She could remember George as she remembered the house in Fifty-seventh Street or her wedding-gown which Miss Polly had made; she could say to herself, "I loved him when I married him," or, "It was in such a year that he left me"; but the empty phrases awoke no responsive echoes in her heart; and it would have been impossible to imagine a woman less crushed or permanently saddened by the wreck of her happiness. "I suppose it's hard work that keeps me from thinking about the past," she reflected while she watched Patty's beautiful face framed by the pale gold of her hair. "I suppose it's work that has driven everything else out of my thoughts."

"Have you any idea what became of Florrie?" she asked, moved by a passing curiosity.

"She left George for a very rich man she met in London. I believe he had a wife already, but things like that never stood in Florrie's way."

"It's queer, isn't it, because she really has a kind heart."

"Yes, she is kind-hearted when you don't get in her way, but she was born without any morality just as some people are born without any sense of smell or hearing. I know several women over here who are like that—American women, too—and, do you know, they are all surprisingly successful. Nobody seems to suspect their infirmity, least of all the men who become their victims."

"I sometimes think," observed Gabriella cynically, "that men like women to be without feeling. It saves them so much trouble."

The next day Patty fluttered off like a brilliant butterfly, and Gabriella began to suffer acute homesickness for the house in Twenty-third Street and her children. Not once during her stay in Paris did the thought of O'Hara enter her mind; and so completely had she ceased to worry about his friendship for Archibald that it was almost a shock to her when, after landing one September afternoon, she drove up to the gate and found the man and the boy standing together beside a flourishing border of red geraniums, which appeared almost to cover the yard.

"Oh, look, Ben, there's mother!" cried Archibald; and turning quickly, the two came to meet her.

"My darling, I thought you were still in the country," said Gabriella, kissing her son.

"We've been here almost a week.. The place closed, so we decided to come back to town. It's much nicer here," replied Archibald eagerly. He looked sunburned and vigorous, and it seemed to Gabriella that he had grown prodigiously in six weeks.

"Why, you look so much taller, Archibald!" she exclaimed, laughing with happiness, "or, perhaps, I've been thinking of you as a little boy." Then, while her manner grew formal, she held out her hand to O'Hara. "How do you do, Mr. O'Hara?"

He was standing bareheaded in the faint sunshine, and while her eyes rested on his dark red hair, still moist and burnished from brushing, his tanned and glowing face, and on the tiny flecks of black in the clear gray of his eyes, she was startled by a sensation of strangeness and unreality as if she were looking into his face for the first time.

"Oh, we're well. I've been playing with Archibald. Did you have a good crossing?"

"It was smooth enough, but I got so impatient. I wanted to be with the children."

"Well, I went once, and I was jolly glad to get back again. There was nothing to do over there but loaf and lie around."

There would be nothing else for him, of course, she reflected; and she wondered vaguely if he had ever entered a picture gallery? What would Europe offer to a person possessing neither culture nor a passion for clothes?

The driver had placed her bags inside the gate; and O'Hara took charge of them as if it were the most natural thing in the world to carry for a fellow tenant. Upstairs in the sitting-room he put his burden down, unfastened the straps, and commented upon the leather of a bag she had bought in Paris.

"I'd like to have a grip like that myself. Is there anything else I can help about?"

"No, thank you." She was embracing Fanny, and she did not glance at him as she responded: "You are very kind, but my trunks are arranged for."

At this he went without a word, and Gabriella began a joyous account of her trip to the children.

"Year after next, if you work hard with your French, you may both go with me. Then you'll be big enough to look after each other while I am with the dressmakers."

"Oh, tell me about the dressmakers, mother. What did you bring me?" urged Fanny, prettily excited by the thought of her gifts. "I need dreadfully some dancing frocks. Carlie has a lovely one her mother has just bought for her."

"I have all your autumn dresses, darling; everything you can possibly need at Miss Bradfordine's."

Fanny's eager face grew suddenly fretful. "Am I really to go away to school, mother?"

"Really, precious, both you and Archibald. Think of your poor lonely mother." Breaking off with a start she glanced inquiringly about the room, and turned a hurt look on Miss Polly. "Why, where is Archibald? I thought he was in the room."

"I reckon he must have gone down after Mr. O'Hara. They had just got back from a ball game, and I 'spose they felt like talking about it. He'll be up again in a minute, because Mr. O'Hara goes out at six o'clock."

"But I've just come home." Her lip trembled. "I should think Archibald would rather be with me."

"Oh, he won't stay, and you'll have him all the evening. Archibald is just crazy about gettin' you back."

Taking off her hat, a jaunty twist of black velvet from Paris, Gabriella went into her bedroom and changed to a gown of clear blue crape, which she took out of the new bag. When she came out again, with her arms filled with Fanny's gifts, there was a flush in her usually pale face, and her eyes were bright with determination.

"I put these in my bag, Fanny, so you wouldn't have to wait for the trunks. Try on this little white silk."

"Oh, mother, you look so sweet in that blue gown!"

"I got it for almost nothing, dear, but the colour is lovely." Turning restlessly away, she walked to the window and stood looking over Miss Polly's window box down on the brilliant border of red geraniums.

"Has Archibald come upstairs yet, Miss Polly?"

"Not yet, but he'll be up directly. Don't you worry."

For an instant Gabriella hesitated; then crossing the room with a resolute step, she turned, with her hand on the knob, and looked back at the startled face of the little seamstress, who was fastening Fanny's white gown.

"Well, I'm going after him," she said sternly; "I am going straight downstairs to find him."

# CHAPTER VII

## READJUSTMENTS

For a minute Gabriella stood outside the door of what had once been the drawing-room of the house, while she listened attentively to the sound of animated voices within. Then suddenly Archibald's breezy laugh rang out into the hail, and raising her hand from the knob, she knocked softly on the white-painted panel of the door.

"Come in!" called O'Hara's voice carelessly; and Gabriell entered and imperatively held out her hand to her son, who was standing by the window.

"Come, Archibald, I want you," she said gravely. "You went off without seeing your gifts." She had invaded the sitting-room of a strange man, but her purpose was a righteous one, and there was no embarrassment in her manner.

"Oh, mother, are they upstairs? I'll run up and see them!" cried, Archibald delightedly. "I thought they were all in the trunks."

Darting past her in a flash, he bounded up the staircase, while Gabriella stood facing O'Hara, who had risen and thrown away his cigar at her entrance. The room was still fragrant with tobacco; there was a light cloud of smoke over the mignonette in the window box, and beyond it, she could see the dim foliage of the elm tree waving over the flagged walk to the gate. With an eye trained to recognize the value of details, she saw that the sitting-room was furnished with the same deplorable taste which had selected the golden-oak hatrack and the assortment of ornamental walking-sticks. The woodwork had been stained to match the oak of the barbarous writing-table, which held a distorted bronze lamp, with the base composed of a heavily draped feminine figure, a massive desk set, also of bronze, a pile of newspapers, a dictionary, and several dull-looking books with worn covers and dog's eared pages. She noticed that the chairs were all large and solid, with deep arms and backs upholstered in red leather, which looked as if it would never wear out, that the rug was good, and that, except for a few meretricious oil paintings on the greenish walls, the room was agreeably bare of decoration. After her first hesitating glance, she surmised that a certain expensive comfort was the end sought for and achieved, and that in the furnishing beauty had evidently been estimated in figures.

"Mr. O'Hara," she began firmly, "I wish you would not take my son away from me."

He did not lower his gaze, and she saw, after an instant in which he appeared merely surprised, a look of amusement creep into his expressive eyes. Within four walls, in his light summer clothes, with the gauzy drift of tobacco smoke over his head, he looked larger and more irrepressibly energetic than he had done out of doors.

"I am sorry you feel that way," he returned very slowly after a pause. Already she had discovered that he had great difficulty with his words except when he was stirred by excitement into self-forgetfulness. At other times he seemed curiously inarticulate, and she saw now that, while she waited for his answer, he was groping about in his mind for a suitable phrase in which to repel her accusation.

"I appreciate your interest in him," she resumed smoothly, "but he is with you too much. I do not know you. I know nothing in the world about you."

"Well—" Again he hesitated as if over an impediment in his speech. Then, finding with an effort the words he needed, he went on more easily: "If there's anything you'd like to know, I guess you can ask me."

She frowned slightly, and leaving the door moved resolutely to the writing-table, where she stopped with her hand on the pile of newspapers. Against the indeterminate colour of the walls her head, with its dark, silver-powdered hair, worn smooth and close after the Parisian fashion, showed as clear and fine as an etching. In her blue summer gown she looked almost girlish in spite of the imperious dignity of her carriage; and from her delicate head to her slender feet, she diffused an air of fashion which perplexed and embarrassed him, though he was unaware of the conscious art which produced it.

"The only thing I'd like to know about you," she answered, "is why you have taken so sudden a fancy to my son?"

At this he laughed outright, with a boyish zest which dispelled the oppressive formality of her manner. He was completely at his ease again, and while he ran his hand impatiently through his hair, he answered frankly:

"Well, you see, when it comes to that, I didn't take any sudden fancy, as you call it—I didn't take any fancy at all—it was the other way about. The boy is a nice boy—a bully good boy, anybody can see that—and I like boys, that's all. When he began trotting round after me, we got to be chums in a way, but it would have been the same with any other boy who had come to the house— especially," he added with a clean blow given straight from the shoulder, "if he'd been a decent chap that a parcel of women were making into a muff."

For a minute anger, righteous anger, kept her silent; then she responded with stateliness: "I suppose I have a right to decide how my son shall be brought up?"

He met her stern gaze with a smile; and in the midst of her resentment she was distinctly aware of the impeccable honesty of his judgment. The peculiar breeziness she had always thought of as "Western" sounded in his voice as he answered:

"By George, I'm not so sure that you have!"

Before his earnestness she felt her anger melt slowly away. The basic reasonableness of her character—her passion to investigate experience, to examine facts, to search for truth—this temperamental attitude survived the superficial wave of indignation which had swept over her.

"So you think I am making a mistake with Archibald?" she asked quietly; and growing tired of standing, she sank instinctively into one of the capacious leather-covered chairs by the table. "But the question is—are you able to judge?"

"Well, I'm a man, and I hate to see a boy coddled. It's going to be devilish hard on the kid when he grows up."

"Perhaps you're right"—her manner had grown softer—"and because I've thought of this, I am going to send him away to school this autumn—in a few weeks. Much as it will hurt me to part with them, I am going to send both of my children away from me. I have made the arrangements."

Insensibly the note of triumph had crept into her voice. By the simple statement of her purpose she had vindicated her motherhood to this man. She stood clear now of his aspersions on her wisdom and her devotion.

"I don't know much about girls," he replied, seating himself on the opposite side of the table, where the green light from the shaded lamp fell directly on his features. "I can't remember ever noticing one until I grew up, and then I was afraid to death of them, particularly when they were young—but I've been a boy, and I know all about boys. There isn't a blooming thing you could tell me about boys!" he concluded with animation.

"And you think that all boys are alike?"

"More or less under the skin. Of course some are washed and some are dirty—I was dirty— but they're all boys, every last one of them, and all boys are just kids. With the first money I made out West, I started a lodging-house for them—the dirty ones—down in the Bowery," he added. "They can get a wash and a supper and a night's lodging in a bed with real sheets any night in the year."

She was suddenly interested. "Do you care for boys just because you were a boy yourself?" she asked.

"Because I was such a God-forsaken little chap, I guess. You were never down in a cellar, I suppose, the kind of cellar people live in? Well, I was born in one, and my father had killed himself the week before because he was ill with consumption, and couldn't get work. He'd been a teamster, and he lost his job when he came down with pneumonia, and after they let him out of the hospital, he looked such a scarehead that nobody would employ him. After he died, my mother struggled on somehow, taking in washing or scrubbing floors—God knows how she managed it!—and by the time I was five, and precious big for my age, I was in the street selling papers. I used to say I was seven when anybody asked me, but I wasn't more than five; and I remember as plain as if it was yesterday, the way mother used to take me to a corner of Broadway, and put a bundle of papers in my arms, and how I used to hang on to the coppers when the bigger boys tried to get 'em away from me. Sometimes I'd get an extra dime or nickel, and then we'd have Irish stew or fried onions for supper. After my mother died, when I was about eight, I still kept on selling papers because I didn't know what else to do, but I didn't have any place to sleep then so I used to crawl into machine shops or areas (he said 'aries') or warehouses, when the watchmen weren't looking. In summer I'd sometimes hide under a bush in the park, and the policeman would never see me until I slipped by him in the morning. There was one policeman I hated like the devil, and I used to swear that I'd get even with him if it took me all the rest of my life." For a moment he paused, brooding complacently. "I did get even with him, too," he added, "and it didn't take me more than twenty years."

"You never forget anything?"

"Forget?" he laughed shortly. "When you find a thing I forget, it'll be so small you'll have to put on spectacles to recognize it!"

She nodded comprehendingly. "And after that?"

"After that they caught me and sent me to school, and I learned to read and write and do sums—I always had a wonderful head for figures—but after school I went on selling papers so I'd have something to eat—"

The door burst open, and Archibald rushed in to show the evening clothes Gabriella had brought him from Paris.

"They are jolly, mother! May I keep them on?"

"If you like, dear, but they'll have to be altered a little. The coat doesn't quite fit across the shoulders."

"You're a dandy, kid, a regular dandy," observed O'Hara, with humorous gravity.

After a few moments Archibald rushed off again, and Gabriella made an uncertain movement to follow him. "I must go," she said, without rising, and added abruptly: "So you got on in spite of everything?"

"Right you are!" He leaned back in his chair and regarded her with benevolent optimism. "You can always get on if the stuff is in you. I meant to get on, and a steam engine couldn't have kept me back. It's the gospel truth that I believe I came into the world meaning to get out of that cellar, and it was the same thing with areas and ash-bins. I knew all the time I wasn't going to keep grubbing a living out of an ash-bin. I was always growing, shooting up like one of those mullein stalks out there, and eating? Great Scott! I used to eat so much when I was a kid that mother starved herself near to death so as to give me a square meal. By the time I was twelve I had grown so fast that I got a job at cleaning the streets—my first job from the city. But I never went hungry. As far as I recollect I never went hungry except the time I beat my way out to Chicago—"

Without moving, without lowering her eyes from his face, Gabriella listened, while she clasped and unclasped the hands in her lap. There is a personality that compels attention, and she realized for the first time that O'Hara possessed it. A new vision of life had opened suddenly before her, and she felt, with the illuminating intensity of a religious conversion, that the world she had been living in was merely a fiction. In spite of her experience she had really known nothing of life.

"Yes, a lot of 'em went hungry, but I never did," he resumed in a tone of frank congratulation. "Sometimes, of course, I'd go without supper or breakfast, but that was nothing—that was not being really hungry, you know. I always managed, even when I was at school, to make enough to keep satisfied. What I minded most," he added musingly, "was not having a regular place to go home to at night, and that's why I started that lodging-house. When you've slept in holes and on benches, and under freight cars, and hidden away in machine shops, you know there's nothing on God's earth—not a blessed thing—that can take the place of a real sure enough bed with real sure enough sheets and pillow cases on it."

"But how did you come out of it? How did you succeed? For you have succeeded beyond your dreams, haven't you?"

"Beyond my dreams?" He threw back his big, bright head, laughing happily. "Did any man alive ever succeed beyond his dreams? Why, I used to dream of being President, and I guess I shan't be President this side of the Great Divide, shall I? But I made money, if that's what you mean. Why, I have a million to-day to every dollar I had when I was twenty. Do you mind my smoking? I can't talk unless I've got hold of a cigar."

While he struck a match, she noticed with surprise how very neat and orderly he was about the ashes of his cigars, which lay in an exact gray heap in the massive bronze ash-tray. What a pity, she thought, moved by a feeling of compassion, that he had had no advantages!

"I'll tell you how I got on," he pursued after a minute, leaning forward with the cigar in his hand—it was a good cigar, she knew from the smell of it. "Do you see this room?"—he glanced proudly about him—"do you know why I keep this place even when I am in the West?" She shook her head, and he went on with a kind of half-ashamed, whimsical tenderness: "Well, a man lived here once you never heard of—a common Irishman—just a common Irish politician—the Tammany sort, just the sort the newspapers are so down on. I guess he wasn't strong on civic morality as they call it, and the social conscience and all the other new-fashion catchwords, but he found me out there in the snow one night selling newspapers without any overcoat, and he brought me in and gave me one of his. He was a little fellow—not big as the Irish usually grow—and I could wear his clothes, though I wasn't thirteen at the time. The coat wasn't an old one, either," he explained with retrospective complacency; "no, sirree, he had just bought it, and he made me take it off after I'd tried it on and sit down at the table in that back room there—it's all just as he left it—and eat supper with him—the best supper I ever had in my life before or since, you may take my word for it. Then when I'd finished he gave me a dollar and told me to go out and rent a bed—" He broke off, glanced about the room with the pride of ownership, and added softly: "Who'd ever have thought on that night that this place would one day belong to me?"

"Did you see him again?"

"After that he never lost sight of me. He got me a room, he sent me to school—not that he thought much of education, the more's the pity—and when I was through with school he got me into the Mechanics' Institute, and gave me a job at engineering. But the job was too small for me, and so was New York—there ain't room enough here to get on without stepping on somebody's toes—and when I was twenty I set out to beat my way to Chicago, and went clean out to Arizona. That's a long story—I'll tell you that some day, for I've been everything on earth you can be in order to keep alive, and done pretty much everything you can do with two hands that will earn you a square meal. I've cut corn and ploughed fields, and greased wheels, and chopped wood, and mended machinery, and cleaned the snow away, and once out in some little town in Arizona, I even dug a grave because the sexton was down with pneumonia. I've been brakesman, and freightman, and, after that, freight agent. That was just before I struck it rich in Colorado. I was one of the first men at Bonanza City, and when I went there with the railroad—I was on the very first train that ever ran there—the whole town was just a row of miners' shacks near the foot of old Bonanza. It's the richest mineral streak in the State, and yet twenty-five years ago, before the C.A. & F.W. tapped it, there wasn't even a saloon out there at Bonanza. City. When you wanted a drink—and that didn't worry me, for I haven't tasted anything but water since I was twenty-five—you had to go all the way to Olympia to get it; and what was worse, all the ore had to go to Olympia, too, on a little no account branch road to be shipped over the main line. Well, as soon as I discovered Bonanza City I said that had to change, and it did change. I guess I did as much to make that town as any man out there, and to-day I own about two thirds of it. I've got a house on Phoenix Avenue, and I gave the town a church and a theatre and the ground for a library. We've got one of the handsomest churches in the State," he proclaimed with his unconquerable optimism, "and we've just begun growing. Why, in ten years more Bonanza City will be in the race with Denver."

"And what about your friend?" she asked, finding it difficult to become enthusiastic over the most progressive town in Colorado, a State which she always pictured imaginatively as a kind of rocky desert, inhabited by tribes of gregarious invalids, which one visited for the sake of the scenery or the climate, when one had exhausted the civilized excitements of Europe.

"I am coming back to him," he responded with a manner of genial remonstrance. "You just give me time. But I'd honestly like you to see Bonanza City. Why, it would take your breath away if I told you it hadn't even begun to grow twenty years ago. You people in New York don't know what progress means. Why, out there in Bonanza City we do things while you're thinking about doing them. But to come back to Barney—that was his name, Barney McGoldrick—after I made my pile out of Bonanza, I used to strike here once in a while to see how he was getting along, and when he died I took these rooms just as he left 'em. There wasn't a chick or a child to come after him, but he had a string of pensioners as long as the C.A. & F.W. His money—it must have been half a million—all went to charity, but I kept on in the rooms."

"What kind of man was he?" she asked, sincerely interested.

"What kind?" He pondered the question with deep puffs of his cigar. "Well, do you know, I don't believe, to save my life, I could tell you. The more you know of men, and of women, too, for they're all alike, the more you understand, somehow, that you can't judge unless you've been right in the other man's place—unless you know exactly what they've had to pull up against and how hard they have pulled. Now, if I was drawing my last breath, and you asked me what I thought of Barney McGoldrick, I'd be obliged to answer that he was the best man I ever knew, though there are others in this town, I guess, and the newspapers among 'em, who would tell you that he was—" He broke off abruptly, and she waited without speaking, until he solaced himself with his cigar, and went on less boisterously: "It's a downright shame, isn't it, that the same man can't manage to corner all the virtues. I can't explain how it is, but I've noticed that the virtues don't seem able to work along peaceably in one another's company, for if they did, I guess we'd have pure saints or pure sinners instead of the mixed lot we've got to make a world out of. I've seen a man who wouldn't have lied or stolen to save his wife from starving, and who was the first in the pew at church every Sunday, grind the flesh and blood out of his factory girls until they were driven into the streets, or crush the very life out of the little children he put to work in his mills. Yes, and I've seen a tombstone over him with 'I know that my Redeemer liveth' carved an inch deep in the marble. Well, Barney wasn't like that, but he had his weaknesses, and they were the kind people don't raise marble tombstones over. I never had a taste for politics myself, but it seems to be like any other weakness, and to drag a man a little lower down if it once gets too strong a hold on him. It's all right, of course, if you keep it in moderation, but there's precious few chaps, particularly if it's in their blood, and they're Irish, who can keep the taste under control. Barney was the most decent man to women I ever knew. He wouldn't have hurt one for a million dollars, in a factory or out of it, and he was faithful to his old wife up to the day of her death and long after. He grieved for her till he died, and I don't believe any woman ever asked his help without getting it. His private life was absolutely clean, but his public morality—well, I guess that wasn't exactly spotless. At any rate, they had an investigation—there was a committee of citizens appointed to sit in judgment on his record. The chairman was a pillar of the church and a public benefactor; he had led every political reform for a generation; and I happened to know that he kept two mistresses up somewhere in the Bronx, and his wife, who was old and ugly, wore herself to a shadow because he neglected her. Mark you, I'm not upholding Barney, but, good Lord! ain't it queer how easy men get off when they just sin against women and not against men or against the State?"

"It's all queer." She rose from the leather chair, and held out her hand. "I'm glad I came in, Mr. O'Hara. Some day you must tell me the rest."

"The rest?" His embarrassment had descended upon him, and he was awkwardly stammering for words, with her cool hand in his grasp. As long as his enthusiasm had lasted he had talked fluently and naturally, swept away from his self-consciousness; but with the return of the formal amenities he became as ill at ease and shy as a boy. "There ain't anything more except that we're building a railroad out there, and I'm going back to finish it next spring if I'm alive."

The September breeze entered from the dim stretch of yard, under the waving elm boughs, and in an instant the room was filled with the fragrance of mignonette.

"But you won't be if you never get your dinner," she retorted, as she smiled brilliantly. Then, turning quickly, she crossed the threshold, and went down the hall to the staircase.

She was tremendously excited, and while she mounted the stairs she felt that she had not been so alive, so filled with energy since her girlhood in Richmond. It was as if a closed door into the world had been suddenly flung open, and she knew that she had passed beyond the narrow paths of convention into the sunny roads and broad fields of vision. In a moment of enlightenment she saw deeper and farther than she had ever dreamed of seeing before. "It teaches one not to judge," she thought, with a stab of self-reproach, "it teaches one not to judge others until one really knows." Twice before to-night, on the day when she resolved for the sake of Jane's children to go to work, and again on the June evening when George returned to her, she had felt this sudden quickening of life, this magical sense of the unexplored mystery and beauty of the world that surrounded her. But she had been very young then, and on that June evening she had been deeply in love. To-night, she assured herself, there was no touch of personal romance. In some inexplicable way the talk with O'Hara had renewed her broken connection with her Dream, and she felt closer in sympathy to Arthur than she had been able to feel for months. No, this awakening was utterly different from the awakening of love, for it shed its illumination not on a single person, but on the whole of humanity. O'Hara had moved her, not as a man, but as a force—a force as impersonal as the wind or the sea, which had swept her intellect away from its anchorage in the deeps of tradition. She had thought herself free, but she understood now that she had never really broken away—that in spite of her struggles to escape, the past had still held her. To-night it was more than an awakening, it was a conversion through which she was passing, and she knew she could never again believe as she had believed a few hours ago, that she could never judge again as unintelligently as she had judged yesterday. "So that is a man's world," and then with a rush of impulse: "What a mean little life I have been living—what a mean little life!" For she really knew nothing of life except dressmaking; she was familiar with no part of it except the way to Dinard's. She had been living a little life, with little standards, little creeds, little compromises. And yet, though the personality of O'Hara had enlarged her vision of the world, it had not altered her superficial view of the man. She still saw him outwardly at least without the glamour of romance—she still thought of him as boisterous, uneducated, slangy—but she was beginning almost unconsciously to distinguish between the faults of manner and the faults of character; she was beginning to be tolerant.

From Fanny's open door a humming voice floated out to her, and going inside, she found the girl, in a new frock, practising a dance step before the mirror. "This is the lame duck, mother, but it's different from the one we danced last year."

"Yes, dear, it's very pretty." Stopping before the dressing-table, Gabriella frowned on the photograph of a young man in a silver frame—a young man with a fascinating smile and inane features.

"Fanny, where did you get this?"

"Oh, mother, I didn't mean you to see it. I meant to put it away."

"Where did you get it?"

"He sent it to me. I wrote and asked him for it, and it has his autograph. Isn't he handsome? That's just the way he looked in 'Stolen Sweets' last winter."

"Well, he looks like a calf, I think," returned Gabriella severely. "I suppose you may keep it out until you get tired of it, but please try to be sensible, Fanny." Though she spoke jestingly, she was secretly disturbed by the discovery of the photograph. "If she were not pretty, it wouldn't matter," she thought, "but she is so pretty that almost any man might be tempted to begin a flirtation. Thank Heaven, she didn't take a fancy to Mr. O'Hara. That would have been a calamity." For, in spite of the fact that she had become personally reconciled to O'Hara, she was as firmly resolved as ever to keep Fanny out of his sight. "You know so many nice boys, dear," she resumed after a minute, "that I think you might be content to let actors alone."

"But boys are so stupid, mother." Fanny's tone was withering in its disdain. "They are wrapped up in sports, and I despise sports."

"Then you oughtn't to tease them as you do. You're too young to have fancies."

"I am sixteen."

"Well, that is much too young for anything of that sort. I like you to have boy friends, but I don't like you to be foolish. What has become of that attractive boy, Carlie's brother? He doesn't come here any more, and I'm afraid you've hurt his feelings."

"Oh, mother," hummed Fanny to the music of the lame duck as she practised before the mirror, "how can you really hurt a man?"

The next morning when Gabriella, in a Parisian gown of black taffeta and one of the absurdly small hats of the autumn, started for Dinard's, she found herself thinking, not of Fanny's flirtation, but of her long talk with O'Hara. She cast a friendly glance on the golden-oak hatrack as she passed—for O'Hara had risen in her regard since she had discovered that he had not selected the furniture on the first floor—and then stopping for a few moments on the front steps, she closed her eyes, and inhaled the fragrance of the mignonette in the window box. The yard was brilliant in the early sunshine; and at the gate she saw the wife of the caretaker, who had looked after the flowers in her absence. Detaining the woman by a gesture, she joined her in the street, and the two started together to walk the long blocks that stretched to Fifth Avenue.

"You are going home early to-day, Mrs. Squires."

"Yes, ma'am; it's Johnny's birthday and I promised to take him up to the Bronx. Mr. O'Hara had his breakfast at seven, and I got through earlier than usual. He is so tidy that there ain't much to do except to dust around a little."

She was a neat, red-faced woman, in rusty mourning for a child she had lost in the early summer, and while she talked, Gabriella felt an irresistible impulse to question her about O'Hara. "She has known him for thirty years, and I can find out more from her than I could discover for myself in six months," she thought; but she only said indifferently:

"You've worked at this house a long time, haven't you?"

"For thirty years—ever since I came here at eighteen as housemaid to Mr. McGoldrick. My husband was coachman for Mr. McGoldrick, you know—he drove the prettiest pair of bays in New York—and that was how I met him. When we married, Mr. McGoldrick set us up, and John drove his carriage for him as long as he lived. I often wonder what the old gentleman would think of everybody having automobiles. They were just beginning to come into fashion when he died."

"You knew Mr. O'Hara then?"

"Oh, yes, he was a great deal with Mr. McGoldrick. After he went West we didn't see much of him for a time—that was while he was making his money. Then he came back and brought his wife to a place here to be treated—"

"His wife?"

"Didn't you know? She died a few years ago, but before that he used to keep her with some doctor over on Long Island, and he went regularly to see her every Sunday afternoon as long as she lived."

"What was the matter?"

"Drugs. Drugs and drink, too, they said, though I never knew for certain about that. But they couldn't do anything with her. They tried all the cures anybody ever heard of, and she went back every time. No sooner would one thing fail, however, than Mr. O'Hara would hear of something or other over in Europe, and make them begin trying it. Finally for the last ten or twelve years she was quite out of her mind—clean crazy they said, and didn't know anybody. But he still went to see her every Sunday when he was staying in town, and he still made the doctors go on trying new things. He never gave up till the very last. Mr. McGoldrick used to say of him that he was the sort that would go on hoping in hell."

"Who was she? Where did he meet her?"

"God only knows. He never would say much about her even to Mr. McGoldrick, but John always stuck it out that she was never the right sort in the beginning, and that Mr. O'Hara got tangled up with her somewhere in a mining town out West, and couldn't get out. I've heard she was a chambermaid or a barmaid or something in a miners' hotel, but I don't know, and nobody else knows, for Mr. O'Hara never opened his mouth about her. All we know positive is that she must have been a drug fiend long before he ever married her, and that he stuck to her for better or for worse until she died and was buried. Some men are like that, you know, a few of 'em. When a thing once belongs to 'em, no matter what it is or how little it's worth, they'll go through fire and water for the sake of it—and it makes no difference whether it's a woman or a railroad or a dog or a mine. They've got the sense of responsibility like a disease. You see, Mr. O'Hara is that sort, and you might as well try to turn a steam roller as to start to reason him out of a notion. It would have been as easy as talking for him to have got a divorce. Time and again Mr. McGoldrick used to go after him about it, and talk himself hoarse; but it didn't do any good, not a particle. Instead of getting free out there in the West where it was easy, he kept on lugging that crazy woman back and forth, trying to cure her long after everybody else had given up hope and was wishing that she was dead."

"Well, I suppose he loved her."

"No, ma'am, that's the funny part, but it didn't look like love to me—not like what men call love, anyway. If it had been love, it would have worn itself out long ago. Who on earth could love a crazy, yellow, shrieking, cursing creature like that? I saw her sometimes when he'd send me to take things down to her, and I tell you it wasn't love—not man's love, anyhow—that made him do what he did."

"Then it must have been something finer even than love," Gabriella acquiesced after a moment. "It's strange, when we come to think of it, how often we find spirituality in places where we'd never expect it to be."

"I don't know that I'd call Mr. O'Hara spiritual exactly," replied Mrs. Squires thoughtfully. "I don't believe he ever puts his foot inside a church, and I've heard him swear when he got ready till you'd expect the roof to drop in on you, but when you come to think of it," she concluded, "I guess there's a good deal of religion floating around outside of walls."

At the next corner they parted, and as the caretaker stopped to shake hands with Gabriella and thank her for a birthday present for Johnny, she added nervously: "I hope I haven't said anything that I oughtn't to have said, Mrs. Carr. Mr. O'Hara has been as good as gold to me, and I shouldn't like him to hear I'd been talking about him."

"He shan't hear, I promise you"; and while Mrs. Squires hurried, reassured, to her home in Sixth Avenue, Gabriella walked briskly with the crowd which was streaming along Twenty-third Street into Broadway.

A week ago she would scarcely have noticed the people about her. For ten years she had gone every morning to her work through the streets, and she had felt herself to be as aloof from the masses as the soaring skyscraper at the corner of Broadway. The psychology of the crowd had not touched her; even when she walked with it, when she made a part of it, she had felt herself to be detached from its purposes.

To-day, however, a change had come over her, and she was happy with a large and impersonal happiness which seemed to belong less to herself than to the throng which surged about her and gathered her in. Her little standards, her little creeds, had become a part of the larger standards and creeds of humanity. In Broadway, moving onward with the other workers who were returning to the day's work, she was aware of an invisible current of joy which flowed from the crowd into her thoughts and through her thoughts back again into the crowd. For the first time she was feeling and thinking in unison with the multitude.

That night, when she sat alone with Miss Polly, she said to her suddenly:

"I believe I was wrong to wish Archibald not to see anything of Mr. O'Hara. Yesterday we had a long talk, and I think he must have some very fine traits."

"Maybe," replied Miss Polly, a little snappishly. "I never could see what set you so against him, Gabriella."

"Oh, he is dreadfully slangy, and, of course, he isn't educated. I suppose if I mentioned Hamlet to him, he'd think I was talking about some town in Oklahoma."

"Well, I reckon he's been his own Hamlet," retorted Miss Polly; "and knowing about Hamlet don't make a man, anyhow. George knew all about Hamlet, but it didn't make him easy to live with."

"Yes, that's just it. What did George's advantages do for him? I used to think it was love that mattered most," she said musingly after a pause, "and then, when love failed, I began to think it was culture. But I see now that it is something else. Do you ever wonder what the essential thing really is, Miss Polly?"

"No, I never wonder," responded Miss Polly tartly, "but when you stew it down to the bones, I reckon it's just plain character."

"Yes, if you can't have both culture and character, of course character is the more important. But think how much that man might have made of the university training that was wasted on George." While she spoke there came back to her in snatches a conversation she had had with an Englishman on the boat last summer, and she remembered that he had alluded to Judge Crowborough as "a man of the broadest culture." Surely the "broadest culture" must include character, and yet she could feel even now the casual and business-like clasp of the judge, she could see again the admiring gleam in his small, fishy eyes. "After all, I suppose it is a kind of spiritual consciousness that makes character," she said aloud, "and you can't train that into a man if he isn't born with it."

"It seems to me that Mr. O'Hara has done mighty well, all things considered," pursued Miss Polly, and she inquired suspiciously: "Did Mrs. Squires ever tell you anything about his marriage?"

"I met her this morning on my way to work, and she told me about it."

"Well, what do you make of it? Don't it beat anything you ever heard?"

"It does. There's not the slightest doubt of it. And, do you know," Gabriella went on hurriedly, "that story made a remarkable impression on me—I've been thinking about it ever since. It made me see everything differently, and I've even asked myself if I had enough patience with George. If I wasn't too hard and intolerant with him in the beginning?"

"I shouldn't worry about that, honey, because I don't believe it would have made any difference if you'd been gentler. It's the stuff in a man, I reckon, that counts more than the way a woman handles him. You couldn't have saved George any more than that other woman could ruin the man downstairs."

"Perhaps not." Rising from her chair, Gabriella drew the pins from the smooth, close coil of her hair. "But I see things so differently since I had that talk with Mr. O'Hara. I am glad to have him for a friend," she added generously, "but of course I still feel the same about Fanny. I hope he won't begin to notice Fanny."

"Well, he won't. He ain't thinkin' about it. I declare, Gabriella," the little woman went on with a change of tone, "your head don't look much bigger than a pincushion with your hair fixed that way. It makes you seem mighty young, but there ain't many women that could stand it."

"It's the fashion in Paris. I have to be smart. Do you suppose many people guess that I wear extreme styles," she added laughingly, "because they are so hard to sell?"

"You certainly do look well in 'em. I never saw anybody with more natural style. Why, you can put on those slouchy things without a piece of corset and look as if you'd just stepped out of a fashion plate."

"When you aren't pretty, you're obliged to be smart."

"Well, of course you never had the small features and pink and white colouring that Jane had; but you always had a way of your own even as a girl, and you're handsomer now than you ever were in your life. If you were to ask Mr. O'Hara, I bet you he'd say you were a heap better lookin' than Fanny."

A gasp broke from Gabriella, and she turned from the mirror to stare blankly at the seamstress. "Mr. O'Hara! Why, what in the world made you think of him?"

But Miss Polly had grown suddenly impenetrable. "Oh, nothin'," she responded evasively; "I've just seen him look at you both when you were together."

Gabriella laughed brightly. "Oh, he looks at everything. I never saw such eyes."

There was the note of accomplishment, of success, in her voice, and she brushed her fine, soft hair with long, vigorous strokes which had in them something of this same quality of unwavering confidence. To look at her as she sat, relaxed yet dominant, before the glass, was to recognize that she was a woman who had achieved the purpose of her life, who had succeeded in whatever she had undertaken. Not a great purpose, perhaps—there were hours when her purpose seemed to her to be particularly trivial—but still, great or small, she had accomplished it. She was not only directing Dinard's now—she *was* Dinard's. Without her the business would collapse like a house of cards, and it was because she knew this, because Madame also knew this, that she had been able to perfect the arrangements she had planned that May afternoon after her depressing visit to Judge Crowborough. For she managed the house of Dinard's now by an arrangement which gave her one third of the profits; and in the last six months, since this scheme had gone into effect, the business had grown tremendously in certain directions. The millinery department, for instance, which Madame had once treated with such supercilious disdain, had become to-day the most fashionable hat shop in Fifth Avenue. The work was hard, but the returns were wonderful; and with a strange gloating, she told herself that she was making money—always more money for the children. "When Fanny finishes school year after next, we'll take a large apartment in Park Avenue, and spend every summer in Europe," she concluded.

In the morning she rather expected to see O'Hara, but a month passed before she met him one evening in October, when she came home late from work. The autumn rains had come and gone, destroying the fugitive bloom of

Miss Polly's flower-beds, and scattering the leaves of the elm tree in a moist, delicately tinted carpet over the grass. An hour ago the sun had set in a purple cloud, and beneath the electric lights, which shone through the fog with a wan and spectral glimmer, the dark outlines of the city assumed an ominous vagueness. There was no light in the house; and the deserted yard, silvered from frost and strewn with dead leaves, which lay in wind-drifts along the flagged walk, had the haunted aspect of a place where youth and happiness have passed so recently that the fragrance of them still lingers.

"Archibald went off to school without telling you good-bye," she said in a friendly voice. "He was much disappointed."

Stopping in the walk, he looked at her with unaffected surprise.

"Why, I thought that was what you wanted!"

She met this quite honestly. "Not after I talked to you."

"What in thunder did I say to change your opinion of me?" The strong west wind blowing around him and lifting the roughened red hair from his forehead, appeared to lessen by contrast the breezy animation of his manner.

"It wasn't anything you said," she answered simply. "I found out you were different from what I thought, that is all."

"Then you must have thought something!" he laughed aloud.

"I was afraid at first that you might have a bad influence over Archibald."

"Oh, the kid!" His mirth was as irrepressible as his energy.

"You see I have to be very careful," she went on gently. "I want to do my best by him."

At this he turned on her with sudden earnestness. "You can't do your best by being too careful—take my word for it. If you want him to be a man, don't begin by making a mollycoddle of him. Let him rough it a bit, or it will be twice as hard for him when he grows up."

"But I do—I do. I am sending him away from me. Isn't that right?"

"You bet it is. Let him learn his own strength. I've lived among men ever since I was born, and I tell you, nine times out of ten, the boy who is tied to his mother's apron-strings, loses his grip when he is turned out into the world. At the first knock-down he goes under."

Instinctively she flinched. If only he wouldn't!

"After he leaves school of course he will go to the university," she said.

"That's right," he agreed emphatically, and pursued a little wistfully: "Now, that's what I was cheated out of, and there've been times when I'd have given my right arm to have been through college instead of having to keep my mouth shut and then run home and look up the meaning of things in an encyclopædia. It's a handicap, not knowing things. Nobody who hasn't had to get along in spite of, it knows what a darned handicap it is!"

"But you read, don't you?"

"Not much. Never had time to form the habit. But I've read Shakespeare— at least I've read Julius Cæsar six times," he explained. "I had it in the desert once where there wasn't a newspaper for two months. And I've read the Kings, too—most of 'em."

"But not Hamlet?" She was smiling as she looked from him into the street.

He shook his head with a laugh. "Too much meandering in that. I don't like talk unless it is straight."

Though he was upon the most distant terms of acquaintance with the English language, it occurred to her that he probably possessed a knowledge of men and things which no university training could have given him.

"It is wonderful," she remarked, touched to sympathy by his confession, "that you should have succeeded."

"Oh, any man could have done it—any man, that is, who loved a fight as much as I do. It was half luck and half bulldog grip, I suppose. When I once get my grip on a thing, I'll hold on no matter what happens. There ain't the power this side of Kingdom Come that could make me let go if I don't want to."

She thought of his wife, of his losing fight against the craving for morphine, and she replied very gently: "If you hadn't been a good fighter, I suppose you would have been beaten long ago."

"So long ago," he retorted with jovial humour, "that you wouldn't have known me."

An impulse of curiosity urged her to an utterly irrelevant response. "I wonder if you have known many women?" She felt that she should like to hear his story from him, there in the deserted yard; but when he answered her, he revealed a personal reticence worthy of the aristocratic traditions of Mrs. Carr. "Oh, I haven't had time for them," he replied indifferently.

"Perhaps there aren't so many in Bonanza City?"

"Oh, there're plenty," he rejoined gaily, "if you take the trouble to look for them."

"And you didn't?" They had entered the house, and she spoke merrily as she crossed to the staircase.

"Well, the sort I found didn't take my fancy, you see!" he tossed back playfully from his door.

Her foot was on the lowest step, when, hesitating with a birdlike movement, she looked at him over her right shoulder.

"Well, that's a pity. A woman could have told you a good many things," she observed.

"For instance?" He was still jesting.

Poised for flight, she gazed back at him, challenging his eyes.

"Oh, not to collect gold-headed walking-sticks, not to believe in golden-oak, and not to be so extravagantly—slangy."

As she ran up the staircase, a burst of laughter followed her in the midst of which she distinguished the retort: "Well, I own to the slang, but I inherited the oak, and the sticks were all given me—by women."

The temptation to fling back, "of a sort?" came to her; but she conquered it as she passed demurely into the sitting-room, where Miss Polly was reading the afternoon paper before an open fire. "I mustn't get too friendly," she told herself, reprovingly. "It is better to keep up a certain formality." And she determined that at the next meeting she would be dignified and aloof.

But the next meeting did not occur until January, for O'Hara went West the following day, and for more than two months Miss Polly and Gabriella were alone in the house. Though she was working doubly hard at Dinard's, the loneliness of the winter evenings after the Christmas holidays were over became almost intolerable to Gabriella; and the bleak month of January stretched ahead of her in an interminable prospect of cold and gloom. For the past ten years the children had absorbed her life, after her working hours, so entirely that the parting from them had been an unbearable wrench, and had left her with an aching feeling as if an arm had been cut away. She had had little time to make friends; the streets of the city isolated her as completely as if they had been spaces of uninhabited wilderness; and, except for her casual remarks to Miss Polly, she had lived from day to day without speaking a word that was not directly concerned with the management or the sales of Dinard's. Since her divorce, obeying perhaps some inherited tradition, she had avoided men almost instinctively; and even if she had cared to make friends among them, her life was so narrow that it would have been almost impossible for her to do so. When she was not too tired, she still read as widely as she could; but at thirty-seven books had become but a poor substitute for the more robust human activities. As the theatres and the lecture rooms offered the only opportunities of relaxation and amusement, she went twice a week, accompanied by the little seamstress, who appeared to thrive on self-sacrifice, to see a play that was noticed in the papers, or to listen to explanatory descriptions of the scenery of South America or the grievances of the oppressed natives of Asia.

"You mustn't let yourself mope, honey," urged Miss Polly, one snowy morning in January, when Gabriella was putting on a fur coat, cut in the latest fashion, which had been left on her hands after the mid-winter sales. "The children had to go sooner or later, and it's just as well it happened while you are young enough to get over it. A boy never stays at home anyway, and you know I always told you Fanny was the sort to marry before she is out of her teens."

"Oh, I'm not moping, but of course I can't help missing them. The house seems so empty."

"It's obliged to be empty with only us two women in it. I declare I got such a creepy feelin' about burglars last night that I kept wishin' Mr. O'Hara would hurry up and come home. Mrs. Squires says she was expectin' him all last week, but he didn't turn up, so she is kind of lookin' for him to-day."

"Is she?" Gabriella's voice was charged with sincere thankfulness. Merely to know that there was a man on the first floor afforded a sense of security; and an occasional meeting with him would make, she was aware, a trivial diversion from the monotony of her existence. The loneliness of the winter had driven her like a storm-swept bird back to the enduring refuge of her Dream; but, after all, the flesh and blood presence of O'Hara could not seriously interfere with the tender and pensive visions her memory spun of the past. Every morning, standing beside her window and gazing on the bleak street and the bare elm boughs, she thought of Arthur and of her first love, with a pious and reverent mind—for they occupied in her day the hour and mood which her mother, belonging to a more orthodox generation, piously dedicated to "Daily Strength for Daily Need." But never for an instant would it have occurred to the granddaughter of that sanctified snob, Bartholomew Berkeley, who despised the lower orders and fraternized with the Deity in his pulpit every Sabbath, that the red-blooded and boisterous O'Hara—the man of force and slang—could by any accident usurp the sacred shrine where the consecrated relics of her first love reposed. Before the whirlwind of O'Hara's energy, she would congratulate herself that her Arthur, with the milder fluid of the Peytons in his veins, would never allow himself to be carried away by his impulses.

"Well, I'm glad he's coming back, if it's only to protect us," she said, while she fastened her fur coat. "I wonder what he has been doing out West all this time?"

"Makin' money, I reckon. They say he makes so much he don't know what to do with it."

"We could teach him, couldn't we? But he ought to marry and let his wife spend it for him. Only," she concluded carelessly, "I suppose he'd select some dizzy chorus girl who would bring him to ruin. Men of his kind always pick out chorus girls, don't they?"

"I thought 'twas the other sort that did that," observed Miss Polly, fresh from the perusal of the Sunday newspapers; "Dukes and society men and the sons of millionaires."

"Perhaps. Maybe they're all alike," and taking up her umbrella, Gabriella started bravely out into the storm.

At six o'clock, when she struggled back along Twenty-third Street, the wind had changed, and the storm driving furiously down the long blocks caught her in a whirl of blinding snowflakes. In the swirling whiteness of the distance, the black outlines of the city appeared remote and shadowy, while the waning lights, which shone like dim moons at the crossing, revealed the ghostly figures of a few struggling pedestrians.

The gate was open, and she had almost reached it, when the lurching form of a man, emerging suddenly from the storm, was flung against her with such violence that she fell back for support on the icy railing of the yard. Then, as the obscure figure, drawing away from her with a staggering motion, began fumbling blindly at the gate, she caught sight of a ghastly face, which looked as if it had been stricken by an incurable illness. The man wore no overcoat; a knitted muffler was wrapped tightly about his neck; and she saw that the hands fumbling at the gate were red and trembling from cold.

Steadying herself against the fence, she drew her purse from her muff, and she had already taken out a piece of silver, when she heard her name called in a voice which sounded vaguely familiar, though it awoke no immediate associations in her mind.

"Gabriella! My God! I was looking for you, Gabriella!"

With the money still in her hand, she stooped to look into his face.

"You don't know me. I'm George," he said in an angry voice as if he were about to burst into tears. "I'm George, but you don't know me."

The storm drove him against her, and he clung weakly to her arm, crying softly in a terrified whimper like a child that is awaking from a horrible nightmare. Though she did not realize that he was dying, not of disease, but of drink, the thought shot through her mind: "So this is George. So this is what George has come to—George who took everything that he wanted!"

"Where are you going?" she asked, for the shock had restored him to some poor semblance of sanity.

"I was looking for you. I heard you lived down here, and I knew you'd take me in. I've been ill—I'm ill enough to die, and they turned me out of the hotel. There was a woman who stole everything I had. She stole it and ran off in the night, damn her!"

He shivered violently while he spoke, and she saw a glassy look creep into his eyes and over his face, as if his features had been frozen in an instant of terror. Panic seized her lest he should die there in the street, and she grasped his arm almost roughly as if she would shake him back into life. As she supported him his teeth began to rattle, not as the teeth of the living chatter from fear, but as the teeth of a dead man might rattle when he is jolted in his coffin. For a minute she felt the madness of her panic pass from her pulses to her brain, and her terror of him turned her as cold as the sleet-covered iron railing against which she leaned. A cowardly impulse tempted her to desert him and run for her life, to seek shelter behind bolted doors, to leave him there alone to freeze to death at her gate.

"Gabriella, I'm afraid," he whined, clinging to her arm. "I'm afraid, Gabriella. You can't let go of me!"

An unspeakable loathing swept over her; his very touch seemed contamination; and while she turned toward the gate, she knew that every fibre of her flesh, every quiver of her nerves, revolted against the thing she was doing. But something stronger than her flesh or her nerves—the vein of iron in her soul—decided the issue.

"Come in with me, and I'll take care of you," she said. "There is the step. Don't stumble. Here, steady yourself with the umbrella. We are almost there now." Her voice was cold and hard; but the words were those she might have used to Archibald had she been leading him in out of the storm.

Still whimpering and stumbling, George clung to her with his desperate clutch, while she dragged him up the short walk, which was deep in snow, to the six steps, which appeared to her to reach upward into eternity. As she approached the house, a light shone out suddenly in one of the windows and a sense of safety, of perfect security descended upon her, for she knew that it was the red glimmer of O'Hara's fire. With the sensation, she heard again her mother's voice speaking above the storm: "Gabriella, we'll send immediately for your Cousin Jimmy Wrenn!" So, in the old days of her childhood, Cousin Jimmy had brought her this feeling of relief in the midst of distress.

Opening the door with her latchkey, she dragged George into the hall, where her thankful eyes fell on O'Hara's overcoat, from which the water was, still dripping. For an instant she was tempted to call to him; then checking the impulse, she went on to the staircase, which she ascended with difficulty because George's legs seemed to give way when he tried to lift them to a step. At last, after what she felt to be an eternity, they reached the upper floor, and she pushed her burden into Archibald's room, where he fell like a log on the hearthrug. The sound of his fall shook the house, and when Miss Polly came running in, with a cry of alarm, Gabriella almost expected to see O'Hara behind her. But O'Hara did not come, and before the seamstress could recover from the palpitations the shock had produced, George was on his feet again, and was staring blankly, as if fascinated, at the reflection of the electric light in the mirror.

"It's George," Gabriella explained in a harsh voice. "I found him in the street. He was looking for me, and I couldn't leave him to freeze. I think he's either drunk or ill. I don't know which it is, but it sounds like pneumonia."

"God have mercy!" exclaimed Miss Polly, which was quite as lucid as she ever became in a crisis. Her face had turned blue, she was trembling with terror, and the violence of her palpitations almost exceeded the painful sounds in George's chest. "If there was only a man we could send for," she wailed hysterically. "Oh, Gabriella, if there was only a man!"

"Well, there's the doctor," replied Gabriella shortly. "You'd better telephone for him at once. Get the nearest one. I think his name is McFarland."

"And a nurse? You'll want a nurse, won't you?"

"I'll want anything I can get, and I'll want it quickly. There, hurry, while I find a bathrobe of Archibald's. He's wet through—soaking wet. He must have been out all day in the storm."

Miss Polly vanished into the dimness of the hall, and after a few minutes Gabriella heard her fluttering voice demanding a telephone number as if she were still supplicating the Deity.

"Take off your wet clothes while I get you a drink and some hot blankets!" said Gabriella when she had found one of Archibald's bathrobes in the closet. It occurred to her that George was really incapable of undressing himself, but she felt that she would rather die than touch him again. The loathing which had overpowered her outside in the storm became stronger in the close air of the house. "I can't touch him. I don't care what happens I can't touch him," she told herself, while she placed the flannel robe on the rug, and hurried back to the kitchen. Her whole body was benumbed and chilled, not from cold, but from disgust, yet her mind was almost unnaturally active, and she found herself thinking over and over again: "So this is the man I loved, this is the man I married instead of Arthur!"

When she came back with a cup of broth and some hot blankets, she found George in the flannel gown of Archibald's, with his wet clothes on the floor at his feet, from which he had forgotten to remove his shoes. He drank the soup greedily, while Miss Polly lighted the wood-fire she had laid in the open grate.

"The heat's comin' up all right in the radiator," she said, "but I thought a blaze might make him more comfortable."

"Yes, it's better," replied Gabriella sternly, while she stooped to unlace George's boots. There was no compassion in her heart, and it seemed to her, while she struggled with the wet lacing, that the fumes of whiskey spread contagion and disease over the room. She was not only hard and bitter—she felt that she loathed him with unspeakable loathing.

"I declare, Gabriella, I believe he has gone deranged!" Miss Polly cried out sharply, dropping the poker and starting to her feet in an erratic impulse of flight.

With the flannel gown clutched tightly to his chest, where the dull rattling sounds went on unceasingly, George was staring in fascinated intensity at the reflection of the electric light in the mirror. Then suddenly, with a scream of terror, he lifted the poker Miss Polly had dropped, and flung it over Gabriella's head in the direction of the dressing-table. At the noise of breaking glass, Gabriella rose from her knees, and said in the hard, quiet voice she had used ever since the first shock of the meeting:

"If you are afraid, lock yourself in your room, Miss Polly. I am going downstairs for Mr. O'Hara."

Without waiting for a response, she ran out into the hall and down the staircase, while her eyes clung to the comforting glimmer of light under the drawing-room door. As her feet touched the lowest step, the door opened quickly, and O'Hara stood on the threshold.

# CHAPTER VIII

## THE TEST

"I knew something was wrong," he said, emerging, big and efficient, from the firelight, "and I was just coming up." Before she could answer she felt his warm grasp on her hands, and it seemed to her suddenly that it was not only her hands he enfolded, but her agonized and suffering mind.

"There's a man up there—" she faltered helplessly. "I was once married to him long ago—oh, long ago. Just now I found him in the street and he seems to be out of his mind. We are frightened."

But he seemed not to hear her, not to demand an explanation, not even to wait to discover what she wanted. Already his long stride was outstripping her on the staircase, and while she followed more slowly, pausing now and then to take breath, she realized thankfully that the situation had passed completely away from her power of command. As Miss Polly's strength to hers, so was her strength to O'Hara's.

Faint, despairing moans issued from Archibald's room as she reached the landing; and going inside, she saw George wrestling feebly with O'Hara, who held him with one hand while with the other he waved authoritative directions to Miss Polly.

"Get the bed ready for him, with plenty of hot blankets. He's about at the end of his rope now. It's a jag, but it's more than a jag, too. If I'm not mistaken he's in for a case of pneumonia."

Miss Polly, hovering timidly at a safe distance, held out the blankets and the hot water bottles, while O'Hara carried George across the room to the bed, and then covered him warmly. When he turned to glance about his gaze fell on Gabriella, and he remarked bluntly: "You'd better get out. You aren't wanted."

"But I am obliged to be here. It is my business, not yours," she replied, while a sensation of sickness passed over her.

For a moment he regarded her stubbornly, "Well, I don't know whose business it was a minute ago," he rejoined, "but it's mine now. I am boss of this particular hell, and you're going to keep out of it. I guess I know more about D.T. than you and Miss Polly put together would know in a thousand years."

She was very humble. In the sweetness of her relief, of her security, she would have submitted cheerfully not only to slang, but to downright profanity. It was one of those unforgettable instants when character, she understood, was more effective than culture. Even Arthur would have appeared at a disadvantage beside O'Hara at that moment.

"I think I ought to help you," she insisted.

"Well, I think you oughtn't. Out you go! I guess I know what I'm up against."

Before she could protest, before she could even resist, he had pushed her out into the hall, and while she still hesitated there at the head of the staircase, the door opened far enough to allow the huddled figure of Miss Polly to creep through the crack. Then the key turned in the lock; and O'Hara's voice was heard pacifying George as he might have pacified a child or a lunatic. After a few minutes the shrieks stopped suddenly; the door was unlocked again for a minute, and there floated out the reassuring words:

"Don't stand out there any longer. It's as right as right. I've got him buffaloed!"

"What does he mean?" inquired Gabriella helplessly of the seamstress.

"I don't know, but I reckon it's all right," responded Miss Polly. "He seems to know just what to do, and anyhow the doctor'll be here in a minute. It seems funny to give him whiskey, don't it, but that was the first thing Mr. O'Hara thought of."

"I suppose his heart was weak. He looked as if he were dying," answered Gabriella. "He asked for more whiskey, didn't he?"

"Yes; I'm goin' right straight to get it. Oh, Gabriella, ain't a man a real solid comfort sometimes?"

Without replying to this ejaculation, Gabriella went after the whiskey, and when she came back with the bottle in her hand, she found the doctor on the landing outside the locked door. He was a stranger to her, and she had scarcely begun her explanation when O'Hara called him into the room.

"The sooner you take a look at him the better." Everything was taken out of her hands—everything, even her explanation of George's presence in her apartment.

As there was nothing more for her to do, she went back to the sitting-room, where a fire burned brightly, and began to talk to Miss Polly.

"I don't know what I should have done if he hadn't been here," she said.

"Who? Mr. O'Hara? Well, it certainly was providential, honey, when you come to think of it."

The door of Archibald's room opened and shut, and the doctor came down the hall to the telephone. They heard him order medicines from a chemist near-by; and then, after a minute, he took up the receiver, and spoke to a nurse at the hospital. At first he gave merely the ordinary directions, but at the end of the conversation he said sharply in answer to a question: "No, there's no need of a restraining sheet. He's too far gone to be violent. It is only a matter of hours."

His voice stopped, and Gabriella went out to him. "Will you tell me what you think, Doctor?" she asked.

"Is he your husband?" He had a blank, secretive face, with light eyes, and a hard mouth—so different, she thought from the poetic face of Dr. French.

"I divorced him ten years ago."

He looked at her searchingly. "Well, he may last until morning, but it is doubtful. His heart has given out."

"Is there anything I can do?"

"No. Morphine is the only thing. We are going to try camphorated oil, but there is hardly a chance—not a chance." He turned to go back into the room, then stopped, and added in the same tone of professional stoicism: "The nurse will be here in half an hour, and I shall wait till she comes."

When Gabriella went back to the sitting-room, Miss Polly was weeping. "I followed you and heard what he said. Oh, Gabriella, ain't life too awful!"

"I'll be glad when the nurse comes," answered Gabriella with impatience. Emotionally she felt as if she had turned to stone, and she had little inclination to explore the trite and tangled paths of Miss Polly's philosophy.

The nurse, a stout, blond woman in spectacles, arrived on the stroke of the half-hour, and after talking with her a few minutes, the doctor took up his bag and came to tell Gabriella that he would return about daybreak. "I've given instructions to the nurse, and Mr. O'Hara will sit up in case he is needed, but there is nothing to do except keep the patient perfectly quiet and give the hypodermics. It is too late to try anything else."

"May I go in there?"

"Well, you can't do any good, but you may go in if you'd rather."

Then he went, as if glad of his release, and after Gabriella had prevailed upon Miss Folly to go to bed, she changed her street dress for a tea-gown, and threw herself on a couch before the fire in the sitting-room. An overpowering fatigue weighed her down; the yellow firelight had become an anodyne to her nerves; and after a few minutes in which she thought confusedly of O'Hara and Cousin Jimmy, she let herself fall asleep.

When she awoke a man was replenishing the fire, and as she struggled drowsily back into consciousness, she realized that he was not Cousin Jimmy, but O'Hara, and that he was placing the lumps of coal very softly in the fear of awaking her.

"Hallo, there!" he exclaimed when he turned with the scuttle still in his hand; "so you're awake, are you?"

She started up. "I've been asleep!" she exclaimed in surprise.

"You looked like a kid when I came in," he responded cheerfully, and she reflected that even the presence of death could not shadow his jubilant spirit. "I went back to the kitchen to make some coffee for the nurse and myself, and I thought you might like a cup. It's first-rate coffee, if I do say it. Two lumps and a little cream, I guess that's the way. I rummaged in the icebox, and found a bottle of cream hidden away at the back. That was right, wasn't it?"

A strange, an almost uncanny feeling of reminiscence, of vague yet profound familiarity, was stealing over her. It all seemed to have happened before, somewhere, somehow—the slow awakening to the large dark form in the yellow firelight, O'Hara's sudden turning to look at her, his exuberance, his sanguine magnetism, and even the cup of coffee he made and brought to her side. She felt that it was the most natural thing in the world to awake and find him there and to drink his coffee.

"It's good," she answered; "I had no dinner, and I am very hungry."

"I thought you'd be. That's why I brought a snack with it." He was cutting a chicken sandwich on the tray he had placed under the green shaded light, and after a minute he brought it to her and held the cup while she ate. A nurse could not have been gentler about the little things she needed; yet she knew that he was rough, off-hand, careless—she could imagine that he might become almost brutal if he were crossed in his purpose. She had believed him to be so simple; but he was in reality, she saw, a mass of complexities, of actions and reactions, of intricacies and involutions of character.

"I don't know what I should have done if you hadn't been here," she said gratefully while she ate the sandwich and he sat beside her holding her cup. "But I'm so unused to being taken care of," she added with a trembling little laugh, "that I don't quite know how to behave."

"Oh, you would have got on all right," he rejoined carelessly; "but I'm glad all the same that I was here."

She motioned toward the hall. "Has there been any change?"

"No, there won't be until morning. He'll last that long, I think. We're giving him a hypodermic every four hours, but it really ain't any good, you know. It is merely professional." For a minute he was silent, watching her gravely; then recovering his casual manner, he added: "I shouldn't let it upset me if I were you. Things happen that way, and we've got to take them standing."

She shook her head. "I'm not upset. I'm not feeling it in the least. Somehow, I can't even realize that I ever knew him. If you told me it was all a dream, I should believe you."

"Well, you're a plucky sort. I could tell that the first minute I saw you."

"It's not pluck. I don't feel things, that's all. I suppose I'm hard, but I can't help it."

"Hard things come useful sometimes; they don't break."

"Yes, I suppose if I'd been soft, I should have broken long ago," she replied almost bitterly.

After putting the plate and cup aside, he sat down by the table, and gazed at her attentively for a long moment. "Well, you look as soft as a white rose anyhow," he remarked with a curiously impersonal air of criticism.

A rosy glow flooded her face. It was so long since any man had commented upon her appearance that she felt painfully shy and displeased.

"All the same I've had a hard life," she returned with passionate earnestness. "I married when I was twenty, and seven years later my husband left me for another woman."

"The one in there?"

She shuddered, "Yes, the one in there."

"The darn fool!" he exclaimed briefly.

"There was a divorce, and then I had my two children to support and educate. Because I had a natural talent for dressmaking, I turned to that, and in the end I succeeded. But for ten years I never heard a word of the man I married—until—I met him downstairs—in the street."

"And you brought him in?"

"What else could I do? He was dying."

"Do you know what he was doing out there?"

"He was looking for me, I think. He thought. I would take him in."

"Well, it's strange how things work out," was his comment after a pause. "There's something in it somewhere that we can't see. It's impossible to reason it out or explain it, but life has a way of jerking you up at times and making you stand still and think. I know I'm putting it badly, but I can't talk—I never could. Words, don't mean much to me, and yet I know—I know—" He hesitated, and she watched his thought struggle obscurely for expression. "I know you can't slip away from things and be a quitter, no matter how hard you try. Life pulls you back again and again till you've learned to play the game squarely."

He was gazing into the fire with a look that was strangely spiritual on his face, which was half in shadow, half in the transfiguring glow of the flames. For the second time she became acutely aware of the hidden subtleties beneath his apparent simplicity.

"I've felt that myself often enough," he resumed presently in a low voice. "I've been pulled up by something inside of me when I was plunging ahead with the bit in my teeth, and it's been just exactly as if this something said: 'Go steady or you'll run amuck and bu'st up the whole blooming show.' You can't talk about it. It sounds like plain foolishness when you put it into words, but when it comes to you, no matter where you are, you have to stand still and listen."

"And is it only when you are running amuck that you hear it?" she asked.

"No, there've been other times—a few of them. Once or twice I've had it come to me up in the Rockies when there didn't seem more than a few feet between me and the sky, and then there was a time out on the prairie when I was lost and thought I'd never get to the end of those darned miles of blankness. Well, I've had a funny road to travel when I look back at it."

"Tell me about some of the women you knew in the West." An insatiable curiosity to hear the truth about his marriage seized her; but no sooner had she yielded to it than she felt an impulsive regret. What right had she to pry into the hidden sanctities of his past?

A frown contracted his forehead, but he said merely: "Oh, there wasn't much about that," and she felt curiously baffled and resentful. "I think I'll go and take a look in there," he added, rising and walking softly in the direction of the room at the end of the hall.

He was gone so long that Gabriella, crushing down the revolt of her nerves, went to the door, and opening it very gently, looked cautiously into the room. The window was wide open to the night, where the snow was still falling, and beside the candlestand at the head of the bed the nurse was filling a hypodermic syringe from a teaspoon. By the open window O'Hara stood inhaling the frosty air; and Gabriella crossed the floor so silently that he did not notice her presence until he turned to watch the nurse give the injection.

Then he said in a whisper: "You'd better go out. You can't do any good." But she made an impatient gesture of dissent, and stopping between the bed and the wall, waited while the nurse bared George's arm and inserted the point of the needle. He was lying so motionless that she thought at first that he was already dead; but presently he stirred faintly, a shiver ran through the thin arm on the sheet, and a low, half-strangled moan escaped from his lips. Had she come upon him in a hospital ward, she knew that she should not have recognized him. He was not the man she had once loved; he was not the father of her children; he was only a stranger who was dying in her house. She could feel nothing while she looked down at him. When she tried to remember her young love she could recall but a shadow. That, too, was dead; that, too, had not left even a memory.

As she bent there above him she made an effort to remember what he had once been, to recall his face as she had first seen it, to revive the burning radiance of that summer when they had been lovers. But a gray veil of forgetfulness wrapped the past; and her mind, when she tried to bring back the emotions of seventeen years ago, became vacant. For so long she had stoically put the thought of that past out of her life, that when she returned to it now, she found that only ashes remained. Then a swift stab of pity pierced her heart like a blade, and she saw again, not George her lover, not George her husband, but the photograph Mrs. Fowler had shown her of the boy in velvet clothes with the wealth of curls over his lace collar. So it was that boy who lay dying like a stranger in the bed of his son!

She turned hurriedly and went out without speaking, without looking back when she opened the door.

"If one could only understand it," she said aloud as she entered the sitting-room; and then, with a start of surprise, she realized that O'Hara had followed her. "You walked so softly I didn't hear you," she explained.

"The rugs are thick, and I have on slippers. My boots were soaking when I came in, and I'd just taken them off when you called."

They sat down again in front of the fire; and while she stared silently at the flames, with her chin on her hand and her elbow on the arm of the chair, he burst out so unexpectedly that she caught her breath in a gasp:

"You didn't know that I was married, too, did you?" His words, and even more than his words, his voice, filled with suppressed emotion, awoke her from her reverie in which she had been dreaming of Arthur.

She smiled evasively, remembering her promise to Mrs. Squires.

He hesitated again, and then spoke with an effort. "Well, it was hell!" he said grimly.

"I know"—she was very gentle, full of understanding and sympathy—"but you went through it bravely."

"I stuck to her." His hand clenched while he answered. Then, after a pause in which she watched him struggle against some savage instinct for secrecy, he added quietly: "If she were alive to-day, I'd be sticking to her still."

"You must have loved her." It was all she could think of to say, and yet the words sounded trite and canting as soon as she had uttered them.

Lifting his head quickly, he made a contemptuous gesture of dissent. "No, it wasn't that. I never loved her, except, perhaps, just at the first. But there's something that comes before love, I guess. I don't know what it is, but there's something. It may be just plain doggedness, but after I married her there wasn't anything on top this earth that could have made me give up and let go. As soon as I found what I was up against—it was morphine—I knew I'd either got to fight it out or be a quitter, and I've never been a quitter. Until she got so bad she had to be shut up I kept a home for her out there in Colorado, and I lived with her in hell as long as she wasn't too bad to be out of a hospital. Then I brought her on here and we found a private place down on Long Island where she stayed till she died—"

"And you still saw her?"

"Except when I was out West, and that's where I was most of the time, you know. My work was out there, and there's nothing like hell behind you to keep you running. I made piles of money those years. That's all I ever cared for about money—just making it. I'd fight the devil to get it, but after I've once got it, I'll give it to the first fool who comes begging. But the getting of it is great."

"How long did it last?"

"My marriage? Going on eighteen years. She was down on Long Island for the last ten of them."

"Then you lived with her eight. Was she always—always-"

"Took it before I ever married her, and I found it out in a month. She wasn't so much to blame as you might think," he pursued thoughtfully. "You see she had a tough time of it, and she was little and weak, and everything was against her. She came out West first to teach school, and then she got mixed up with some skunk of a man who pretended to marry her when he had a wife living in Chicago, and after that I guess she went on taking a dope just to keep up her spirits and ease the pain of some spinal trouble she'd had since she was a child. There was nothing bad in her—she was just weak—and I began to feel sorry for her, and so I did it. If I had it to do over again, I'm not so sure I'd act differently. She was a poor little creature that didn't have any man to look after her, and I was just muddling along anyway, thinking about money. Heaven knows what would have become of her if I hadn't happened along when I did."

He had lifted his head toward the light, while he ran his hand through his hair, and again she saw the look, so like spiritual exaltation, transfigure his face. Before this man, who had sprung from poverty and dirt, who had struggled up by his own force, overcoming and triumphing, fighting and winning, fighting and holding, fighting and losing, but always fighting—before this man, who had been born in a cellar, she felt suddenly humbled. Without friends, without knowledge, except the bitter knowledge of the streets, he had fought his fight, and had kept untarnished a certain hardy standard of honour. Beside this tremendous achievement she weighed his roughness, his ignorance of books and of the superficial conventions, and she realized how little these things really mattered—how little any outside things mattered in the final judgment of life. She thought of George, dying a drunkard's death in the room at the end of the hail—of George whose way had been smoothed for him from birth, who had taken everything that he had wanted.

"I wish there was something I could do for you—something to help you," she said impetuously. "But I never saw any one who seemed to need help so little."

His face brightened, and she saw that her words had brought a touching wistfulness into his eyes.

"Well, if you'd let me come and talk to you sometimes" he answered shyly. "There're a lot of things I'd like to talk to you about—things I don't know, things I do know, and things I half know."

From the brilliant look she turned on him, he understood that he must have given her pleasure, and she saw the smile return to his face.

"I'll tell you everything I know and welcome," she replied readily; "but that isn't much. Better than that, I'll read to you."

"If you don't mind, I think I'd rather you'd just talk." Then he rose with one of his abrupt movements, "I'd better look in again now. The nurse might want something."

"I feel that you oughtn't to stay up," urged Gabriella, rising as he turned away from her. "You have done all you can."

His only response was an impatient negative gesture, and without looking at her, he crossed the room quickly and went out into the hall. Hardly a minute had passed, and she was still standing where he had left her, when he returned and said in a whisper:

"He is going now—very quietly. Will you come?"

She shook her head, crying out sharply: "No! no!" Then before something in his face her opposition melted swiftly away, and she added: "Yes, I'll come. He might like to have some one by him who knew him as he used to be."

"After all, he got the worst of it, poor devil!" he answered gently as he opened the door.

By a miracle of memory her resentment was swept out of her thoughts, and she was conscious of an infinite pity. In George's face, while she watched it, there flickered back for an instant the glory of that enchanted spring when she had first loved him. Of his brilliant promise, his ardent youth, there remained only this fading glimmer in the face of a man who was dying. And it seemed to her suddenly that she saw embodied in this wreck of youth and love all the inscrutable mystery not of death, but of life. Her tears fell quickly, and while they fell O'Hara's grasp enfolded her hand.

"It's over now. The best thing that could happen to him has happened," he said, and the touch of his hand was like the touch of life itself, consoling, strengthening, restoring.

In the days that followed it was as if the helpful spirit of Cousin Jimmy had returned to her in the unfamiliar character of O'Hara. The ghastly details of George's burial were not only taken out of her hands, she was hardly permitted to know even that they were necessary. All explanations were made, not by her, but by O'Hara; and when they returned together from the cemetery, Gabriella brought with her a feeling that she had been watching something that belonged to O'Hara laid in the earth. But when she tried to thank him, she found that he was apparently unaware that he had done anything deserving of gratitude.

"Oh, that's nothing. Anybody would have done it," he remarked, and dismissed the subject forever.

For a week after this she did not see him again; and then one Saturday afternoon, when she was leaving Dinard's, they met by chance and walked home together. It was the first time she had been in the street with him, and she was conscious of feeling absurdly young and girlish—she, the mother of a daughter old enough to have love affairs! A soft flush—the flush of youth—tinted her pale cheek; her step, which so often dragged wearily after the day's work, was as buoyant as Fanny's; and her low, beautiful laugh was as gay as if she were not burdened by innumerable anxieties. As they passed a shop window, her reflection flashed back at her, and she thought happily: "Yes, it is true, you are better looking at thirty-seven, Gabriella, than you were at twenty."

"Shall we walk down?" asked O'Hara, and added: "So that was your shop? I am glad that I saw it. But what do you do there all day?"

She laughed merrily. "Put in pins and take them out again. Design, direct, scold, and flatter. We are getting in the spring models now, and it's very exciting."

He glanced down at her figure, noting, as if for the first time, the narrowness at the feet, the large loose waist, and the bunchiness around the hips.

"Did you make that?" he inquired.

"This coat? Oh, no; it came from Paris. It was left on my hands," she explained, "or I shouldn't be wearing it. I wear only what people won't buy, you know."

"No, I didn't know," he returned abstractedly, and she observed humorously after a minute that he was not thinking of her because he was thinking so profoundly about her clothes. It was his way, she had discovered, to concentrate his mind intensely upon the object before him, no matter how trivial or insignificant it might appear. He seemed never to have learned how to divide either his interest or his attention.

"If you could make what you wanted," he remarked, "I should think you'd make them more comfortable. Are you going to wear those hobble skirts this spring?"

"They'll be narrow at the feet but very bunchy at the top—doesn't that sound delightful? I am making a white taffeta for Fanny that has five or six yards of perfectly good material puffed out in the most ridiculous way at the back over a petticoat of silver lace."

Her spirits felt so light, so effervescent, that she wanted to jest, to laugh, to talk nonsense interminably; and after his first moments of bewilderment, when he appeared still unable to detach his mind from his business, he entered gaily and heartily into her mood. His perplexities once disposed of, he gave himself entirely to the enjoyment of the walk with her, and she noticed for the first time his boyish delight in the simplest details of life. With the simplicity of a man to whom large pleasures are unknown, he threw himself whole-heartedly into the momentary diversion of small ones. Every person in the crowd, she discovered, excited his interest, and his humour bubbled over at the most insignificant things—at the grimace of a newsboy who offered him a paper, at the absurd hat worn by a woman in a motor car, at the expression of disgusted solemnity on the face of a servant in livery, at the giggles of an over-dressed girl who hung on the arm of an anemic and exhausted admirer. Never before had she encountered such vitality, such careless, pure, and uncalculating joy of life. There was a tonic quality in his physical presence, and while she walked at his side down Fifth Avenue she felt as if she were swept onward by one of the health-giving, pine-scented winds of Colorado. And she told herself reassuringly that only a man who had lived decently could have kept himself so extraordinarily young and exuberant at forty-five.

The shop windows, particularly those displaying men's shirtings, enchanted him; and he stopped a moment before each one, while she yielded as obligingly as she might have yielded to a fancy of Archibald's, though she was aware that her son would have scorned to look into a window.

"It's so seldom I get out on the Avenue, that's why I like it, I suppose," he remarked while they were surveying a festive arrangement of pink madras.

She smiled up at him, and her smile, gay as it was, held a touch of maternal solicitude. Notwithstanding his bigness and his success and his forty-five years, there was something appealingly boyish about him.

"It would be so easy to get out, wouldn't it?" she asked as they walked on again.

"Well, there ain't much fun when you are by yourself."

"But you know plenty of people."

"Oh, yes, I know people enough in a business way, but that don't mean having friends, does it? Of course, I've men friends scattered everywhere," he added. "The West is full of 'em, but it's funny when you come to think of it—" He broke off, hesitated an instant, and then went on again: "It's funny, but I don't believe. I ever had a woman friend in my life—I mean a friend who wasn't just the wife of some man I knew in business."

The confession touched her, and she answered impulsively: "Well, that's just what I want to be to you—a good friend."

He laughed, but his eyes shone as he looked down on her. "If you'd only take the trouble."

"It won't be any trouble—not a bit of it. After your goodness to me, how could I help being your friend?"

Lifting her eyes she would have met his squarely while she spoke, but he was not looking at her—he appeared, indeed, to be looking almost obstinately away from her.

"There wasn't anything in what I did," he responded in a barely audible voice, and she understood that he was embarrassed by her gratitude.

"But there was something in it—there was a great deal in it," she insisted. It was so easy to be natural with a man, so easy to be candid and sincere when there was no question of sentiment, and, she thought almost gratefully of the elusive and mysterious Alice. The faintest suggestion of romance would have spoiled things in the beginning; but thanks to the hidden Alice, she might be as kind and frank as she pleased. Besides, she was nearly thirty-eight, and a woman of thirty-eight might certainly be trusted to make a friend of a man of forty-five.

With this thought, over which the memory of Arthur brooded benevolently, in her mind, she said warmly: "It will make so much difference to me, too, having a real friend in New York."

He turned to her with a start. "Do you mean that I could make a difference to you?"

"The greatest difference, of course," she rejoined brightly, eager to convince him of his importance in her life. "I can't tell you—you would never understand how lonely I get at times, and now with the children away it is worse than ever—the loneliness, I mean, and the feeling that there isn't anybody one could turn to in trouble."

For a minute he appeared to ponder this deeply. "Well, you could always come to me if you needed anything," he answered at last, and she felt intuitively that for some reason he was distrustful either of himself or of her. "I am not here very much of my time, but whenever I am, I am entirely at your service."

"But that's only half of it." She was determined to reassure him. "A friendship can't be one-sided, can it? And it isn't fair when you give everything, that I should give nothing."

His scruples surrendered immediately to her argument. "You give everything—you give happiness," he said—a strange speech certainly from the twilight lover of Alice. However, as she reasoned clearly after her first perplexity, men were often strange when one least expected or desired strangeness. At thirty-seven, whatever else life had denied her, she felt that it had granted her a complete understanding of men; and it was out of this complete understanding that she observed brightly after a minute:

"Well, if you feel that way, we are obliged to be friends." At least she would prove by her frankness that she was not one of those foolish women who are always taking things seriously.

"Yes, you give happiness. You scatter it, all over the place," he went on, groping an instant after the right words.

"Cousin Jimmy used to say," she laughed back, "that I had a sunny temper."

"That's it—that's what I meant," he replied eagerly; and she was impressed again by his utter inability to make light conversation. When he was once started, when he had lost himself in his subject, she knew that he could speak both fluently and convincingly; but she realized that he simply couldn't talk unless he had something to say. In order to put him at his ease again, she remarked with pleasant firmness: "Do you know there is something about you that reminds me of my Cousin Jimmy. It gives me almost a cousinly feeling for you."

She had the air of expecting him to be interested, but he met it with the rather vague interrogation: "Cousin Jimmy?"

"The cousin who always came to our help when we were in trouble. We used to say that if the bread didn't rise, mother sent for Cousin Jimmy."

Though he laughed readily enough, she could see that his attention was still wandering. "I never had a cousin," he returned after a pause, "or a relation of any sort, for that matter."

His voice was curiously distant, and she was conscious of a slight shock, as if she had run against one of the hard places in his character. "Well, I've done my best," she thought impatiently. "If he doesn't want to be friends he needn't be." Then, with a change of manner, she observed flippantly: "Sometimes one's relatives are useful and sometimes they're not." Really, he was impossibly heavy except in a crisis; and one could scarcely be expected to produce crises in order to put him thoroughly at his ease.

As he made no response to her trite remark, she, also, fell silent, while they turned into Twenty-third Street, and began the long walk to Ninth Avenue. Once or twice, glancing inquiringly into his face, which wore a preoccupied look, she wondered if he were thinking of Alice. Then, as the silence became suddenly oppressive, she ventured warily in the effort to dispel it: "I hope you are not disturbed about anything?"

"Disturbed?" He turned to her with a start. "No, I was only wondering if you knew how much your friendship would mean to me."

It was out at last, and confirmed once more in her knowledge of men, she retorted gaily: "How can I know if you won't take the trouble to tell me?" After all, she reflected cheerfully, the education she had derived from George and Judge Crowborough, though lacking in the higher branches, was fundamentally sound. All men were alike in one thing at least—they invariably disappointed one's expectations.

"I've been trying to tell you for a quarter of an hour," he answered, "and I didn't know how to put it."

"But at last you didn't have to put it at all," she said laughingly; "it simply put itself, didn't it?"

"I am still wondering," he persisted gravely.

"Wondering if I know?" She spoke in the sweetly practical tone of one who is firmly resolved not to permit any nonsense. "Yes, I do know—that is, I know there are ways in which I might be useful to you."

"For instance?"

"Well, there are some little—some very little things I might tell you if we were friends—real friends," she made this plain, "just as two men might be."

"But the very last things two men would tell each other," he was laughing now, "are the little things—the things about slang and walking-sticks and oak furniture."

So he hadn't forgotten! The recollection of her impertinence confused her, and she hastened to make light of it by protesting gaily: "I was only joking. Of course, you didn't take that seriously."

"I don't know how much more seriously," he replied emphatically, "I could have taken it."

"But you haven't thought of it since?"

"What would you say if I told you I hadn't thought of anything else?"

"Then I wish I hadn't said it." She was obviously worried by his admission. "It was horrid of me—perfectly horrid. I ought to have been ashamed of myself. I had no right to criticise you, and you have been so heavenly kind."

"After that"—he appeared to be hammering the idea into her mind—"I was so grateful I'd have done almost anything. Do you know," he burst out with evident emotion, "that was the first criticism—I mean downright honest criticism—I've ever had in my life. Nobody—that is nobody who knew—ever thought enough of me before to tell me where I was wrong."

It was all a pathetic mistake, she saw, but she saw also that it was impossible for her to explain it away. She could not tell him the ugly truth that she had been merely laughing at him when he had believed, in his beautiful simplicity, that she was speaking as a friend. Though she felt ashamed, humbled, remorseful, there was nothing that she could say now which would not hurt him more than the original misunderstanding had done.

In her desire to atone as far as possible, she remarked recklessly: "I only wish I could be of some real help to you."

"You can," he answered frankly. "You can let me come to see you sometimes before I go West again."

"You are going back in the spring?"

He laughed happily, drawing himself erect with a large, free movement as if he needed to stretch his limbs. "I can't stand more than six months of the East, and I've been here a year now, off and on. After a time I begin to want air. I want to breathe."

"Yet you lived here once."

"A sort of life, yes, but that don't count."

"What does count with you, I wonder?" She was smiling up at him, and as they passed under a street light her eyes shone with a misty brightness through her veil of dotted net.

For a minute he thought over her question. "I guess fighting does," he answered at last. "Getting on in spite of hard knocks, and smashing things that stand in your way. I like the feeling that comes after you've put through a big deal or got the better of the desert or the mountains. I got joy in Arizona out of my first silver mine; but I didn't get the joy exactly out of the silver. I don't suppose you understand."

"Oh, yes, I do. I understand perfectly. It's the pure spirit of adventure. Whenever we do a thing for the sake of the struggle, not for the thing itself, it's pure adventure, isn't it?"

"Well, I like money," he said with the air of being entirely honest. "I'm not a romantic chap, don't think that about me. I care a lot about money, only after I've made it, somehow, I never know what to do with it. All I want for myself is a place to sleep and a bite to eat—I'm not over-particular what it is—and clothes to wear, good clothes, too—but I don't give a hang for motor cars except to go long distances in when there are no trains running."

It was the commonplace problem, worked out in intricate detail, of the newly rich, of the uncultivated rich, of the rich whose strenuously active processes of enrichment had permanently closed all other highways to experience. Seventeen years ago the Gabriella of Hill Street would have had only disdain for the newly rich and their problems; but life, which had softened her judgment and modified her convictions, had completely reversed her inherited opinion of such a case as O'Hara's. Though he was as raw as unbaked brick, she was penetrating enough to discern that he was also as genuine; and, so radically had events altered her point of view, that at thirty-seven she found genuine rawness more appealing than superficial refinement. George had wearied her of the sham and the superficial, of gloss without depth, of manner without substance, of charm without character.

"But there is so much that you might do to help," she said presently. "After all, money is power, isn't it?"

"Misused power too often," he answered. "Of course, you can always build lodging-houses and tenements and hospitals; but when you come squarely down to facts, I've never in my life tried to help a man by giving him money that I haven't regretted it. Why, I've ruined men by helping to make their way too easy at the start."

"Perhaps you're right," she admitted; "I don't know much about it, I confess; but I should have been spared a great deal of suffering if I had had something to start with when I was obliged to make my living."

"That's different." His voice had grown gentle in an instant. "I can't think of your ever having had a hard time. You seem so strong, so successful, so happy."

If she had answered straight from her heart, Gabriella would have retorted frankly: "A good deal of that is in the shape of my face and the way I dress," but instead of speaking sincerely, she remarked with impersonal cheerfulness: "Oh, well, happiness, like everything else, is mainly a habit, isn't it? I cultivated the habit of happiness at the most miserable time of my life, and I've never quite lost it."

"But I don't like to think of your ever having worried," he protested.

Of her ever having worried! Was he becoming dangerously sentimental or was it merely a random spark of his unquenchable Western chivalry?

Though she told herself emphatically again that she was not falling in love with O'Hara, though she was perfectly faithful in her heart to the memory of Arthur, still she was vividly aware with every drop of her blood, with every beat of her pulses, of the man at her side. And through her magnetic sense of his nearness there flowed to her presently a deeper and clearer perception of the multitudinous movements of life which surrounded her—of the variable darkness out of which lights flashed and gigantic spectacular outlines loomed against a dim background of sky, of the vague shapes stirring, swarming, creating there in the darkness, and always of the pitiless, insatiable hunger from which the city had sprung. For the first time, flowing like a current from the mind of the man beside her, there came to her an understanding of her own share in the common progress of life—for the first time she felt herself to be not merely a woman who lived in a city, but an integral part of that city, one cell among closely packed millions of cells. Something of the responsibility she felt for her own children seemed to spread out and cover the city lying there in its dimness and mystery.

"But I don't like to think of your ever having worried," he repeated.

"Oh, it's over now," she returned, severely matter-of-fact. "It took me years to make my way, but I've made it at last, and I may settle down to a comfortable middle-age without the dread of the poorhouse to spur me into activity. My business is doing very well; our custom has doubled in the last two or three years."

"But wasn't it a tough pull at one time?"

"It was hard; but what isn't? Of course, when I was obliged to work from nine till six and then come home to cook the children's dinner and teach them their lessons, I used to be tired out by the end of the day—but that lasted only a few years: five or six at the most—and now I can afford to let Fanny wear imported gowns when she goes out to parties."

Though she spoke gaily, making a jest of her struggle, she saw the gravity of his face deepen until his features looked almost wooden.

"And through it all you kept something that so many other women seem to lose when they work for a living," he said. "You've kept your—your charm."

Again she found herself on the point of exclaiming frankly: "heaven knows I've tried to!"—and again, checking herself, she proceeded cautiously: "I've never understood why charm should be merely a hothouse flower."

"I suppose it does depend a good deal upon a sunny temper," he rejoined in his blindness.

They had reached the gate, and stopping him when he would have entered, she said with the directness of a man: "So we're friends, and you're coming to see me?"

"Yes, I'm coming," he replied gravely. Then, standing beside the gate, he watched her while she went up the walk and opened the door with her key.

Upstairs, with her knitting on her lap and her feet on the fender, Miss Polly looked up to observe: "You're late, Gabriella. You must have walked all the way."

"Yes, I walked all the way. Mr. O'Hara joined me."

"Where did you run across him?"

"Just as I left the shop. He was walking down Fifth Avenue."

"Do you reckon he was waitin' outside?"

"Oh, no, he said he had been up to Fifty-ninth Street on business."

"Well, the walk certainly did you good. You are bloomin' like a rose."

"The air was delicious, and I really like talking to Mr. O'Hara. He is quite interesting after you get over the first impression, and he isn't nearly so ignorant about things as I imagined. He has thought a great deal even if he hasn't read very much. It's wonderful, isn't it, what the West can do with a man? Now, if he'd stayed in New York he would have been merely impossible, but because he has lived out of doors he has achieved a certain distinction. I can understand a woman falling in love with him just because of his force and his bigness. They are the qualities a woman likes most, I think."

"He must have made a great deal of money."

"Yes, he's rich, and that's a good thing. I like money tremendously, though I used to think that I didn't. I wonder if he had been poor if I should have liked him quite so much?" she asked herself honestly.

"I don't 'spose you could ever—ever bring yourself to think of him, honey? It would be a mighty good thing in some ways."

Gabriella, being in a candid mood, pondered the question without subterfuge or evasion. "Of course I've passed the sentimental age," she answered. "If Mr. O'Hara had been poor, I suppose I should never have thought of him; but his money does make a difference. It stands for success, achievement, and ability, and I like all those qualities. Then he is rough in many ways, but he isn't a bit vulgar. He has genuine character. There is absolutely no pretence about him."

"You could catch him in a minute," replied Miss Polly hopefully, animated by the inveterate match-making instinct of her class.

Gabriella laughed merrily. "Oh, yes, I might capture him if I went questing for him. I am not a child. But put that out of your head forever, Miss Polly. I have given him clearly to understand that there must be no nonsense, though, for the matter of that, I doubt if he needed the warning. There is an Alice."

"I reckon it would take more than an Alice to stand in the way if you wanted him," insisted the little seamstress, possessed by an obstinate conviction that fate could provide no happiness apart from marriage.

"Perhaps. But you see I don't want him." Gabriella had become perfectly serious, and to Miss Polly's amazement a hint of petulance showed in her manner. "Everything of that kind was over for me long ago. I never think of love now, and if I did there wouldn't be but one—but one—"

"I know, honey," agreed Miss Polly, suddenly softened, "and I'd give anything on earth if you and Arthur could come together again."

"It wouldn't be any use. I made my choice, and I have had to abide by it. He could never forgive me—". She stopped as if she were choking, and Miss Polly said sympathetically:

"Well, I wish he had a chance to, that's all. Why don't you run down to Richmond for a few days this spring to see your folks? Your ma and all would be so glad to see you, and it ain't as if you had the children to keep you back. The thing that worries me," she added with feeling, "is the thought of your spendin' the summer here without the children. If Archibald goes to camp from school and Fanny joins Jane at the White Sulphur Springs as soon as her school is out, you won't have them at all, will you?"

"No, but they will be happy; that is the only thing that matters."

"It seems all wrong to me. What do you get out of life, honey?"

"What do any of us get out of it, dear little Miss Polly, except the joy of triumphing? It's overcoming that really matters, nothing else, and it is the same thing to you and to me that it is to the man downstairs. I am happy because in my little way I stood the test of struggle, and so are you, and so is Mr. O'Hara."

"But you're young yet, and it ain't natural for you to live as you're doin'. Lots of women marry when they're older than you are."

"Oh, yes, if they want to—"

For a minute the little seamstress rattled her newspaper while she looked at her without replying. Then, after folding the paper, and removing her spectacles, she asked grimly: "Can you look me in the eyes, Gabriella, and tell me that you ain't still hankerin' after Arthur?"

The blush of a girl made the business-like Gabriella appear as young and as piquantly feminine as her daughter.

"No, Miss Polly, I cannot," she answered with incomparable directness; "I have loved Arthur all my life."

"That's just what I thought all along, and yet you went off and married somebody else." Excited by the unexpected confession, Miss Polly was quivering with sympathy.

In that supreme instant of self-revelation Gabriella answered this accusation as if it had been uttered by her remorseful conscience. "But that wasn't love," she said slowly; "it was my youth craving experience; it was my youth reaching after the unknown, the untried, the undiscovered. We all go questing for adventure one way or another, I suppose, but it was not the reality."

"I wonder what is," said Miss Polly in a whisper; "I wonder what is, Gabriella?"

"That," replied Gabriella softly, "is what I am still trying to discover."

# CHAPTER IX

## THE PAST

It was the morning of Gabriella's thirty-eighth birthday, and she was standing, with her hat on, before the window of her sitting-room, gazing with dreaming eyes at the young leaves on the elm tree. The day's work was ahead of her, but for a little while, standing there by the open window, she gave herself, with a sense of pleasure, of abandonment, to the rare luxury of regret. Out of her whole year it was the one day when, for a few hours, she permitted herself to think sadly of the past and the future, when she cherished in her heart something of the gentle melancholy of her mother's retrospective philosophy.

In the street, beyond the narrow yard, where the grass lay like a veil, there was a curious deadening of sounds, as if the traffic had become suddenly muffled in the languorous softness of spring. Out of this imaginary stillness floated the sharp twittering of sparrows and the bright laugh of a child at play in one of the neighbouring yards. Above the grim outlines of the city the sky shone divinely clear and blue, flecked by a single cloud, soft as an eagle's feather, which drifted in a mist of light above the horizon. The city, beneath that azure sky, borrowed the transparent brightness of an object that is imprisoned in crystal. White magic had transformed it for an hour, and the street, the houses, the shining elm tree, and the distant frowning brows of the skyscrapers, all seemed as unreal as the vivid yet impalpable images in a dream. And into this world of crystal there drifted, like the essence of spring, the dreamy fragrance from the window box filled with white hyacinths.

While she stood there Gabriella thought pensively of many things. She thought of the day's work before her, of the gown she was designing for Mrs. Pletheridge, of Fanny's latest lover, the brother of a schoolmate, of the clothes she should send the child to the White Sulphur Springs, of her mother, and of Jane's eldest daughter, Margaret; and then very slowly, with the scent of the hyacinths drowning all merely prosaic memories, she began to think hopelessly and tenderly of Arthur Peyton. She thought of him as he had looked on the day when she had told him of her engagement of the sympathetic expression in his eyes, and of his beautiful manner, which she had felt at the time she could never forget. Well, after eighteen years she had not forgotten it. Compared with Arthur, all other men seemed to her as unreal as shadows. "How could Miss Polly imagine that I'd think of Ben O'Hara after a love like that?" she reflected indignantly.

And then, perhaps because for a shadow he was so solidly substantial, she became aware that O'Hara's image was trespassing upon the hallowed soil of her reverie. To be sure, she had seen a great deal of him since George's death, when he had been so wonderfully considerate and helpful. Scarcely a day had passed since then that he had not brightened by some reminder of his friendship. They had spent long evenings together; and occasionally, accompanied by the delighted Miss Polly, they had gone to dinner at a restaurant and later to a concert or a play. That he had been almost too kind it was impossible for her to deny; but she had tried her best to repay him—she had, when one came to the point, done as much as she could to remedy the defects of his education. At first she had given zest, sympathy, eagerness, to her self-appointed task of making him over; then, as the months went by, a sense of doubt, of discouragement, of approaching failure, had tempered her enthusiasm, and at last she had realized that her work, except in the merest details, had been ineffectual and futile. The differences, which she had regarded as superficial, were, in reality, fundamental. It was impossible to make him over because he was so completely himself. He stood quite definitely for certain tendencies in democracy, and by no ingenious manipulation could she twist him about until he presented the sham appearance of moving in the opposite direction. For the logic of her failure was perfectly simple—he couldn't see, however hard he tried, the things she wanted him to look at. The difficulty was far deeper than a mere matter of finish, or even of education—for it was, after all, not one of manner, but of material. Day by day she had realized more clearly that the problem confronting them was one which involved their different standards of living and their individual philosophies. The things which she regarded as essential were to him only the accidental variations of life. He had lived so long in touch with the basic realities—with vast spaces and the stark aspect of desert horizons, with droughts, and winds, and the unquenchable pangs of thirst and hunger, with the vital issues of birth and death in their most primitive forms—he had lived so long in touch with the simplest and most elemental forces of Nature, that his spirit, as well as his vision, had adjusted itself to a trackless and limitless field of view. No, what he was now he must remain, since to change him, except in trivial details, was out of her power.

And of course he had his virtues—she would have been the last to deny him his virtues. Whenever she applied the touchstone of character, she realized how little alloy there was in the pure gold of his nature. He was truthful, he was generous, he was brave, kind, and tolerant; but his virtues, like his personality, were large, flamboyant, and without gradations of colour. Custom had not pruned their natural luxuriance, nor had tradition toned down the violence of their contrasts. They were experimental, not established virtues, as obviously the expression of the man himself as was his uncultivated preference for red geraniums. For he possessed, she admitted, a sincerity such as she had not believed compatible with human designs—certainly not with human achievement. According to the code of the sheltered half of her sex—according to the inflexible code of her mother and Jane—he was not a gentleman. He lacked breeding, he lacked taste, he lacked the necessary education of schools; but in other ways, in ways peculiarly his own, she was beginning dimly to realize that he possessed qualities immeasurably larger than any superficial lack in his nature. In balance, moderation, restraint—in all the gracious attributes with which Arthur was endowed in her memory, in all the attributes she had particularly esteemed in the past—she understood that O'Hara would undoubtedly fall below her inherited standards. But, failing in these things, he had been able to command her respect by the sheer force of his character.

Though he had, as he had confessed to her, gone down into hell, she could not talk to him for an hour without recognizing that he had never lost a natural chivalry of mind beside which the cultivated chivalry of manner appeared as exotic as an orchid in a hothouse. Even Arthur, she was aware, would have lied to her for her own good; but she would have trusted O'Hara to speak the truth to her at any cost. In this, as well as in his practical efficiency, and his crude yet vital optimism, he embodied, she felt, the triumphs and the failures of American democracy—this democracy of ugly fact and of fine ideals, of crooked deeds and of straight feeling, of little codes and of large adventures, of puny lives and of heroic deaths—this democracy of the smoky present and the clear future. "If this is our raw material to-day," she thought hopefully, "what will the finished and signed product of to-morrow be?"

"Gabriella, ain't these lovely?"

Whirling out of the sunshine, she saw Miss Polly holding a rustic basket of primroses and cowslips. "Mr. O'Hara wants to know if he may speak to you for a minute before you go out?"

"Oh, yes, I'm not in a hurry this morning." Then Miss Polly disappeared and an instant later the vacant space in the doorway was filled exuberantly by O'Hara.

"I wanted to be the first to wish you a happy birthday," he began, a little shyly, a little awkwardly, though his face was flushing with pleasure.

"The flowers are wonderful!" For a minute, while she answered him, he seemed to be a part of the unreal intense brightness of the world outside—of that magic world where the elm tree and the grass and the sunny street were all imprisoned in crystal. He diffused a glowing consciousness of success, a sanguine faith in the inherent goodness of experience. For, as she had discovered long ago, O'Hara was one of those who stood not for the elimination of struggle, but for the complete acceptance of life. He had sprung out of ugliness, he had lived intimately with evil; and yet more than any one she had ever known, he seemed to her to radiate the simple, uncalculating joy of living. He was the strongest person she knew, as well as the happiest. He had never evaded facts, never feared a risk, never shirked an issue, never lacked the hardy, adventurous courage of battle. In his own words, life had never "found him a quitter."

He stood in front of her now, fresh, smiling, robust, with his look of suddenly arrested energy, and the dark red of his hair, which was still moist from his bath, striking a vivid note against the cool grays and blues of the background. The sunshine, falling through the open window, warmed the ruddy tan of his face, and made his eyes like pools of clear light in which the jubilant spirit of the spring was reflected. "After all, it isn't what one does, it is what one is, that matters," she thought while she looked at him. "At the end, as Miss Polly said, it is character, not circumstances, that counts."

"I've been all over New York this morning looking for that basket," he said. Though he had been so eager to make light of his services to her in her trouble, she was amused from time to time by a childlike vanity which prompted him to impress her with the value of small attentions; and this she was swift to recognize as the opposite of Arthur's delicacy. It was the only littleness she had observed in O'Hara so far—this reluctance to hide his smaller lights under a bushel—and in its place, it was amusing. Here was an obvious instance where nature unassisted by training appeared to fall short.

"They couldn't be lovelier if you'd gone all over the world," she responded sincerely.

Before answering her he hesitated a moment, and she watched pityingly the struggle he was making toward an impossible self-expression. The thing he wanted to say, the thing struggling so pathetically in the inarticulateness of his feeling, would not, she knew, be uttered in words.

"You are the first woman I ever wanted to send flowers to," he said presently; and added with abject infelicity: "It's strange, isn't it?"

"Yes, it's strange," she assented pleasantly. Though his words were ineffectual, she was aware suddenly of a force before which she felt a vague impulse of flight. Now, if ever, she understood that she must keep their relations as superficial as she had always meant them to be—that she must cling with all her strength to the comfortable surface of appearances. "But you haven't had many women friends, have you?"

"I've wanted to give other things," he went on hurriedly; "but not flowers. I never thought of flowers until I met you."

"That's nice for me." She was growing nervous, and in her nervousness she precipitated the explosion by venturing rashly: "But there's Alice, too, isn't there, to like them?" Her voice was firm and friendly. Once for all she intended him to understand how aloof she stood from any sentimental advances.

"Alice?" For an instant his response hung fire, enveloped in a fog of perplexity. Then, with an air of dispelling the cloud, he made a vigorous gesture of denial, and moved nearer to her with the swiftness and directness of a natural force. "Why, Alice was you! You were Alice all the time!" he exclaimed energetically.

"You mean—" She checked herself in alarm, paralyzed the next instant by the tremendous, unexpected blow of her discovery.

"So you thought there was somebody else!" The delight in his face kept her silent, amazed, incapable of explanation. His arm was still outstretched, as if he were brushing aside the last flimsy barrier between them, and his voice, with its unrestrained and radiant joy, stirred some faintly quivering echoes in the secret depths of her being. It was as if the jubilant spirit of spring had flowered suddenly in his look.

"There wasn't anybody else." He came still nearer, and she stood there, startled, incredulous, powerless either to retreat or to prevent the inevitable instant that was approaching. "At least, there wasn't anybody I ever knew named Alice except a school teacher when I was a kid. She was good and she was pretty like you, and I used to dream about her after school, and every evening at dusk I would go out of my way to speak to her in Sixth Avenue. Once she told me that she'd wait for me to grow up and get rich so I could marry her, and after I went out to Arizona I used to think about her a lot. When I came on you suddenly, standing there in the dusk with your hands full of lilacs, it all came back to me because you, looked like her, with your dark hair and your tall slenderness. Then before I knew what I was, doing I called you by her name. I oughtn't to have done it," he finished ecstatically, "but I'm jolly glad now that I did."

So he also, the man of action and of enterprise, he, the worker and the adventurer, so he also cultivated his garden of dreams!

"I didn't know—I didn't know—" she found herself murmuring faintly in protest.

"But you know now!" His voice rang out exultantly, and, though she felt that the thing she feared and dreaded was coming upon her, she still stood there without moving a step, without lifting a hand, mesmerized, enchanted, by the force of the man. "You know now," he repeated. "You know now, Gabriella, and you knew all along."

It was true. In spite of her surprise, in spite of her shrinking, in spite of her evasion, she confessed it in her heart. She had known all the time. Something deep down in her, something secret and profound and clairvoyant, had discerned the truth from the beginning.

"No! no!" she cried out sharply, for, mistaking her silence, he had stooped to her with the directness which impelled all his movements, which so easily brushed aside and discarded intervening encumbrances, and had kissed her on the lips.

For an instant, in the merciless tenderness of his arms, her resistance melted from her. Beneath the crash of the storm she did not think, she did not struggle, she did not murmur. Her consciousness seemed suspended, and with her consciousness, her memory, her judgment, even her passionate unshaken loyalty to the love of her youth. Then, after the moment of weakness, of passive submission, it was as if her soul and body caught fire at a flash, and a quiver of anger ran through her, enkindling her glance and nerving her spirit.

"But I do not love you! I never meant that I loved you!" she cried.

At her words his arms dropped to his sides, and he stood as if turned to stone, with only his questioning eyes and the vivid red of his hair seeming alive. There was no need now for her to struggle. At her first movement to escape he had released her and drawn to a distance.

"You don't love me?" he stammered. "Why, I saw it. I've seen it for weeks. I see it now in your face."

"You see nothing—nothing." She denied it bitterly. "I liked you as a friend. I did not think of this. I never suspected it. I don't love you. I don't love you in the least."

He was very still. The jubilant spirit of the spring had ebbed away from his look, and even in the height of her anger she was struck by the change in his face.

"I don't believe you," he said gravely after a minute. "I don't believe you."

"You must believe me. I don't love you. I have never thought of you except as a friend. I have loved another man all my life."

Her voice rose accusingly, triumphantly, and so fervent was her look that she might have been repeating a creed. It was as if she hoped by convincing him to persuade her own rebellious heart of the truth she proclaimed.

Now at last he understood. She had been lucid enough even for the crystalline lucidity of his thought.

"I am sorry. I made a mistake," he said quietly, and after the exultant note of a few moments ago there was a dull level of flatness in his voice. "I am sorry. There don't seem to be anything else that I can say or do, but—but it wouldn't have happened if I had understood—" He paused, looked at her closely for a minute, and then added stubbornly, with an echo of the old confidence in his tone: "I still don't believe it."

"It is true, nevertheless." She was trembling with indignation, and this indignation, in spite of her natural fairness, was not directed against herself, against her own blindness and folly. Though she knew that she was to blame, she was furious, not with herself, but with O'Hara. He had insulted her, and she resolved bitterly that she would never forgive him. Even now, whenever she was silent, she could still feel his kiss on her mouth, and the vividness of the sensation stung her into passionate anger. She was no longer the reasonable and competent Gabriella, who had so successfully "managed her life"; she was primitive woman in the grip of primitive anger; and balance, moderation, restraint, had flown from her soul. The very mystery of her feeling, its complexity, its suddenness, its remorselessness—these emotions worked together to deepen the sense of insult, of injury, with which she burned.

"It is true, and you have no right to doubt it. You have no right." She caught her breath sharply, and then went on with inexcusable harshness: "Even if there hadn't been any one else, I should never—I could never in the world—"

Her loss of self-control gave him an advantage, which he was either too generous or too stupid to perceive. "Well, forget all about it. I am going now," he answered quietly.

While she watched him moving away from her, she was conscious of an inexplicable longing to stab him again more deeply before she lost him forever. It was intolerable to her that he should leave her while she was still indignant, that he should evade her just resentment by the natural cowardice of flight.

"I can't forget it," she said; "how can you expect me to?"

For an instant he seemed on the point of smiling. Then, turning, at the door, he walked back to where she was standing, and said gravely: "When I came in here it was to ask you to marry me, and, if it's the last word I ever speak, I thought you understood—that you knew how I felt. I was even fool enough to think you would be willing to marry me. That's all I can say. I haven't any other excuses."

For the second time he went to the door, opened it, and then turning quickly, came back again. "I am not the sort to change, and I shan't change about this. You are a free woman, and if you ever feel that you made a mistake, if you ever want me or need me, you can just come to me. I shan't stop caring for you, and if you choose to come, I'll be waiting. I believed you were meant for me when I first saw you—and I believe it now. In spite of all you say, I am going to keep on believing it—"

He went out, closing the door softly, and five minutes later, feeling extraordinarily young, she watched him pass through the gate, and walk as buoyantly as ever in the direction of Broadway. While she looked after him she wondered suddenly why novelists always dropped their heroines as soon as they passed twenty-seven? "If I'd been in a play, they'd have put me in the background, dressed in lavender, and made me look on and do fancywork," she thought humorously, "but this is real life, and I've just had a real love scene on my thirty-eighth birthday. He couldn't have been more romantic if I'd been Fanny," she mused with an agreeable complacency. "It's only in books and plays that people stop falling in love when they pass the twenties. I don't believe they ever stop in real life. I believe it goes on forever." And glancing at the glass, she added truthfully: "I want love more to-day than I wanted it when I was twenty—and so does Ben O'Hara."

A sensation of stifling, as if her throat were closing together, oppressed her suddenly, and picking up her hand-bag, she ran downstairs and out of the house.

By the time she reached Broadway her anger had ebbed, but the oppression, the feeling that she was being slowly smothered, was still in her throat and bosom. After all, seen in the sober light of reason, why had she been so indignant? There had been a misapprehension; he had thought that she was in love with him, and thinking so, he had kissed her. That was the case plainly stated; and what was there in this to send a burning, rush of anger to her heart? What was there in this that had made her turn and insult him? For the first time in her life she had lost her temper without cause, and had raged, she told herself sternly, like a fury. And beneath her rage she had been conscious always of some vague, incomprehensible disloyalty to Arthur—of a feeling of, humiliation, of self-reproach, which appeared ridiculous when she remembered that she had been kissed against her will and without warning. But, in spite of this, she knew intuitively, with a knowledge deeper than reason, that the glory of her Dream had paled in the moment when she lay in O'Hara's arms.

A subtle change had come over the spirit of spring since she had left the elm tree and the emerald veil of the grass. It was no longer jubilant, but languorous, wistful, haunting, as if it eternally pursued, through the fugitive seasons, an immortal and ineffable beauty. The enchanted crystal had been shattered in an instant, and she saw life now, not imprisoned in magical sunshine, but gray, sordid, monotonous, as utterly hopeless as the faces thronging in Broadway. Yet not many months ago she had seen in these, same faces the inward hope, the joy in sadness, the gaiety in disappointment, which had brightened the world for her. Then she had been aware of an invisible current flowing from the crowd to herself; but to-day this shining current was broken or turned aside, and she felt detached, adrift, and distrustful of the future. That mental correspondence with the mood of the crowd, with the life of the city, which had come to her first on the brilliant morning in September, and then again when she walked home with O'Hara in the winter's dusk—which had released a new faculty in her soul, and had given her a fresh perception of human responsibilities—this had deserted her so utterly that she could barely remember its miraculous visitation. Then her personal life had seemed to become a part of the life of the street, of the sky, of the mysterious city outlined against the gray background of dusk. To-day she walked alone and without sympathy through the crowd. Her feet dragged, and she felt dully that she had lost her share in both the street and the sky. The very faces of the men and women around her—those lethargic foreign faces which crowded out the finer American type—awoke in her the sensation of hopeless revolt which one feels before the impending destruction of higher forms by masses of inert and conscienceless matter. She thought gloomily: "I have lost the vision—there is no hope either for me or for America except in the clear vision of the future." And while she spoke there passed over her the vague feeling of loss, of something missing, as if a precious possession had slipped from her grasp.

Her morning's work was unusually trying, and at one o'clock, when she put on her hat before going out to lunch, she asked herself dejectedly: "What can be the matter with me? Before I go home I'll take a taxicab and drive up Riverside for an hour. If only the children were here, I should not feel so depressed." She remembered regretfully that Archibald and Fanny would be away all summer; and then from thinking of her children, she passed by almost insensible degrees of despondency to meditating pensively about Arthur Peyton. What a wreck, what an inconceivably stupid wreck she had made of her happiness!

As she entered the outer showroom on her way to the street, she heard the voice of Miss Murphy attuned to a cooing pitch, and glancing around a little, painted cabinet, filled with useless ornaments, which stood in the centre of the floor, she beheld a dazzling head of reddish gold before one of the elaborately decorated French mirrors. While she advanced the red-gold waves, worn with extreme flatness over a forehead of pearly whiteness, were submerged for a minute in the smallest and roundest hat in the shop, and from a fashionable figure, reminding her vaguely of an ambulatory dressmaker's model, there issued a high, fluting note of delighted ejaculation.

"This is just exactly what I've been looking all over New York for! Now, isn't it too funny for anything that I should have found it right here the very minute I came in?" As Gabriella's face flashed back from the mirror the fashionable figure sprang suddenly to life, and the voice, still fluting delightedly, exclaimed:

"Why, Gabriella! Where on earth did you come from?"

For a minute sheer amazement kept Gabriella clinging helplessly to the ridiculous cabinet, from the top of which an artificial rose-bush seemed to shower artificial pink petals down on her head. Then, recovering herself, with a sharp effort of will, she went forward a few steps beyond the shelter of the cabinet, and said composedly:

"How do you do, Florrie? I did not recognize you at first."

For it was Florrie herself, Florrie in the flesh, Florrie, glowing, sparkling, prosperous, victorious. Her figure, conforming to the latest mode, had lost its pinched protuberances, and was long, slender, sinuous in its perfection of line. Beneath the small round hat, her hair, glossy with brilliantine, was like melted gold in the large loose waves which revealed the rosy tips of her ears. She was thirty-nine, and she looked scarcely a day over twenty-five. The peach-blossom texture of her skin was as unlined by care or pain as if she had spent the last ten years immured in a convent; for in this case, at least, Gabriella realized while she looked at her, the retribution which awaits upon sinners had been tardy in its fulfilment.

As she moved toward her, without noticing the friendly hand that Florrie held out, Gabriella was conscious of an ironical inclination to laugh. Though she felt no bitter personal resentment against Florrie—for, after all, Florrie had not been able to hurt her—there struggled in her bosom an indignation more profound, more moving, than any merely personal emotion could be. Her resentment was directed not against Florrie, but against some abstract destiny which had permitted Florrie to have her way without paying the price. For on the pinnacle of a destructive career, unsinged by the conflagration she had so carelessly started, Florrie was poised securely, crowned, triumphant, rejoicing. On her dazzling height, successful and happy, she was as far removed as one could imaginably be from the repentant Magdalen of tradition. The memory of George's face as it looked in death, floated before the austere mental vision of Gabriella, and she reflected grimly that tradition was not always the mirror of life. For in this one case at least, the man, not the woman, had been the victim of natural law, and Florrie, fool though she was, had shown herself at the hour of requital to be stronger than fate. By that instinctive wisdom, which is so much older, so much truer than civilization, she had triumphed over the ordination of life. In refusing to suffer she had blunted every weapon with which Nature might have punished her in the end. Not by virtue, since she had none, but by pure insensibility, she had escaped the wages of sin. She was a sensualist whose sensuality, hard, metallic, glittering, encased her like armour.

At Gabriella's approach Miss Murphy fluttered off cooingly in the direction of a fresh customer, and only the festively garlanded French mirror witnessed the meeting of the two who had been schoolgirls together. Swift as an arrow there shot through Gabriella's mind, "I wonder what Ben O'Hara would think of her?" Then she checked the dangerous flight of her fancy, for she remembered that O'Hara's thoughts about anything no longer concerned her.

"Are you buying a hat?" inquired Florrie curiously.

"No, I belong here. I am Madame Dinard."

"You don't mean it! I never should have believed it! The idea of your being a dressmaker. That's why you look so smart, I suppose. You're the smartest thing I've seen anywhere, but you look older, Gabriella."

"Well, you don't." It was perfectly true. Except for the gaudy decorations and the twanging accents of the arrogant young women, Gabriella might have imagined herself in the last century atmosphere of Broad Street in the middle 'nineties.

"I must tell you about the things I use." Florrie was always generous. "But, I declare if I'd known this place was yours, I'd have got my hats here ages ago. Of course I knew it was dreadfully swell, but I thought the prices were beyond anything."

"They are," responded Gabriella with business-like brevity, while she glanced about for the flitting Miss Murphy.

"Look here, Gabriella, I hope you don't bear me any malice," Florrie burst out solicitously, for her frankness, like her sensuality, was elemental in its audacity. "You oughtn't to if you know what I saved you from," she proceeded convincingly. "Anyway, we were chums long before either of us ever thought about a man, and I didn't really do you a bit of harm. It wasn't as if you cared about George, was it?"

"No, it wasn't as if I'd cared about him." Gabriella was answering the appeal as truthfully as if Florrie had been the most excellent of her sex. "You didn't harm me in any way—not in any way," she repeated with firmness.

"That's just the way I told mother you'd look at it. I knew you were always so broad-minded even as a girl. Then there isn't any reason we shouldn't be friends just as we used to be."

Gabriella shook her head, polite but implacable in her refusal. "It isn't what you did to me, Florrie," she answered gently, "it's what you are that I can't forgive. I can imagine that a good woman might do almost anything—might even run off with another woman's husband, but you aren't good. You wouldn't be good if you'd spent your life in a convent."

A quick flush—the flush of temper—stained the pearly whiteness of Florrie's skin. "Oh, of course, if you don't want to," she retorted, a little shrilly, though she tried to subdue her rebellious voice to the pitch of Fifth Avenue. "I only thought that being a working woman, you wouldn't have so very many friends, and you might get lonely. I had seats at the opera every night last winter, and time and again I'd have been glad to have given them to you. Then, too, I might have been able to bring you some custom. I know any number of rich women who don't think anything of paying a thousand dollars for a dress—"

Her insolence was so evidently the result of anger that Gabriella, without interrupting the flow, waited courteously until she paused.

"No, you cannot do anything for me, Florrie." Though Gabriella's voice was crisp and firm, her face looked suddenly older, and little lines, stamped by weariness and regret, appeared at the corners of her still brilliant eyes. "I don't wish you any harm," she went on more softly. "If you were in trouble I'd do what I could for you, but somehow I don't seem able to forgive you for being what you are. Would you like to look at anything else?" she inquired in her professional tone. "Miss Murphy is waiting to show you some hats."

Her cheeks were burning when she passed out of the ivory and gold door, saluted deferentially by the attendant in livery. "The effrontery!" she thought, "the barefaced effrontery!" and then, as her eyes fell on Florrie's trim little electric coupé beside the curb, she exclaimed mentally, recalling George's animated perplexity about the pearl necklace, "I wonder how in the world she does it?"

The meeting with Florrie appeared to her, as she walked home that afternoon, to be the last touch needed to push her into a state of utter despondency. The oppressive languor of the day had exhausted her strength, and when she left Dinard's she felt too indifferent, too spiritless even for the drive in the Park. It was still light when she got out of the stage at Twenty-third Street, and while she strolled listlessly down the blocks on the West Side, she had again that curious sensation of smothering which had come to her after her talk with O'Hara.

At the corner of Sixth Avenue a young Italian, with the face of a poet, was roasting peanuts in a little kerosene stove beside a flickering torch which enkindled the romantic youth in his eyes. Farther away some ragged children were dancing to the music of a hand-organ, which ground out a melancholy waltz; and from a tiny flower stall behind the stand of a bootblack there drifted the intense sweetness of hyacinths. An old negro, carrying a basket of clothes, passed her in the middle of the block, and she thought: "That might have been in Richmond—that and the hand-organ and the perfume of hyacinths." A vision of Hill Street floated before her—the long straight street, with the sudden drop of ragged hill at the end; the old houses, with crumbling porches and countless signs: "Boarders Wanted" in the windows between the patched curtains; the irregular rows of tulip poplar, elm, or sycamore trees throwing their crooked shadows over the cobblestones; the blades of grass sprouting along the edges of the brick pavement—the vision of Hill Street as she remembered it twenty years ago in her girlhood; and then the image of her mother's face gazing out beneath the creamy blossoms and the dark shining leaves of the old magnolia tree. "Everything must have changed, I'd hardly recognize it," she thought. "Nobody we know lives on that side now, mother says. Yes, it has been a long time." She sighed, and then a little laugh broke from her lips, as she remembered that Charley, who had recently been West on a business trip, had brought home the good news that Richmond was as progressive as Denver. "At least it seems so to Charley," Mrs. Carr had hastened to add, "but you know how proud Charley is of all our newness. He says there is not a street in the West that looks fresher or more beautiful than Monument Avenue, and I am sure that is a great comfort. Cousin Jimmy says it shows what the South can do when it tries."

"I'd like to go back," mused Gabriella, walking more and more slowly. "I haven't been home for eighteen years, and I am thirty-eight to-day." With the fugitive sweetness of the hyacinths there rushed over her again the feeling that life was slipping, slipping, and that she was missing something infinitely precious, something infinitely desirable. It was the panic of fleeting youth, of youth unsatisfied, denied, and still insatiable.

As she entered the gate she saw that O'Hara's windows were dark, and while a sigh of relief escaped her, she felt a swift contraction of her throat as if she had become suddenly paralyzed and was unable to swallow. "I hope he has gone," she said to herself in a whisper. "If he has gone, everything will be so much easier." But even to herself she could not explain what it was that would be made easier. Her relief was so vague that when she endeavoured to put it into words it seemed to dissolve and evaporate.

Miss Polly was watering the flowers in the window box, and turning, with the green watering-pot in her hand, she stared at Gabriella in silence for a minute before she exclaimed anxiously: "Mercy on us, Gabriella, what on earth, is the matter?"

"Nothing. I've had a hard day, and I'm tired."

"Well, you lie right straight down as soon as you take off your hat. I declare you look ten years older than you did this morning."

"I have seen Florrie for a minute."

"I reckon that was enough to upset anybody. Did she say she was sorry?"

"Sorry! She looked as if she had never been sorry for anything in her life. She was handsomer than ever—don't you remember how much you always admired her figure?—and she didn't look a day over twenty-five. I don't believe she has ever known what it is to feel a regret."

"Well, you just wait, honey," responded Miss Polly consolingly, "you just wait. She'll be punished yet as sure as you're born."

"Oh, I'm not waiting for that. I don't wish her to be punished. Why should I? She is what she is."

"Do you s'pose she knows about George?"

"I doubt it. She didn't speak of his death. She is quite capable of forgetting that she ever knew him, and if she does, think of him, it is probably as a man who betrayed her innocence. You may be sure she has twisted it all about until every shred of the blame rests on somebody else. Florrie isn't the only woman who is made like that, but I believe," she reasoned it out coolly, "that it is her way of keeping her youth."

Miss Polly had put down the watering-pot, and she came presently with a bottle of camphor to the sofa where Gabriella was lying. "Are you sure you wouldn't like me to rub your head?" she inquired. "Dinner will be ready in a minute, but I shouldn't change my dress if I were you."

Gabriella rose slowly to a sitting position, and then stood up while she pushed the camphor away. "I hate the smell of it," she answered; "it makes me think of one of Jane's attacks. And, besides, I don't need it. There is nothing in the world the matter with me." A moment later, to Miss Polly's unspeakable amazement, she sank down again, flung her arms over the back of the sofa, and burst into tears.

"Well, I never!" ejaculated Miss Polly, rooted to the spot. "Well, I never!" In the ten years she had lived with Gabriella she had never seen her cry—not even after George's flight—and she felt as if the solid ground on which she stood had crumbled without warning, and left her insecurely balanced in space. "Something certainly must be wrong, for it ain't like you to give way. Are you real sure you ain't got a pain somewhere?"

Shaking her head, and swallowing her sobs with an effort, Gabriella rose to her feet. "I'm just tired out, that's all," she said, strangely humble and deprecating.

"You must have been working too hard. It ain't right." For a minute or two the little seamstress brooded anxiously; then guided by an infallible instinct, she added decisively: "It's been a long time since you've seen your ma, and she's gettin' right smart along. Why don't you run down home for a few days while the flowers are blooming?"

A change passed over Gabriella's face, and drying her eyes, she looked down on Miss Polly with a lovely enigmatical smile.

"I wonder if I might?" she said doubtfully.

"There ain't any earthly reason why you shouldn't. To-morrow's Friday, and they can get along without you at Dinard's perfectly well till the first of the week."

"Oh, yes, they can get along. I was only wondering"—a faint breeze stole in through the window, wafting toward her the scent of wet flowers—"I was only wondering"—her eyes grew suddenly radiant, and lifting her arms, she made a gesture as of one escaping from bondage—"I was only wondering if I might go to-morrow," she said.

# CHAPTER X

## THE DREAM AND THE REALITY

At the upper station a little group stood awaiting her, and as the train pulled slowly to the platform, Gabriella distinguished her mother's pallid face framed in the hanging crape of her veil; Jane, thin, anxious, anæmic, with her look of pinched sweetness; Chancy, florid, portly, and virtuously middle-aged, and their eldest daughter Margaret, a blooming, beautiful girl. Alighting, Gabriella was embraced by Mrs. Carr, who shed a few gentle tears on her shoulders.

"Gabriella, my child, I thought you would never come back to us," she lamented; "and now everything is so changed that you will hardly recognize it as home."

"Well, if she can find a change that isn't for the better, I hope she'll point it out and let me make a note of it," boasted Charley, with hilarity. "I tell you what, Gabriella, my dear, we're becoming a number one city. Everything's new. We haven't left so much as an old brick lying around if we could help it. If you were to go back there to Hill Street, you'd scarcely know it for the hospitals and schools we've got there, and as for this part of the town—well, I reckon the apartment houses will fairly take your breath away. Apartment houses! Well, that's what I call progress—apartment houses and skyscrapers, and we've got them, too, down on Main Street. I'll show them to you to-morrow. Yes, by George, we're progressing so fast you can hardly see how we grow. Why, there wasn't a skyscraper or an apartment house in the city when you left here, and precious few hospitals. But now—well, I'll show you! We're the hospital city of the South, and more than that, we're becoming a metropolis. Yes, that's the word—we're becoming a metropolis. If you don't believe me, just watch as we go up Franklin Street to Monument Avenue. I suppose you thought of us still as a poor folksy little Southern city, with a lot of ground going to waste in gardens and green stuff. Well, you just wait till you see Monument Avenue. It's the handsomest boulevard south of Washington. It's all new, every brick of it. There's not a house the whole way up that isn't as fresh as paint, and the avenue is just as straight as if you'd drawn it with a ruler—"

But the change in the city, Gabriella reflected while she embraced Jane, was as nothing compared to the incredible change in Charley himself. Middle-age had passed over him like some fattening and solidifying process. He was healthy, he was corpulent, he was prosperous, conventional, and commonplace. If Gabriella had been seeking, with Hogarthian humour, to portray the evils of torpid and self-satisfied respectability, she could scarcely have found a better picture of the condition than Charley presented. And the more Charley expanded, the more bloodless and wan Jane appeared at his side. Her small, flat face with its yellowish and unhealthy tinge, its light melancholy eyes, and its look of lifeless and inhuman sanctification, exhaled the dried fragrance of a pressed flower. So disheartening was her appearance to Gabriella that it was a relief to turn from her to the freshness of Margaret, handsome, athletic, with cheeks like roses and the natural grace of a young animal.

"Oh, Aunt Gabriella, I hadn't any idea you were like this!" cried the girl with naïve enthusiasm.

"You thought of me as gray-haired and wearing a bonnet and mantle?"

"No, not that, but I didn't dream you were so handsome. I thought mother was the beauty of the family. But what a wonderful dress you have on! Are they wearing all those flounces around the hips?"

"There is no doubt about it, you are getting a lot better looking as you grow older," observed Charley, with genial pleasantry.

"She keeps herself up. There is a great deal in that," remarked Jane, and the speech was so characteristic of her that Gabriella tossed back gaily:

"Well, I'm not old, you know. I am only thirty-eight."

"She married so young," said Mrs. Carr mournfully. "I hope none of your girls will marry young, Jane. Gabriella must be a warning to them and to clear little Fanny."

"But you married young, mother, and so did I," replied Jane, a trifle tartly.

For some incommunicable reason Jane's sweetness had become decidedly prickly. Charley's reformation had left her with the hurt and incredulous air of a missionary whose heathen have been converted under his eyes by a rival denomination: and obeying an entirely natural impulse, she appeared ever so slightly, and in the most refined manner possible to revenge herself on the other members of her family. Though she had of late devoted her attention to the Associated Charities and the Confederate Museum, neither of these worthy objects provided so agreeable an opportunity for the exercise of her benevolent instincts as did the presence of a wayward husband in the household. For there could be no question of the thoroughness of Charley's redemption. The very cut of his clothes, the very colour of his necktie, proclaimed a triumph, for the prohibition party.

At last they were packed tightly in the touring car, and Charley, after imparting directions with the manner of a man who regards himself as the fount of wisdom, began expounding the noisy gospel of progress to Gabriella. Mrs. Carr, who had never been active, and was now over seventy, was visibly excited by the suddenness with which she had been whisked from the platform, and while they shot away from the station, she clutched her crape veil despairingly to the sides of her face, and fixed her blank and terrified stare on her son-in-law. After a whispered conference with Jane, Gabriella discovered that her mother was less afraid of an accident than she was of fresh air. "She's afraid of neuralgia," whispered Jane, "but the doctor says the air can't possibly do her any harm."

In Franklin Street the trees were in full leaf, and the charming vista through which Gabriella looked at the sunset, softened mercifully the impending symbols of the ironic Spirit of Progress. It was modern; it was progressive; yet there was the ancient lassitude of spring in the faint sunshine; and the women passing under the vivid green of the elms and maples moved with a flowing walk which one did not see in Fifth Avenue. On the porches, too, groups were assembled in chairs after the Southern fashion, while children, in white frocks and gay sashes, accompanied by negro nurses wheeling perambulators, made a spring pageant in the parks. Though the gardens had either disappeared or dwindled to mere emerald patches of grass, a few climbing roses, of modern varieties, lent brightness and fragrance to the solid, if undistinguished, architecture of the houses.

"That's the finest apartment house in the city!" exclaimed Charley, with enthusiasm. "Looks pretty tall, doesn't it? But it's nothing to the height of some of the buildings downtown. As for changes—well, I hope Jane will take you on Broad Street to-morrow, and then you'll see what we're doing. Why, there's not a shop left there now where you used to deal. Brandywine's—you recollect old Brandywine & Plummer's, don't you?—isn't there any longer. Got a new department store, with a restaurant and a basement in the very spot where it used to be. Look sharp now, we're coming to a hospital. That belongs to Dr. Browning. You don't remember Dr. Browning. After your day, I reckon. He's a young chap, but he's got his hospital like all the rest, and every bed filled—he told me so yesterday. But they've all got their hospitals. Darrow—you recollect Darrow who used to be old Dr. Walker's assistant—well, he's got his, too, just around the corner on the next street. They say he cuts up more people than any man in the South except Spendlow—".

"I miss the old-fashioned flowers," said Gabriella to her mother in one of Charley's plethoric pauses. "The microphylla roses and snowballs."

"Everybody is planting crimson ramblers and hydrangeas now," responded Mrs. Carr, with something of her son-in-law's pride in the onward movement of her surroundings.

"Here are the monuments!" cried Charley, who had treated each apartment house or hospital as if it were a bright, inestimable jewel in the city's crown. "You don't see many streets finer than this in New York, do you?"

"It looks very pretty and attractive," answered Gabriella, as they swung dangerously round a statue, and then started in a race up the avenue, "but I miss the shrubs and the flowers."

"Oh, there are flowers enough. You just wait till you get on a bit. We've got some urns filled with hydrangeas, that queer new sort between blue and pink. But what do you want with shrubs? All they're good for is to get in your way whenever you want to look out into the street. Mrs. Madison was telling me only yesterday that she cut down the lilac bushes in her front yard because they kept her from recognizing the people in motor cars. Look at that house now, that's one of the finest, in the city. Rushington built it—he made his money in fertilizers, and the one next with the green tiles belongs to Hanly, the tobacco trust fellow, you know, and this whopper on the next square is where Albertson lives. He made his pile out of railroad stocks—he's one of the banking firm of Albertson, Jacobstein, Moss & Company. Awfully clever fellows, but too tricky for me, I give them a wide berth when I go out to do business—"

"But where are the old people—the people I used to know?"

"Oh, they're scattered about everywhere, but they haven't got most of the money. A lot of 'em live up here, and a lot are down in Franklin Street in the same old houses."

"Tell me about Cousin Jimmy."

"He's up here, too. Pussy planned that red brick house with the green shutters next door to us. I reckon Jimmy is about as prosperous as is good for him, but he's getting on. He must be over seventy now. He has a son who is a chip of the old block, and his youngest daughter was the prettiest girl who ever came out here. Margaret will tell you about her."

"And the Peytons?" Her voice trembled, and she looked hastily away from the keen eyes of Margaret.

"They are still in the old home—at least Arthur lives there with his Cousin Nelly. You know Mrs Peyton died about nine or ten years ago?"

"Yes, I heard it."

"She was getting on, but it was a great loss to Arthur. Somehow, I could never make up my mind about Arthur. He was bright enough as a young chap, and we used to think he would have a brilliant future; but when the time came, he never seemed to catch on. He wasn't progressive, and he has never amounted to much more than he did when he left college. What I say about him is that he had the wrong ideas—Yes, Jane, I mean exactly what I say, he had the wrong ideas. He doesn't know what he is driving at. No progress, no push, no punch in him."

"Why, Charley," murmured Mrs. Carr reproachfully, while Jane, recovering her nagging manner with an accession of spirit, remonstrated feelingly: "Charley, you really must be more careful what you say."

"Oh, fudge!" retorted Charley, with playful rudeness. "You see she's at it still, Gabriella," he pursued, winking audaciously. "If it isn't one thing, it's another, but she wouldn't be satisfied with perfection. Well, here we are. There are the hydrangeas. I hope you're pleased."

"I declare, those waste papers have blown right back again on the grass, and I had them picked up the last thing before I left," said Jane in a tone of annoyance.

"Never mind the papers; Gabriella isn't looking for papers," returned Charley, while he helped Mrs. Carr out of the motor and up the steps. "So here you are, mother, and the air didn't kill you."

"I may have neuralgia to-morrow. You never can tell," replied Mrs. Carr. "I shouldn't worry about the papers, Jane. Nobody can help the way they blow about. I want Gabriella to see the children the first thing."

As they entered the house Jane's children, a flock of five girls and two boys, fluttered up to be introduced, and among them Gabriella discovered the composed baby of Jane's tragic flight. It seemed an age ago, and she felt not thirty-eight, but a thousand.

After dinner Charley, who had eaten immoderately, unfolded the evening paper under the electric lamp in the library, and dozed torpidly while the girls plied their aunt with innumerable questions about New York and the spring fashions. "It will be lovely to have Fanny with us at the White Sulphur. I know her clothes will be wonderful," they chirped happily, clustering eagerly about the sofa on which Gabriella was sitting. Jane's children, deriving from some hardy stock of an earlier generation, were handsome, vigorous, optimistic in blood and fibre, and so uncompromisingly modern that Gabriella wondered how Mrs. Carr, with her spiritual neuralgia and her perpetual mourning, had survived the unceasing currents of fresh air with which they surrounded her.

"Yes, things have changed. It is the age," thought Gabriella; and presently, when Cousin Jimmy and Cousin Pussy came in to welcome her, she repeated: "Yes, it is the age. There is no escaping it."

"Why, my dear child, you are looking splendidly," trilled Cousin Pussy, with her old delightful manner and her flattering vision so different from Florrie's. She was still trim, plump, and rosy, though her hair was now snow white and her pretty face was covered with cheerful wrinkles. "You're handsomer than you ever were in your life, and the dash of gray on your temples doesn't make you look, a day older—not a day. Some people turn gray so very young. I remember Cousin Becky Bollingbroke's hair was almost white by the time she was thirty-five. It runs like that in some families. But you look just as girlish as ever. It's wonderful, isn't it, Cousin Fanny, the way the women of this generation stay girls until they are fifty? I don't believe you'll ever look any older, Gabriella, than you do now. Of course, I suppose your business has something to do with it, but if I met you for the first time, it would never cross my mind that you were a day over twenty-five."

"Well, well, so little Gabriella went to New York and became a dressmaker," observed Jimmy, who was seldom original, "and she's the same Gabriella, too. I always said, you know, that she was the sort you could count on."

Age, though it had not entirely passed him by, had, on the whole, treated him with great gentleness. He was a remarkably handsome old man, with a distinguished and courtly presence, a head of wonderful white hair, which looked as if it had been powdered, a ruddy unwrinkled face, and the dark shining eyes of the adventurous youth he had never lost.

"Of course, she couldn't have been a dressmaker here where everybody knows her," purred Cousin Pussy, with her arm about Gabriella, "but in New York it is different, and they tell me that even titled women are dressmakers in London."

"Well, she has pluck," declared Cousin Jimmy, as he had declared eighteen years ago at the family council. "There's nothing like pluck when it comes to getting along in the world."

Then they sat down in Jane's library, which, contained most of the things Gabriella associated with the old parlour in Hill Street, and Cousin Pussy asked if Gabriella had found many changes.

"A great many. Everything, looks new to me except this room. The only thing I miss here is the horsehair sofa."

"I keep that in the back hall," said Jane. "The town does look different up here, but the Peytons' house is just as you remember it—even the scarlet sage is in the garden. Miss Nelly plants it still every summer."

A lovely light shone in Gabriella's eyes, and Cousin Pussy watched it tenderly, while a smile hovered about the corners of her shrewd though still pretty mouth.

"It has been such a disappointment that Arthur hasn't done more in his profession," she said presently, "but, as I was saying to Mr. Wrenn only the other day, I have always felt that dear Gabriella was to blame for it."

"The trouble with Arthur," observed Charley, awaking truculently from his doze, "is that he's got the wrong ideas. When a man has the wrong ideas in these days, he might as well go out and hang himself."

"Well, I don't know that I'd call his ideas wrong exactly," reasoned Cousin Jimmy, with the judicial manner befitting the best judge of tobacco in Virginia; "I shouldn't call them wrong, but they're out of date. They belong to the last century."

"I always say that dear Arthur is a perfect gentleman of the old school," remonstrated Mrs. Carr, meekly obstinate. "There aren't many of them left now, so I tell myself regretfully whenever I see him."

"And there'll be fewer than ever by the time you Suffragists get your rights," remarked Charley, with bitterness, while Mrs. Carr, incensed by the word, which she associated with various indelicacies, stared at him with an indignant expression.

"Charley, be careful what you say," nagged Jane acridly from her corner. "Now that so many of our relatives have gone in for suffrage, you mustn't be intolerant."

"I cannot help it, Jane. I shall never knowingly bow to one even if she is related to me," announced Mrs. Carr more assertively than Gabriella would have believed possible.

"Well, for my part, Cousin Fanny, I can't feel that it hurts me to bow to anybody," said Pussy, with her unfailing kindness of heart. "Why, I even bowed to Florrie Spencer last winter. I wanted to cut her, but I just couldn't bring myself to do it when I met her face to face. I hope you don't mind, dear," she whispered to Gabriella. "I suppose I oughtn't to have mentioned her, but I forgot."

"Oh, it doesn't matter in the least," responded Gabriella cheerfully. "I bowed to her myself the day before I left New York."

Though she tried to be independent, to be advanced and resolute, she felt the last eighteen years receding slowly from her consciousness. The family point of view, the family soul, had enveloped her again, and, in spite of her experience and her success, she seemed inwardly as young and ignorant as on the evening when she broke her engagement to Arthur. The spirit of the place had defeated her individual endeavour. Except for the wall paper of pale gray, and the Persian rugs on the floor, Jane's library might have been the old front parlour in Hill Street, and it was as if the French mirror, the crystal candelabra, the rosewood bookcases, with their diamond-shaped panes lined with fluted magenta silk, the family portraits, the speckled engravings of the Burial of Latané and of the groups of amiable children feeding chickens and fish—it was as if these inanimate objects exuded a spiritual anodyne which enfeebled the will. Across the hall, in the modern pink and gray drawing-room, the five girls were playing bridge with several young men whom Gabriella remembered as babies, and the sounds of their voices floated to her now and then as thinly as if they had come out of a phonograph. "There is nothing better than peace, after all," she thought, while her, eyes rested tenderly on the simple, affectionate face of Cousin Jimmy. "Goodness and peace, these things are really worth while."

Then the telephone rang gently, and after a minute Margaret, who had gone to answer it, came in with a roguish smile on her lips. "Aunt Gabriella, Mr. Peyton wishes to come to-morrow at five," she said; and the roguish smile flitted from her lips to the lips of Cousin Pussy, and from Cousin Pussy to each sympathetic and watchful face in the group.

"You may say what you please," argued Charley, still truculent, "the whole trouble with Arthur is that he has got the wrong ideas."

At five o'clock the next day the family crowded into the touring car for an excursion, and left Gabriella in a deserted house to receive the lover of her girlhood. Before going Mrs. Carr had embraced her sentimentally; Charley had dropped one of his broad jokes on the subject of the reunion; Jane had murmured sweetly that there was no man on earth she admired as much as she did Arthur; and the girls had effusively complimented Gabriella on her appearance. Even Willy, the baby of eighteen years ago, had prophesied with hilarity that "Old Arthur Peyton wasn't coming for nothing." One and all they appeared to take her part in the romance for granted; and while she waited in the drawing-room, gazing through the interstices of Jane's new lace curtains into the avenue, where beyond the flying motor cars the grassy strip in the middle of the street was dappled with shadows, she wondered if she also were taking Arthur's devotion for granted. She had not seen him for eighteen years, and yet she was awaiting him as expectantly as if he were still her lover. Would his presence really quiet this strange new restlessness in her heart—this restlessness which had come to her so suddenly after her meeting with Florrie? Was it true that her youth was slipping from her before she had grasped all the happiness that life offered? Or was it only the stirring of the spring winds, of the young green against the blue sky, of the mating birds, of the roving, provocative scents of flowers, of the checkered light and shade on the grassy strip under the maples? Was it all these things, or was it none of them, that awoke this longing, so vague and yet so unquenchable, in her heart?

A car stopped in the street outside, the bell rang, and she watched the figure of a trim mulatto maid flit through the hall to the door. An instant later Arthur's name was announced, and Gabriella, with her hands in his clasp, stood looking into his face. It had been eighteen years since they parted, and in those eighteen years she had carried his image like some sacred talisman in her breast.

"How little you've changed, Gabriella," he said after a moment of silence in which she told herself that he was far better looking, far more distinguished than she had remembered him. "You are larger than you used to be, but your face is as girlish as ever."

"And I have two children nearly grown," she replied with a trembling little laugh; "a daughter who is already thinking of the White Sulphur."

They sat down in the pink chairs on the gray carpet, and leaned forward, looking into each other's faces as tenderly as they had done when they were lovers.

"It's hard to believe it," he answered a little stiffly, in his dry and gentle voice, which held a curious note of finality, of failure. For the first time, while he spoke, she let her eyes rest frankly upon him, and there came to her, as she did so, a vivid realization of the emptiness and aimlessness of his life. He looked handsomer than ever; he looked stately and formal and impressive; but he looked old—though he was only forty-five—he looked old and ineffectual and acquiescent. The fighting strength, such as it was, had gone out of him, and the stamp of failure was on him, from his high, pale, intellectual forehead, where the fine brown hair had retreated to the crown of his head, to his narrow features, and his relaxed slender limbs, with their slow and indolent movements. He was one of those, she felt intuitively, who had stood aloof from the rewards as well as from the strains of the struggle, who had withered to the core, not from age, but from an inherent distrust of all effort, of all endeavour. For his immobility went deeper than any physical habit: it attacked, like an incurable malady, the very fibre and substance of his nature. With his intellect, his training, his traditions, she discerned, with a flash of insight, that he had failed because he lacked the essential faith in the future. He had lost, not because he had risked, but because he had hesitated, not because he had loved ease, but because he had feared effort. For fear of a misstep, he had not dared to go forward; from dread of pain, he had refused the opportunity of happiness. She knew now why he had never come to her, why he had let her slip from his grasp. All that was a part of his failure, of his distrust of life, of his profound negation of spirit.

"Yes, it is hard," she assented; and there came over her like a sudden sense of discomfort, of physical hardship, the knowledge that, in the very beginning, she was trying to make conversation. Meeting his sympathetic smile—the smile that still delighted the impressionable hearts of old ladies—she told herself obstinately, with desperate determination, that she was not disappointed, that he was just as she had remembered him, dear and lovable and kind and conventional. When she recalled what he had been at twenty-seven, it appeared inevitable to her that at forty-five he should have settled a little more firmly into the mould of the past, that his opinions should have crystallized and imprisoned his mind immovably in the centre of them.

She told him what she could about Archibald and Fanny—about her choice of schools, her maternal pride in Archibald's intellect and Fanny's appearance, her hopeful plans for the future—and he listened attentively, with his manner of slightly pompous consideration, while he passed one of his long narrow hands over his forehead. When she had finished her vivacious recital, he began to talk slowly and gravely about himself, with the tolerant and impersonal detachment of one who has reduced life to a gesture, a manner. "I wonder if he has ever really cared about anything—even about me?" she questioned, after a minute; but while the thought was still in her mind, he mentioned his mother's name, and it was impossible to doubt the sincerity of his sorrow and his tenderness. "I have seemed only half alive since I lost her," he said; and the words were like a searchlight which flashed over his character and illumined its obscurities. Did his whole attitude of immobility and negation result from the depth and the intensity of his feeling, from the exquisite reticence and sensitiveness of his soul?

"I know, I know," she murmured in a voice of sympathy. After all, she was not disappointed in him. He was as tender, as chivalrous, as noble as she had believed him to be. The Dream was true; and yet in spite of its truthfulness, it seemed to evaporate slowly while she sat there in Jane's pink satin chair and looked out at the sunlight. Only the restlessness, the inappeasable longing in her heart had not changed. Looking across the hall into the library she could see the old French mirror reflecting the bronze candelabra, with crystal pendants, and the thought flitted into her brain: "It is all real. I am here, talking to Arthur. It is every bit true." But her words failed to convince her, and she had a curious sensation of vagueness and thinness, as if their low, gentle voices were issuing from shadows.

"I should like to show you some of our improvements," he said presently, with a faintly perceptible ripple of animation. "I wonder if you would care to come out in my car? We might go up Monument Avenue into the country."

The idea was delightful, she told him with convincing enthusiasm; and while she ran upstairs to put on her hat, he went out to the car, which was standing in front of the house. So preoccupied was he with his reflections, that when Gabriella appeared, he started almost as if he had forgotten that he was waiting for her.

The air was as soft and fragrant as summer; the grassy strip under the young maples was diapered with sunlight, and an edge of rosy gold was tinting the far horizon. As they sped up the avenue Arthur pointed out the houses to her as possessively as Charley had done the afternoon before, and in the pride with which he told her the cost of them she recognized an admirable freedom from envy or bitterness. If, he had not achieved things, his attitude seemed to say, it was because he had never been in the race, because he had preferred to stand aside and enjoy the reposeful entertainment of the spectator.

The avenue, which swept on indefinitely after the houses had stopped, dwindled at last to two straight and narrow walks binding the town to the country with bands of concrete. The pines had fallen in blackened ruins, and where Gabriella remembered thickets of wildflowers there were masses of red clay furrowed by cart wheels.

"You see, we're developing all this property now," observed Arthur, in a gratified tone as they whirled past an old field intersected by a concrete walk which informed the curious that it was "Arlington Avenue." "Honeysuckle Lane has gone, too, and we're grading a street there now in front of the old Berkeley place."

"The growth has been wonderful," said Gabriella, a little pensively; "but do you remember how lovely Honeysuckle Lane used to be? That's where we went for wild honeysuckle in the spring."

"Oh, we'll find plenty of honeysuckle farther out. I gathered a big bunch of it for Cousin Nelly yesterday."

For a while they sped on in silence. Arthur was intent on the wheel, and Gabriella could think of nothing to say to him that she had not said in Jane's drawing-room. When at last they left the desolation of improvement, and came out into the natural country, the sun was already low, and the forest of pines along the glowing, horizon was like an impending storm. Once Arthur stopped, and they got out to gather wild honeysuckle by the roadside; then with the sticky, heavily scented blossoms in her lap, they went on again toward the sunset, still silent, still separated by an impalpable barrier. "He is just what I thought he would be," she thought sadly. "He is just where I left him eighteen years ago, and yet it is different. In some inexplicable way it is different from what I expected." And she told herself that the fault was her own—that she had changed, hardened, and become hopelessly matter-of-fact—that she had lost her youth and her sentiment.

Suddenly, as if the action had been forced upon him by the steady pressure of some deep conviction, some inner necessity, Arthur turned his face toward her, and asked gently: "Gabriella, do you ever think of the past?"

Facing the rosy sunset, his features looked wan and colourless, and she noticed again that he seemed to have dried through and through, like some rare fruit that has lain wrapped in tissue paper too long.

She looked at him with wistful and sombre eyes. Now that the desired moment had come, she felt only that she would have given her whole future to escape before it overtook her, to avoid the inevitable, crowning hour of her destiny.

"I think of it very often," she answered truthfully, while she buried her face in the intoxicating bloom of the honeysuckle.

"Do you remember my telling you once that I'd never give you up—that I'd never stop caring?"

"Yes, I remember—but, oh, Arthur, you mustn't—" She sat up with a start, gazing straight ahead into the rose and gold of the afterglow. From the deserted road, winding flat and dun-coloured in the soft light, she heard another voice— the strong and buoyant voice of O'Hara—saying: "I'm not the sort to change—" and then over again, "I'm not the sort to change—"

"I suppose it's too late," Arthur went on, with his patient tenderness. "Things usually come too late for me or else I miss them altogether. That's been the way always—and now—" With his left hand he made a large, slow, commemorative gesture.

"You're the best—the kindest—" An urgent desire moved her to stop him before he put into words the feeling she could see in his face. Though she knew that it was but the ghost of a feeling, the habit of a desire, which had become interwoven with his orderly and unchangeable custom of life, she realized nevertheless that its imaginary vividness might cause him great suffering. A vision of what might have been eighteen years ago—of their possible marriage—rose before her while she struggled for words. How could her energetic nature have borne with his philosophy of hesitation, her imperative affirmation of life with his denial of effort, her unconquered optimism with his deeply rooted mistrust of happiness?

There was beauty in his face, in his ascetic and over-refined features, in his sympathetic smile and his cultured voice; but it was the beauty of resignation, of defeat nobly borne, of a spirit confirmed in the bitter sweetness of renouncement. "It would make an old woman of me to marry him," she thought, "an old, patient, resigned woman."

"Most things have slipped by me," he resumed presently, while they raced down a long hill toward the black pines and the fading red of the afterglow. In a marshy pond near the roadside frogs were croaking, while from the darkening fields, encircled with webs of mist, there floated the mingled scents of freshly mown grass, of dewy flowers, of trodden weeds, of ploughed earth, of ancient mould—all the fugitive and immemorially suggestive odours of the country at twilight. And at the touch of these scents, some unforgotten longing seemed to stir in her brain as if it had slept there, covered by clustering memories, from another lifetime. She wanted something with an unbearable intensity; the vague and elusive yearning for happiness had become suddenly poignant and definite. In that instant she knew unerringly that she was in love not with a dream, but with a fact, that she was in love not with Arthur, but with O'Hara. For days, weeks, months, she had been blindly groping toward the knowledge; and now, in a flash of intuition, it had come to her like one of those discoveries of science, which baffle investigators for years, and then miraculously reveal themselves in a moment of insight. Her first antagonism, her injustice, her unreasonable resentments and suspicions, she recognized now, in the piercing light of this discovery, as the inexplicable disguises of love. And she was not old—she was not even middle-aged—she was as young as Fanny, as young as the eternal, ageless spirit of romance, of adventure. This was life in her pulses, in her brain, in her heart—life, not pale, not bitter sweet, but sparkling, glowing, bubbling like wine.

At the foot of the long hill Arthur turned the car, and they flew back between the dim fields where the croaking of frogs sounded louder in the darkness. Ahead of them the lights of the car flitted like golden moths over the dust of the road, and in the sky, beyond the thin veil of mist, the stars were shining over the city. Spring, which possessed the earth, bloomed in Gabriella's heart with a wonderful colour, a wonderful fragrance. She was young again with the imperishable youth of magic, of enchantment. To love, to hope, to strive, this was both romance and adventure.

"Is it too late, then, Gabriella?" asked Arthur, after a long silence, and in his voice there was the sound of suffering acquiescence.

"I'm afraid it is, dear Arthur," she answered softly, and they did not speak again until the lights blazed over them, and they ran into Monument Avenue. After all, it was too late. What could she have added to the answer she had given him?

When they reached the house, he did not come in with her, and tears stained her face while she went slowly up the steps, and stood beside Jane's hydrangeas with her hand on the bell. Then, as the door opened quickly, she saw her mother waiting, with an eager, expectant look, at the door of the library, and heard her excited voice murmur: "Well, dear?"

"We had a lovely drive, mother. Arthur is just as I remembered him, except that he has grown so much older."

A disappointed expression crossed Mrs. Carr's face. "Is that all?" she asked regretfully.

Gabriella laughed happily. "That is all—only I found out exactly what I wanted to know."

For the rest of the week she devoted herself to her mother with a solicitude which aroused in the brain of that melancholy lady serious apprehensions of a hastening decline; and when her visit was over, she packed her trunks, with girlish, delicious thrills of happiness, and started back to New York.

"Do you really think I am failing so rapidly, Gabriella?" Mrs. Carr inquired anxiously while they waited for the train on the platform of the upper station.

"Failing? Why, no, mother. You look splendidly," Gabriella assured her, a little surprised, a little startled. "Why should you ask me such a thing?"

"Oh, nothing, dear. I had a fancy," murmured Mrs. Carr meekly; and then as the train rushed into view, she kissed her daughter reproachfully, and stood gazing after her until the last coach and the last white jacket of the dining-car attendants vanished in the smoky sunshine of the distance.

Through the long day, lying back in her chair, with her eyes on the flying green landscape, Gabriella thought of the discovery she had made while she was driving with Arthur. The restlessness, the uncertainty, the vague yet poignant longing for an indefinite good, had passed out of her happy and exultant heart. In obedience to the law of her nature, which decreed that she should move swiftly and directly toward the end of her destiny, she was returning to O'Hara as resolutely, as unswervingly, as she had fled from him.

"It's strange how little I've ever understood, how little I've ever known myself," she thought, staring vacantly at a severe spinster, with crimped hair and a soured expression, who sat before the opposite window. "I've gone on in the dark, making mistakes and discoveries from the very beginning, undoing and doing over again, creating illusions and then destroying them—always moving, always changing, always growing in new directions. A year ago I'd have laughed at the idea that I could love any man but Arthur—that of all men I could love

Ben O'Hara; and to-day I know that he is the future for me—that he is the beginning again of my youth. A year ago I thought only how I might change him, how I might make him over, and now I realize that I shall never change him, that I shall never make him over, and that it doesn't really matter. It isn't the vital thing. The vital thing is character, and I wouldn't change that if I could. For the rest, I shall probably always wish him different in some ways, just as I wish myself different. I'd like to have him more like Arthur on the surface, just as I'd like to have myself more like Fanny. I'd like to give him Arthur's manner just as I'd like to give myself Fanny's complexion. But it isn't possible. He will always be what he is now, and, after all, it is what he is—it is not something else that I want—"

With a glimmer of the clairvoyant insight which had come to her on the country road, she understood that O'Hara was for her an embodied symbol of life—that she must either take him or leave him completely and without reserve or evasion. He was not an ideal. In the love she felt for him there was none of the sentimental glamour of her passion for George. She saw his imperfections, but she saw that the man was bigger than any attributes, that his faults were as nothing compared to the abundance of his virtues, and that, perfect or imperfect, the tremendous fact remained that she loved him.

In the opposite chair, the severe spinster had taken a strip of knitted silk out of her bag, and was working industriously on a man's necktie of blue and gray. From her intent and preoccupied look, from the nervous twitching of her thin lips, the close peering of her near-sighted eyes, through rimless glasses which she wore attached by a gold chain to her hair, she might have found in the act of knitting a supreme consolation for the inexorable denials of destiny. "I wonder if it satisfies her, just knitting?" thought Gabriella. "Has she submitted like Arthur to chance, to the way things happen when one no longer resists? Is she really contented merely to knit, or is she knitting as a condemned prisoner might knit while he is waiting for the scaffold?" And while she watched the patient fingers, she added: "One must either conquer or be conquered, and I will never be conquered."

It was eight o'clock when she reached New York, and as she drove the short distance to West Twenty-third Street she began to wonder when she should see O'Hara, and what she should say to him. In the end she decided that she would wait for a chance meeting, that she would let it happen when it would without moving a step or lifting a hand. Before many days they would be obliged to meet in the yard or the hall, and some obscure, consecrated tradition of sex, some secret strain of her mother's ineradicable feminine instinct, opposed the direct and sensible way. "As soon as I meet him—and in the end I shall surely meet him—everything will be right," she thought, with her eyes on the streets where the spring multitude of children were swarming. And from this multitude of children, of young, ardent, and adventurous life, there seemed to emanate a colossal and irresistible will—the will to be, to live, to love, to create, and to conquer.

The taxicab turned swiftly into Twenty-third Street, and while it stopped beside the pavement, she saw that Mrs. Squires was standing, with her arms on the gate, staring into the street. As Gabriella alighted, the woman came forward and said, with suppressed emotion, while she wiped her eyes on the back of her hand: "You came just a minute too late to say good-bye to Mr. O'Hara."

"Good-bye? But where has he gone?"

"He has gone to Washington to-night. To-morrow he is starting to the West."

"When is he coming back? Did he tell you?"

At this Mrs. Squires broke down. "He ain't ever coming back, that's what I'm crying for. He's given up his rooms, and his furniture all went to the auction yesterday. He says he's going to live out in Colorado or Wyoming for the rest of his life, and he didn't even tell me where I could write to him. It's a great loss to me, Mrs. Carr. I'd got used to him and his ways, and when you've once got used to a man, it ain't easy to give him up."

She sobbed audibly as she finished; and it seemed to Gabriella that a lifetime of experience passed in the instant while she stood there, with her pulses drumming in her ears, her throat contracting until she struggled for breath, and the lights of the city swimming in a nebulous blur before her eyes. Yet in that instant, as in every crisis of her life, she turned instinctively to action, to movement, to exertion, however futile. While she walked across the pavement to the waiting cab, for the crowning and ultimate choice of her life, she abandoned forever the authority and guide of tradition. Tradition, she knew, bade her sit and wait on destiny until she withered, like Arthur, to the vital core of her nature; but something mightier than tradition, something which she shared with the swarming multitude of children in the streets—the will to live, to strive, and to conquer—this had risen superior to the empty rules of the past. With her hand on the door of the taxicab, she spoke rapidly to the driver: "Drive back to the station as fast as you can, there is not a minute to lose."

When the cab started, she leaned forward, with her hands clasped on her knees, and her eyes on the street, where the children were playing. Because of the children, they drove very slowly, and once, when the traffic held them up for a few minutes, she felt an impulse to scream. Suppose she missed him, after all! Suppose she lost him in the station! Suppose she never saw him again! And beside this possibly it seemed to her that all the other suffering of her life— George's desertion, her humiliation, her struggle to make a living for her children, the loneliness of the long summers, her poverty and hunger and self-denial—that all these things were merely superficial annoyances. "If we don't go on, I shall die," she said aloud suddenly; "if we don't go on, I shall die," and when at last the cab started again, she heard the words like an undercurrent beneath the innumerable noises of the street, "If we don't go on, I shall die."

The taxicab stopped; a porter ran forward to take her bag, and while she thrust the money into the driver's hand, she heard her voice coolly and calmly giving directions.

"I must catch the next train to Washington."

"Have you got your ticket, Miss?"

She stared back at him blankly. Though she saw his lips moving, it was impossible for her to distinguish the words because she was still hearing in a muffled undercurrent the roar of the streets.

"Have you got your ticket?" They were passing through the station now, and he explained hurriedly: "You can't go through the gate without a ticket."

She drew out her purse, and panic seized her afresh while she waited before the window behind a bald-headed man who counted his change twice before he would move aside, and let her step into his place. Then, when the ticket was given to her, she turned and ran after the porter through the gate and down the steps to the platform. As she ran, her eyes wavered to the long platform, and the little groups gathered beside the waiting train, which seemed to shake like a moving black and white picture.

"Suppose I miss him, after all! Suppose I never see him again!" she thought, and all that was young in her, all that was vital and alive, strained forward as her feet touched the platform. Except for several coloured porters and a woman holding a child by the hand, the place was deserted. Then a man stepped quickly out of one of the last coaches, and by his bigness and the red of his hair, she knew that it was O'Hara. At the first sight of him the panic died suddenly in her heart, and the old peace, the old sense of security and protection swept over her. Her face, which had been lowered, was lifted like a flower that revives, and her feet, which had stumbled, became the swift, flying feet of a girl. It was as if both her spirit and her body sprang toward him.

At the sound of his name, he turned and stood motionless, as if hardly believing his vision.

"I came back because I couldn't help it," she said.

But he was always hard to convince, and he waited now, still transfixed, still incredulous.

"I came back because I wanted you more than anything else," she added.

"You came back to me?" he asked, slowly, as if doubting her.

"I came back to you. I wanted you," she repeated, and her voice did not quaver, her eyes did not drop from his questioning gaze. It was all so simple at last; it was all as natural as the joyous beating of her heart.

"And you'll marry me now—to-night?"

It was the ultimate test, she knew, the test not only of her love for O'Hara, but of her strength, her firmness, her courage, and of her belief in life. The choice was hers that comes to all men and women sooner or later—the choice between action and inaction, between endeavour and relinquishment, between affirmation and denial, between adventure and deliberation, between youth and age. One thought only made her hesitate, and she almost whispered the words:

"But the children?"

He laughed softly. "Oh, the children are always there. We're not quitters," and in a graver tone, he asked for the second time: "Will you come with me now—to-night, Gabriella?"

At the repeated question she stretched out her hands, while she watched the light break on his face.

"I'll come with you now—anywhere—toward the future," she answered.